PRIMER

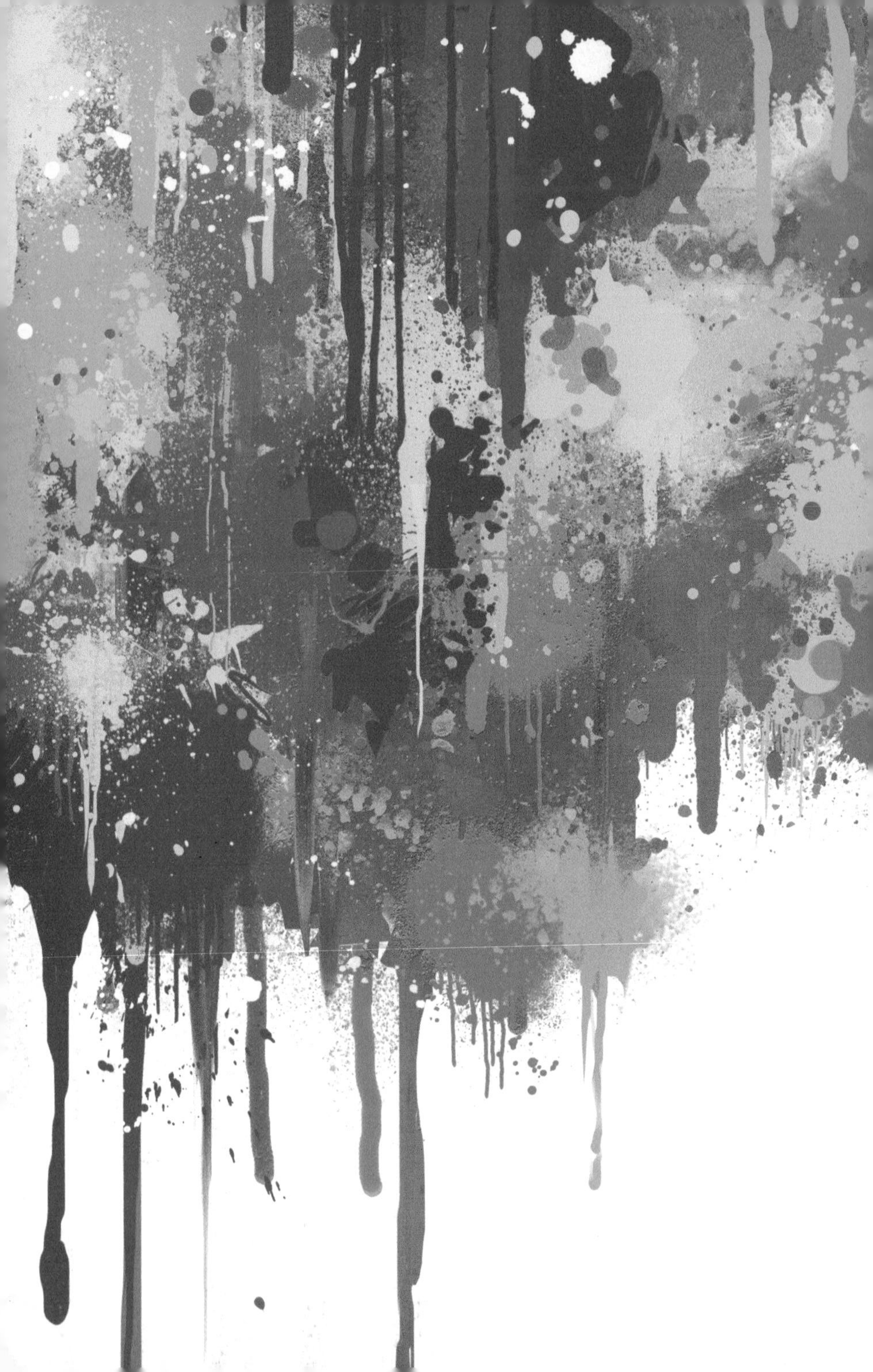

PRIMER

written by
Jennifer Muro & Thomas Krajewski

art by
Gretel Lusky

letters by
Wes Abbott

Jim Chadwick Editor
Diego Lopez Associate Editor
Steve Cook Design Director – Books
Monique Narboneta Publication Design

Bob Harras Senior VP – Editor-in-Chief, DC Comics
Michele R. Wells VP & Executive Editor, Young Reader

Dan DiDio Publisher
Jim Lee Publisher & Chief Creative Officer
Bobbie Chase VP – New Publishing Initiatives
Don Falletti VP – Manufacturing Operations & Workflow Management
Lawrence Ganem VP – Talent Services
Alison Gill Senior VP – Manufacturing & Operations
Hank Kanalz Senior VP – Publishing Strategy & Support Services
Dan Miron VP – Publishing Operations
Nick J. Napolitano VP – Manufacturing Administration & Design
Nancy Spears VP – Sales
Jonah Weiland VP – Marketing & Creative Services

PRIMER

DC Comics - a WarnerMedia Company

DC Comics, 2900 West Alameda Ave., Burbank, CA 91505
Printed by LSC Communications, Crawfordsville, IN, USA.
5/15/20. First Printing. ISBN: 978-1-4012-9657-5
Library of Congress Cataloging-in-Publication Data

Names: Muro, Jennifer, writer. | Krajewski, Thomas, writer. | Lusky, Gretel, artist. | Abbott, Wes, letterer.
Title: Primer : a superhero graphic novel / written by Jennifer Muro & Thomas Krajewski ; art by Gretel Lusky ; letters by Wes Abbott.
Description: Burbank, CA : DC Comics, [2020] | Summary: While living with her latest set of foster parents, Ashley Rayburn mistakenly applies some found body paints which give her a wide range of special powers, but soon the military discovers what happened to their secret weapon and this puts Ashley and her newfound family and friends in danger. | Audience: Ages 8-12 (provided by DC Comics) | Audience: Grades 4-6 (provided by DC Comics)
Identifiers: LCCN 2020000356 (print) | LCCN 2020000357 (ebook) | ISBN 9781779504449 (ebook) | ISBN 9781401296575 (paperback)
Subjects: LCSH: Graphic novels. | CYAC: Graphic novels. | Ability--Fiction. | Superheres--Fiction.
Classification: LCC PZ7.7.M86 (ebook) | LCC PZ7.7.M86 Pr 2020 (print) | DDC 741.5/973--dc23

TABLE OF CONTENTS

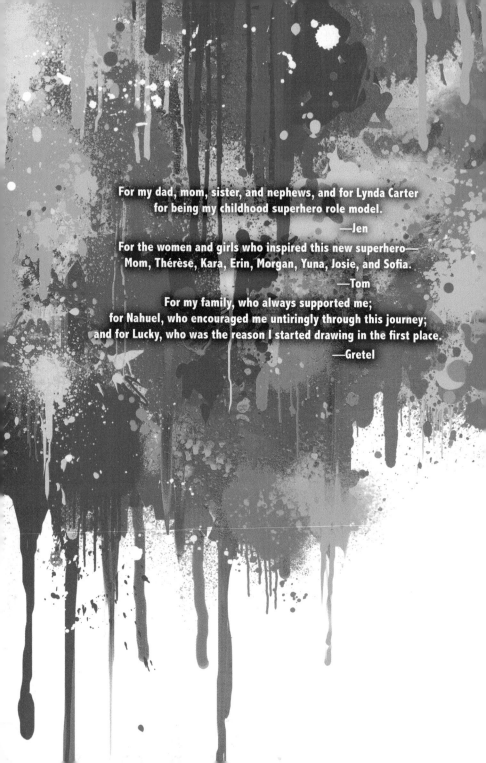

For my dad, mom, sister, and nephews, and for Lynda Carter
for being my childhood superhero role model.

—Jen

For the women and girls who inspired this new superhero—
Mom, Thérèse, Kara, Erin, Morgan, Yuna, Josie, and Sofia.

—Tom

For my family, who always supported me;
for Nahuel, who encouraged me untiringly through this journey;
and for Lucky, who was the reason I started drawing in the first place.

—Gretel

chapter 1
Primary Colors

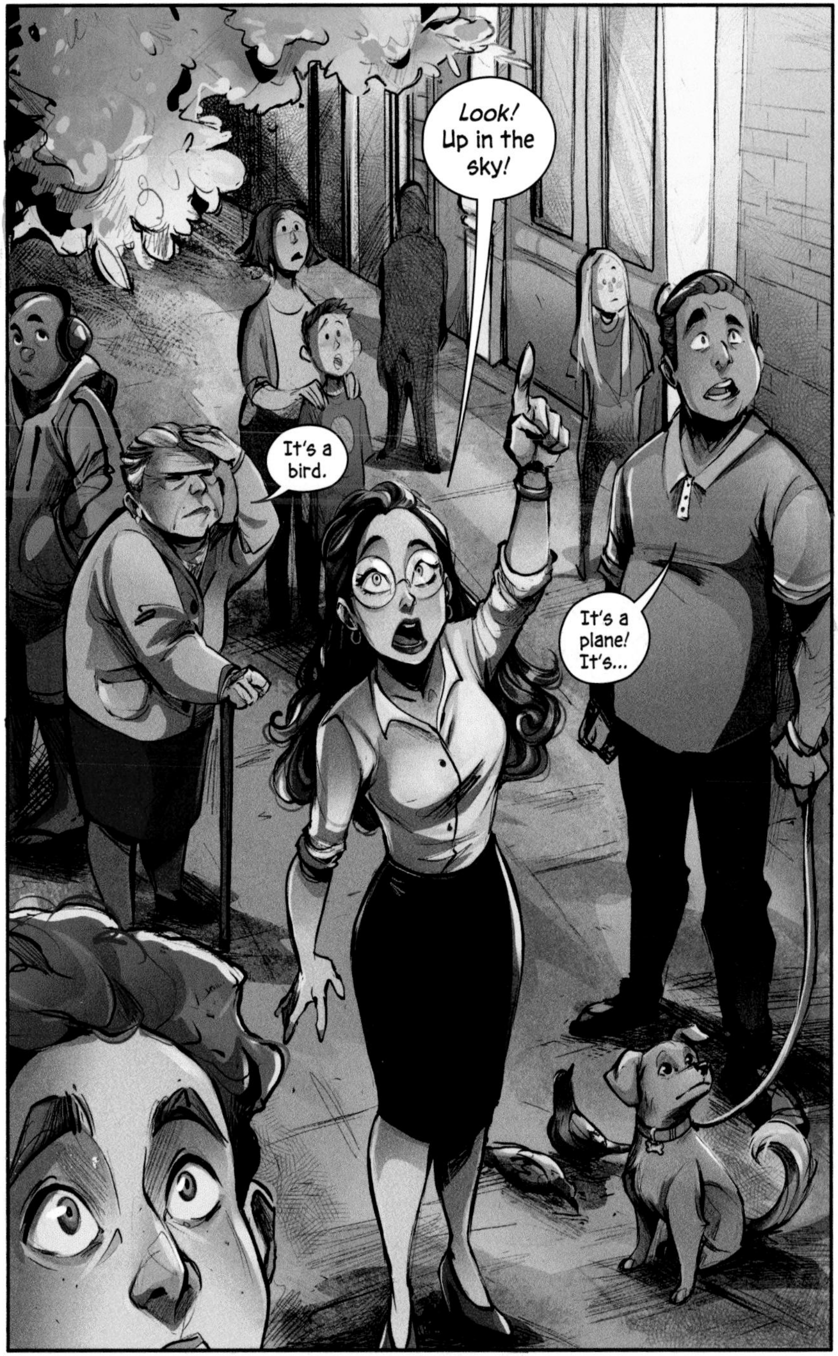
Look! Up in the sky!
It's a bird.
It's a plane! It's...

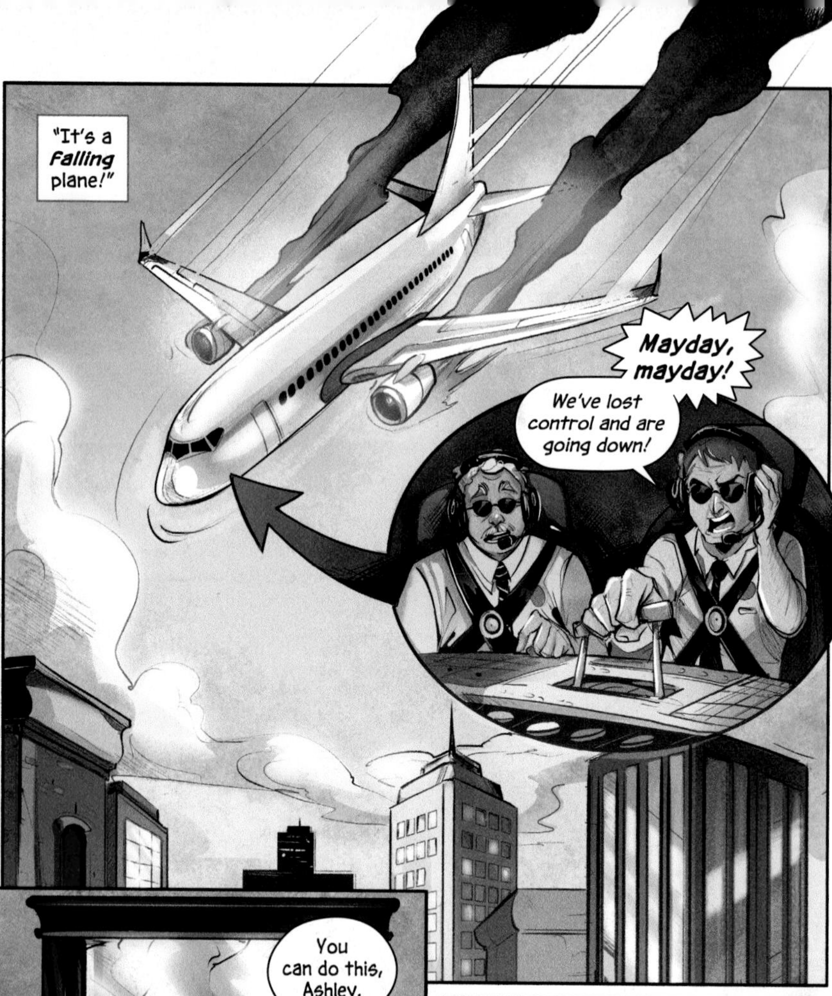
"It's a *falling* plane!"
Mayday, mayday!
We've lost control and are going down!

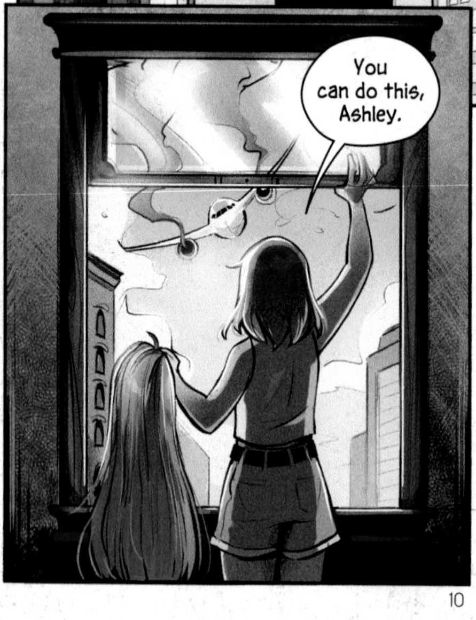
You can do this, Ashley.

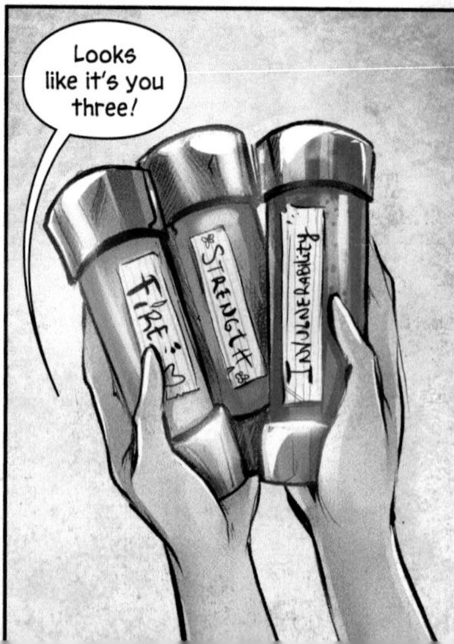
Looks like it's you three!
FIRE
STRENGTH
INVULNERABILITY

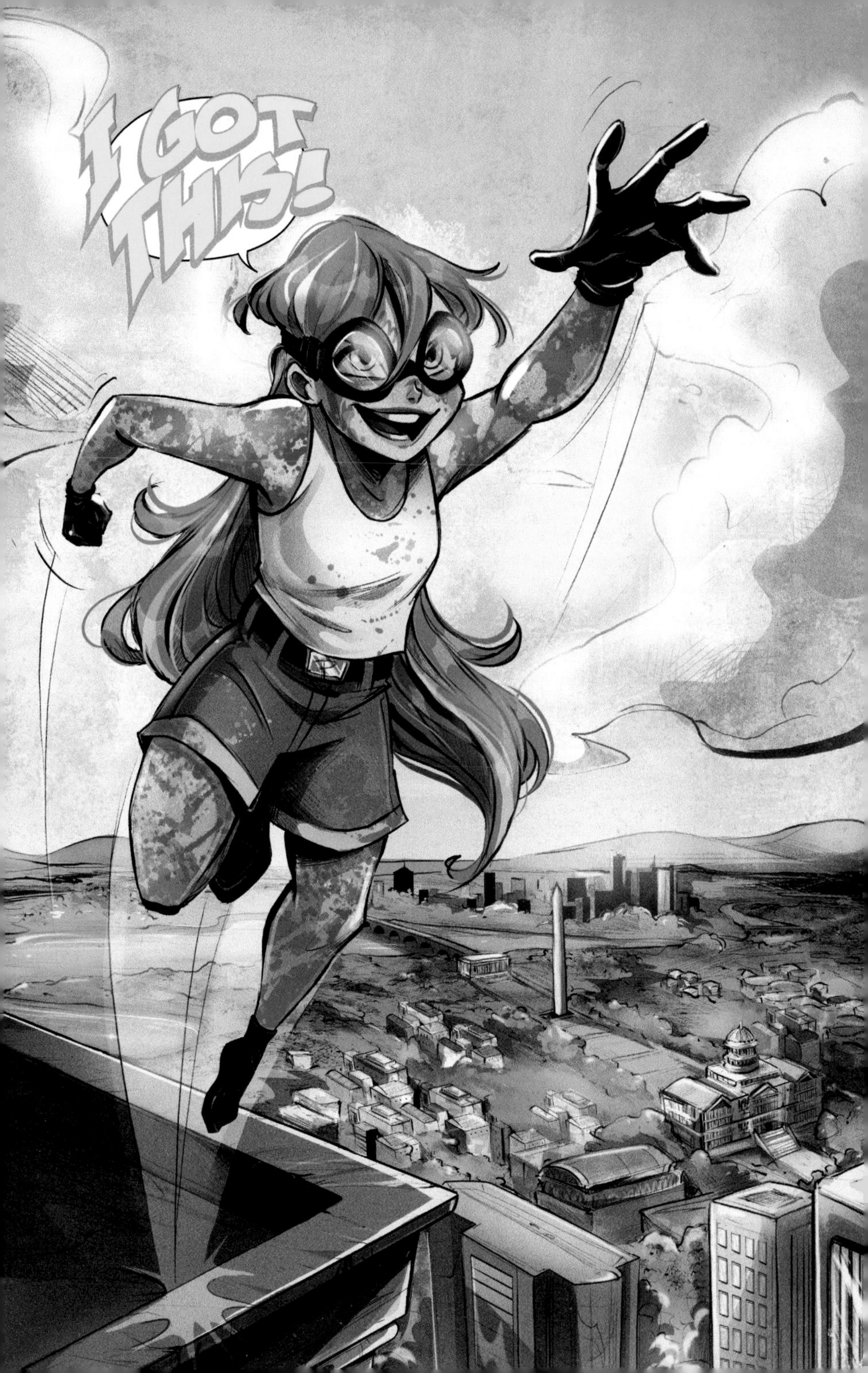
I GOT THIS!

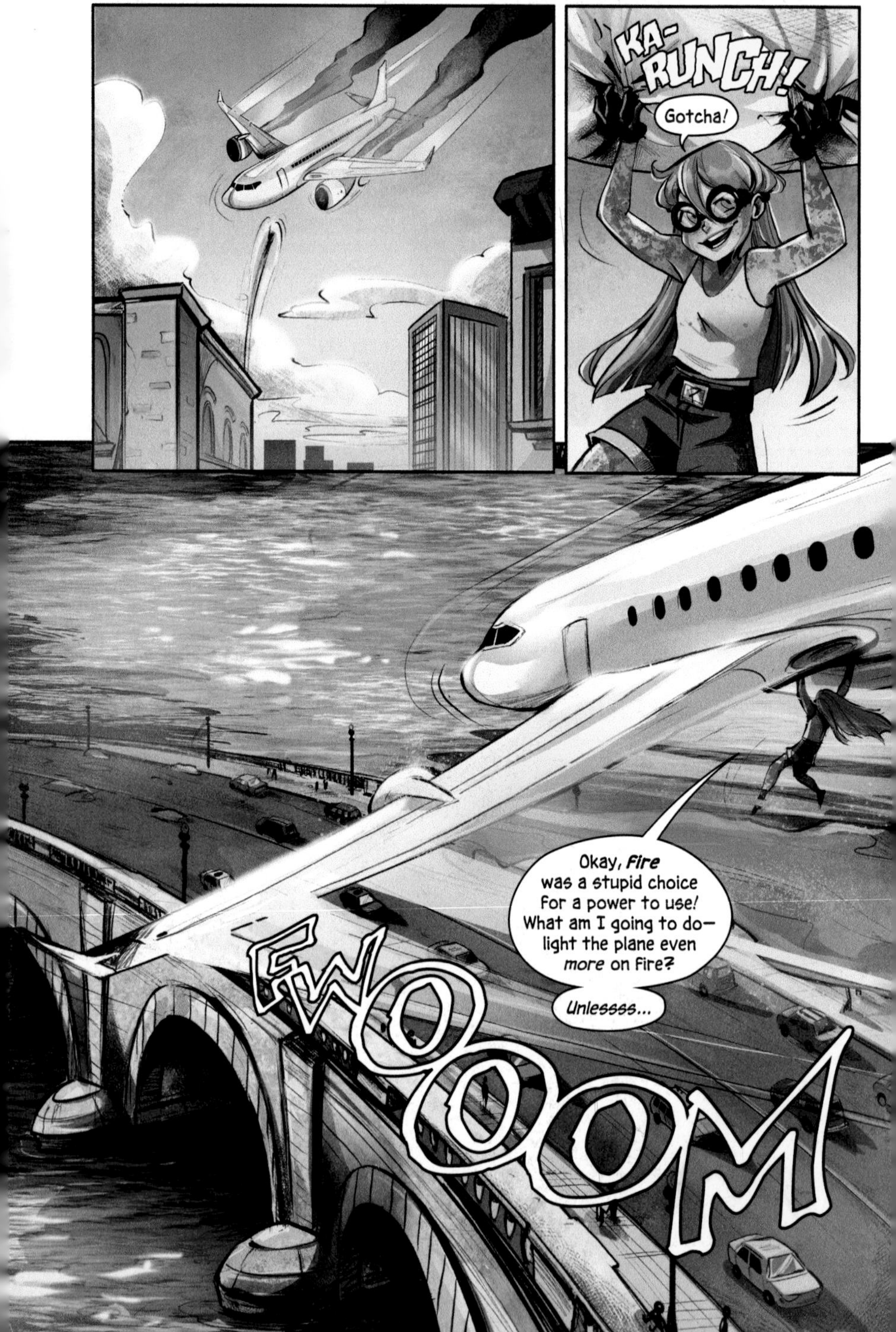
KA-RUNCH!
Gotcha!
Okay, *Fire* was a stupid choice for a power to use! What am I going to do— light the plane even *more* on fire?
Unlessss...
FWOOOOM

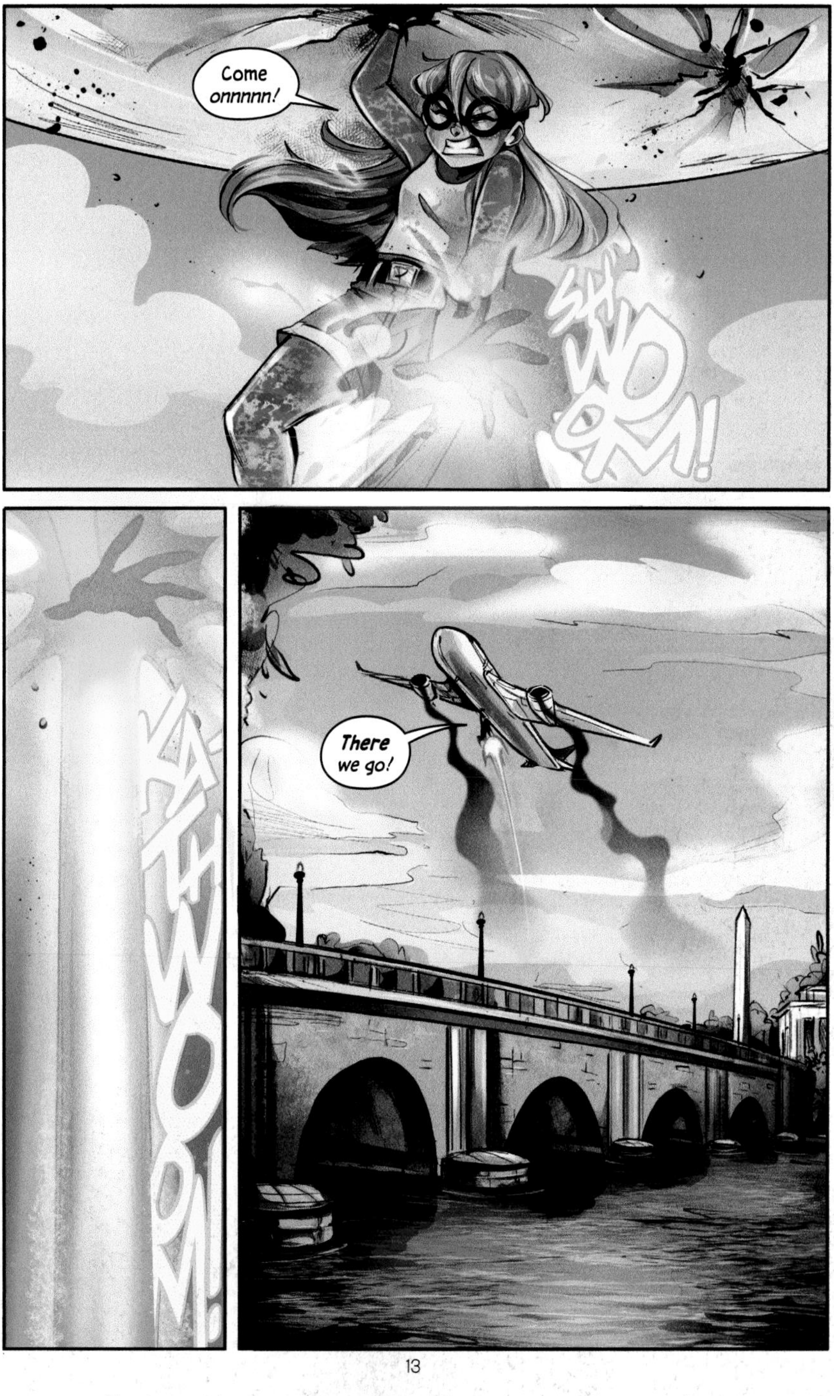
Come onnnnn!
SHWOOM!
KA-WOOM!
There we go!

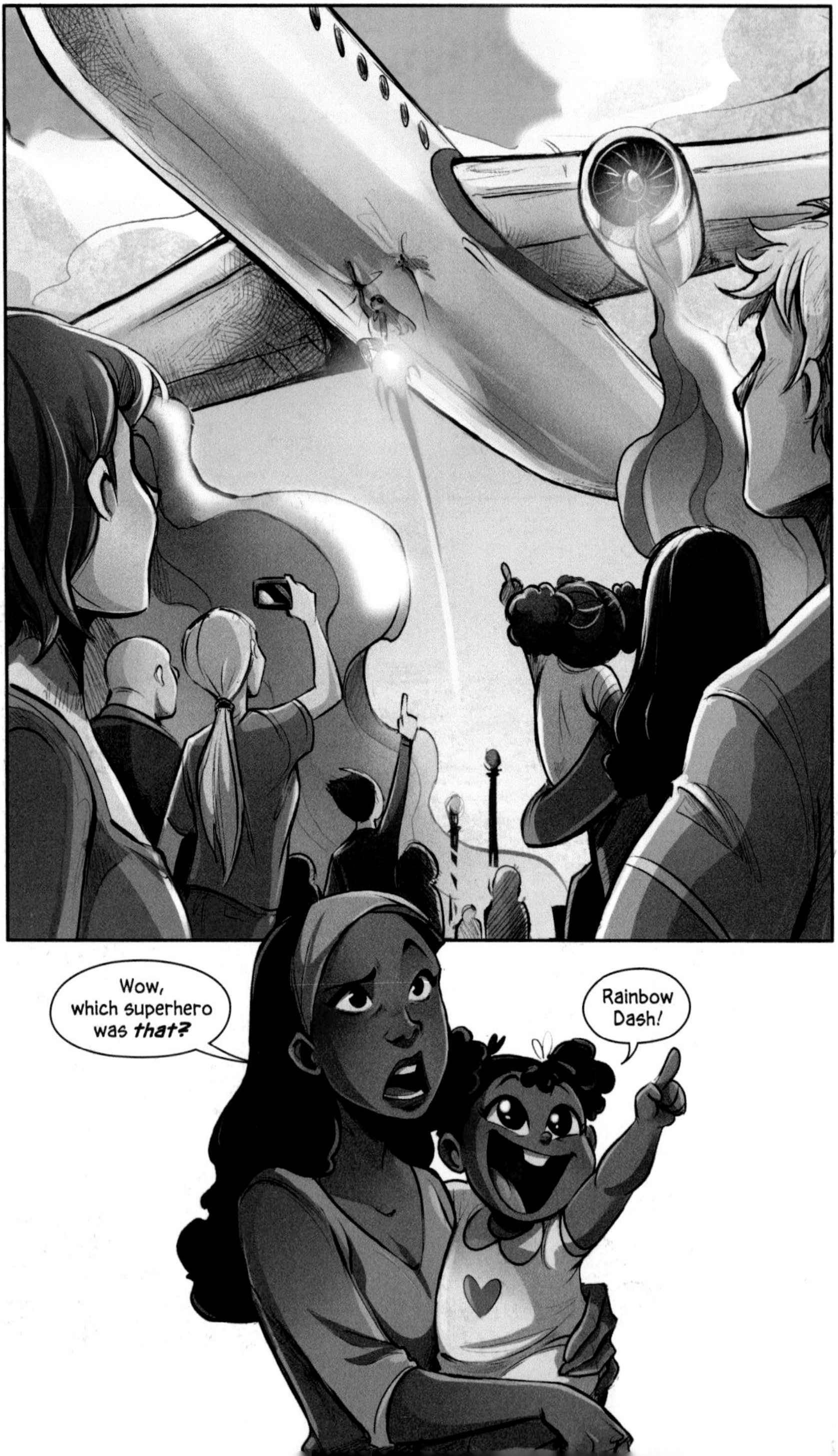
Wow, which superhero was *that?*
Rainbow Dash!

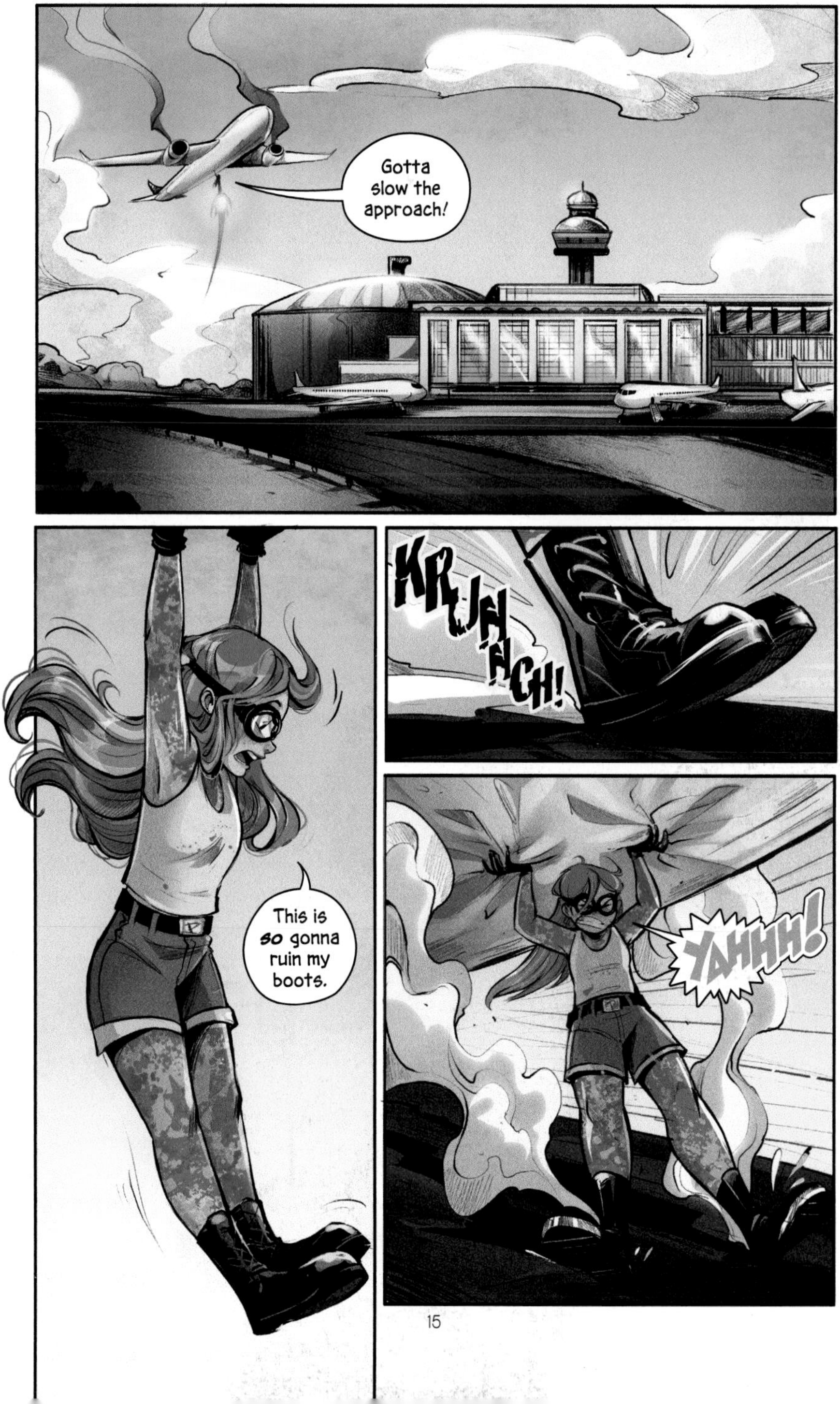
Gotta slow the approach!
This is *so* gonna ruin my boots.
KRUNNCH!
YAHHH!

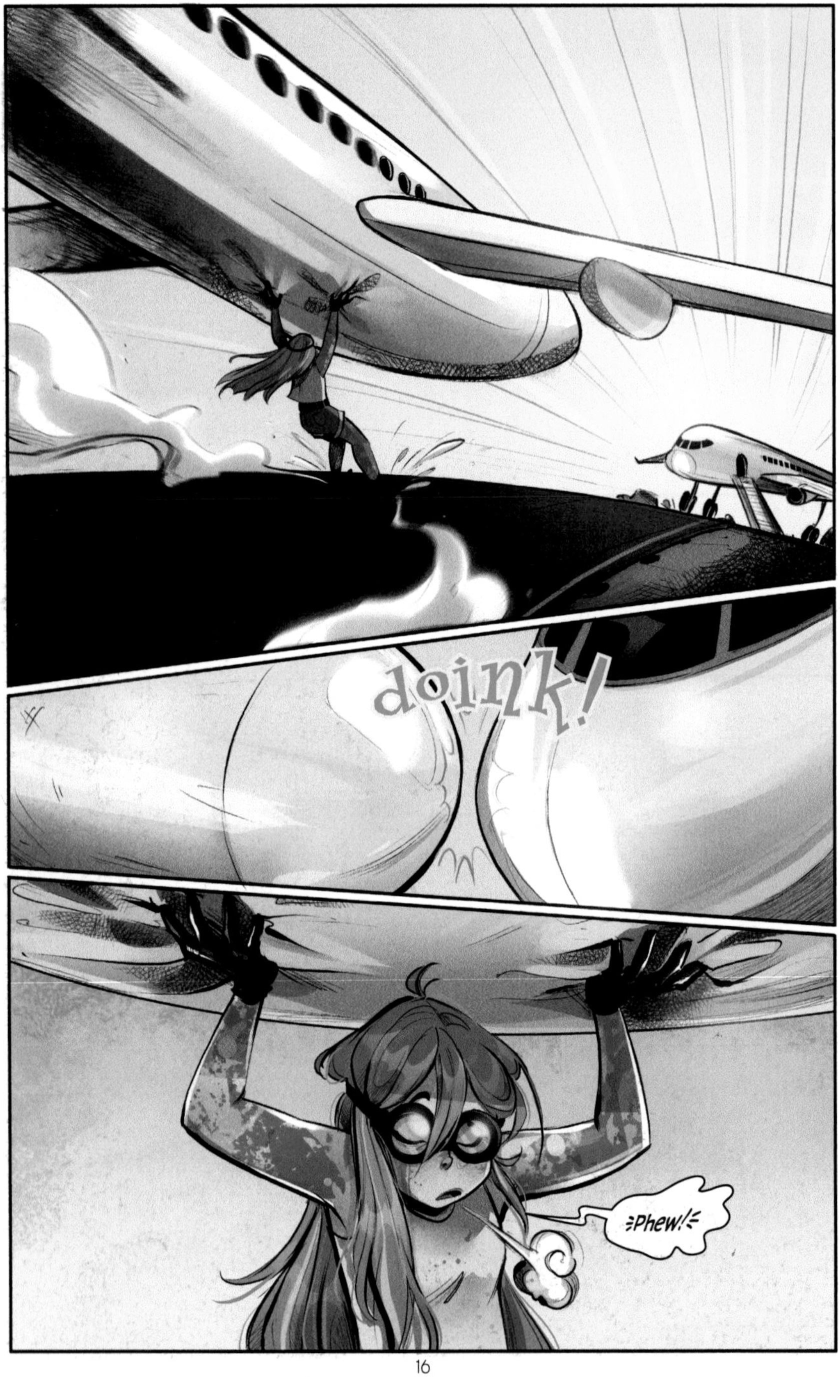
doink!
Phew!

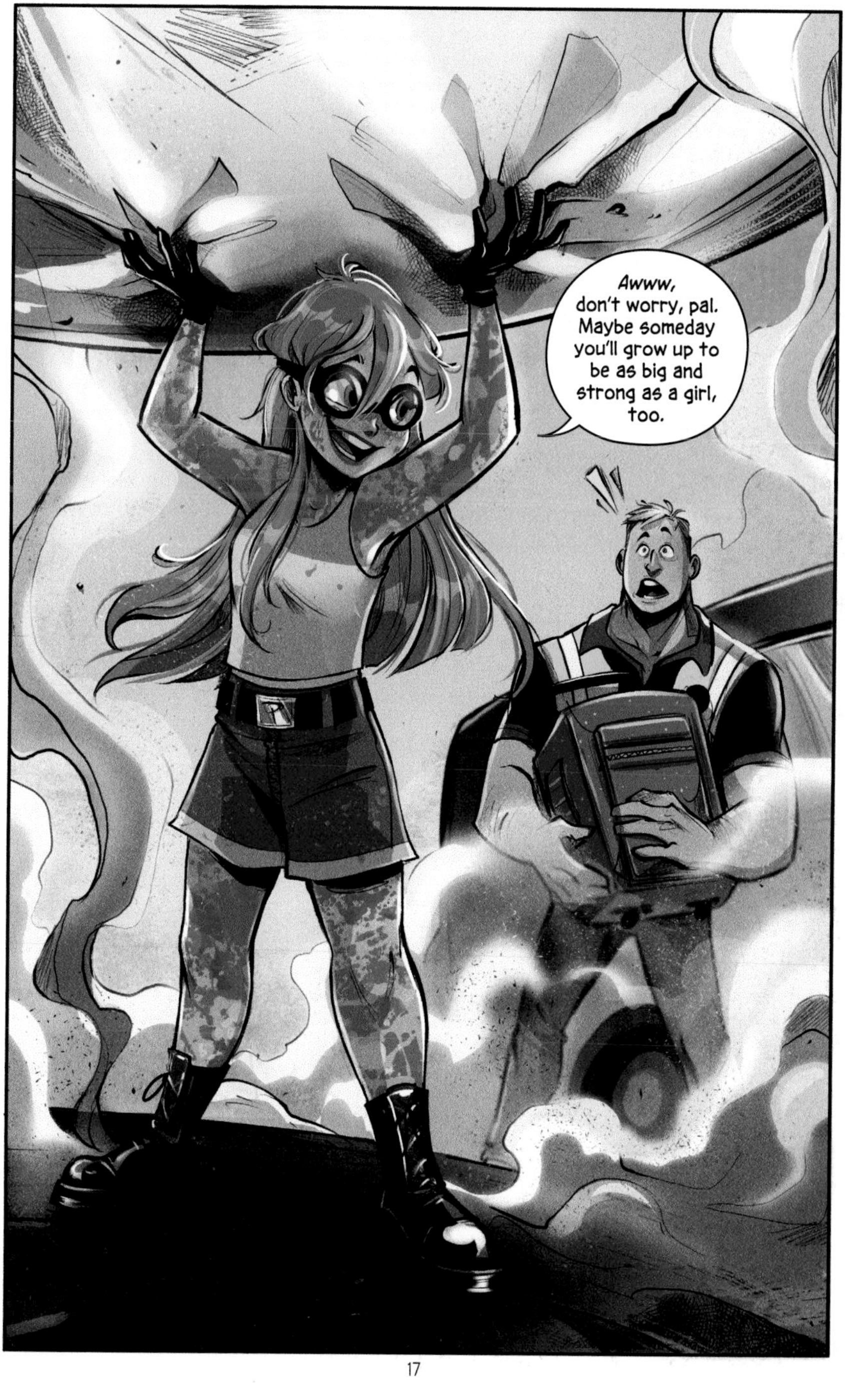
Awww, don't worry, pal. Maybe someday you'll grow up to be as big and strong as a girl, too.

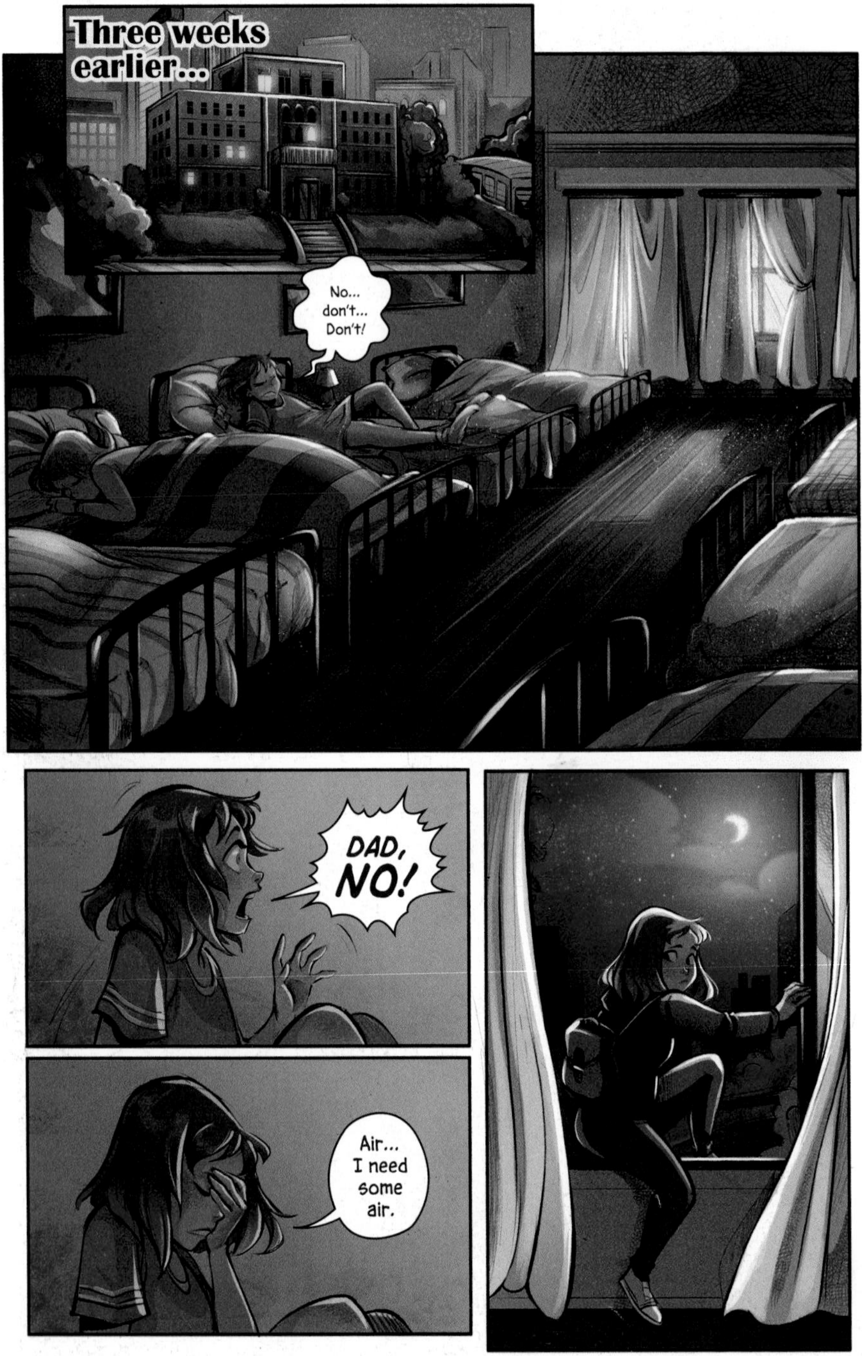
Three weeks earlier...
No... don't... Don't!
DAD, NO!
Air... I need some air.

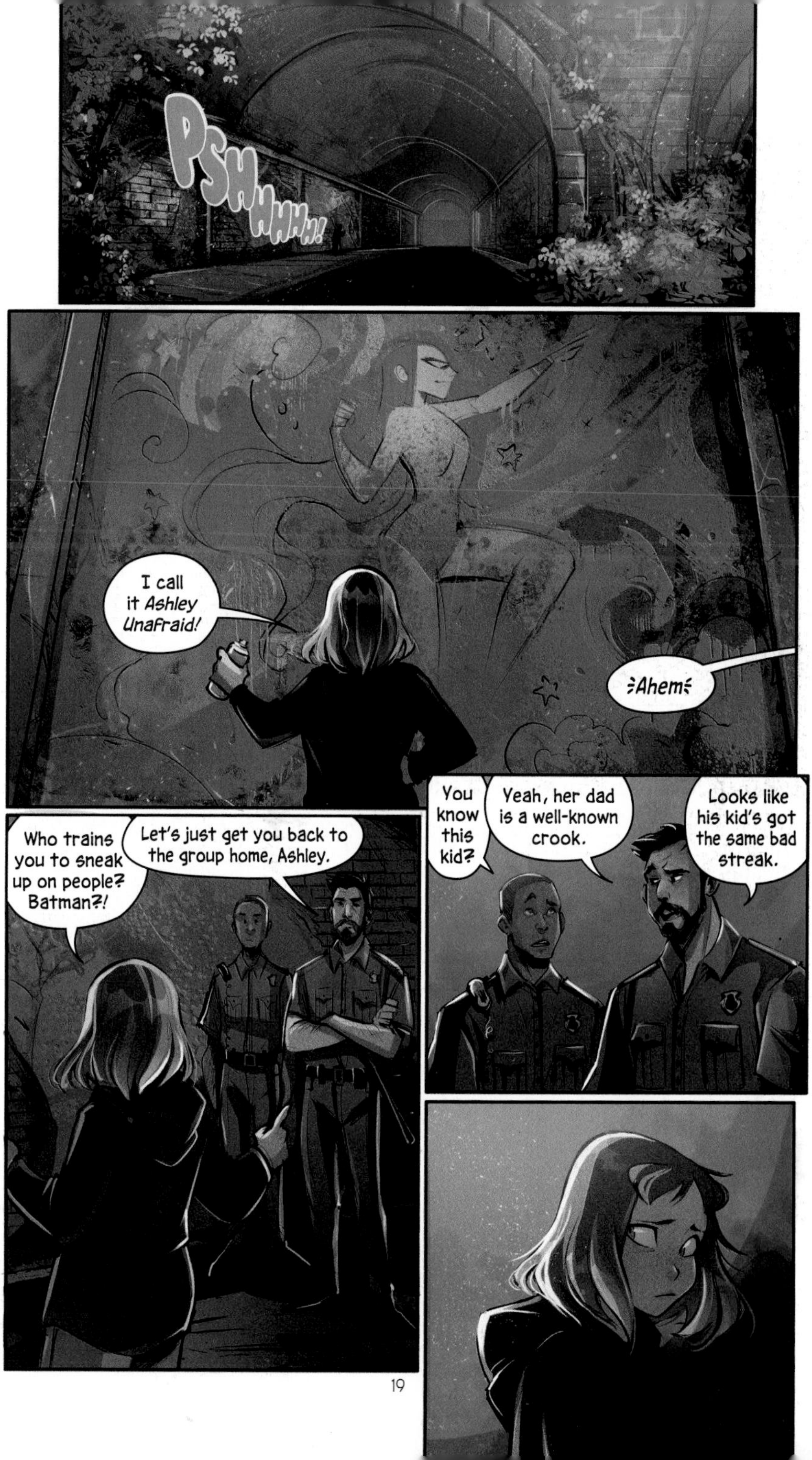
PSHHHHH!
I call it Ashley Unafraid!
Ahem
Who trains you to sneak up on people? Batman?!
Let's just get you back to the group home, Ashley.
You know this kid?
Yeah, her dad is a well-known crook.
Looks like his kid's got the same bad streak.

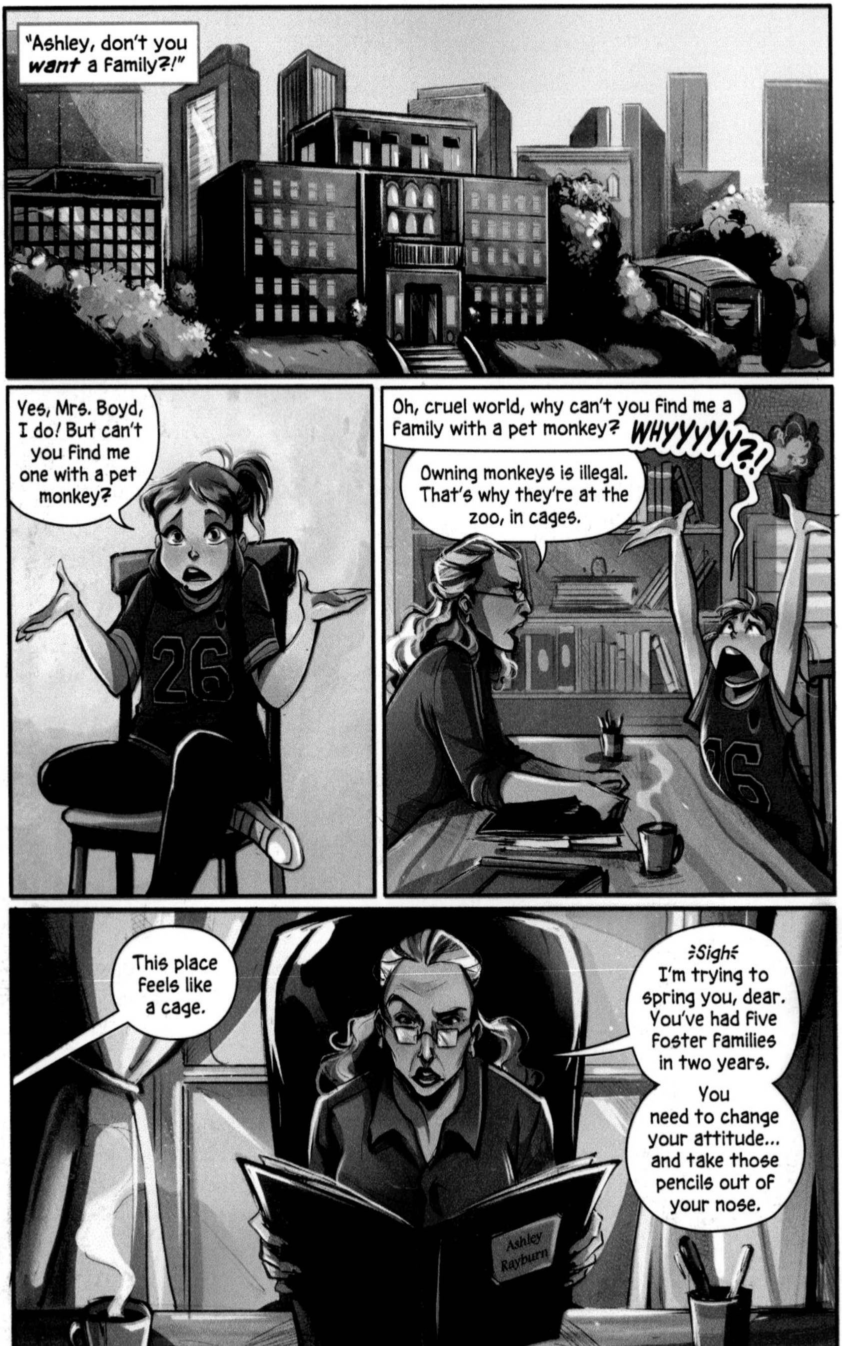

"Ashley, don't you *want* a family?!"
Yes, Mrs. Boyd, I do! But can't you find me one with a pet monkey?
Oh, cruel world, why can't you find me a family with a pet monkey?
WHYYYYY?!
Owning monkeys is illegal. That's why they're at the zoo, in cages.
This place feels like a cage.
Sigh
I'm trying to spring you, dear. You've had five foster families in two years.
You need to change your attitude... and take those pencils out of your nose.
Ashley Rayburn

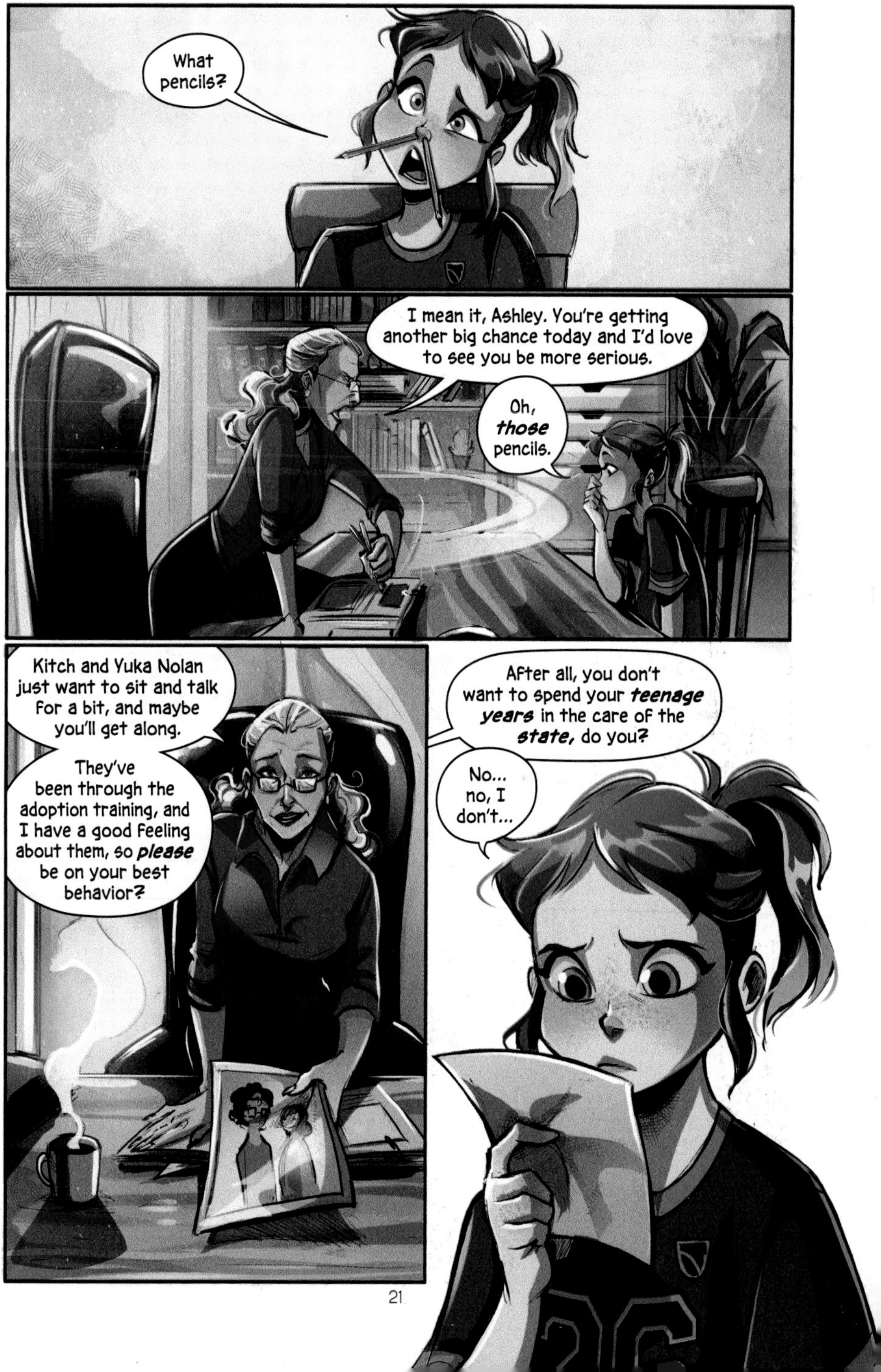
What pencils?
I mean it, Ashley. You're getting another big chance today and I'd love to see you be more serious.
Oh, *those* pencils.
Kitch and Yuka Nolan just want to sit and talk for a bit, and maybe you'll get along.
They've been through the adoption training, and I have a good feeling about them, so *please* be on your best behavior?
After all, you don't want to spend your *teenage years* in the care of the *state,* do you?
No... no, I don't...

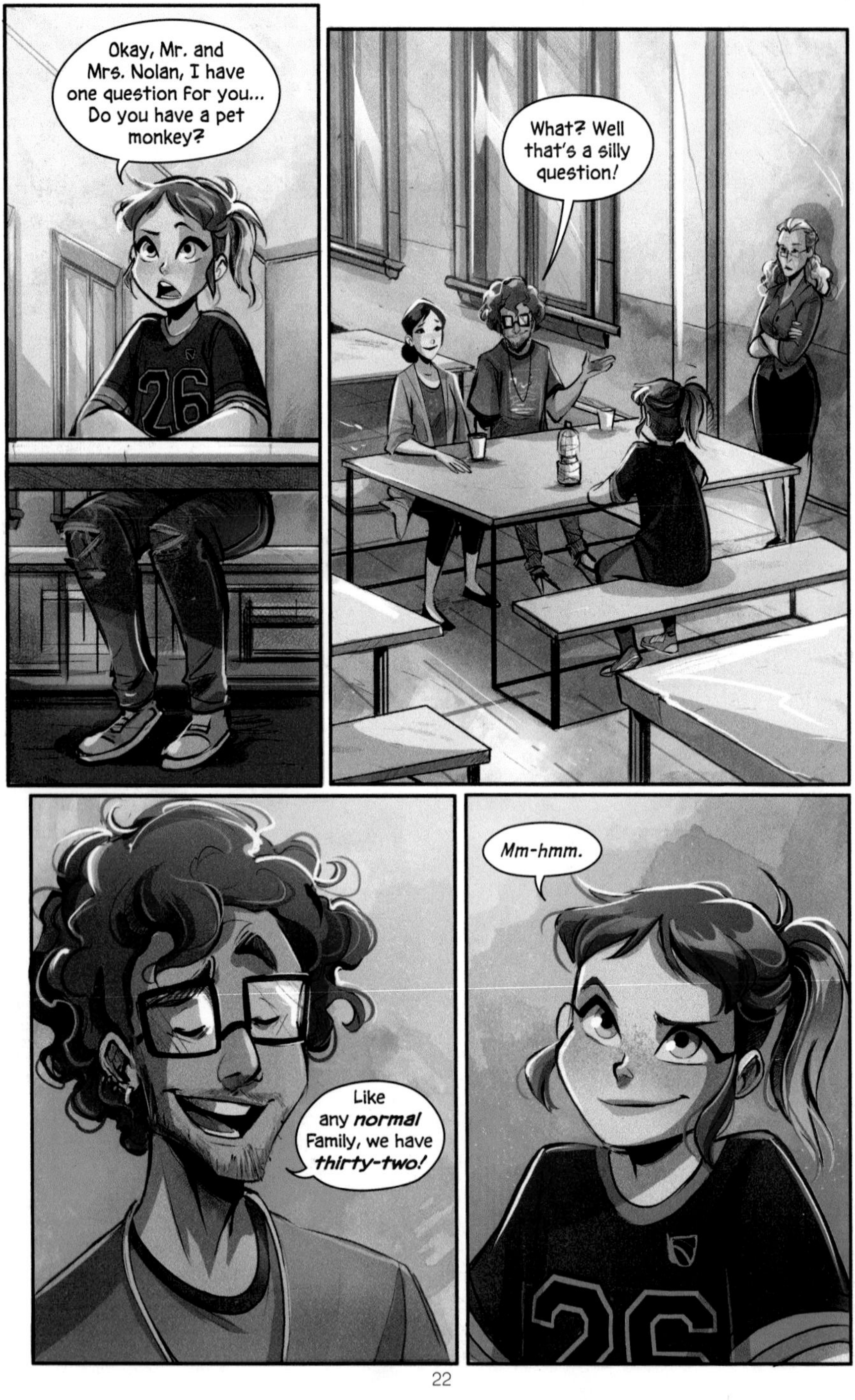
Okay, Mr. and Mrs. Nolan, I have one question for you... Do you have a pet monkey?
What? Well that's a silly question!
Like any *normal* family, we have *thirty-two!*
Mm-hmm.

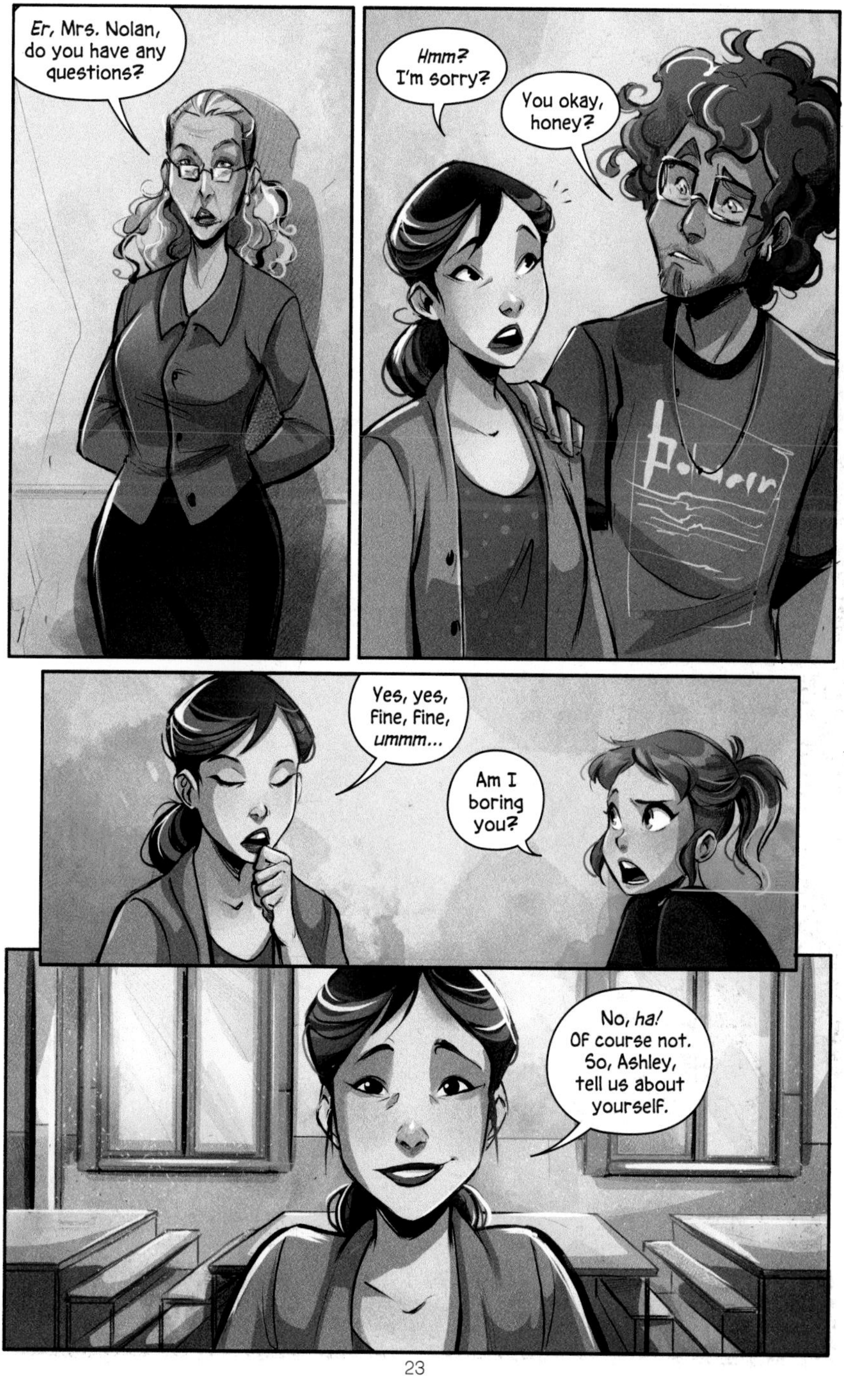

Er, Mrs. Nolan, do you have any questions?
Hmm? I'm sorry?
You okay, honey?
Yes, yes, fine, fine, ummm...
Am I boring you?
No, ha! Of course not. So, Ashley, tell us about yourself.

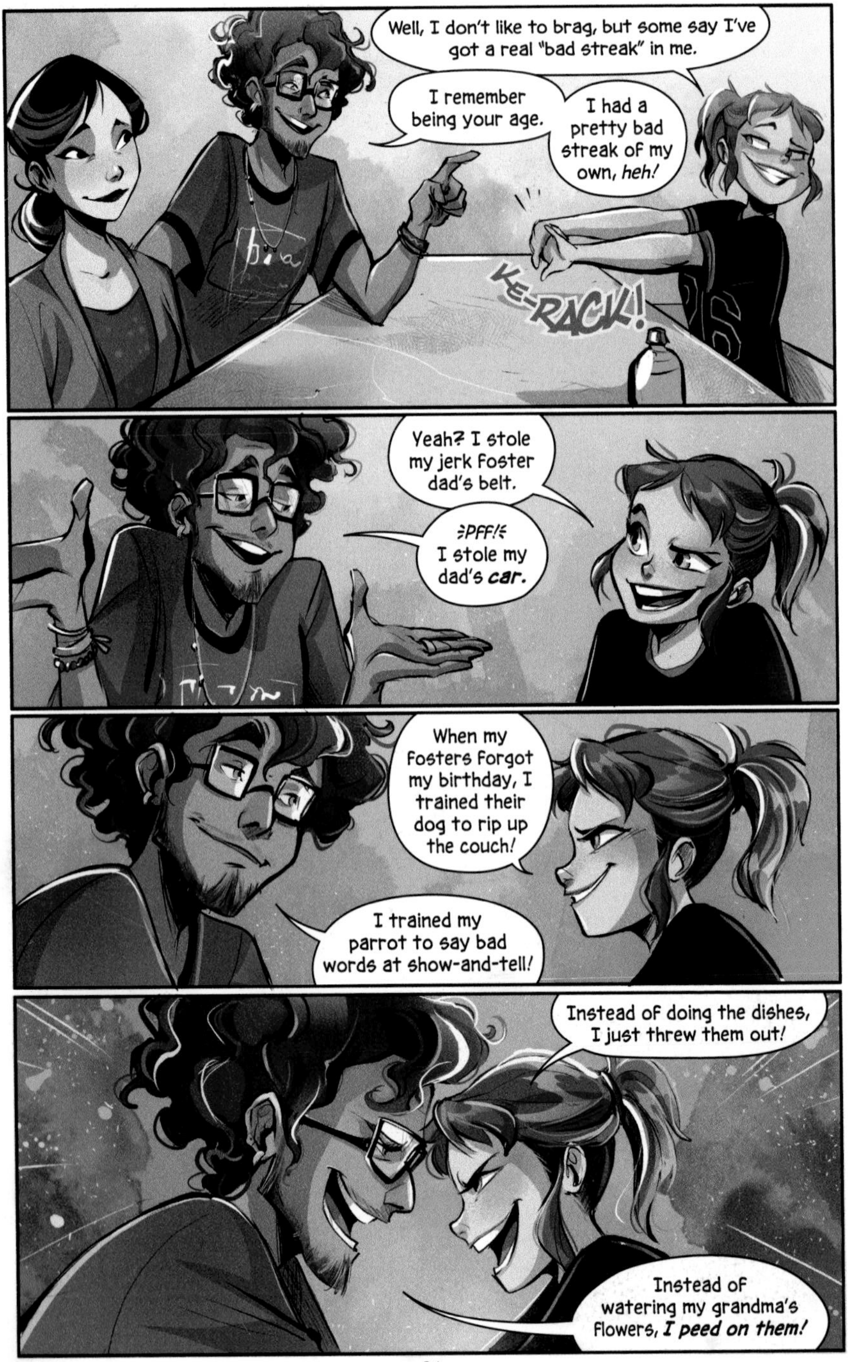
Well, I don't like to brag, but some say I've got a real "bad streak" in me.
I remember being your age.
I had a pretty bad streak of my own, *heh!*
KE-RACK!
Yeah? I stole my jerk foster dad's belt.
PFF! I stole my dad's **car.**
When my fosters forgot my birthday, I trained their dog to rip up the couch!
I trained my parrot to say bad words at show-and-tell!
Instead of doing the dishes, I just threw them out!
Instead of watering my grandma's flowers, ***I peed on them!***

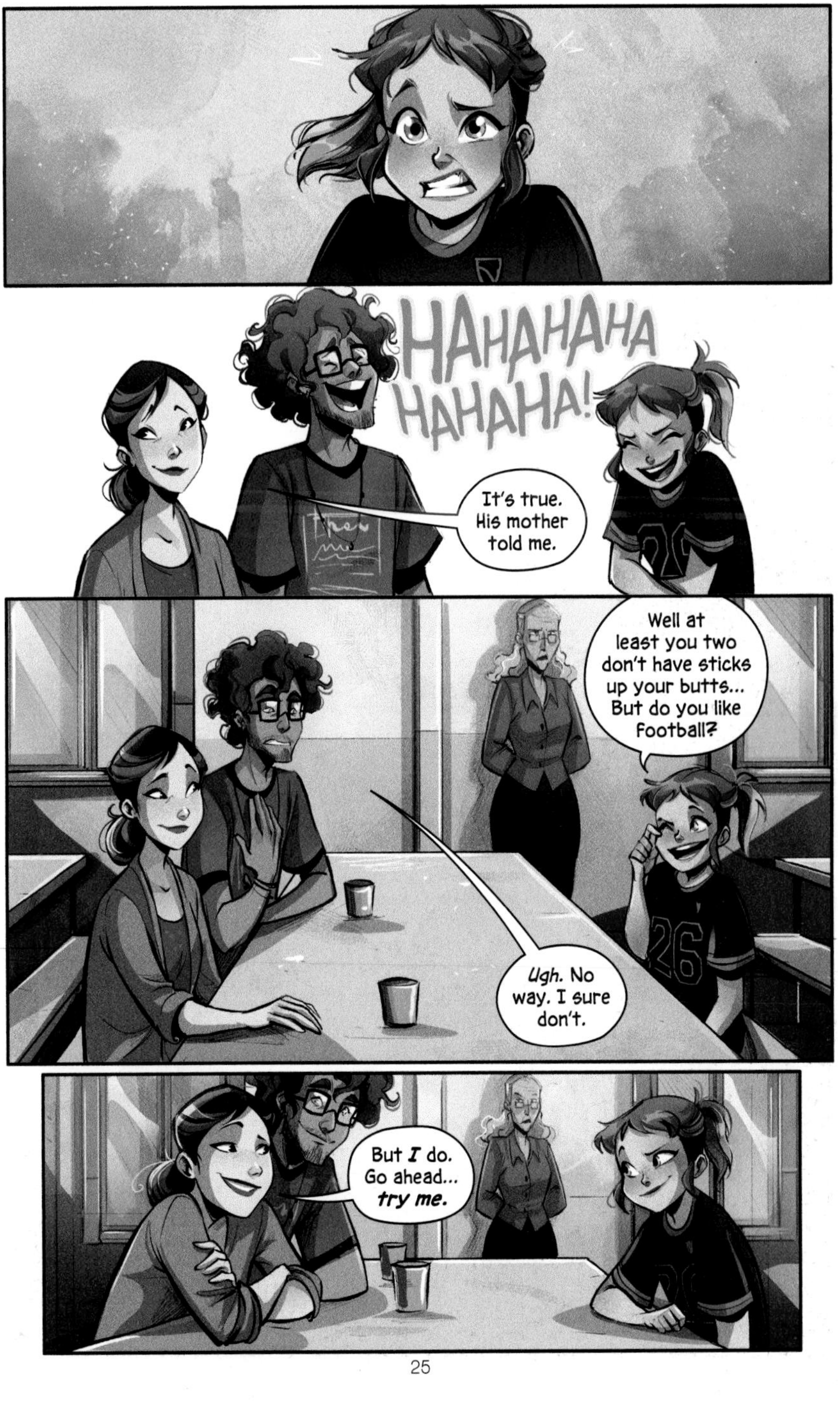
HAHAHAHA HAHAHA!
It's true. His mother told me.
Well at least you two don't have sticks up your butts... But do you like football?
Ugh. No way. I sure don't.
But I do. Go ahead... try me.

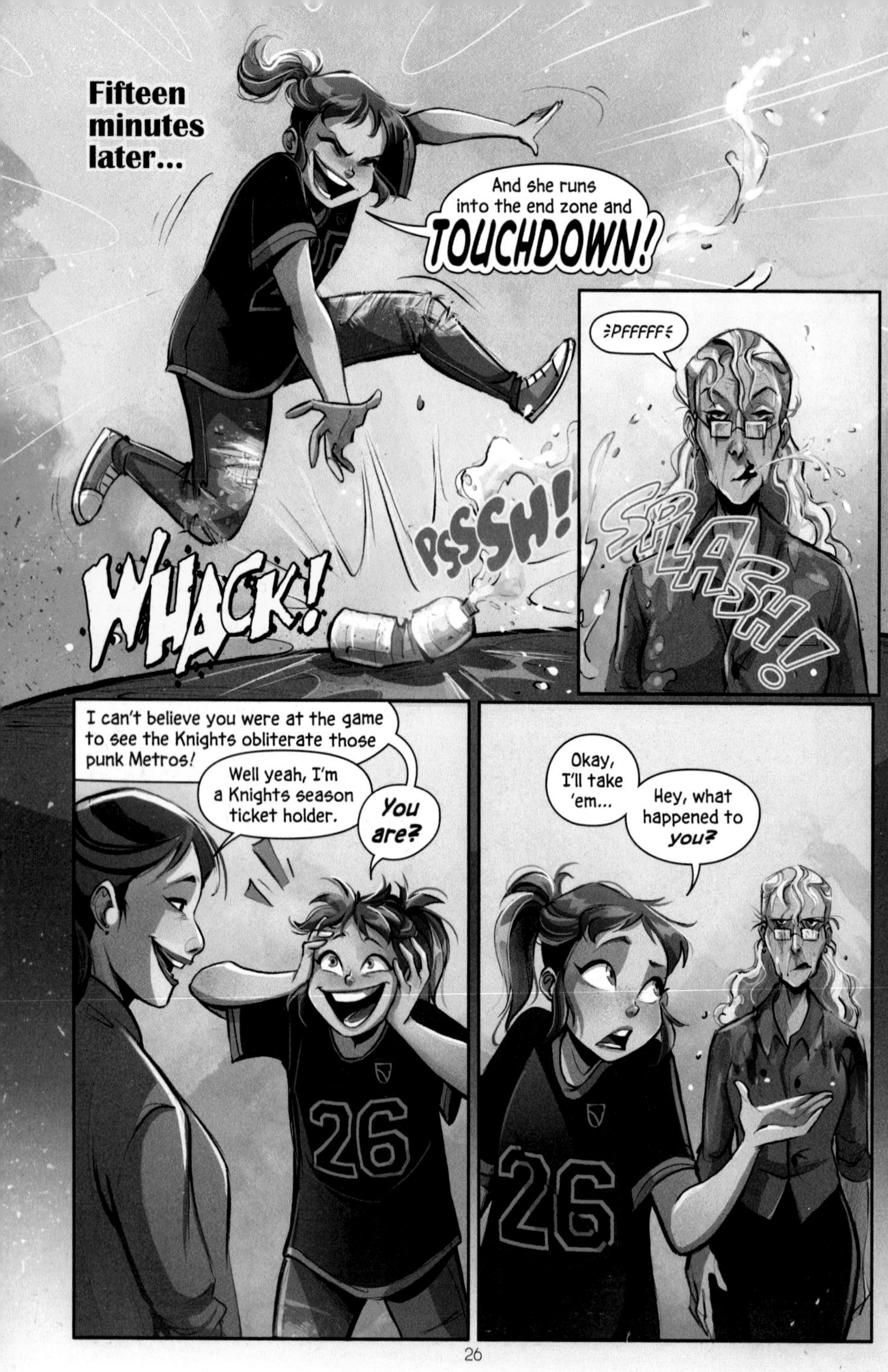
Fifteen minutes later...
And she runs into the end zone and TOUCHDOWN!
WHACK!
PSSSH!
PFFFFF
SPLASH!
I can't believe you were at the game to see the Knights obliterate those punk Metros!
Well yeah, I'm a Knights season ticket holder.
You are?
Okay, I'll take 'em...
Hey, what happened to you?
26
26

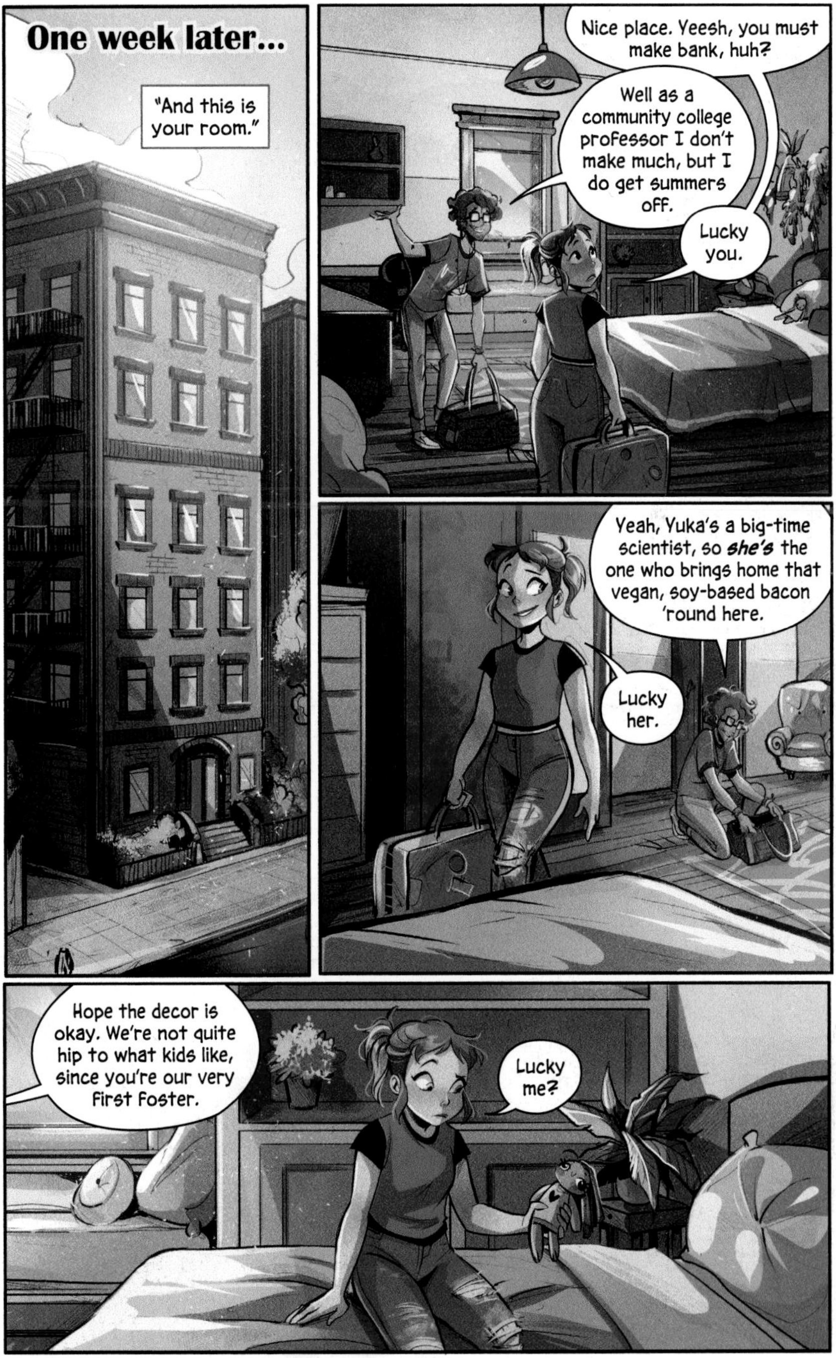
One week later...
"And this is your room."
Nice place. Yeesh, you must make bank, huh?
Well as a community college professor I don't make much, but I do get summers off.
Lucky you.
Yeah, Yuka's a big-time scientist, so *she's* the one who brings home that vegan, soy-based bacon 'round here.
Lucky her.
Hope the decor is okay. We're not quite hip to what kids like, since you're our very first foster.
Lucky me?

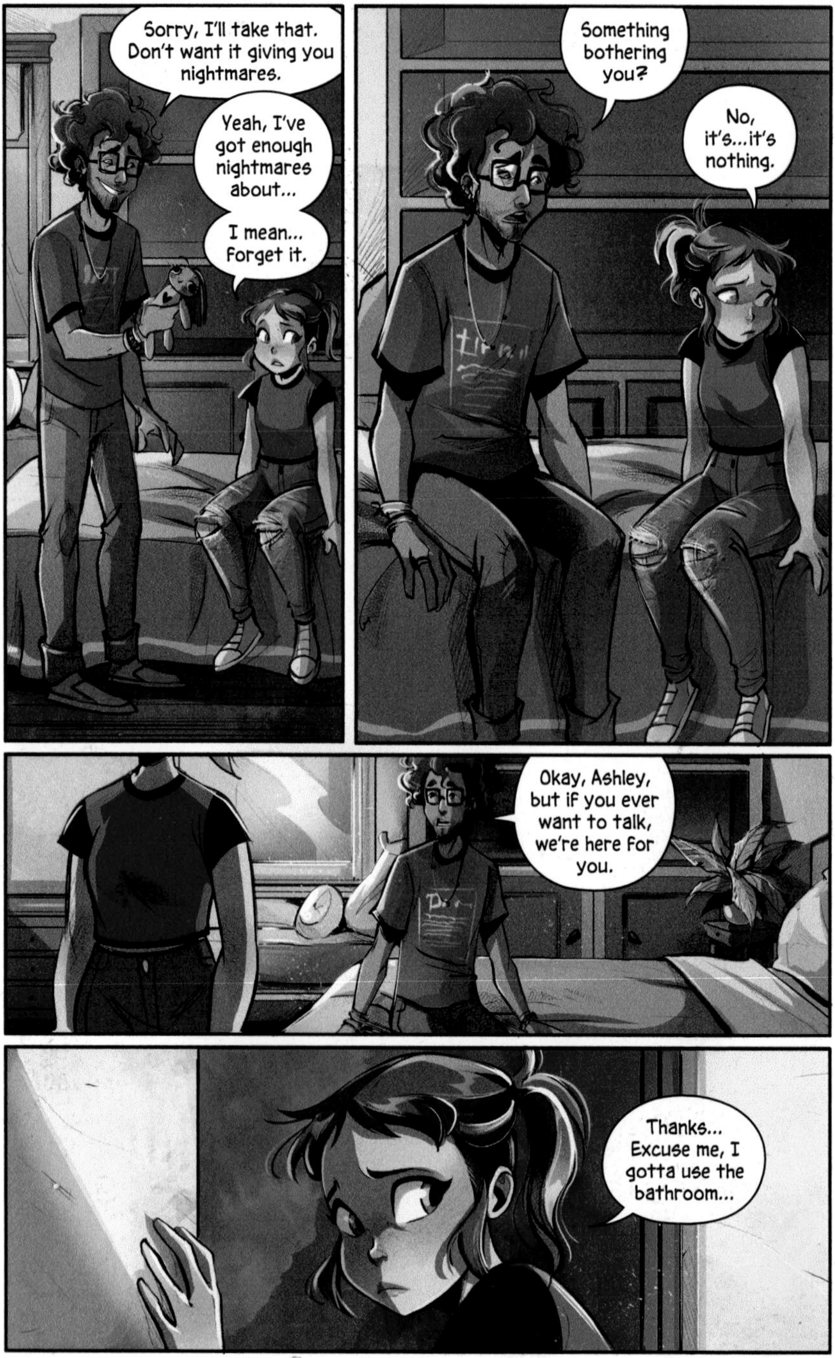

Sorry, I'll take that. Don't want it giving you nightmares.
Yeah, I've got enough nightmares about...
I mean... Forget it.
Something bothering you?
No, it's...it's nothing.
Okay, Ashley, but if you ever want to talk, we're here for you.
Thanks... Excuse me, I gotta use the bathroom...

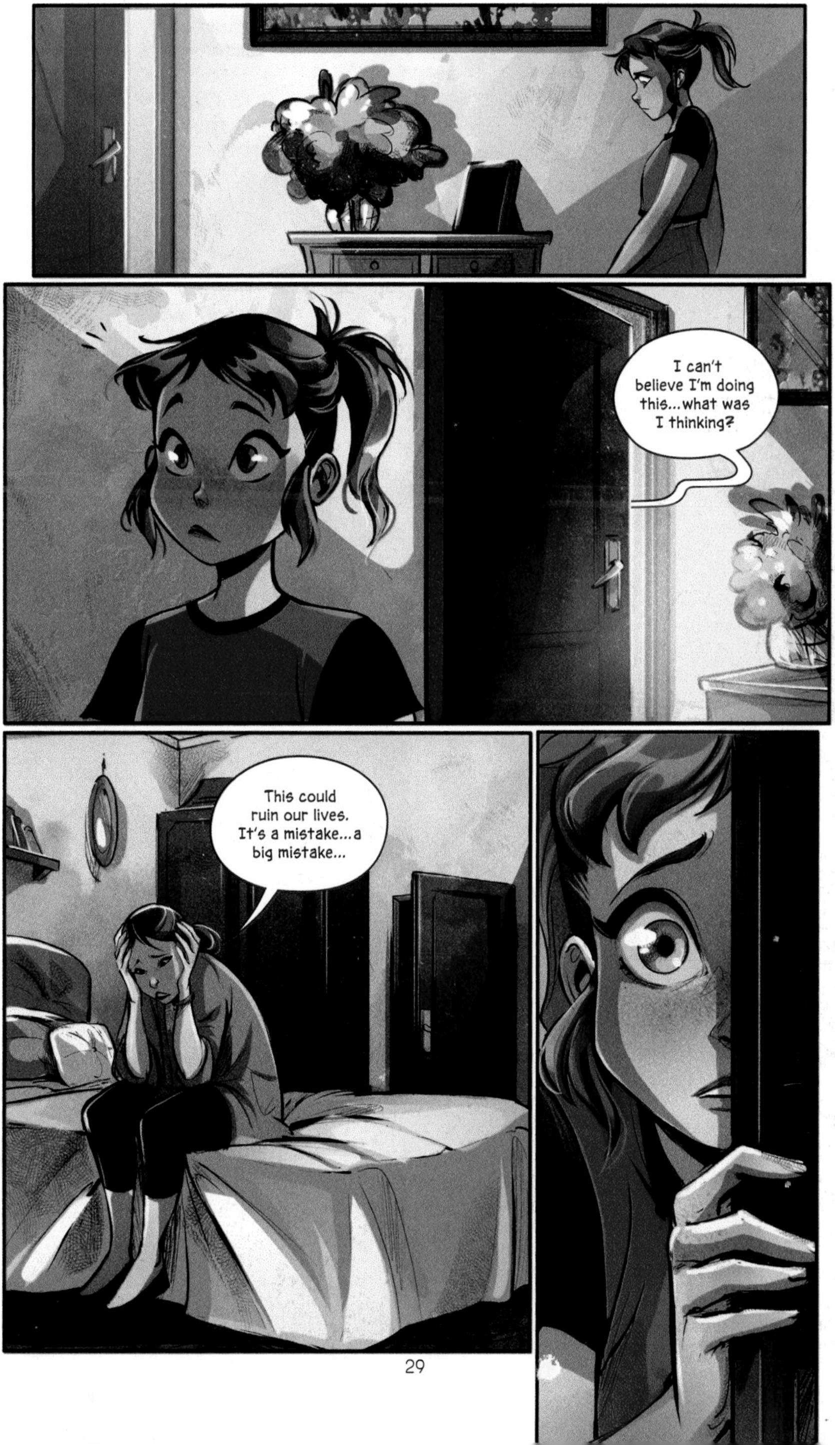
I can't believe I'm doing this...what was I thinking?
This could ruin our lives. It's a mistake...a big mistake...

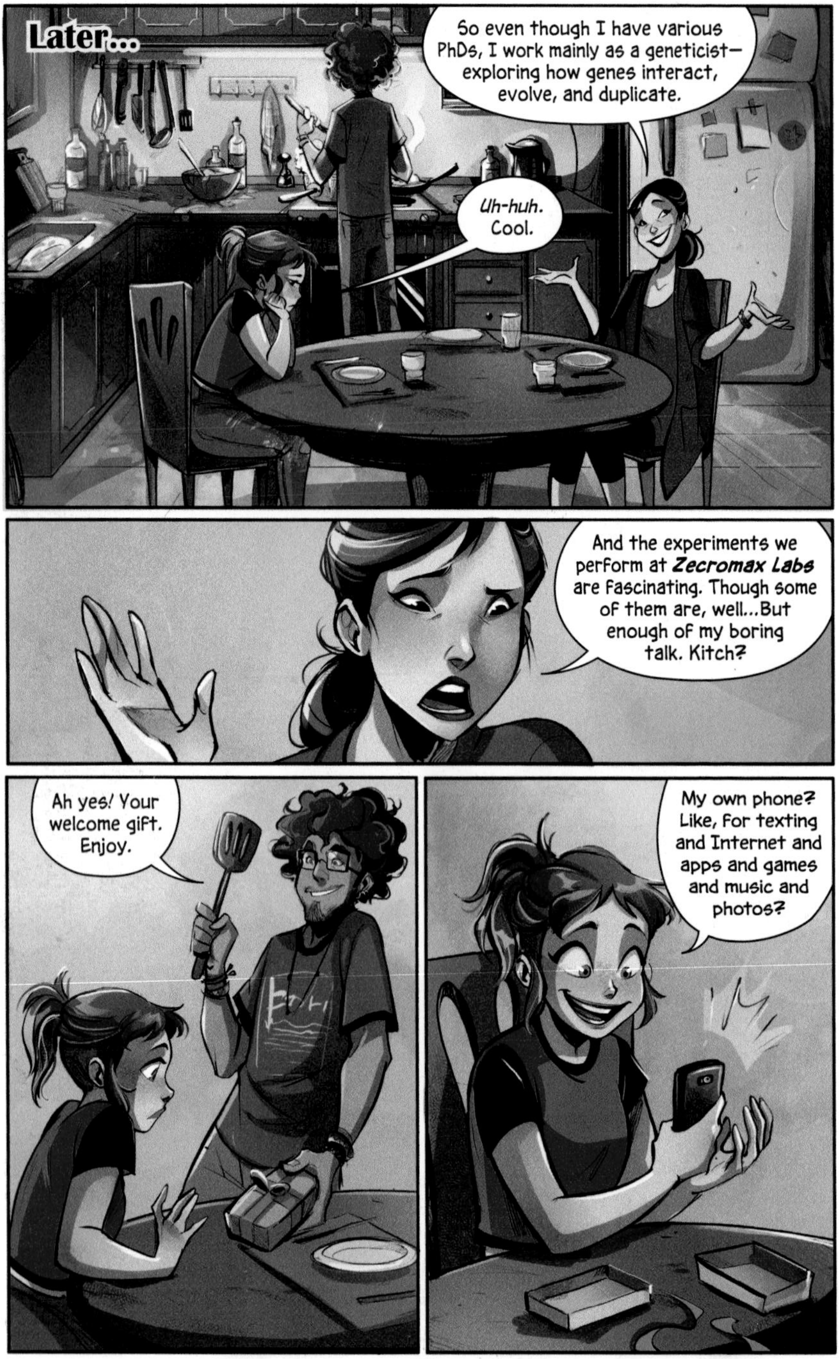
Later...
So even though I have various PhDs, I work mainly as a geneticist—exploring how genes interact, evolve, and duplicate.
Uh-huh. Cool.
And the experiments we perform at Zecromax Labs are fascinating. Though some of them are, well...But enough of my boring talk. Kitch?
Ah yes! Your welcome gift. Enjoy.
My own phone? Like, for texting and Internet and apps and games and music and photos?

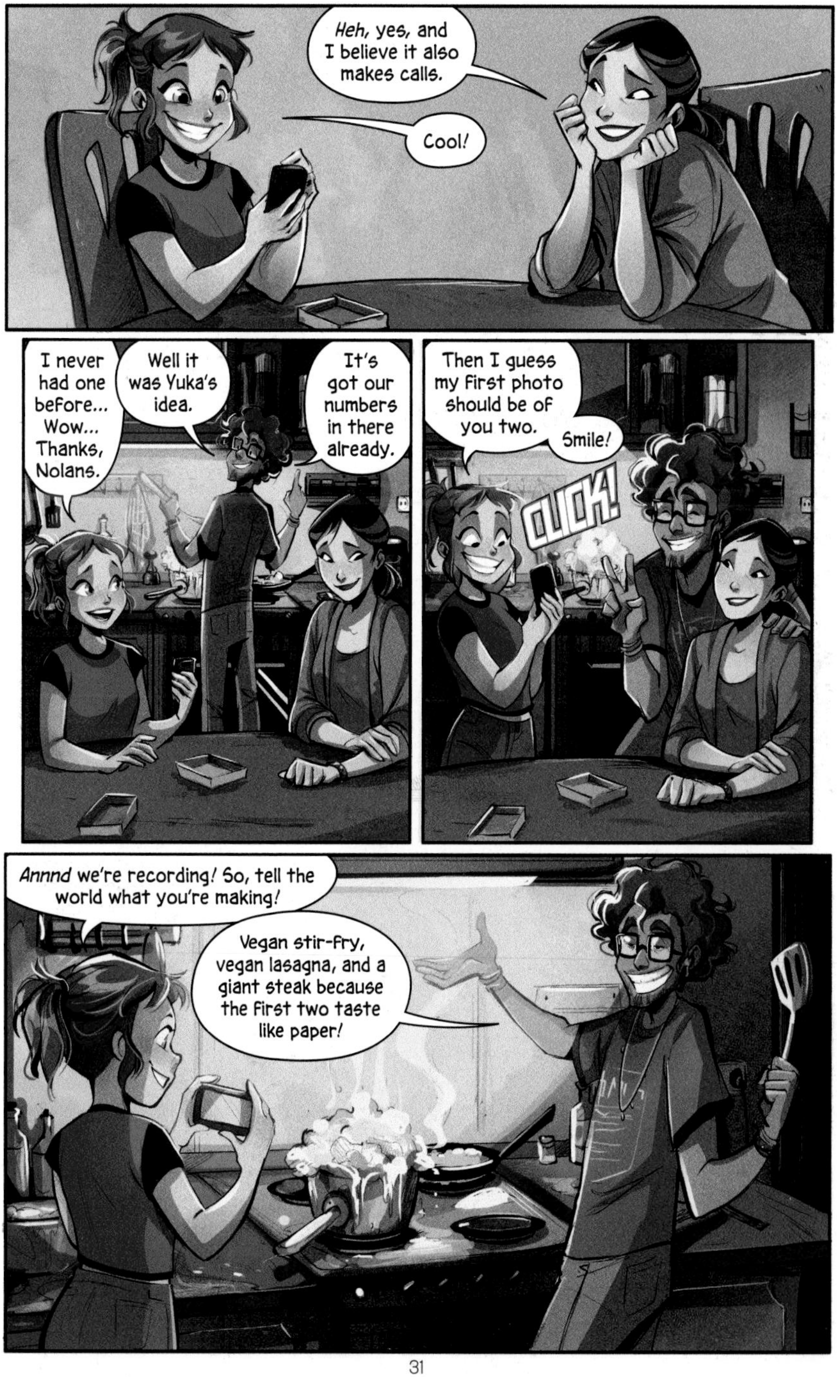

Heh, yes, and I believe it also makes calls.
Cool!
I never had one before... Wow... Thanks, Nolans.
Well it was Yuka's idea.
It's got our numbers in there already.
Then I guess my first photo should be of you two.
Smile!
CLICK!
Annnd we're recording! So, tell the world what you're making!
Vegan stir-fry, vegan lasagna, and a giant steak because the first two taste like paper!

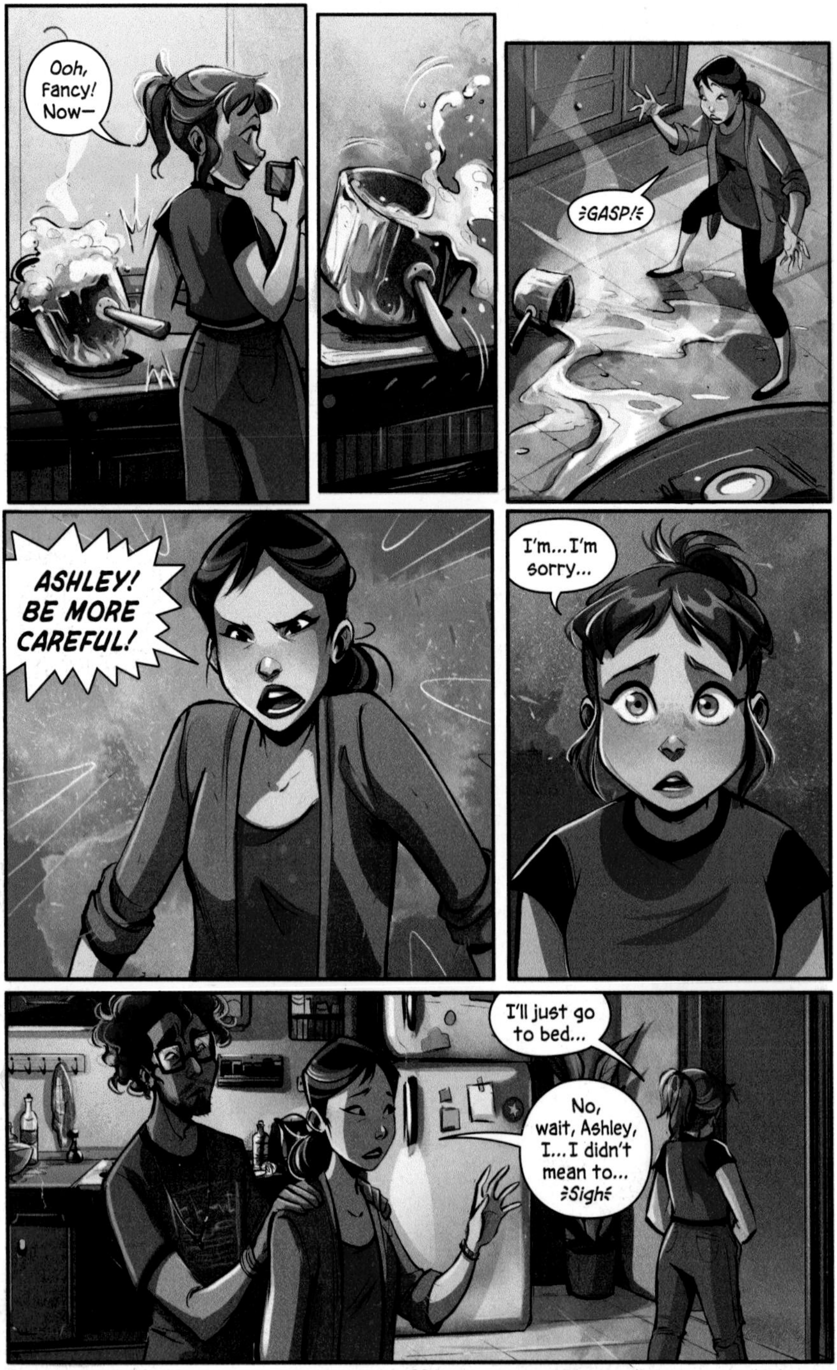
Ooh, fancy! Now—
GASP!
ASHLEY! BE MORE CAREFUL!
I'm... I'm sorry...
I'll just go to bed...
No, wait, Ashley, I... I didn't mean to...
Sigh

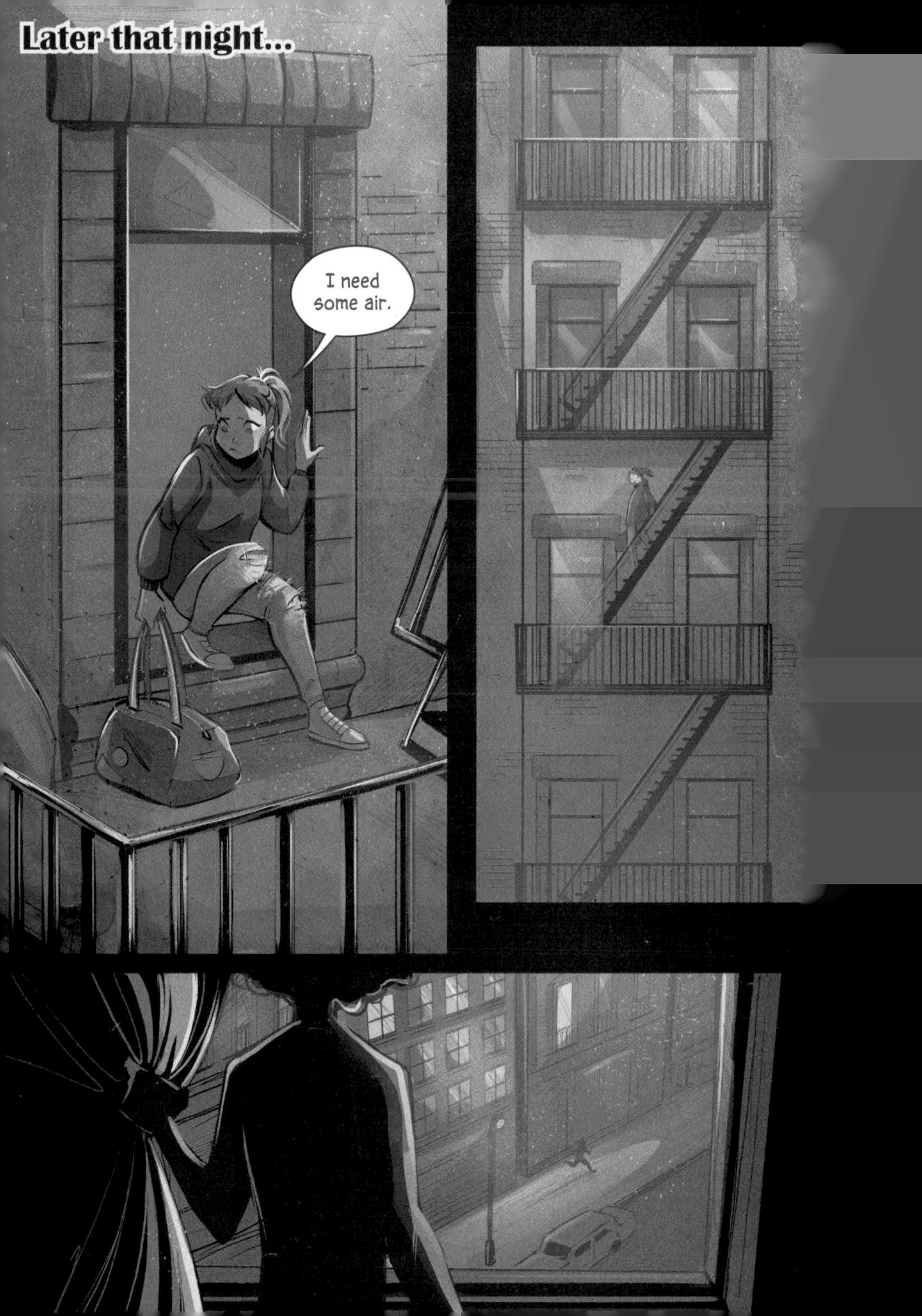
Later that night...
I need some air.

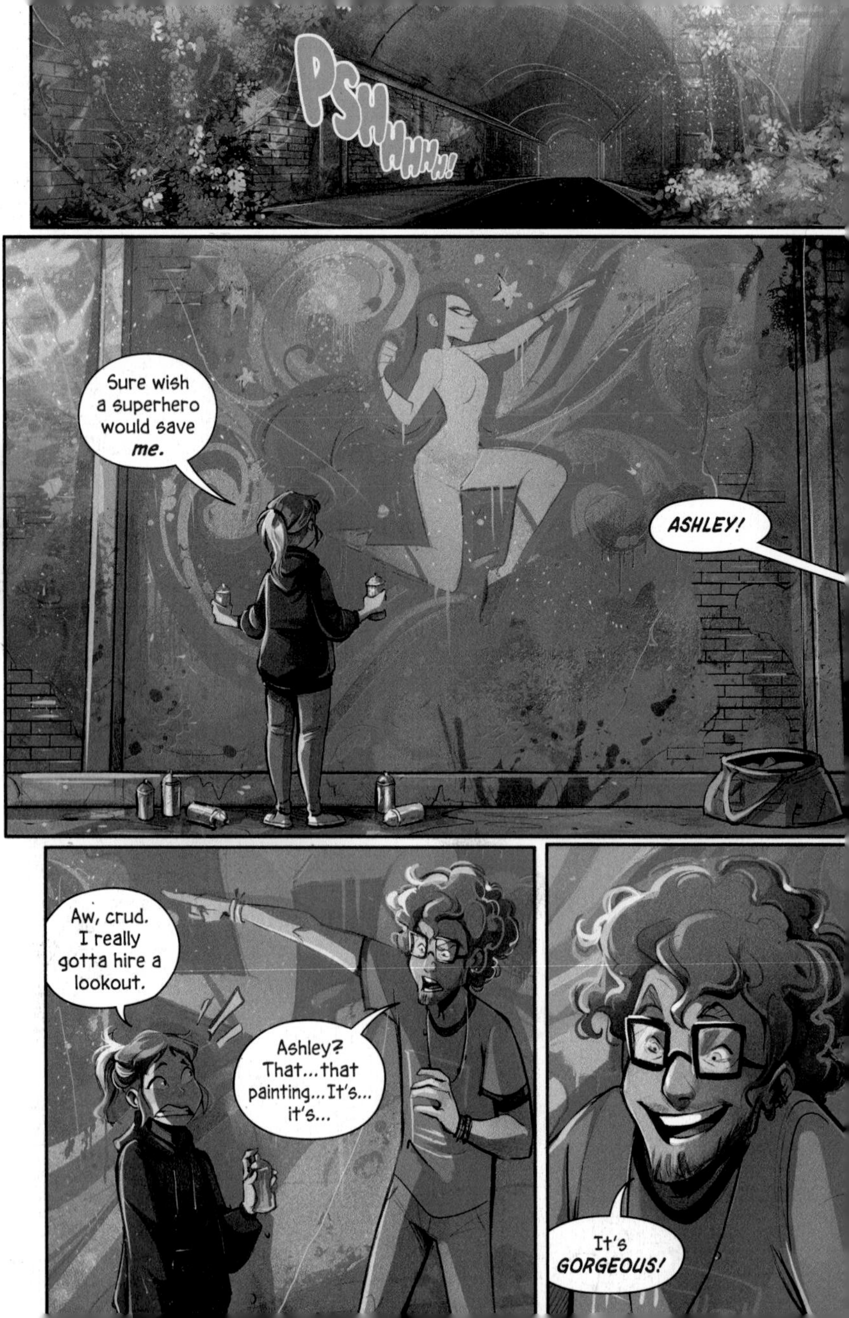
PSHHHHH!
Sure wish a superhero would save *me.*
ASHLEY!
Aw, crud. I really gotta hire a lookout.
Ashley? That...that painting...It's... it's...
It's GORGEOUS!

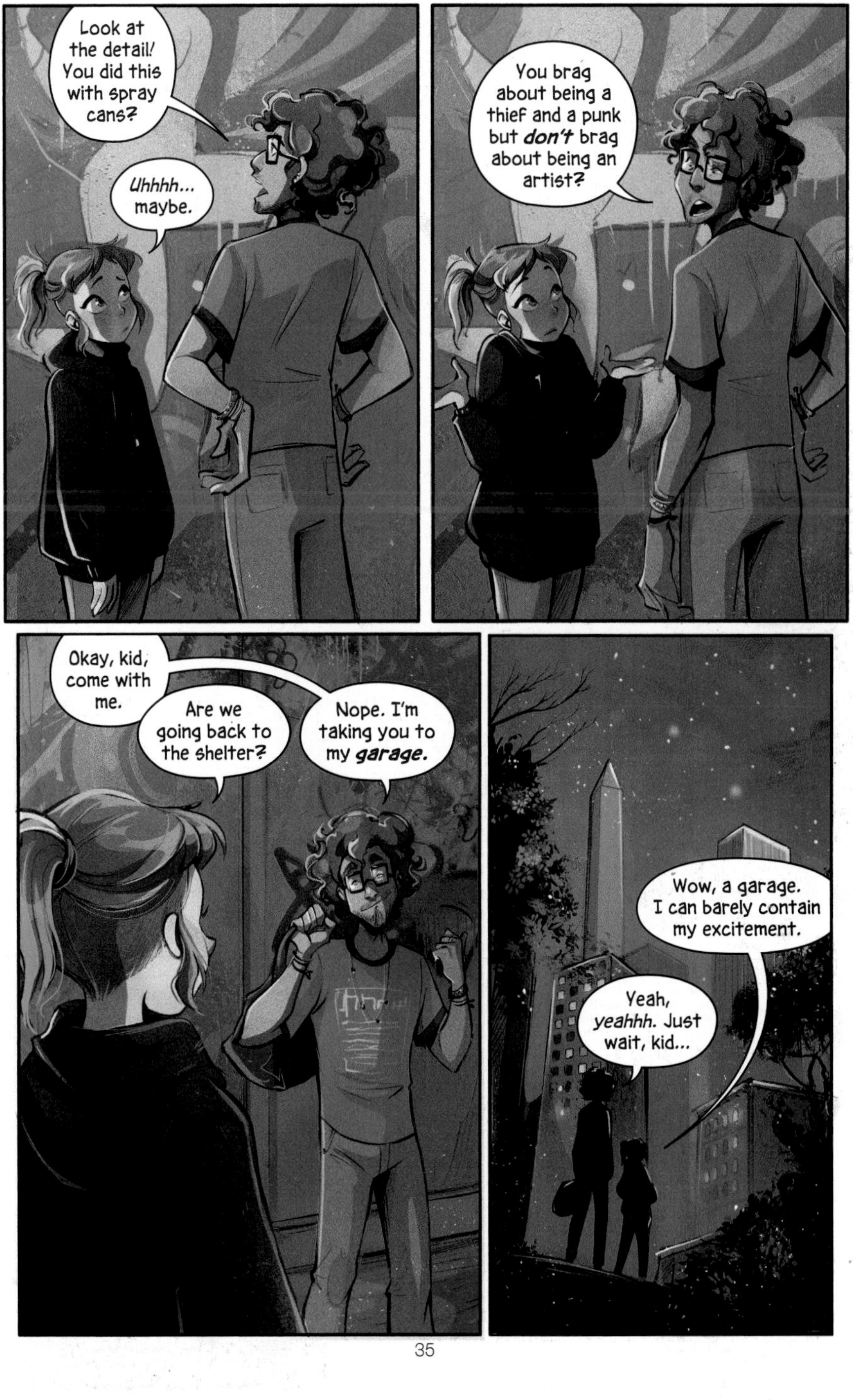
Look at the detail! You did this with spray cans?
Uhhhh... maybe.
You brag about being a thief and a punk but don't brag about being an artist?
Okay, kid, come with me.
Are we going back to the shelter?
Nope. I'm taking you to my garage.
Wow, a garage. I can barely contain my excitement.
Yeah, yeahhh. Just wait, kid...

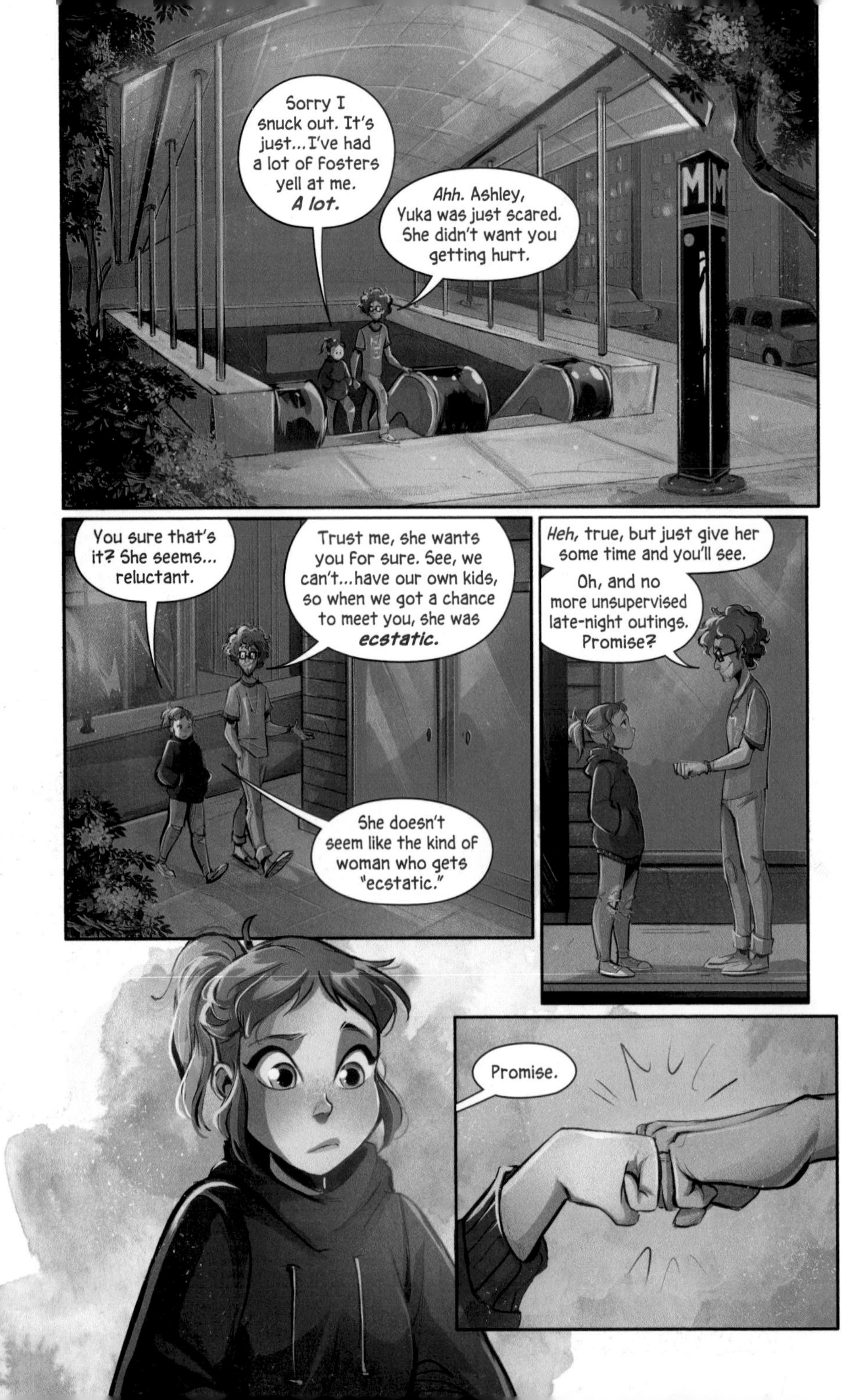

Sorry I snuck out. It's just...I've had a lot of fosters yell at me. *A lot.*
Ahh. Ashley, Yuka was just scared. She didn't want you getting hurt.
MM
You sure that's it? She seems... reluctant.
Trust me, she wants you for sure. See, we can't...have our own kids, so when we got a chance to meet you, she was *ecstatic.*
She doesn't seem like the kind of woman who gets "ecstatic."
Heh, true, but just give her some time and you'll see.
Oh, and no more unsupervised late-night outings. Promise?
Promise.

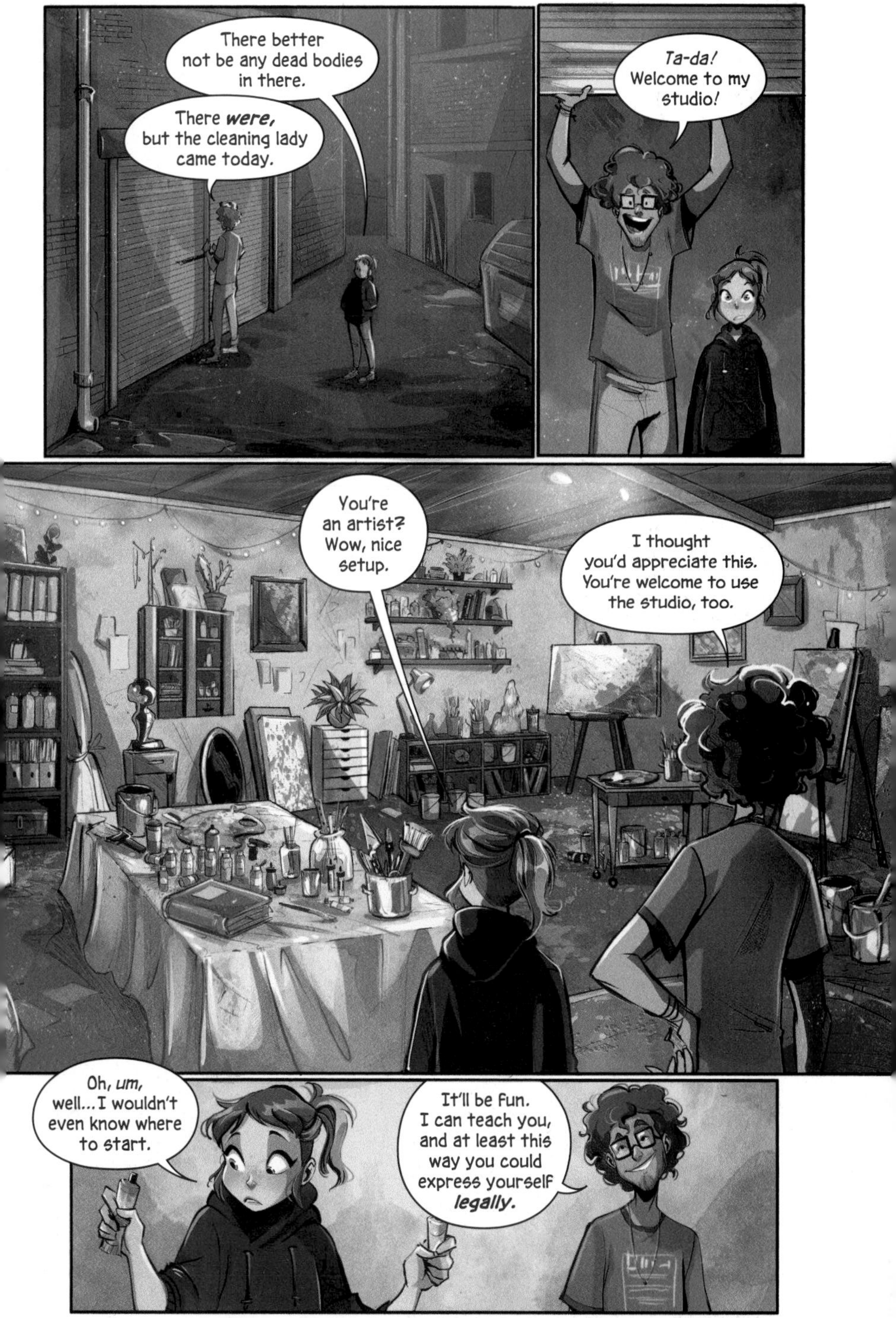
There better not be any dead bodies in there.
There *were,* but the cleaning lady came today.
Ta-da! Welcome to my studio!
You're an artist? Wow, nice setup.
I thought you'd appreciate this. You're welcome to use the studio, too.
Oh, *um,* well...I wouldn't even know where to start.
It'll be fun. I can teach you, and at least this way you could express yourself ***legally.***

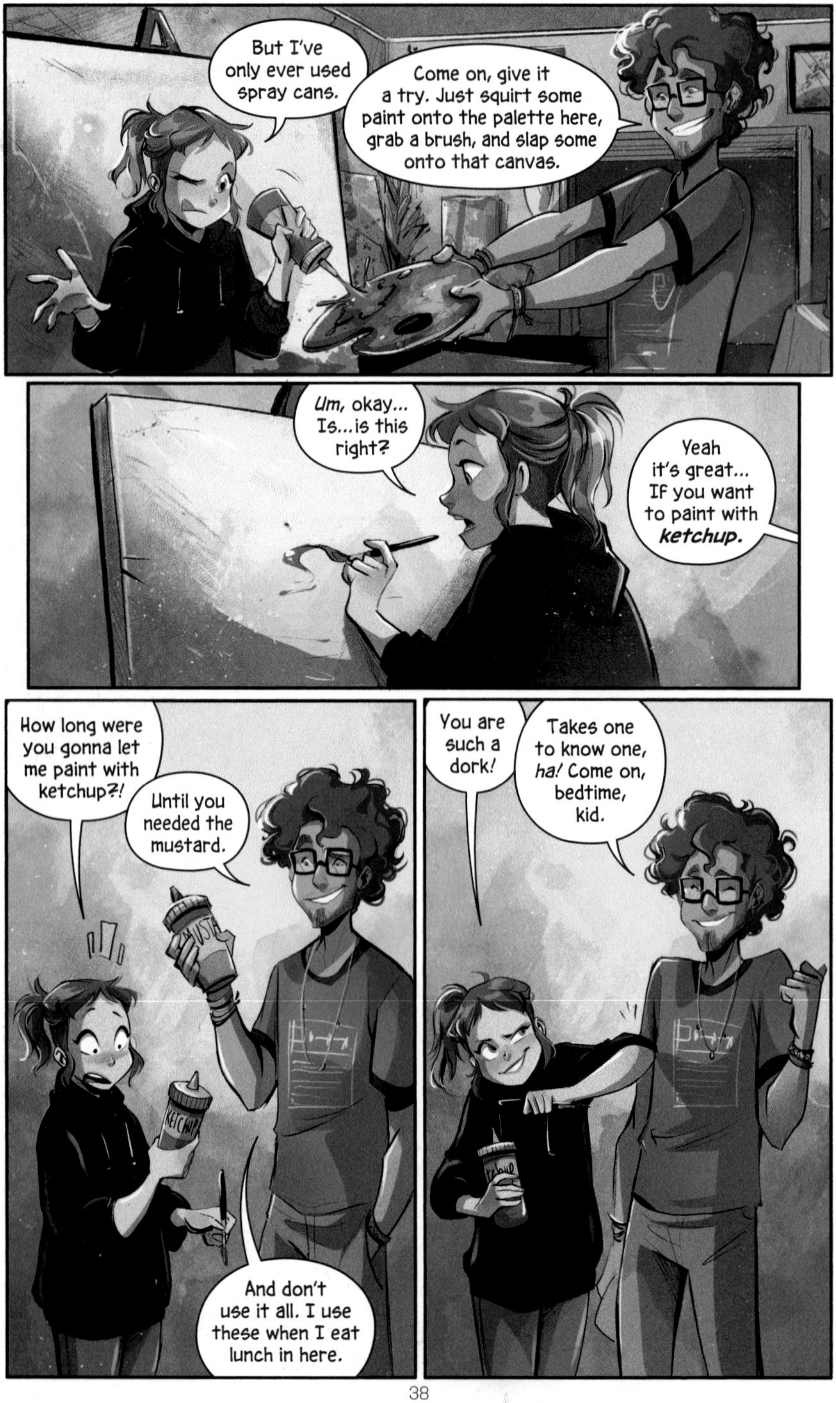
But I've only ever used spray cans.
Come on, give it a try. Just squirt some paint onto the palette here, grab a brush, and slap some onto that canvas.
Um, okay... Is...is this right?
Yeah it's great... If you want to paint with ***ketchup.***
How long were you gonna let me paint with ketchup?!
Until you needed the mustard.
!!
MUSTA
KETCHUP
And don't use it all. I use these when I eat lunch in here.
You are such a *dork!*
Takes one to know one, *ha!* Come on, bedtime, kid.

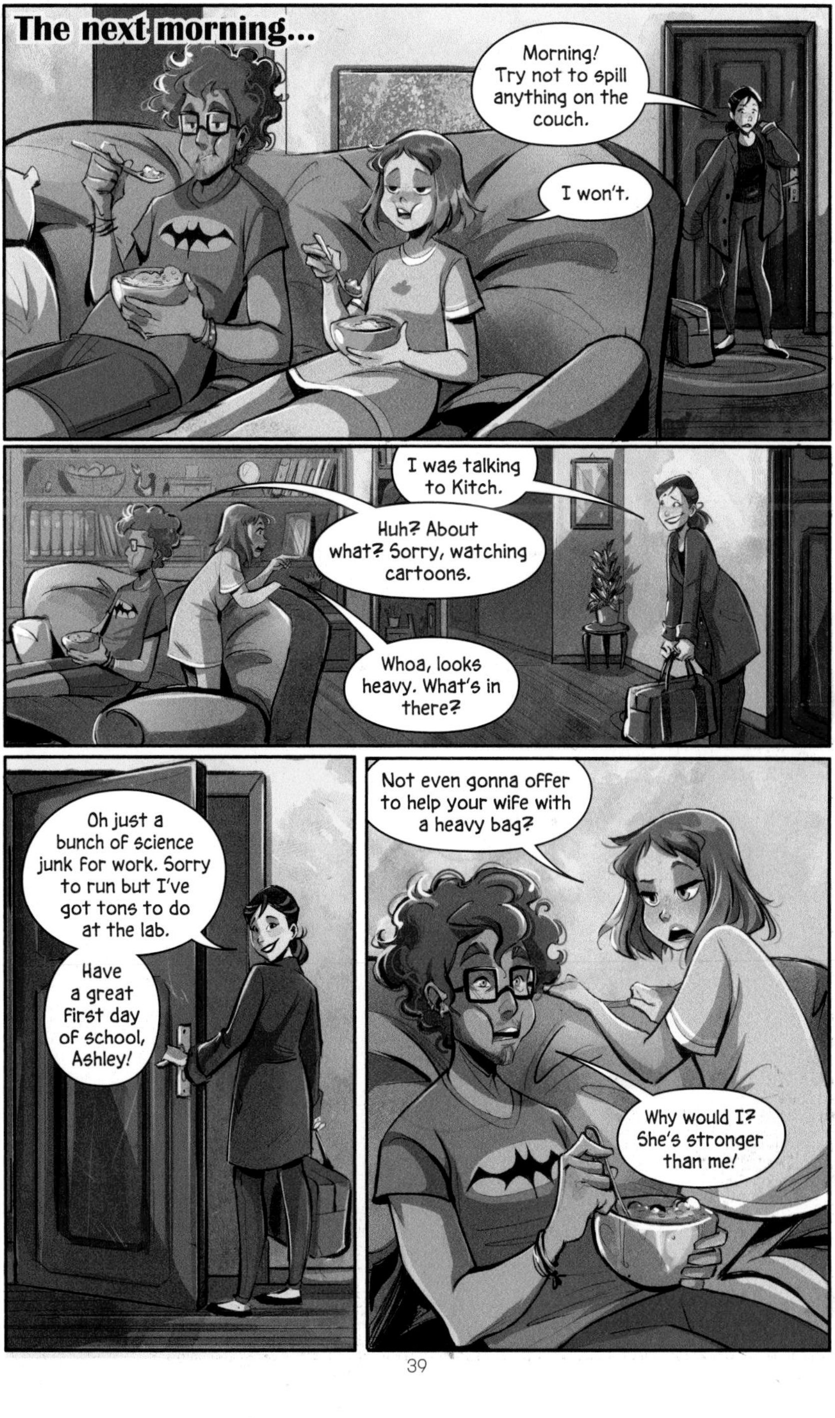
The next morning...
Morning! Try not to spill anything on the couch.
I won't.
I was talking to Kitch.
Huh? About what? Sorry, watching cartoons.
Whoa, looks heavy. What's in there?
Oh just a bunch of science junk for work. Sorry to run but I've got tons to do at the lab.
Have a great first day of school, Ashley!
Not even gonna offer to help your wife with a heavy bag?
Why would I? She's stronger than me!

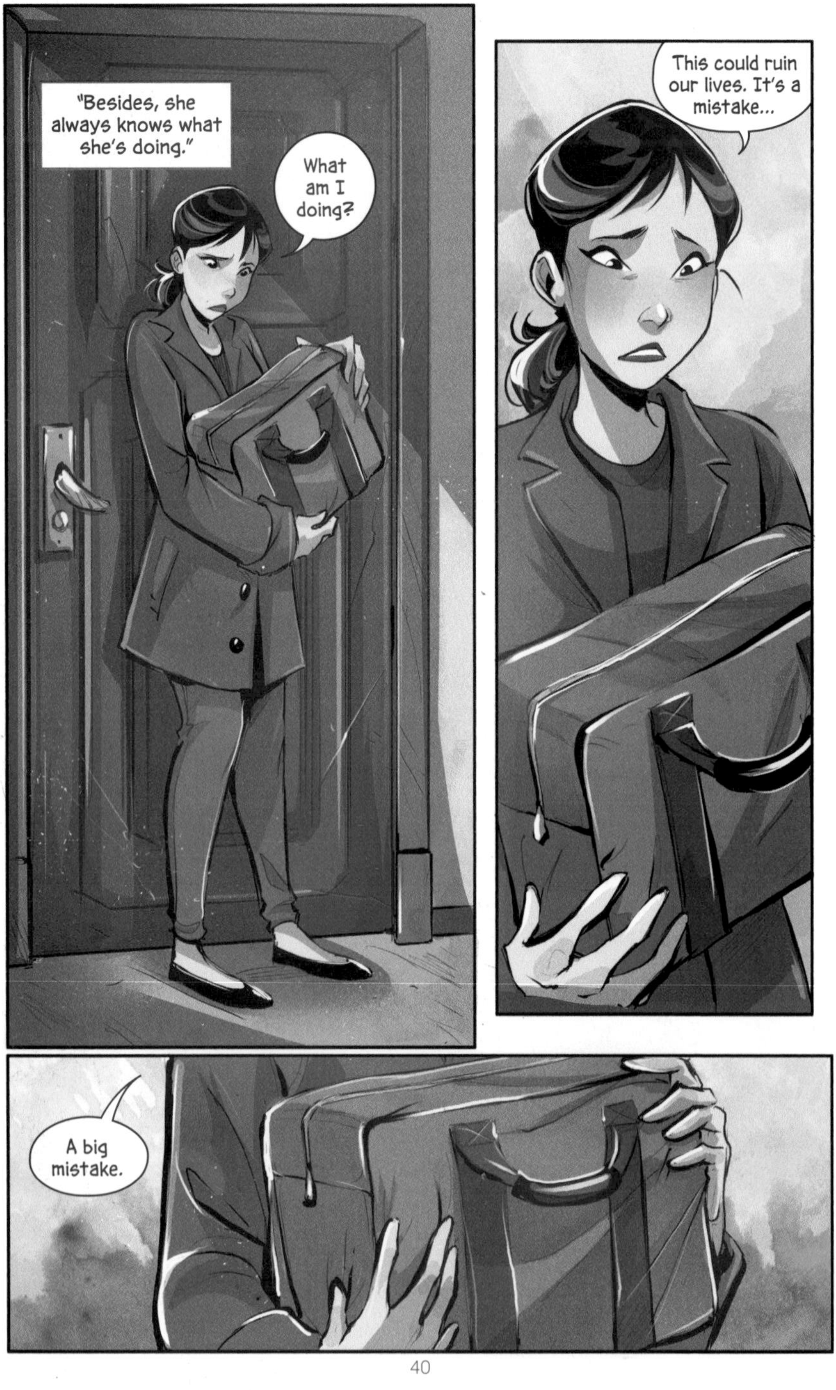
"Besides, she always knows what she's doing."
What am I doing?
This could ruin our lives. It's a mistake...
A big mistake.

chapter 2
No Paints, No Gain

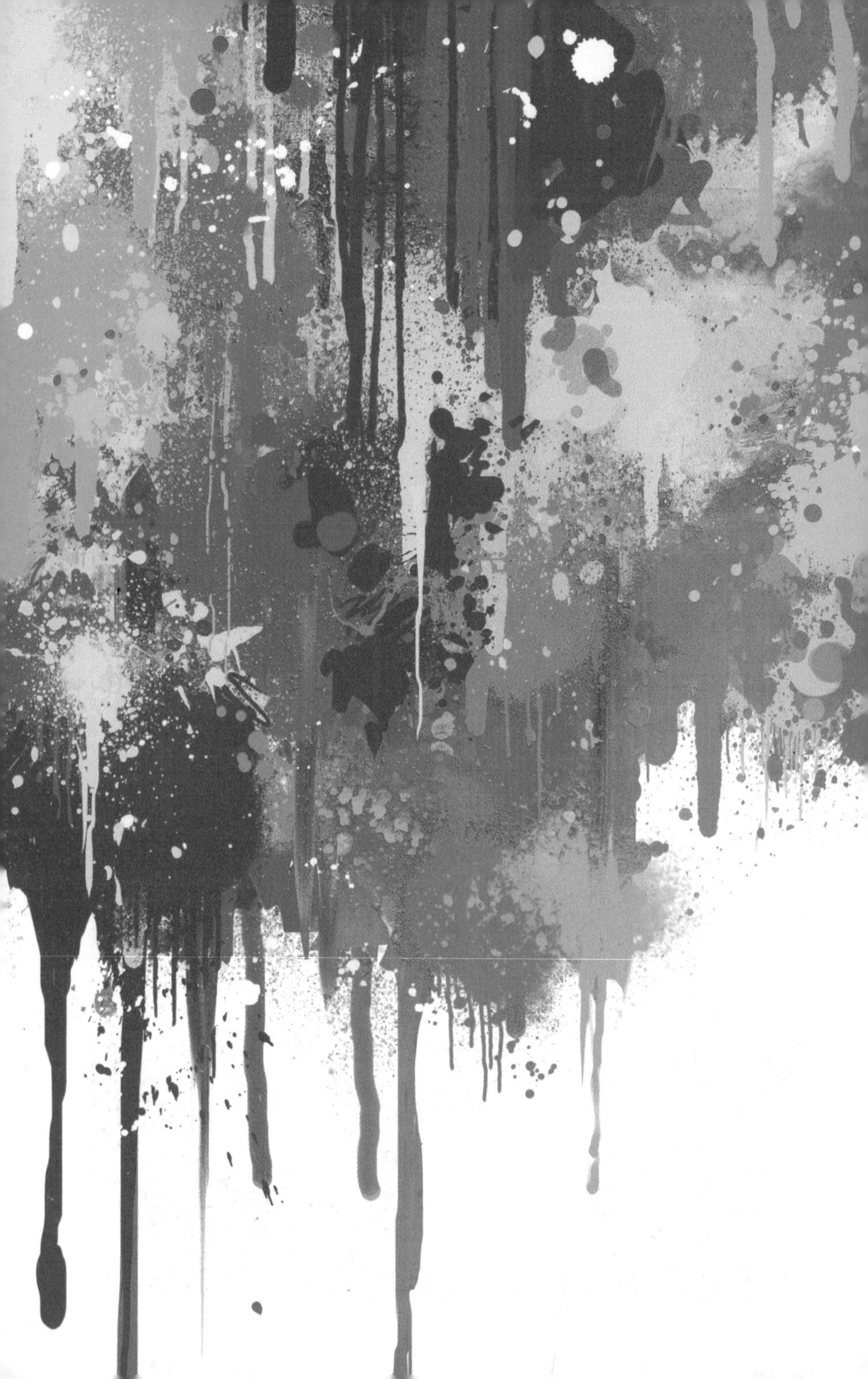

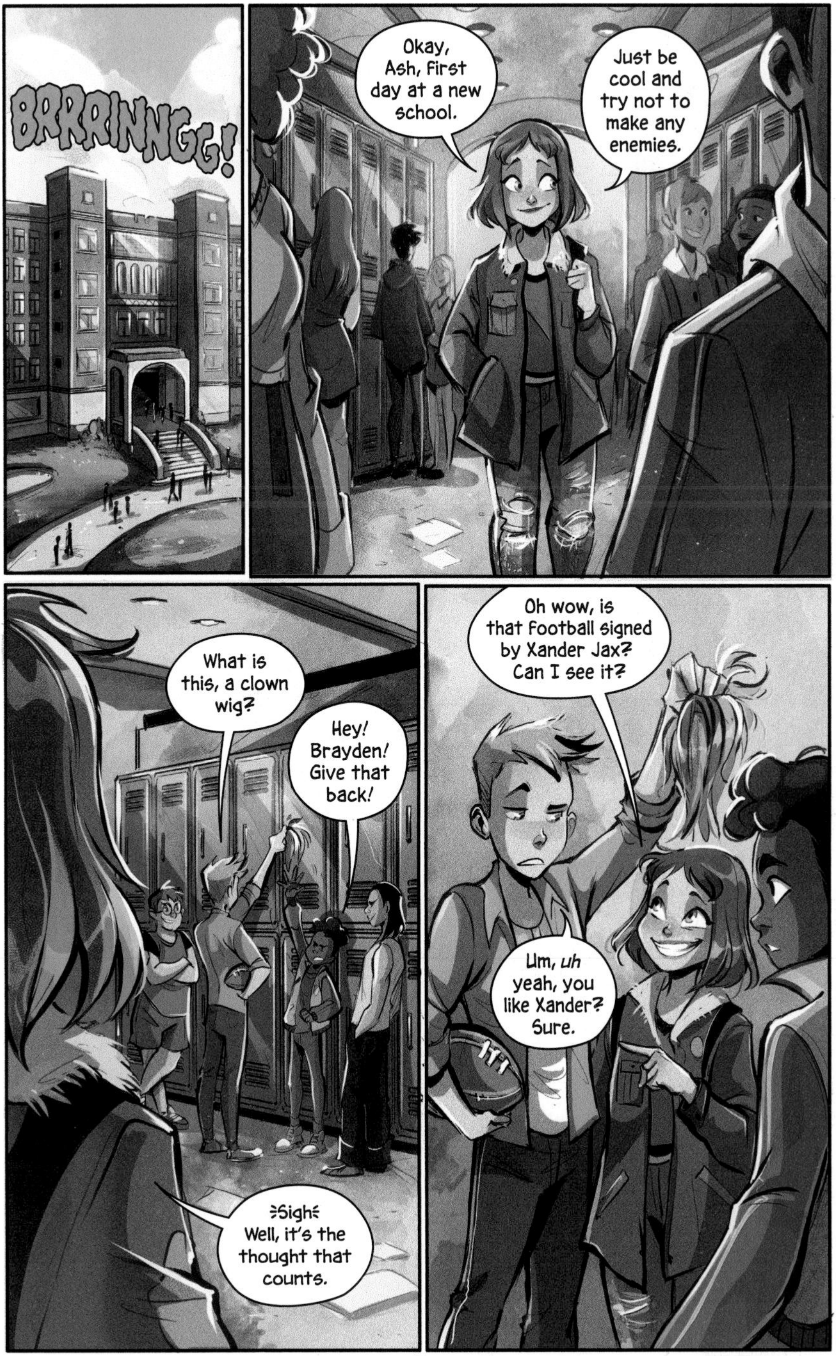
BRRRINNGG!
Okay, Ash, first day at a new school.
Just be cool and try not to make any enemies.
What is this, a clown wig?
Hey! Brayden! Give that back!
≶Sigh≶ Well, it's the thought that counts.
Oh wow, is that football signed by Xander Jax? Can I see it?
Um, *uh* yeah, you like Xander? Sure.

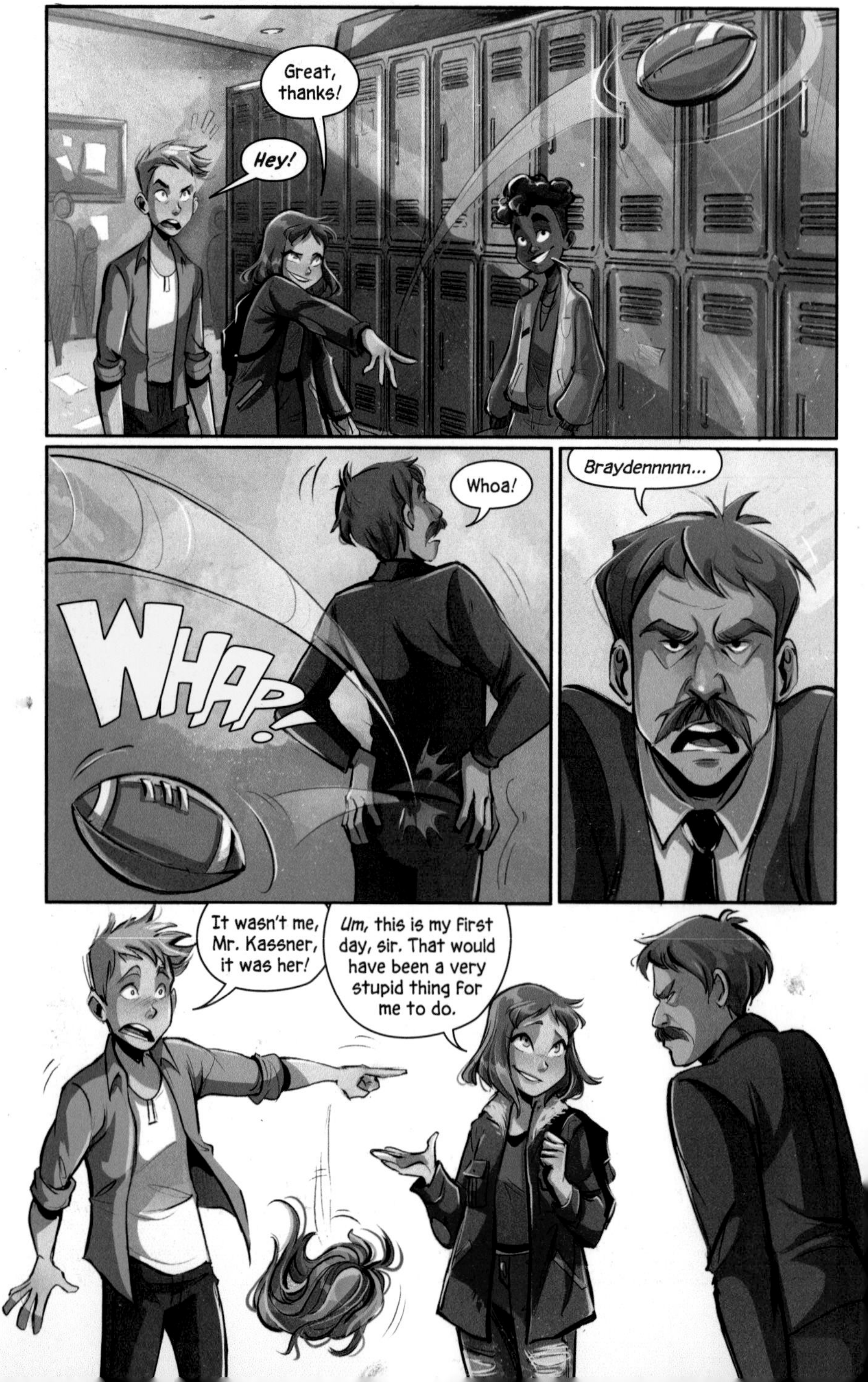
Great, thanks!
Hey!
Whoa!
WHAP!
Braydennnnn...
It wasn't me, Mr. Kassner, it was her!
Um, this is my first day, sir. That would have been a very stupid thing for me to do.

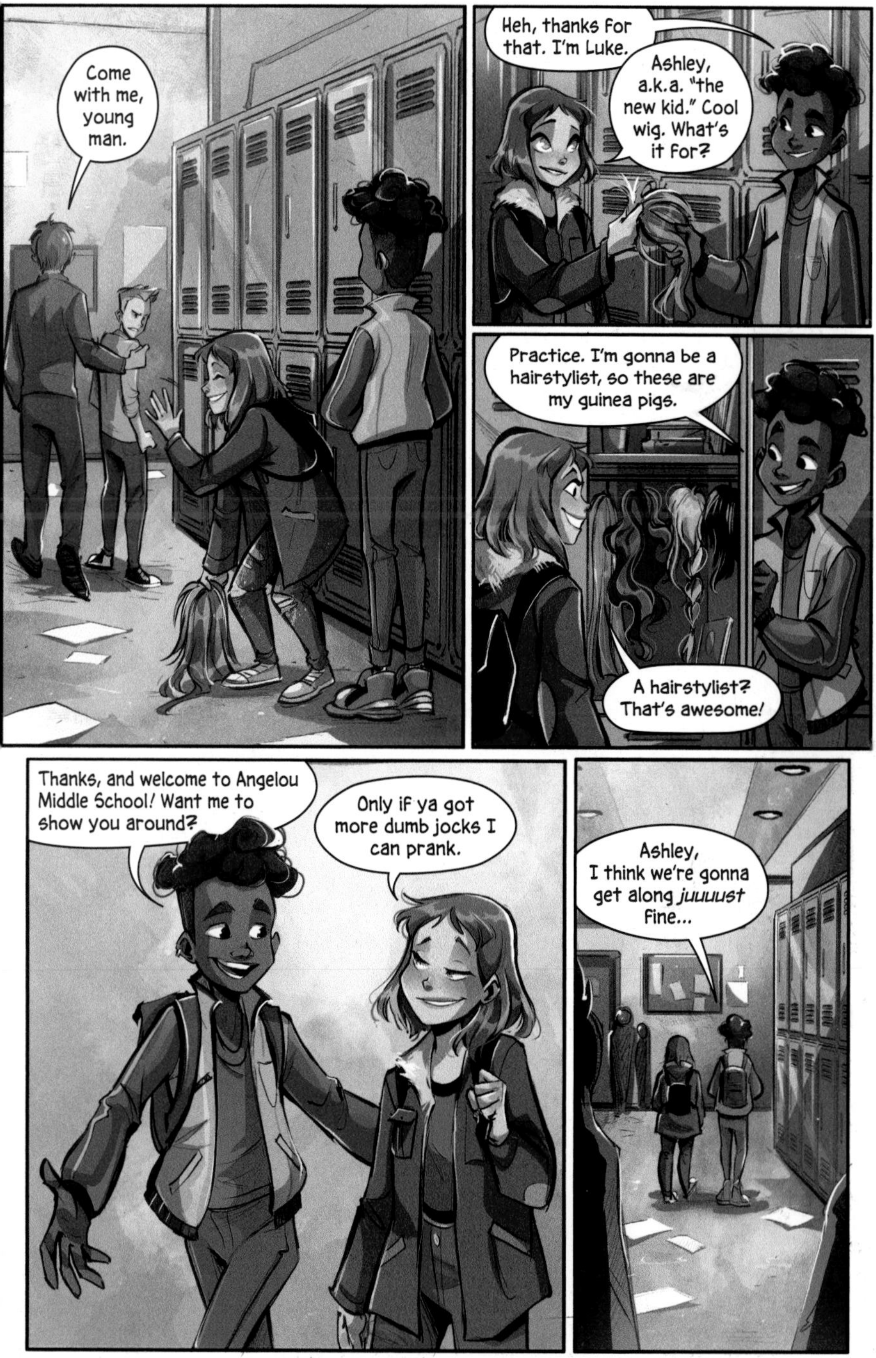
Come with me, young man.
Heh, thanks for that. I'm Luke.
Ashley, a.k.a. "the new kid." Cool wig. What's it for?
Practice. I'm gonna be a hairstylist, so these are my guinea pigs.
A hairstylist? That's awesome!
Thanks, and welcome to Angelou Middle School! Want me to show you around?
Only if ya got more dumb jocks I can prank.
Ashley, I think we're gonna get along *juuuust* fine...

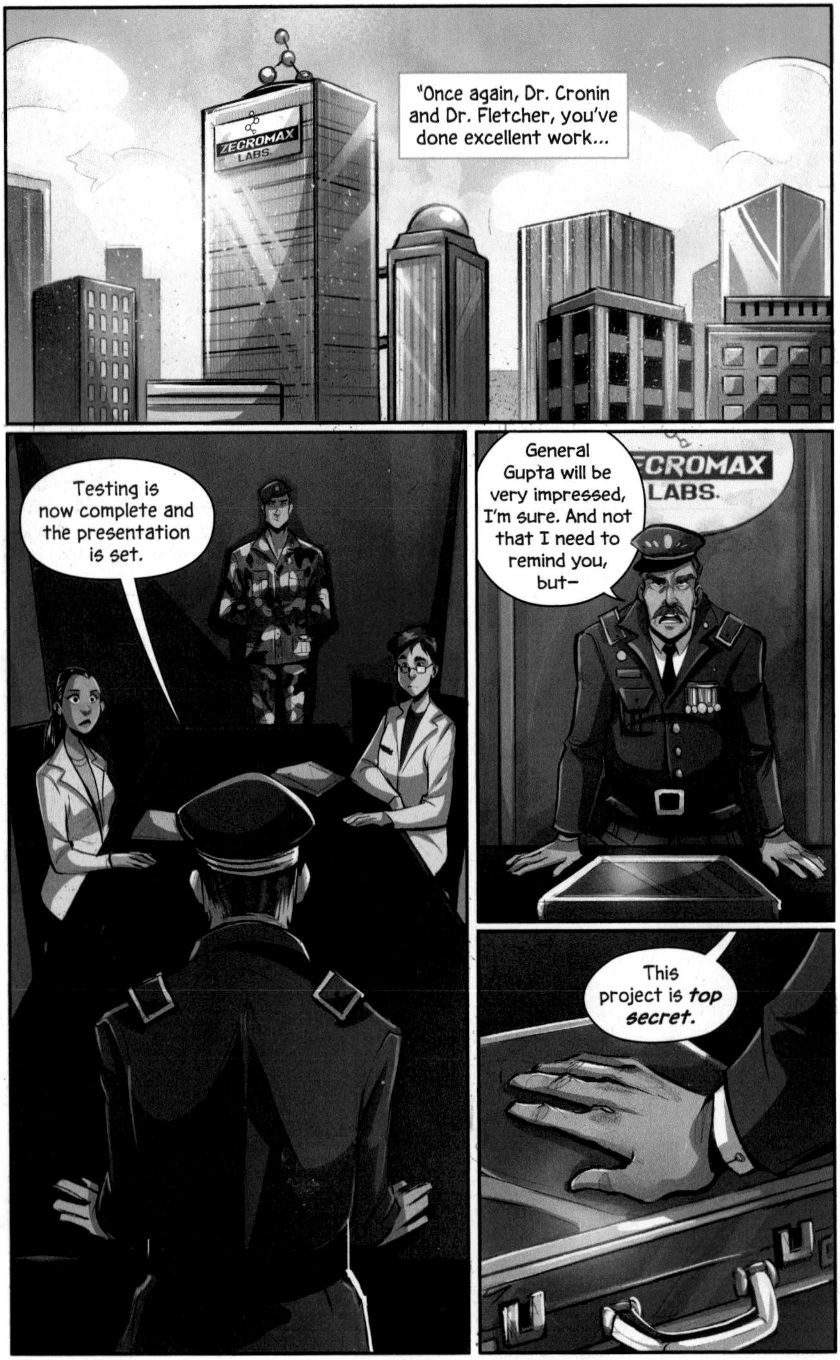
ZECROMAX LABS.
"Once again, Dr. Cronin and Dr. Fletcher, you've done excellent work...
Testing is now complete and the presentation is set.
General Gupta will be very impressed, I'm sure. And not that I need to remind you, but–
This project is *top secret.*

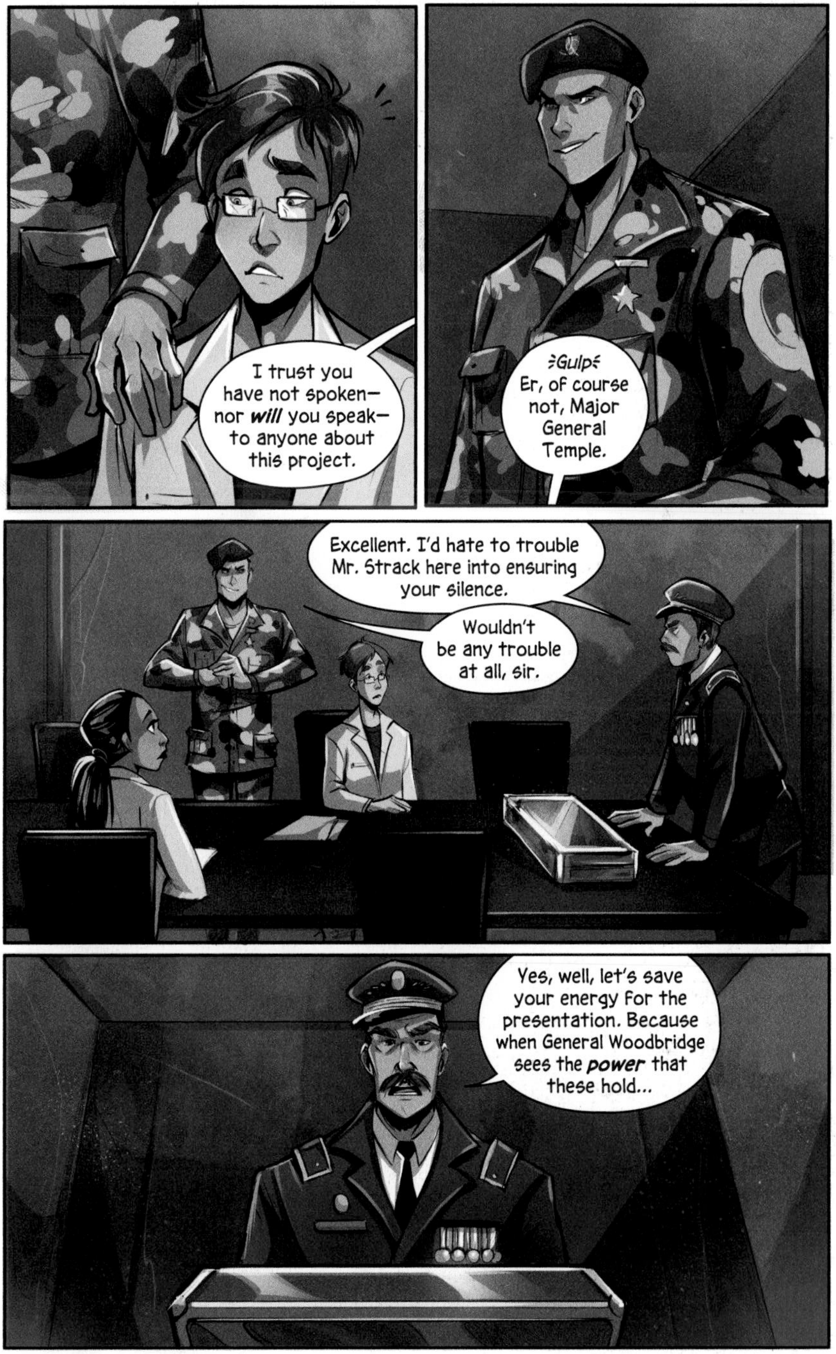
I trust you have not spoken—nor *will* you speak—to anyone about this project.
Gulp
Er, of course not, Major General Temple.
Excellent. I'd hate to trouble Mr. Strack here into ensuring your silence.
Wouldn't be any trouble at all, sir.
Yes, well, let's save your energy for the presentation. Because when General Woodbridge sees the *power* that these hold...

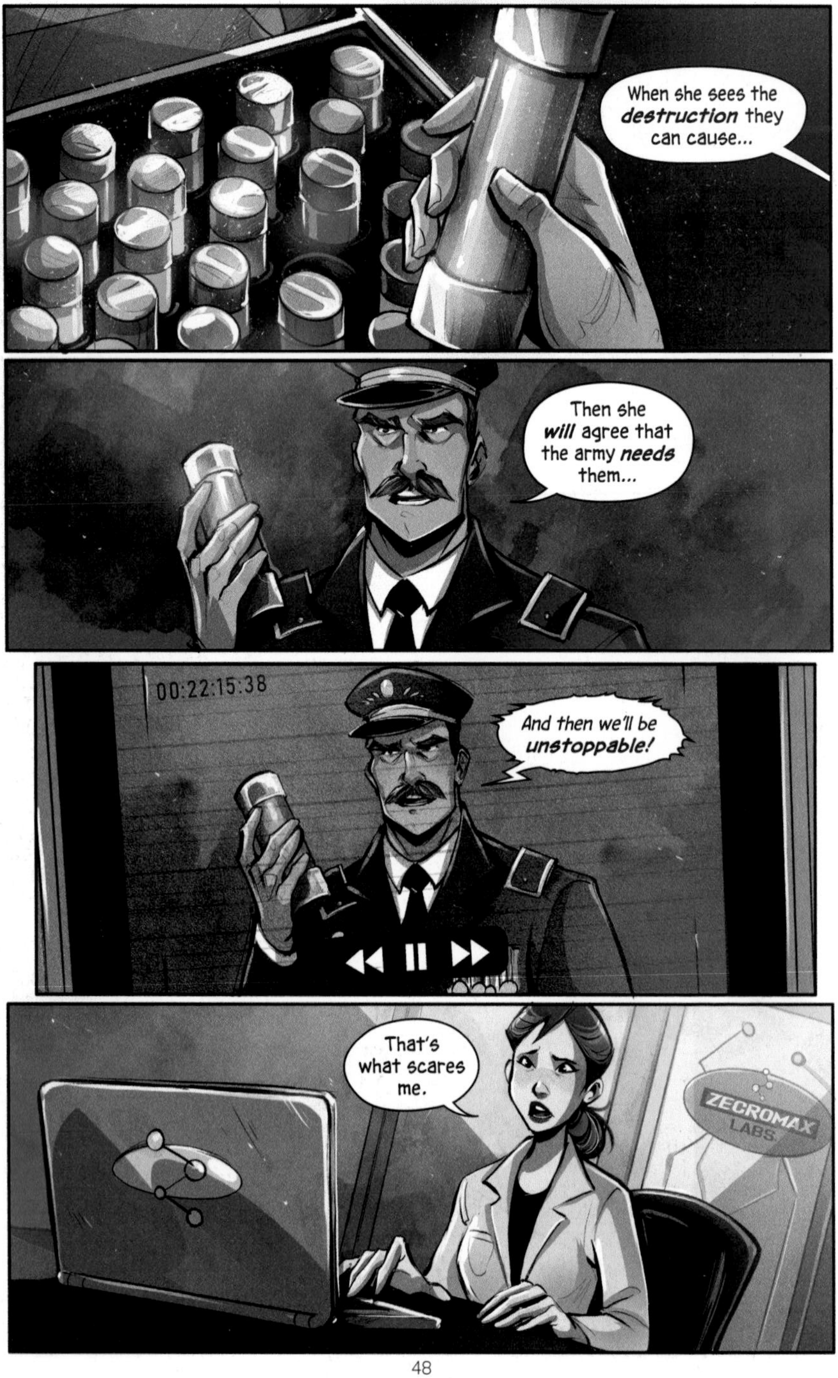
When she sees the ***destruction*** they can cause...
Then she ***will*** agree that the army ***needs*** them...
00:22:15:38
*And then we'll be **unstoppable!***
That's what scares me.
ZECROMAX LABS

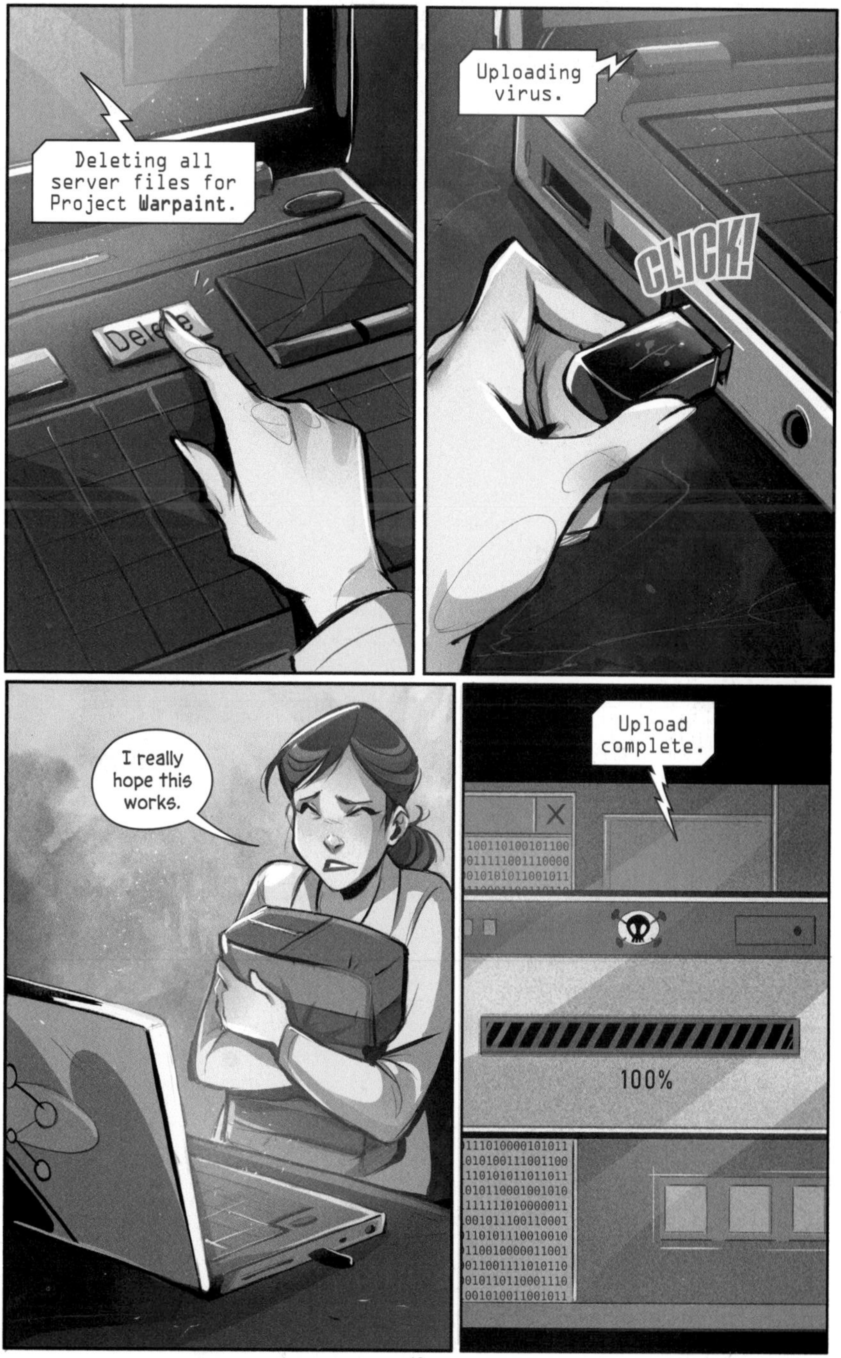
Deleting all server files for Project Warpaint.
Delete
Uploading virus.
CLICK!
I really hope this works.
Upload complete.
100%

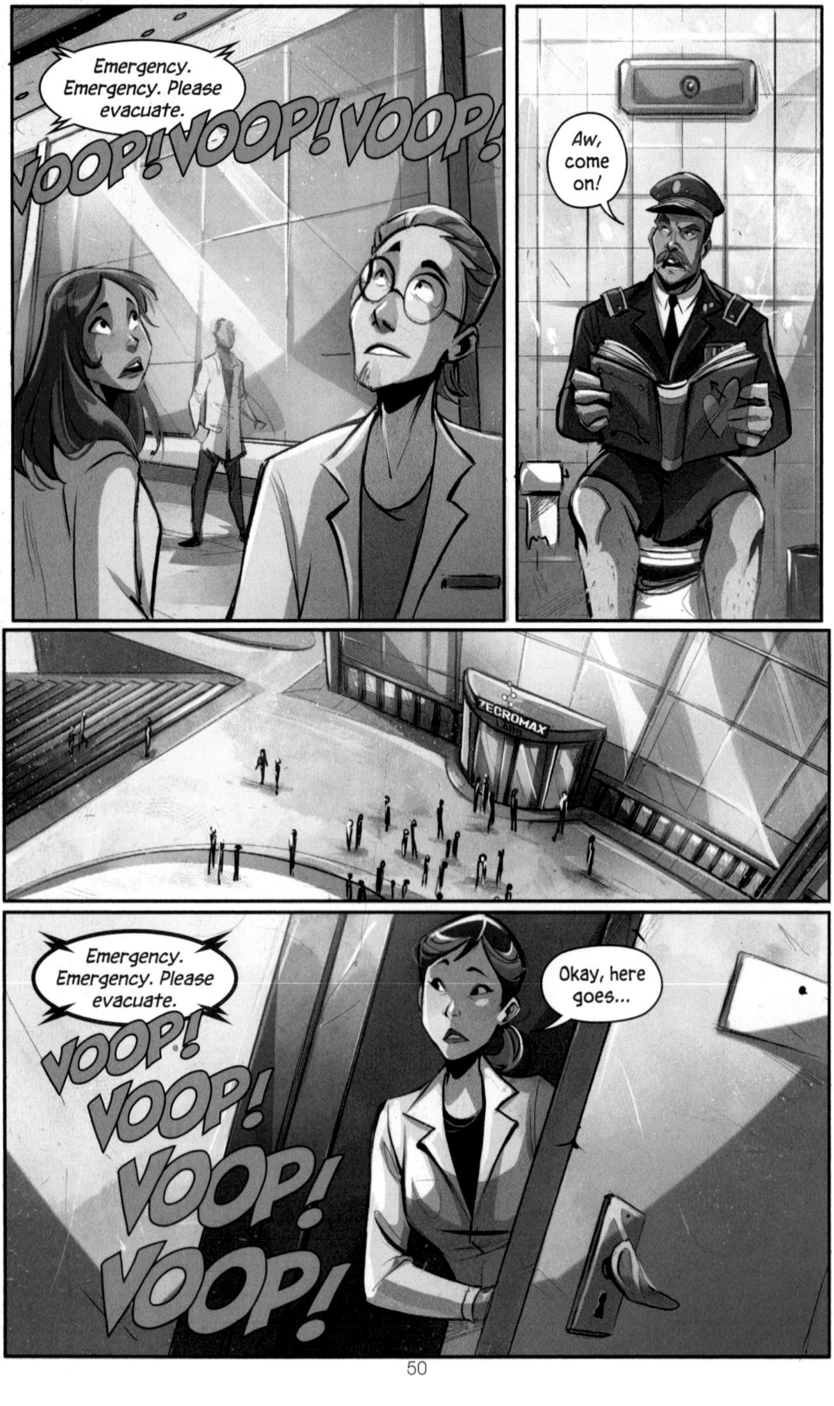
Emergency. Emergency. Please evacuate.
VOOP! VOOP! VOOP!
Aw, come on!
ZECROMAX LABS
Emergency. Emergency. Please evacuate.
Okay, here goes...
VOOP! VOOP! VOOP! VOOP!

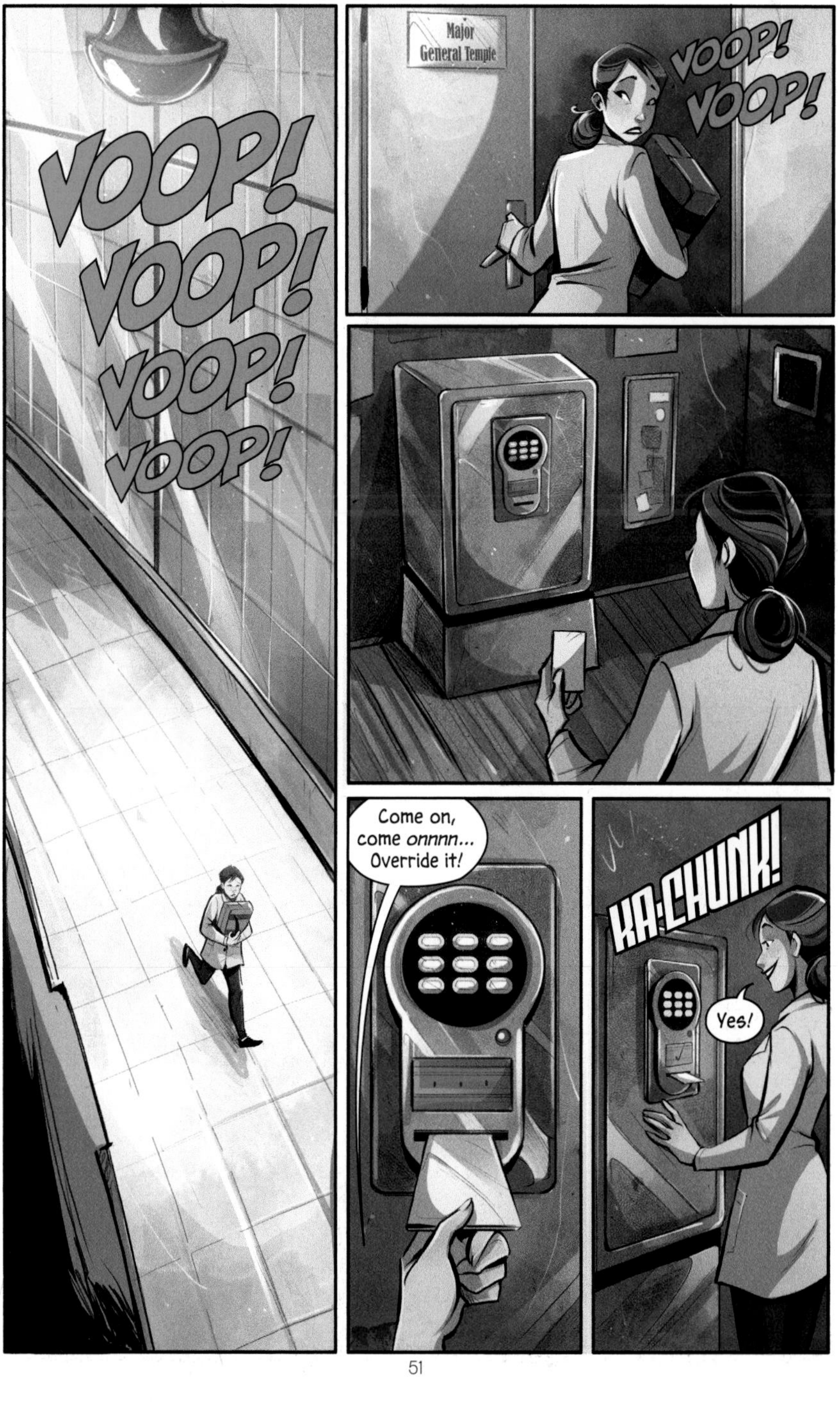
VOOP!
VOOP!
VOOP!
VOOP!
Major General Temple
VOOP!
VOOP!
Come on, come onnnn... Override it!
KA-CHUNK!
Yes!

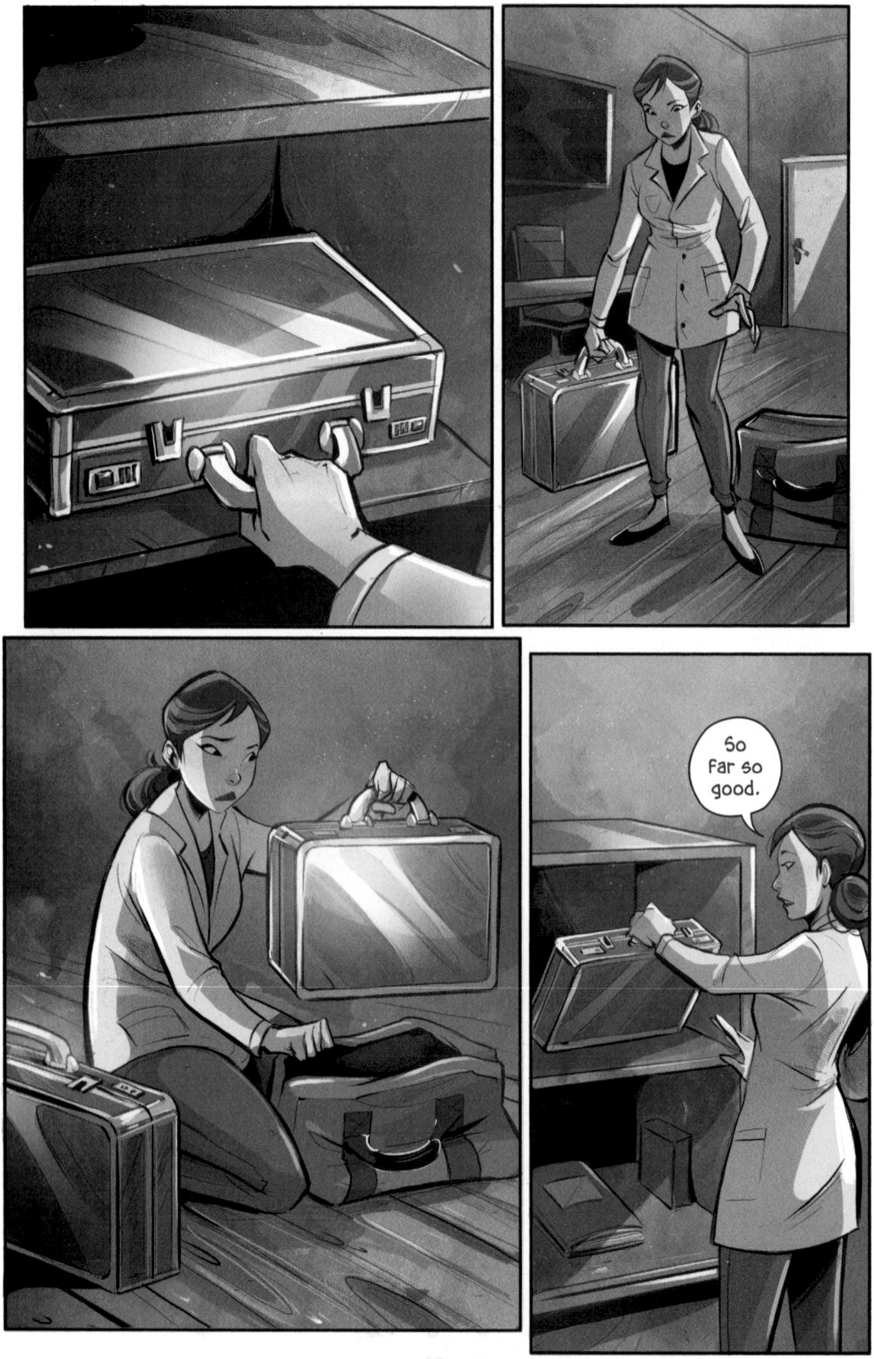
So far so good.

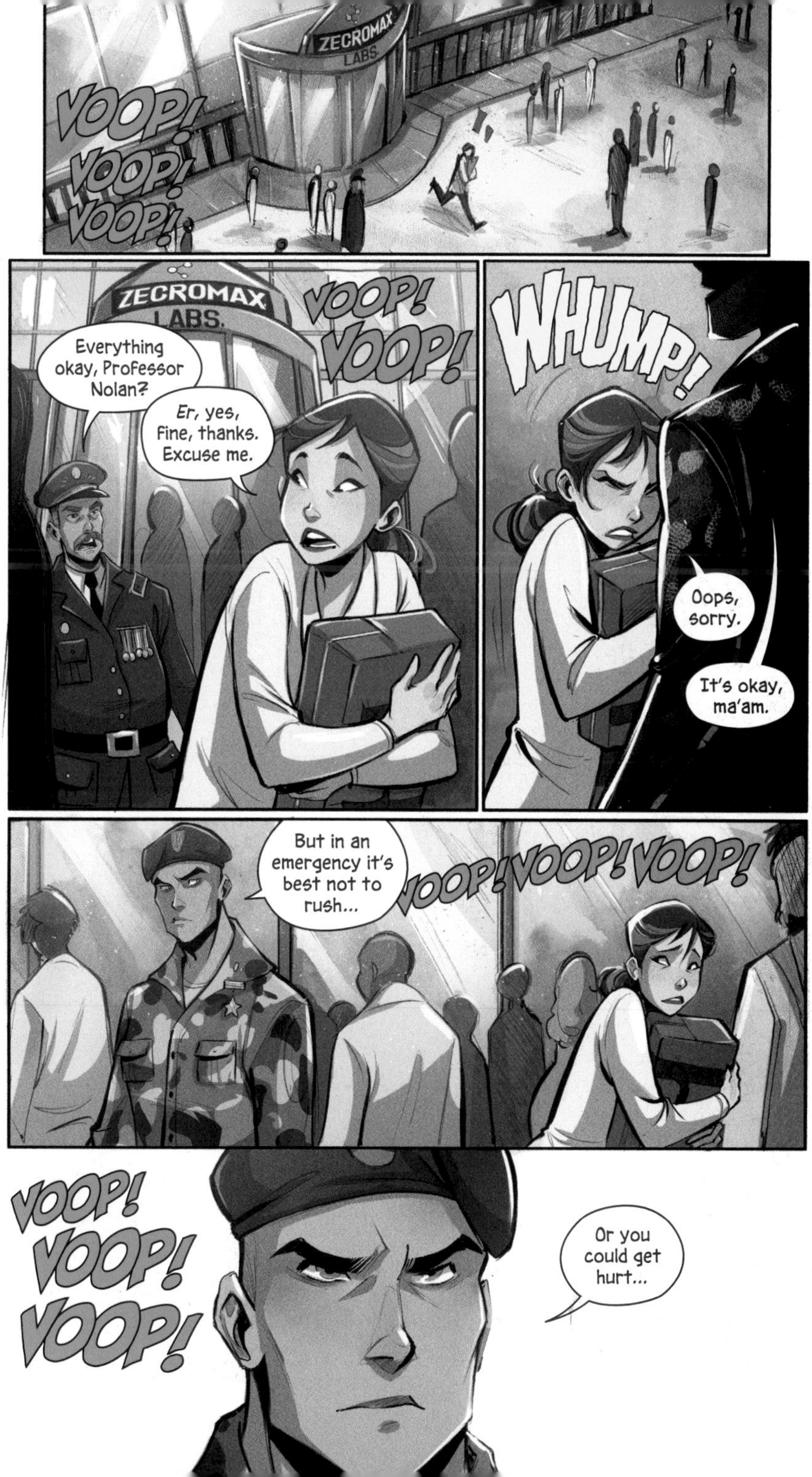
ZECROMAX LABS.
VOOP! VOOP! VOOP!
ZECROMAX LABS.
VOOP! VOOP!
Everything okay, Professor Nolan?
Er, yes, fine, thanks. Excuse me.
WHUMP!
Oops, sorry.
It's okay, ma'am.
But in an emergency it's best not to rush...
VOOP! VOOP! VOOP!
VOOP! VOOP! VOOP!
Or you could get hurt...

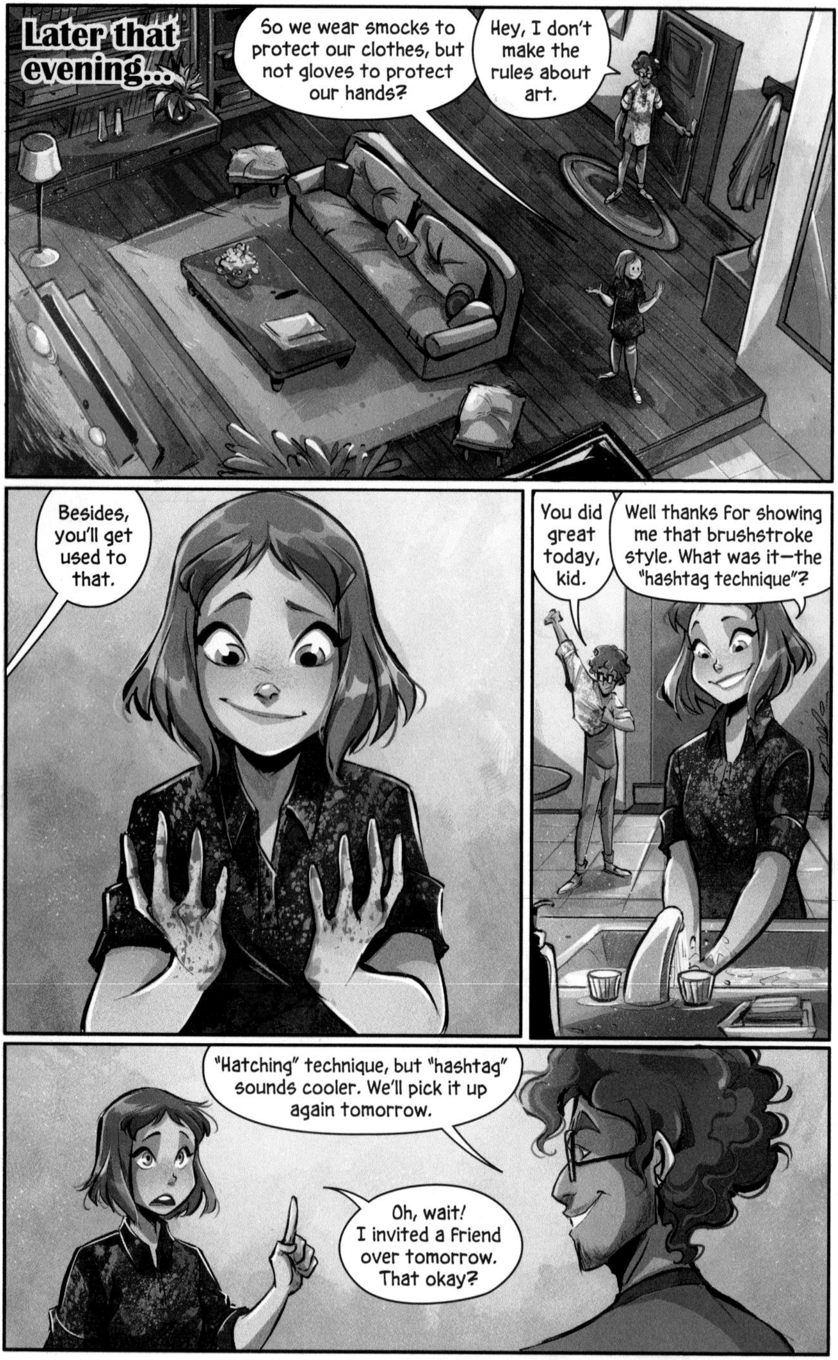
Later that evening...
So we wear smocks to protect our clothes, but not gloves to protect our hands?
Hey, I don't make the rules about art.
Besides, you'll get used to that.
You did great today, kid.
Well thanks for showing me that brushstroke style. What was it—the "hashtag technique"?
"Hatching" technique, but "hashtag" sounds cooler. We'll pick it up again tomorrow.
Oh, wait! I invited a friend over tomorrow. That okay?

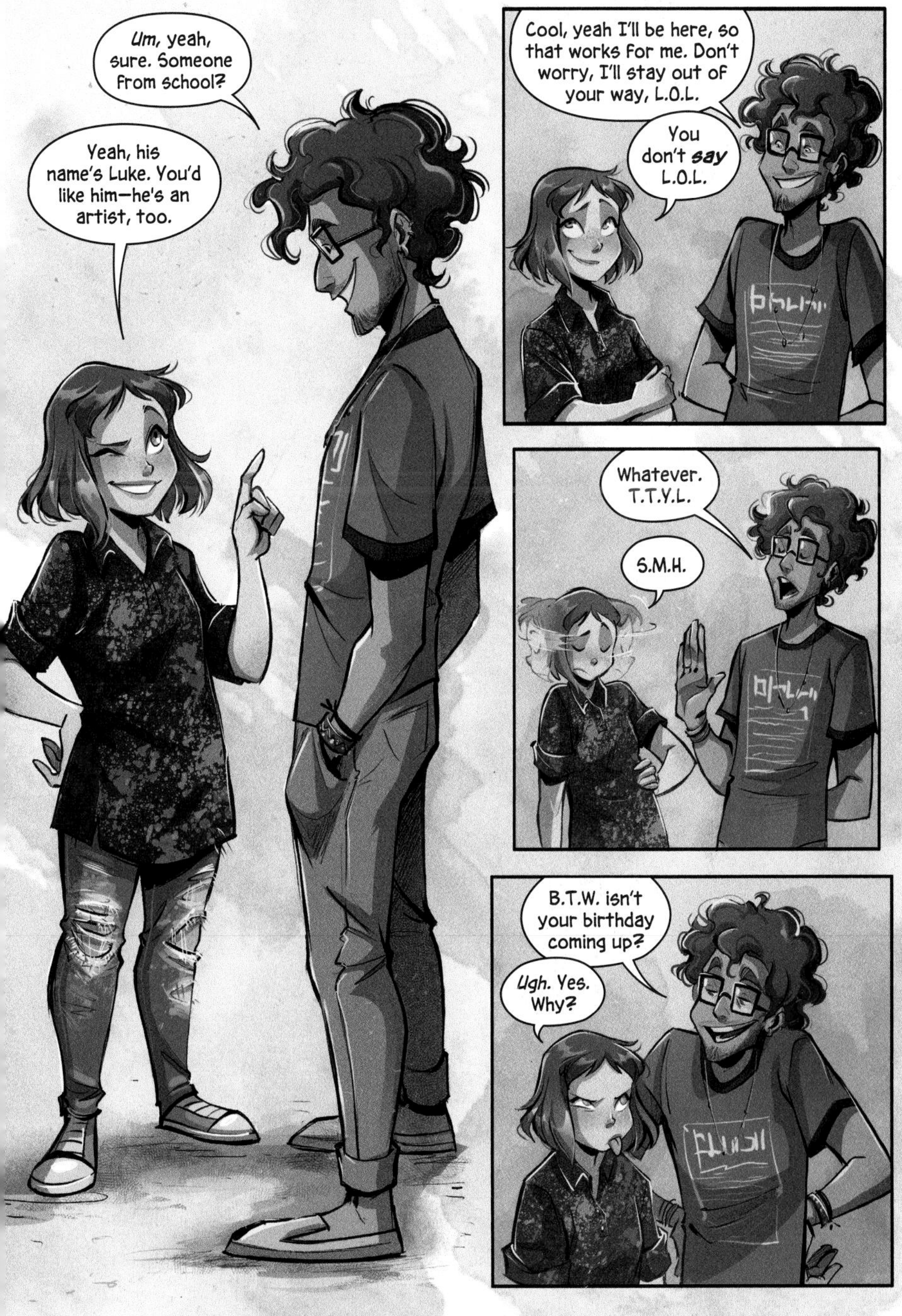
Um, yeah, sure. Someone from school?
Yeah, his name's Luke. You'd like him—he's an artist, too.
Cool, yeah I'll be here, so that works for me. Don't worry, I'll stay out of your way, L.O.L.
You don't say L.O.L.
Whatever. T.T.Y.L.
S.M.H.
B.T.W. isn't your birthday coming up?
Ugh. Yes. Why?

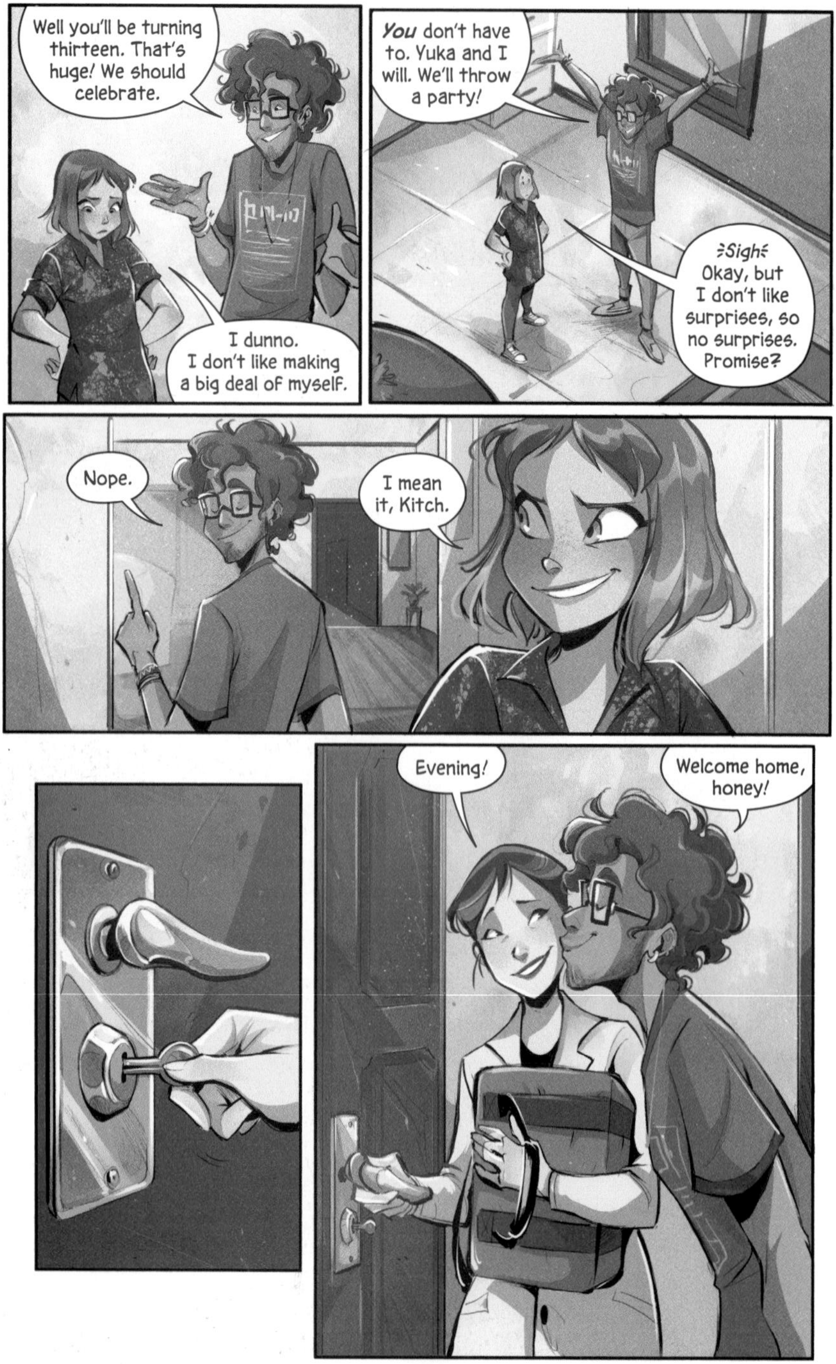
Well you'll be turning thirteen. That's huge! We should celebrate.
I dunno. I don't like making a big deal of myself.
You don't have to. Yuka and I will. We'll throw a party!
⸗Sigh⸗ Okay, but I don't like surprises, so no surprises. Promise?
Nope.
I mean it, Kitch.
Evening!
Welcome home, honey!

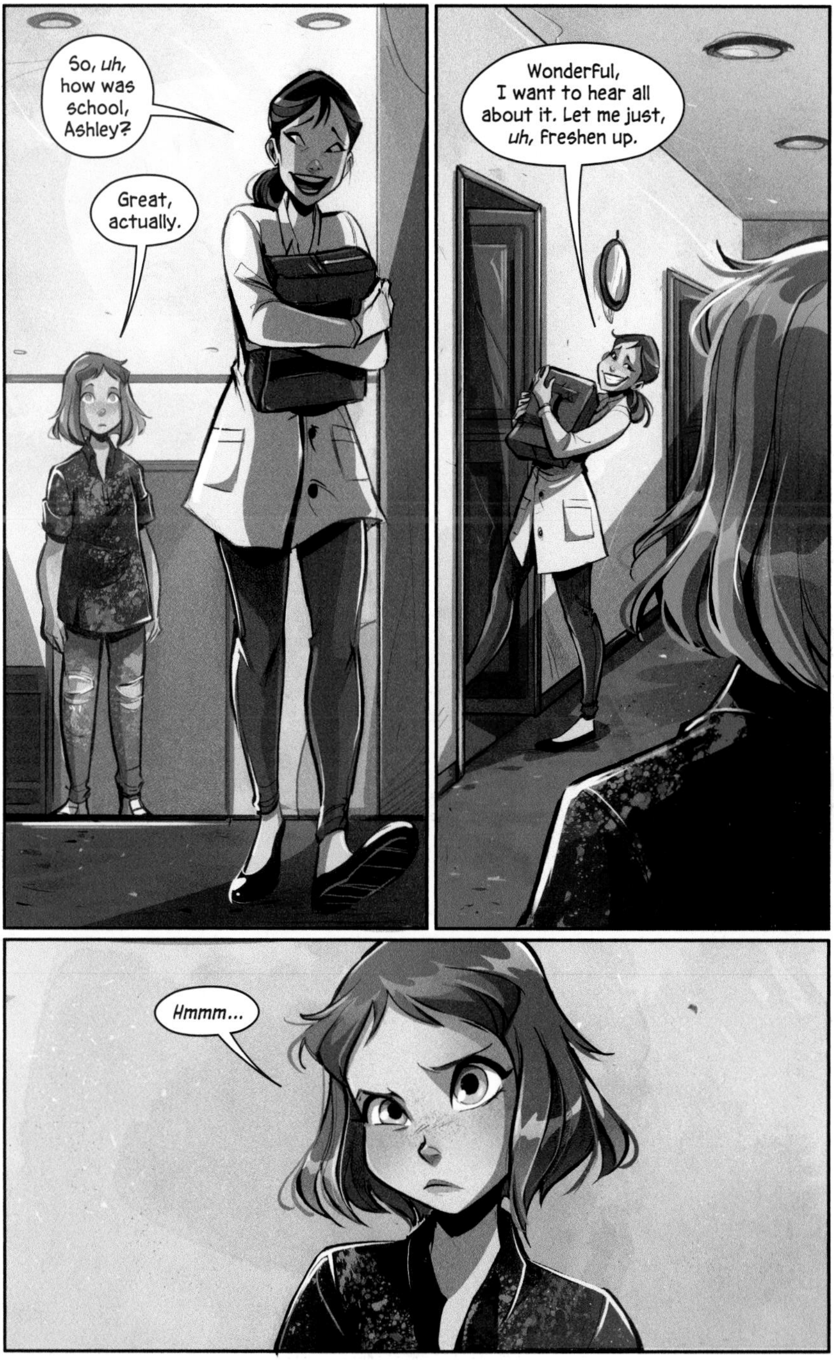
So, *uh*, how was school, Ashley?
Great, actually.
Wonderful, I want to hear all about it. Let me just, *uh*, freshen up.
Hmmm...

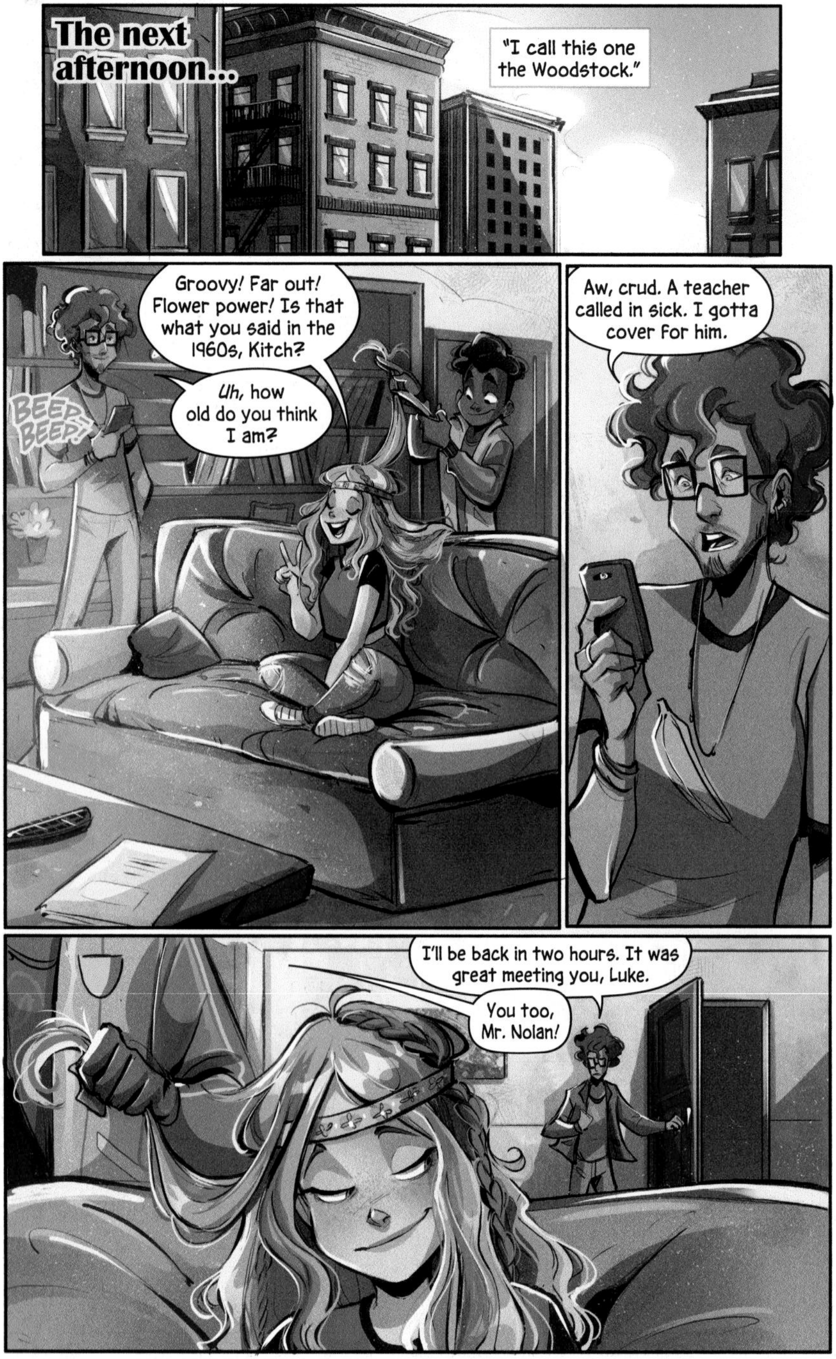
The next afternoon...
"I call this one the Woodstock."
Groovy! Far out! Flower power! Is that what you said in the 1960s, Kitch?
Uh, how old do you think I am?
BEEP-BEEP!
Aw, crud. A teacher called in sick. I gotta cover for him.
I'll be back in two hours. It was great meeting you, Luke.
You too, Mr. Nolan!

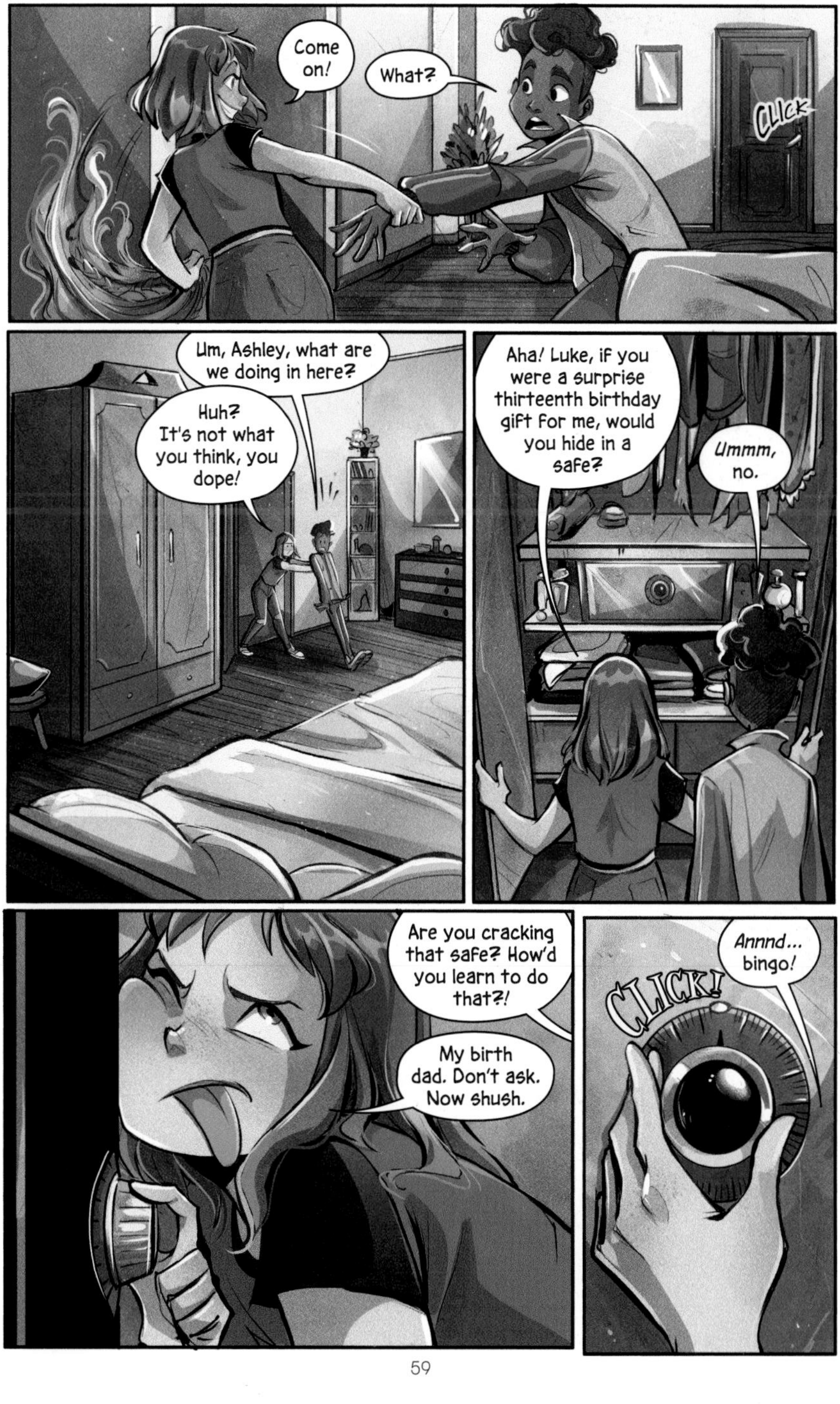

Come on!
What?
CLICK
Um, Ashley, what are we doing in here?
Huh? It's not what you think, you dope!
Aha! Luke, if you were a surprise thirteenth birthday gift for me, would you hide in a safe?
Ummm, no.
Are you cracking that safe? How'd you learn to do that?!
My birth dad. Don't ask. Now shush.
CLICK!
Annnd... bingo!

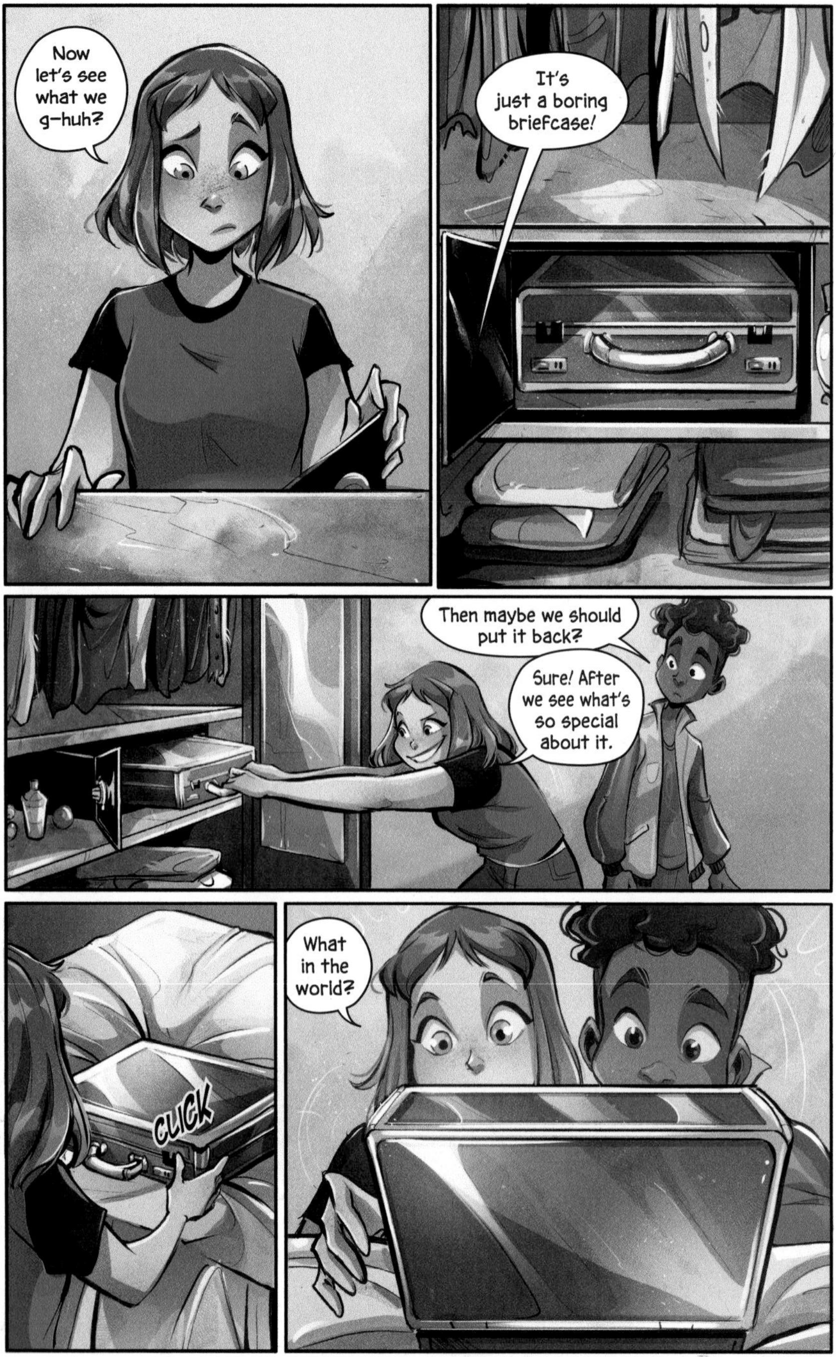
Now let's see what we g–huh?
It's just a boring briefcase!
Then maybe we should put it back?
Sure! After we see what's so special about it.
CLICK
What in the world?

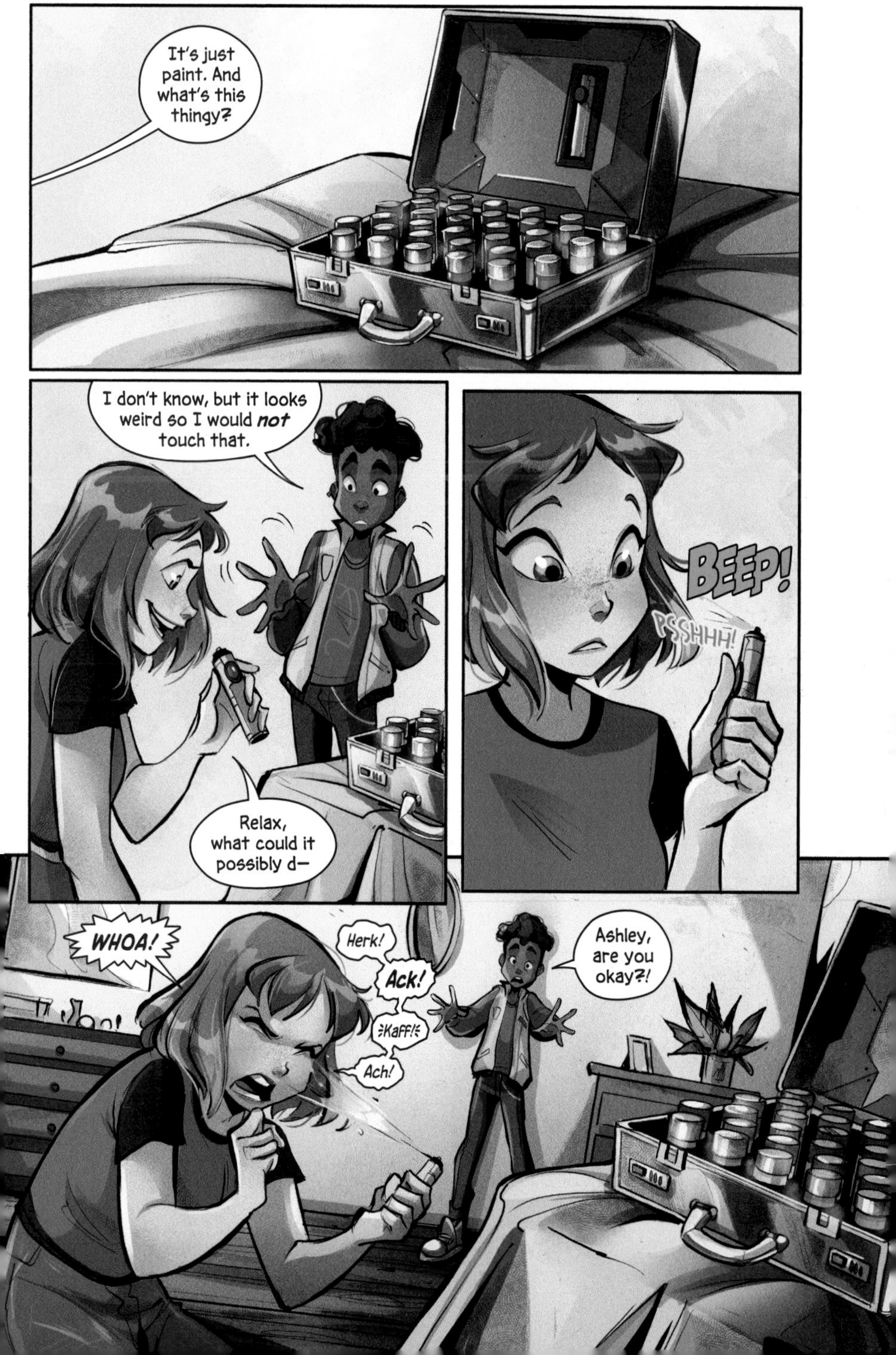
It's just paint. And what's this thingy?
I don't know, but it looks weird so I would *not* touch that.
Relax, what could it possibly d—
BEEP!
PSSHHH!
WHOA!
Herk!
Ack!
Kaff!
Ach!
Ashley, are you okay?!

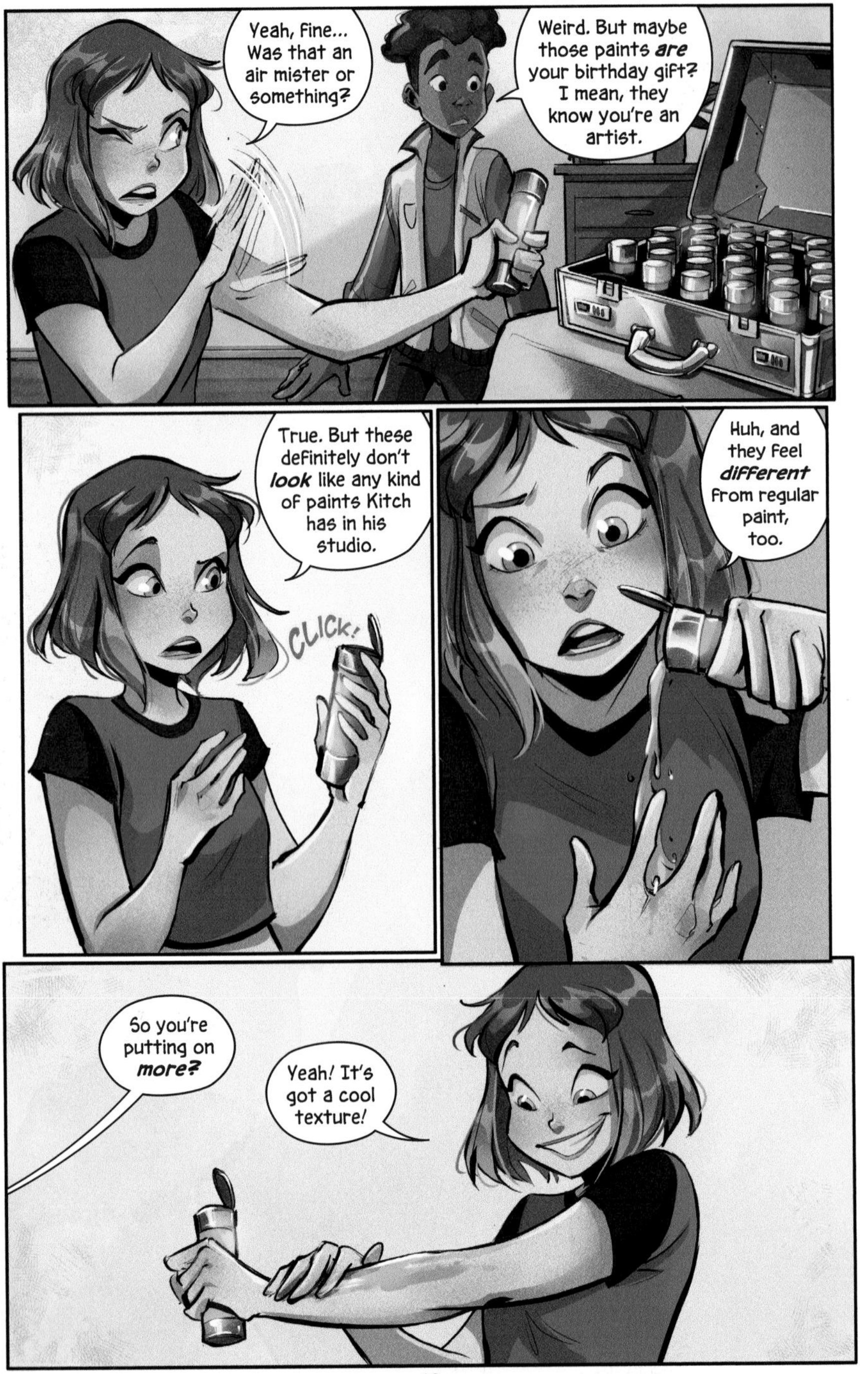
Yeah, fine... Was that an air mister or something?
Weird. But maybe those paints *are* your birthday gift? I mean, they know you're an artist.
True. But these definitely don't *look* like any kind of paints Kitch has in his studio.
CLICK!
Huh, and they feel *different* from regular paint, too.
So you're putting on *more?*
Yeah! It's got a cool texture!

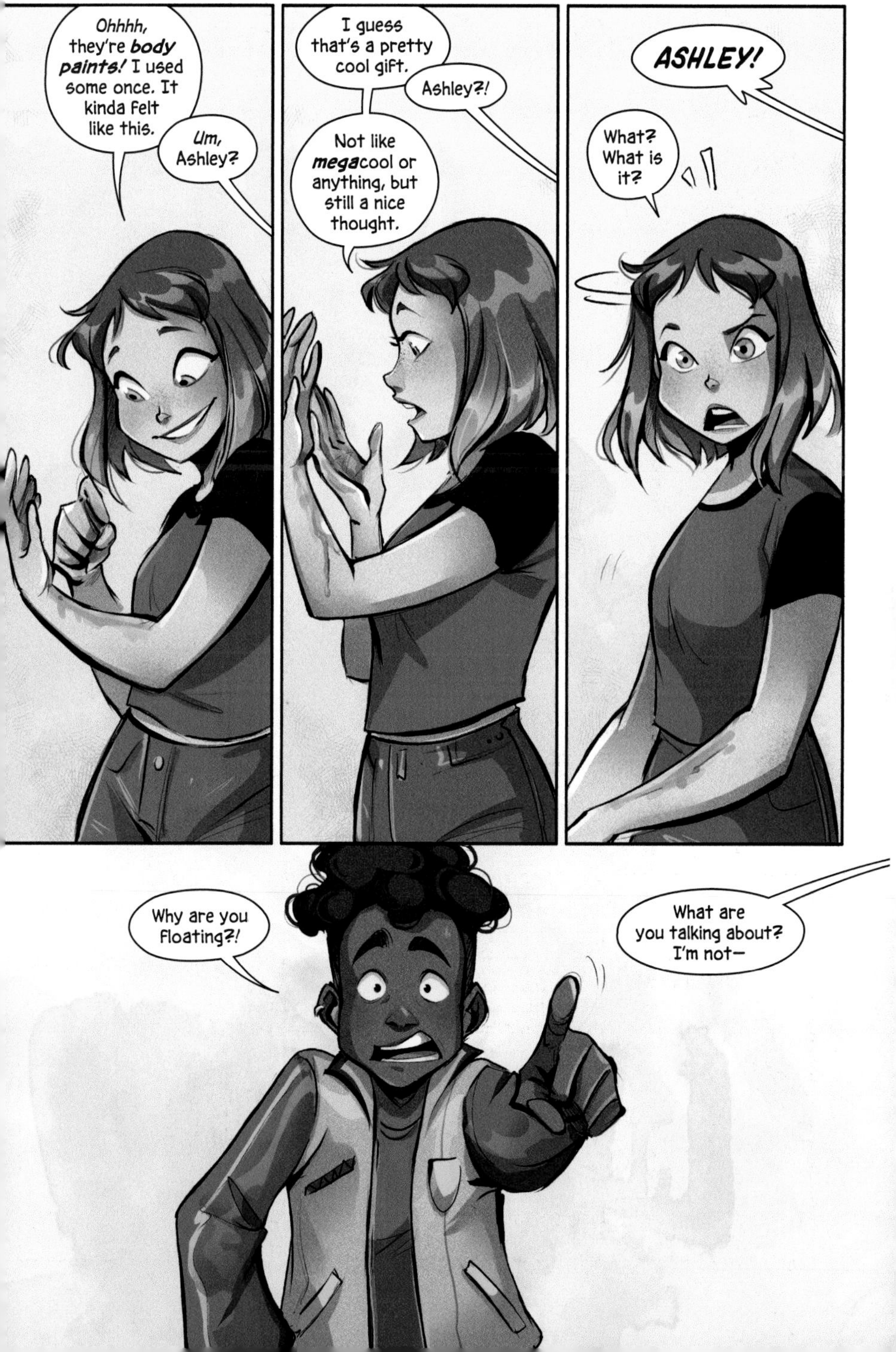

Ohhhh, they're **body paints!** I used some once. It kinda felt like this.
Um, Ashley?
I guess that's a pretty cool gift.
Ashley?!
Not like ***mega***cool or anything, but still a nice thought.
ASHLEY!
What? What is it?
Why are you Floating?!
What are you talking about? I'm not—

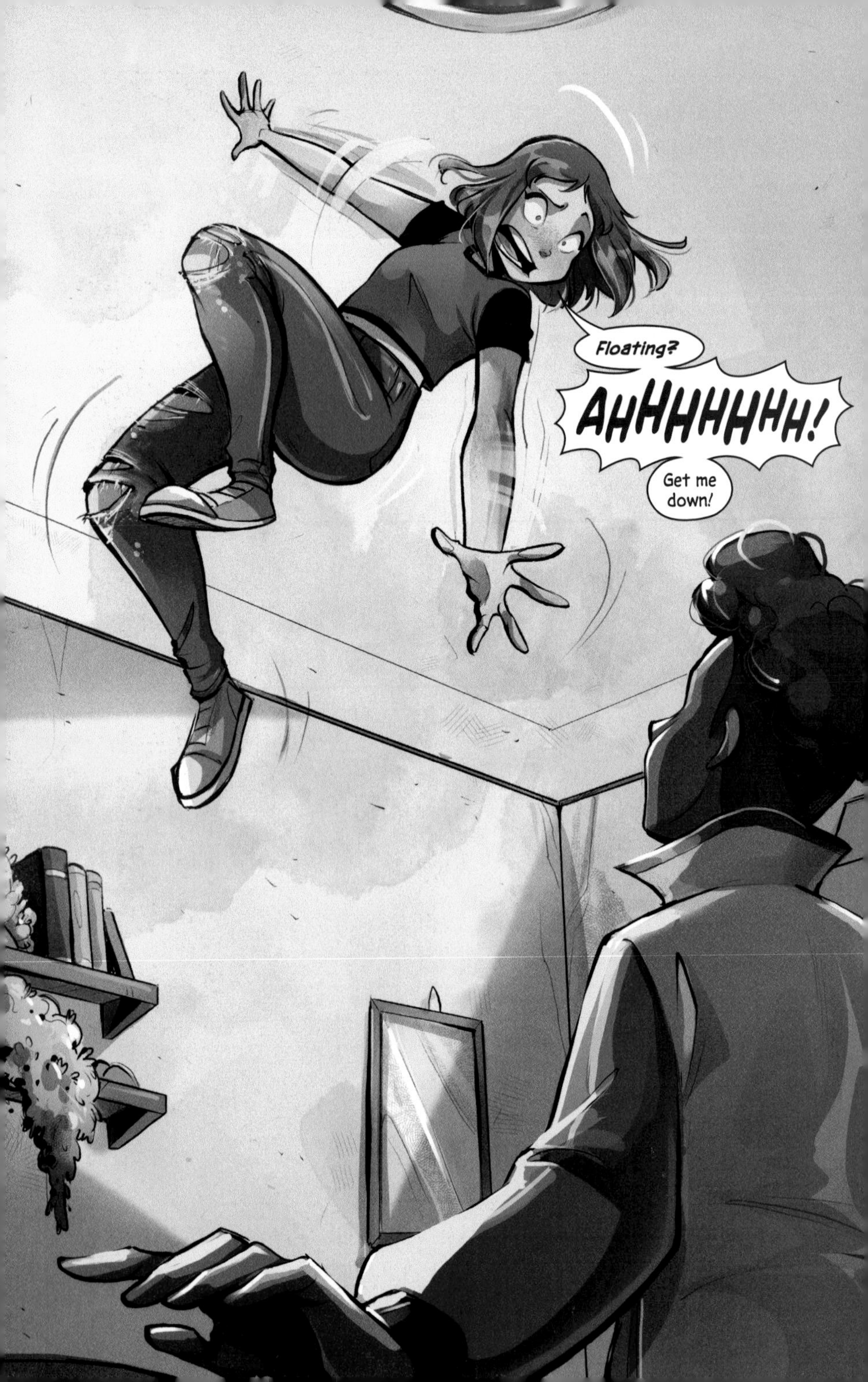
Floating?
AHHHHHHH!
Get me down!

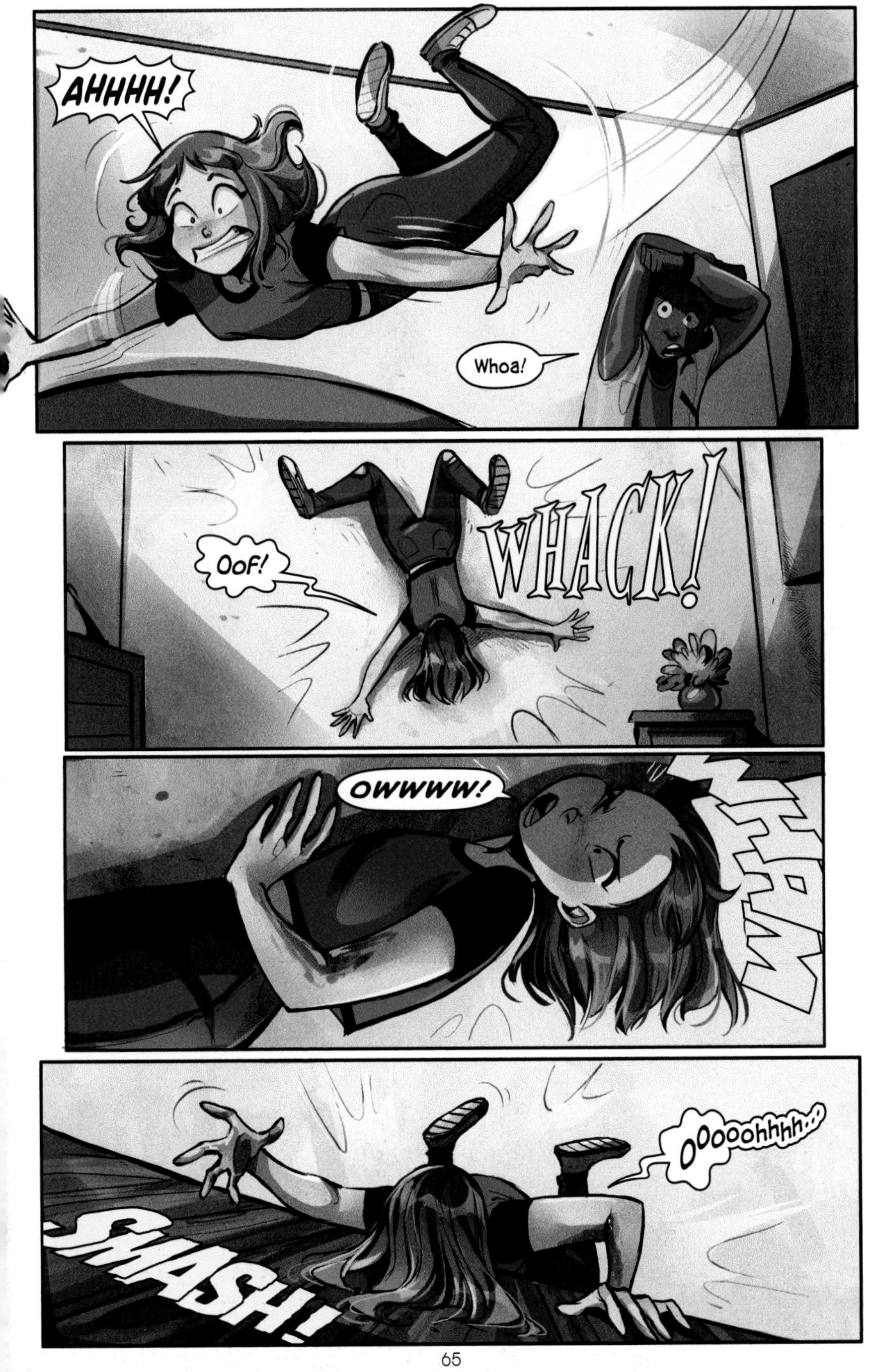

AHHHH!
Whoa!
Oof!
WHACK!
OWWWW!
WHAM
Ooooohhhh...
SMASH!

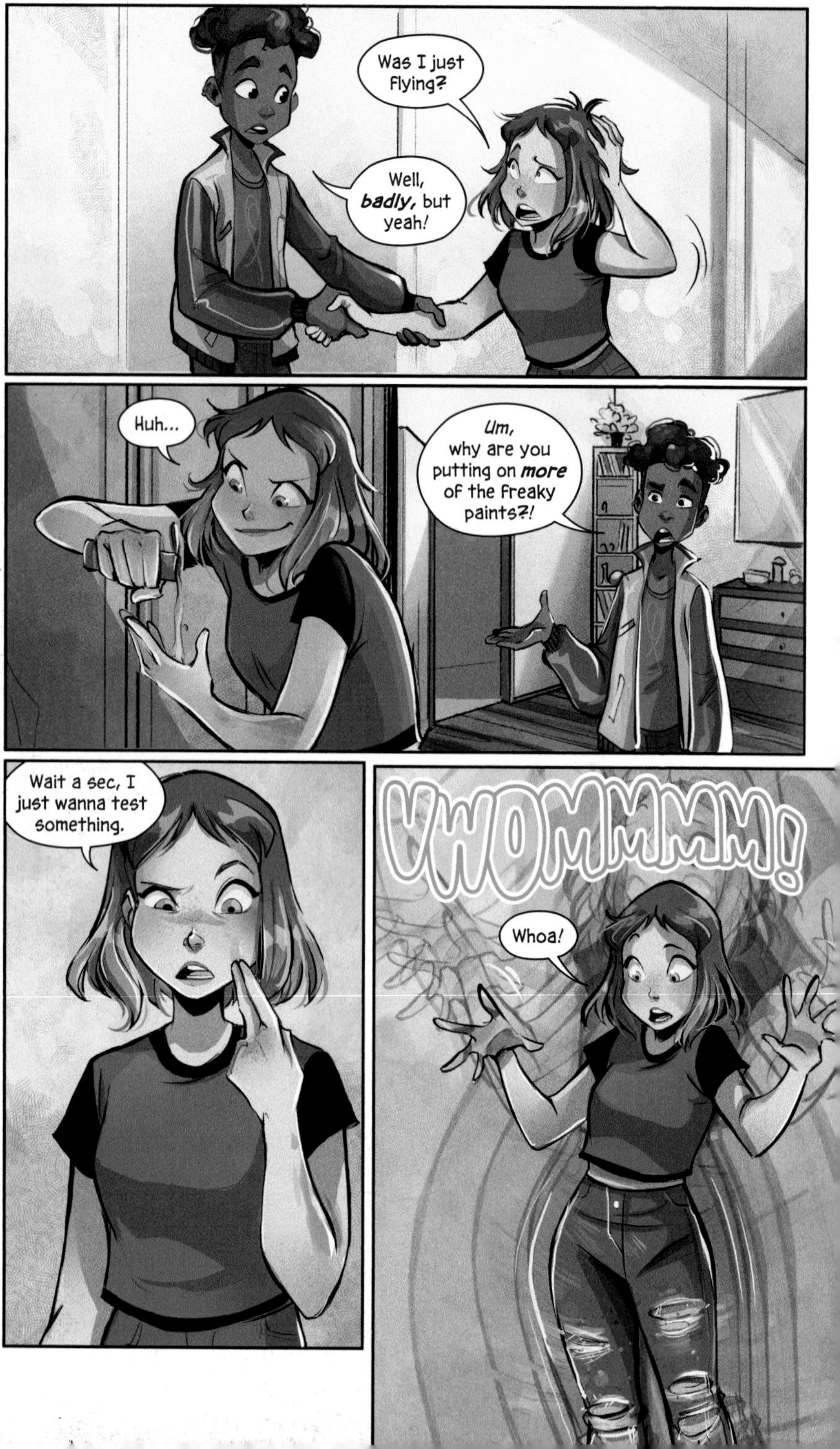
Was I just flying?
Well, *badly,* but yeah!
Huh...
Um, why are you putting on *more* of the freaky paints?!
Wait a sec, I just wanna test something.
VWOMMMMM!
Whoa!

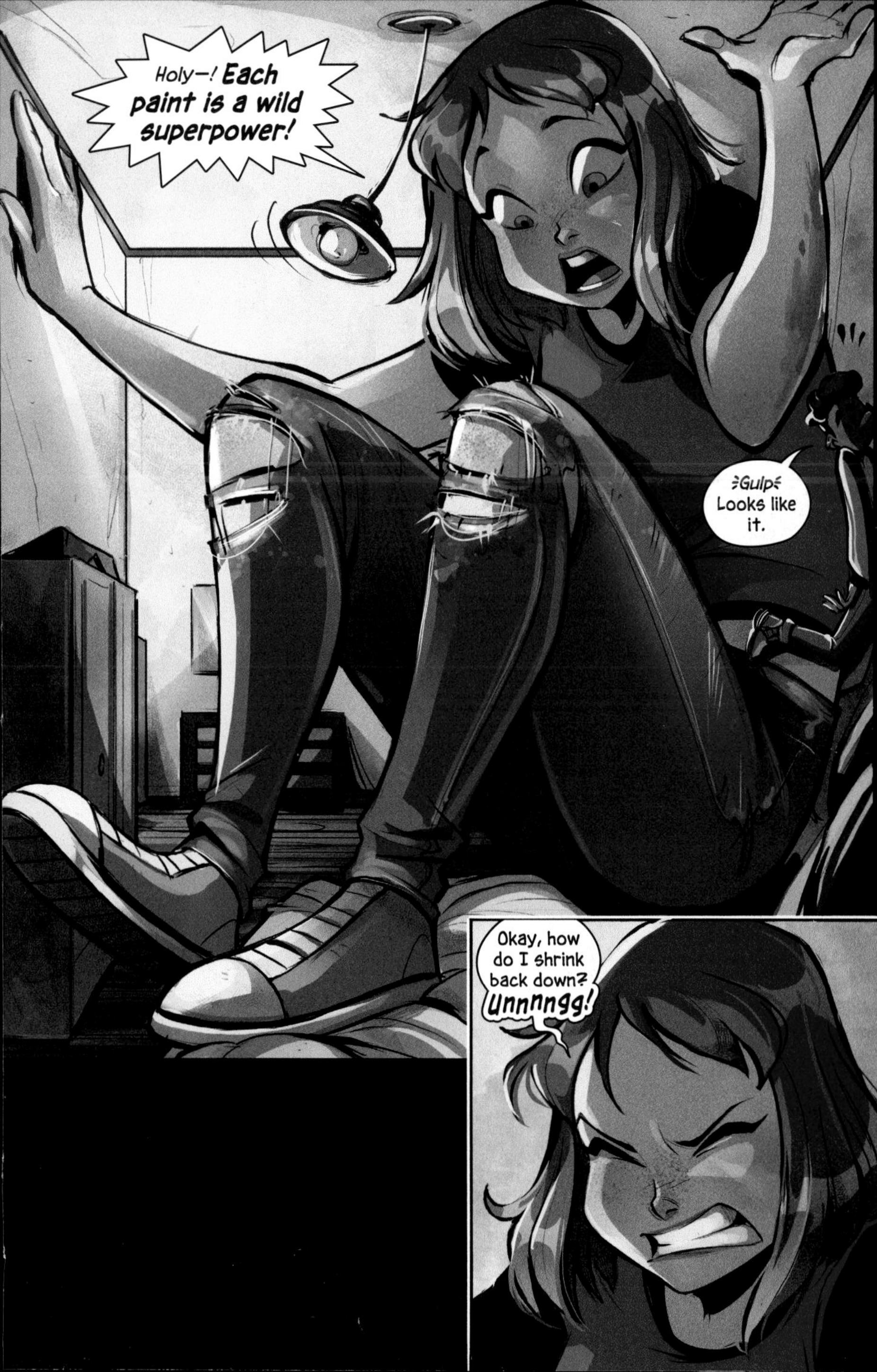
Holy—! **Each paint is a wild superpower!**
Gulp Looks like it.
Okay, how do I shrink back down? **Unnnngg!**

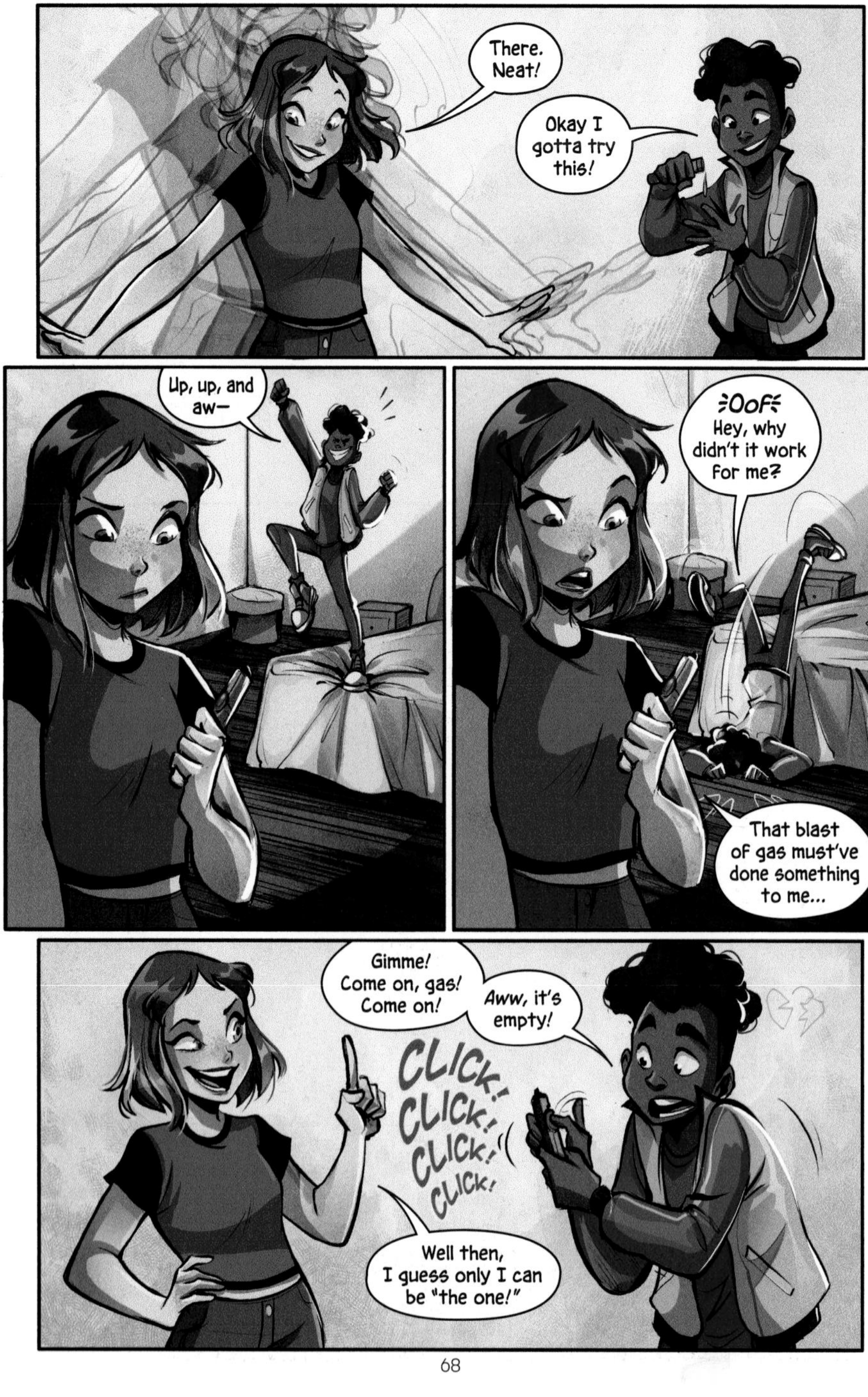
There. Neat!
Okay I gotta try this!
Up, up, and aw—
OOF
Hey, why didn't it work for me?
That blast of gas must've done something to me...
Gimme! Come on, gas! Come on!
Aww, it's empty!
CLICK! CLICK! CLICK! CLICK!
Well then, I guess only I can be "the one!"

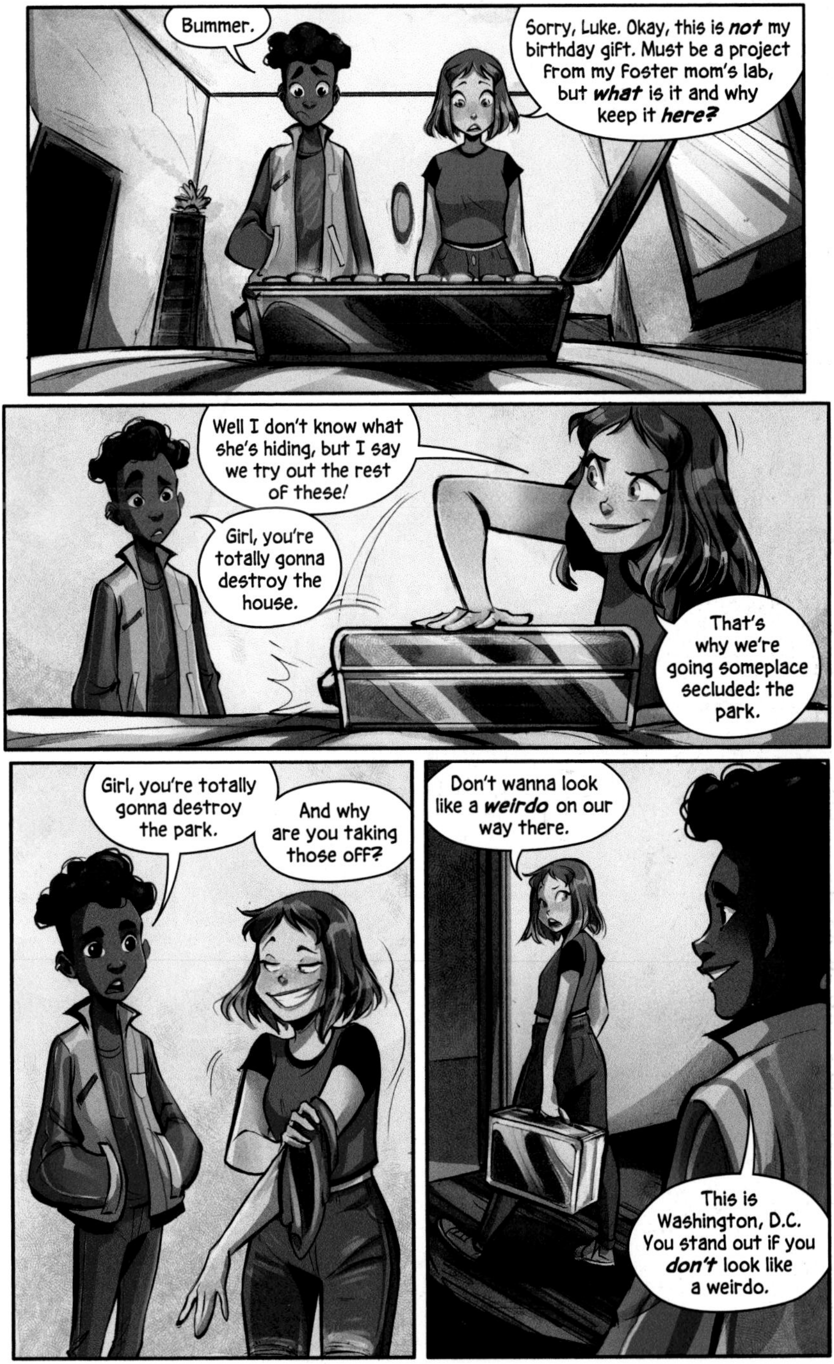
Bummer.
Sorry, Luke. Okay, this is ***not*** my birthday gift. Must be a project from my foster mom's lab, but ***what*** is it and why keep it ***here?***
Well I don't know what she's hiding, but I say we try out the rest of these!
Girl, you're totally gonna destroy the house.
That's why we're going someplace secluded: the park.
Girl, you're totally gonna destroy the park.
And why are you taking those off?
Don't wanna look like a ***weirdo*** on our way there.
This is Washington, D.C. You stand out if you ***don't*** look like a weirdo.

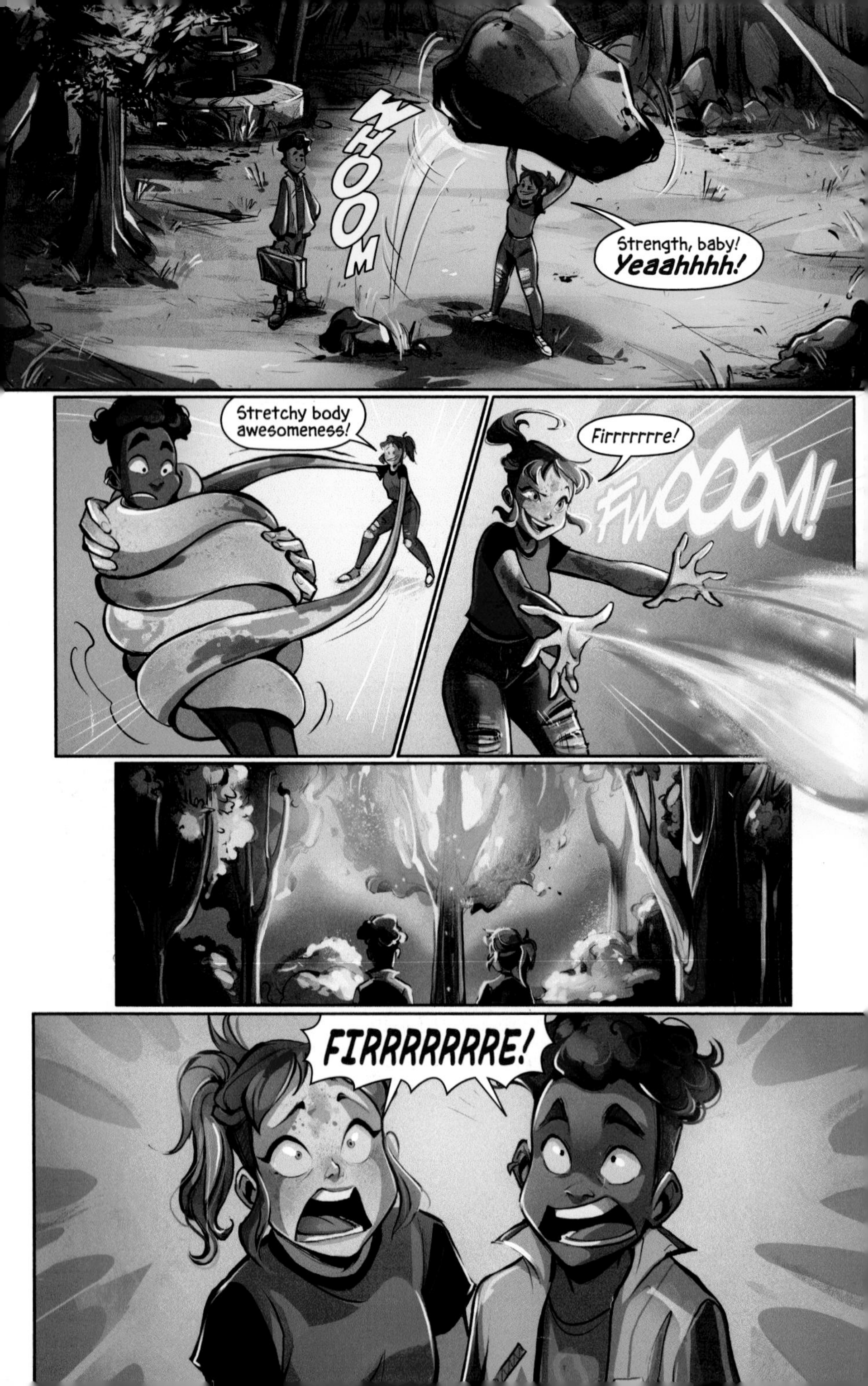
WHOOM
Strength, baby! Yeaahhhh!
Stretchy body awesomeness!
Firrrrrrre!
FWOOOM!
FIRRRRRRRE!

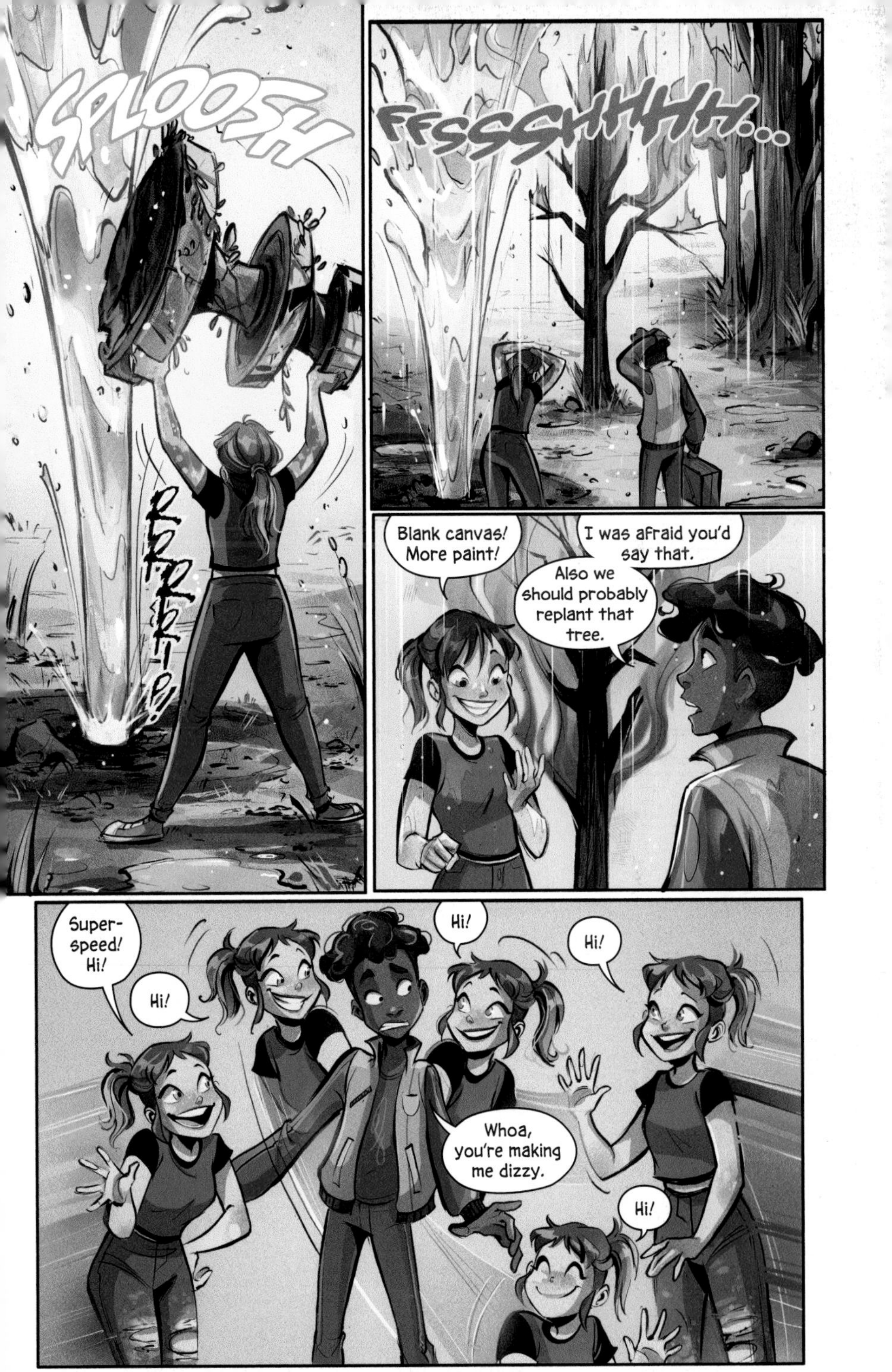
SPLOOSH
RRRRRIIIPP
FFSSSHHHHH...
Blank canvas! More paint!
I was afraid you'd say that.
Also we should probably replant that tree.
Super-speed! Hi!
Hi!
Hi!
Hi!
Whoa, you're making me dizzy.
Hi!

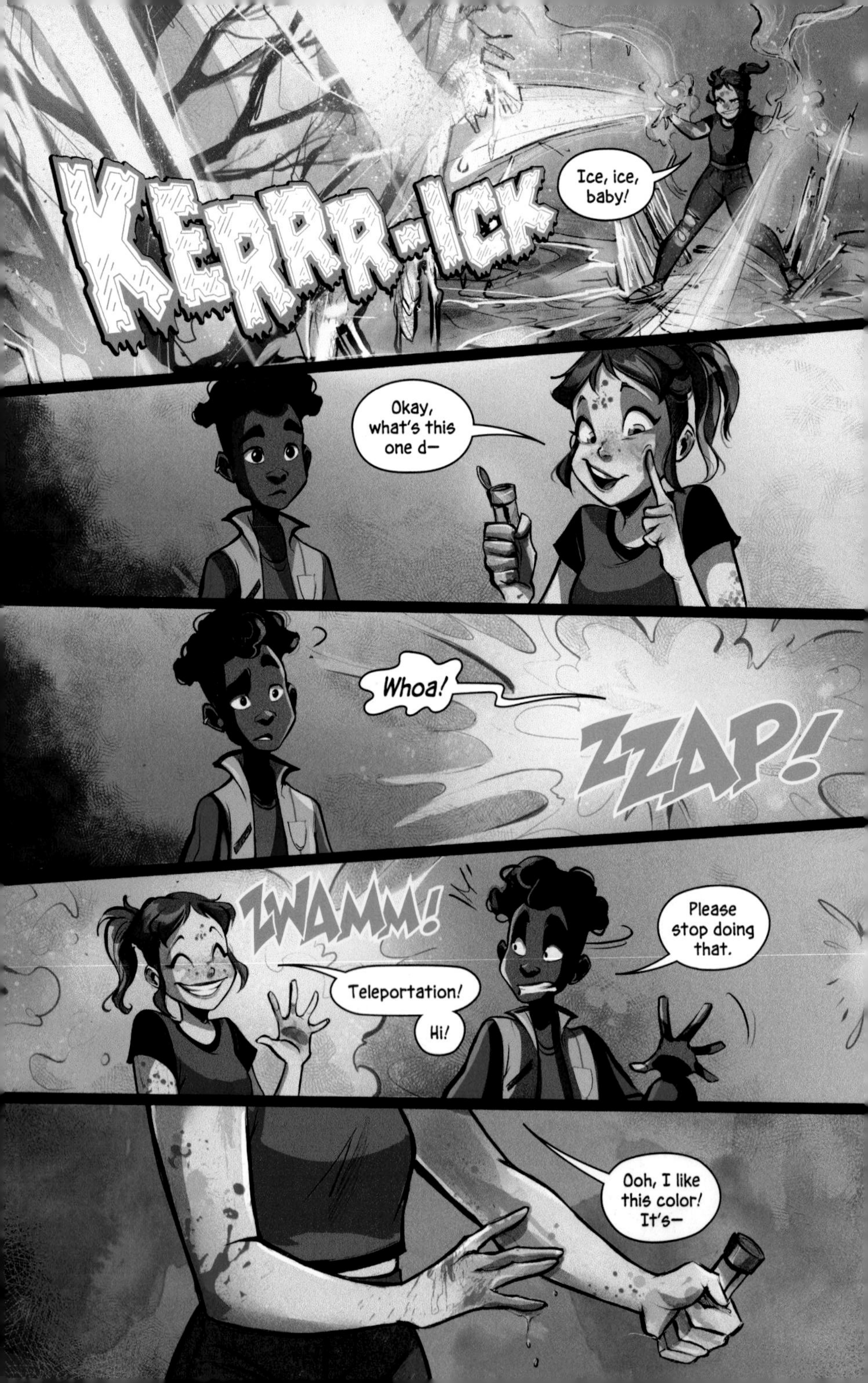
KERRR-ICK
Ice, ice, baby!
Okay, what's this one d—
Whoa!
ZZAP!
ZWAMM!
Teleportation!
Hi!
Please stop doing that.
Ooh, I like this color! It's—

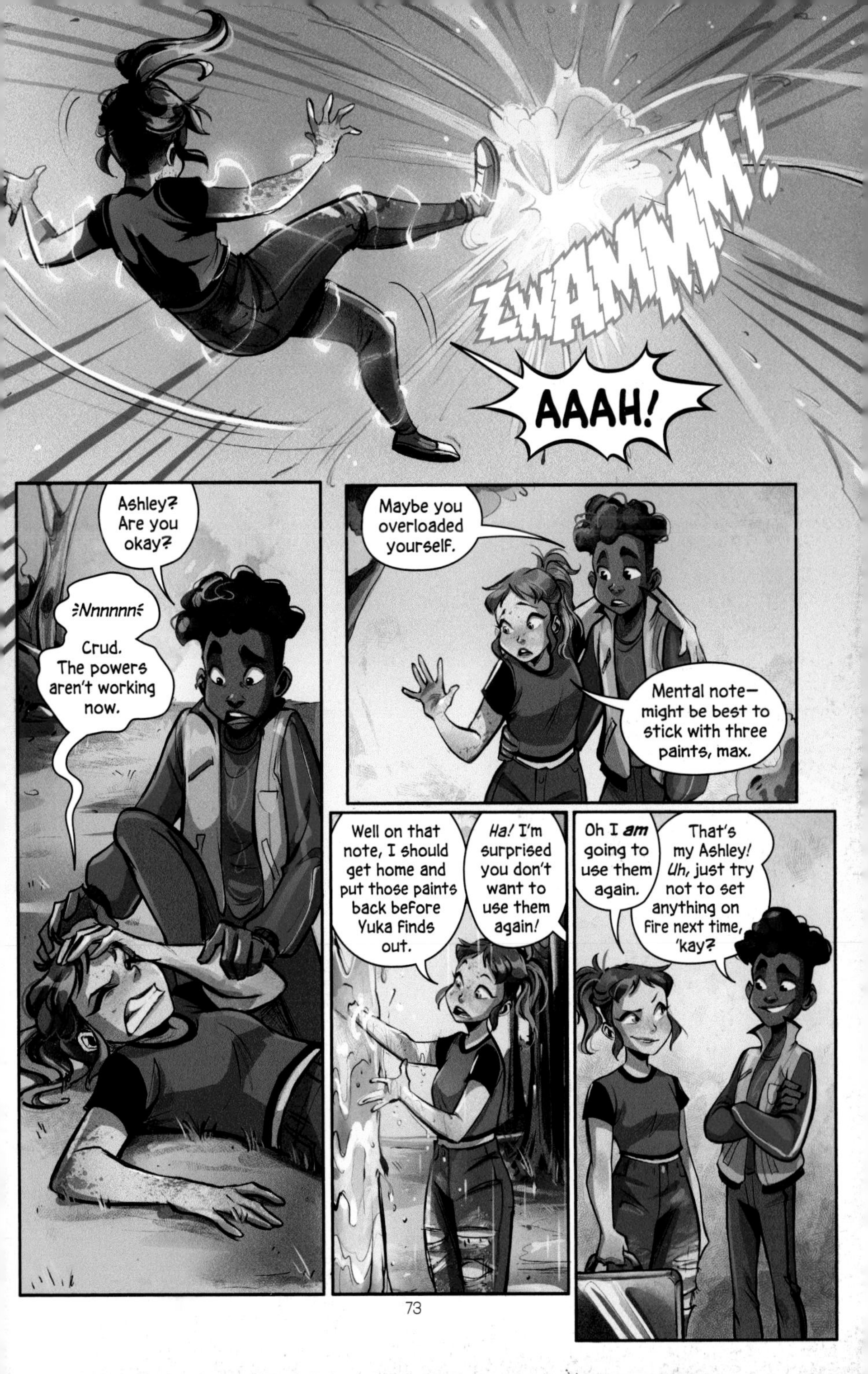
ZWAMMM!
AAAH!
Ashley? Are you okay?
Nnnnnn
Crud. The powers aren't working now.
Maybe you overloaded yourself.
Mental note—might be best to stick with three paints, max.
Well on that note, I should get home and put those paints back before Yuka finds out.
Ha! I'm surprised you don't want to use them again!
Oh I ***am*** going to use them again.
That's my Ashley! *Uh,* just try not to set anything on fire next time, 'kay?

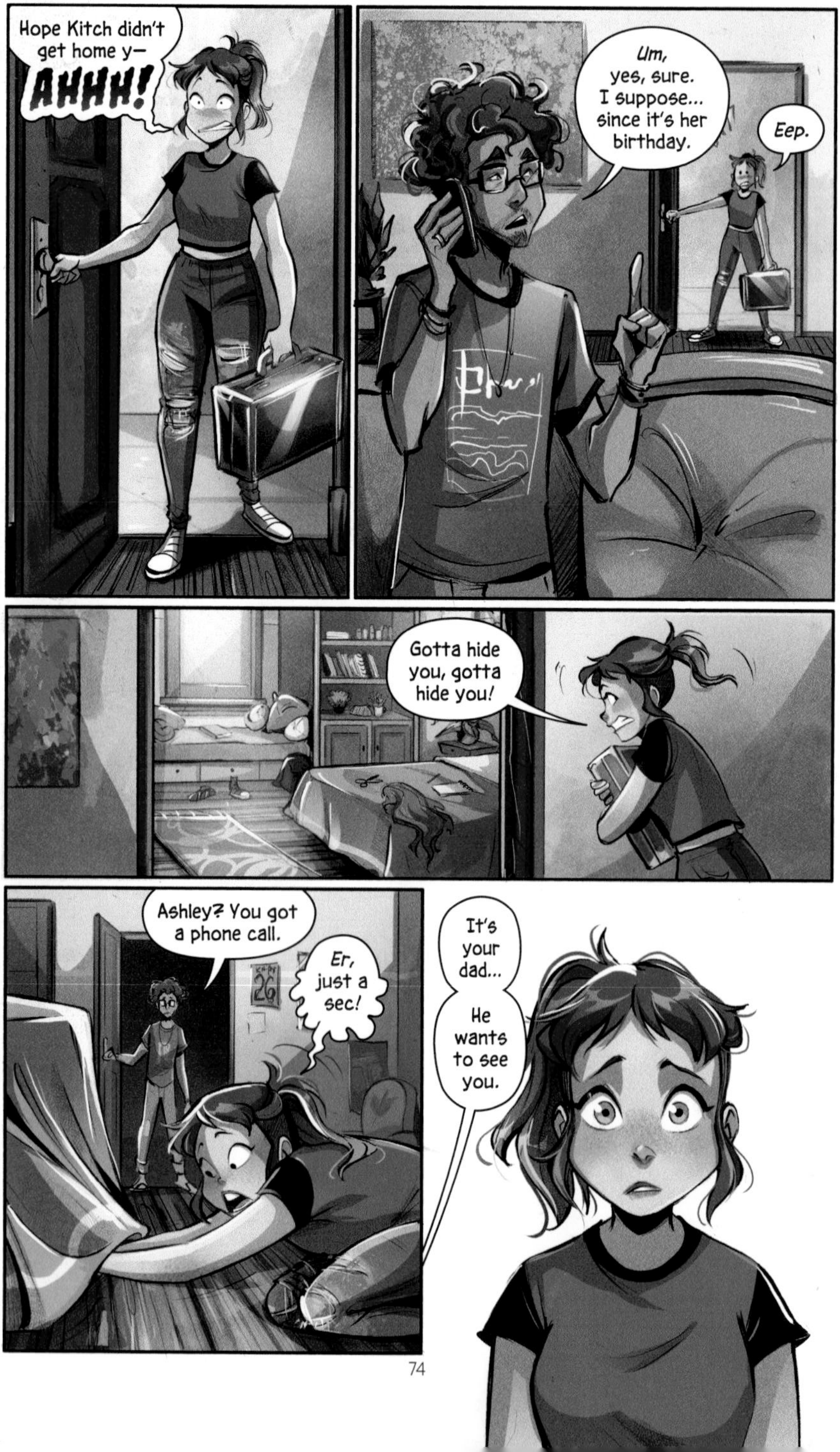
Hope Kitch didn't get home y—
AHHH!
Um, yes, sure. I suppose... since it's her birthday.
Eep.
Gotta hide you, gotta hide you!
Ashley? You got a phone call.
Er, just a sec!
It's your dad...
He wants to see you.

chapter 3
Red, White, and Bruised

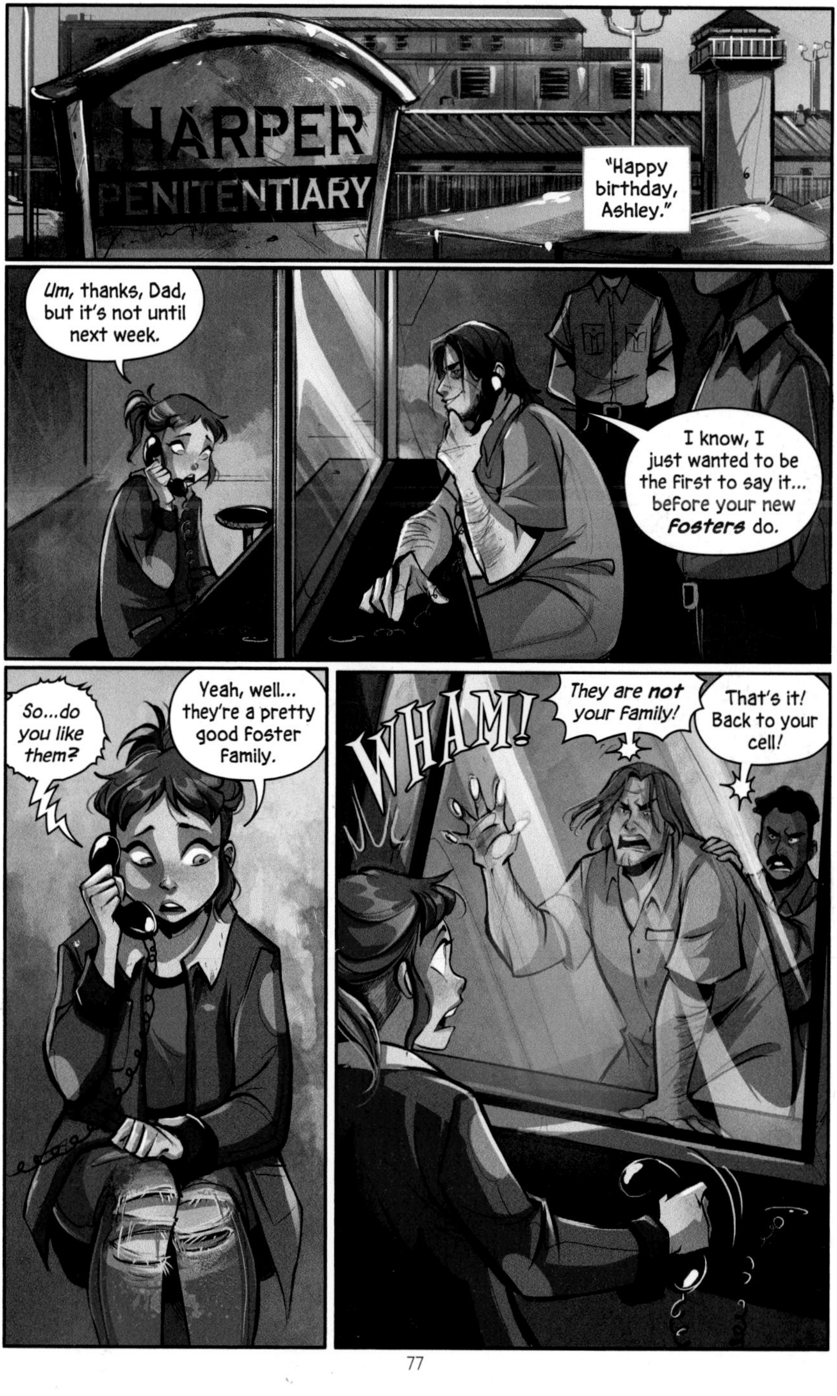
HARPER
PENITENTIARY
"Happy birthday, Ashley."
Um, thanks, Dad, but it's not until next week.
I know, I just wanted to be the first to say it... before your new fosters do.
So...do you like them?
Yeah, well... they're a pretty good foster family.
WHAM!
They are not your family!
That's it! Back to your cell!

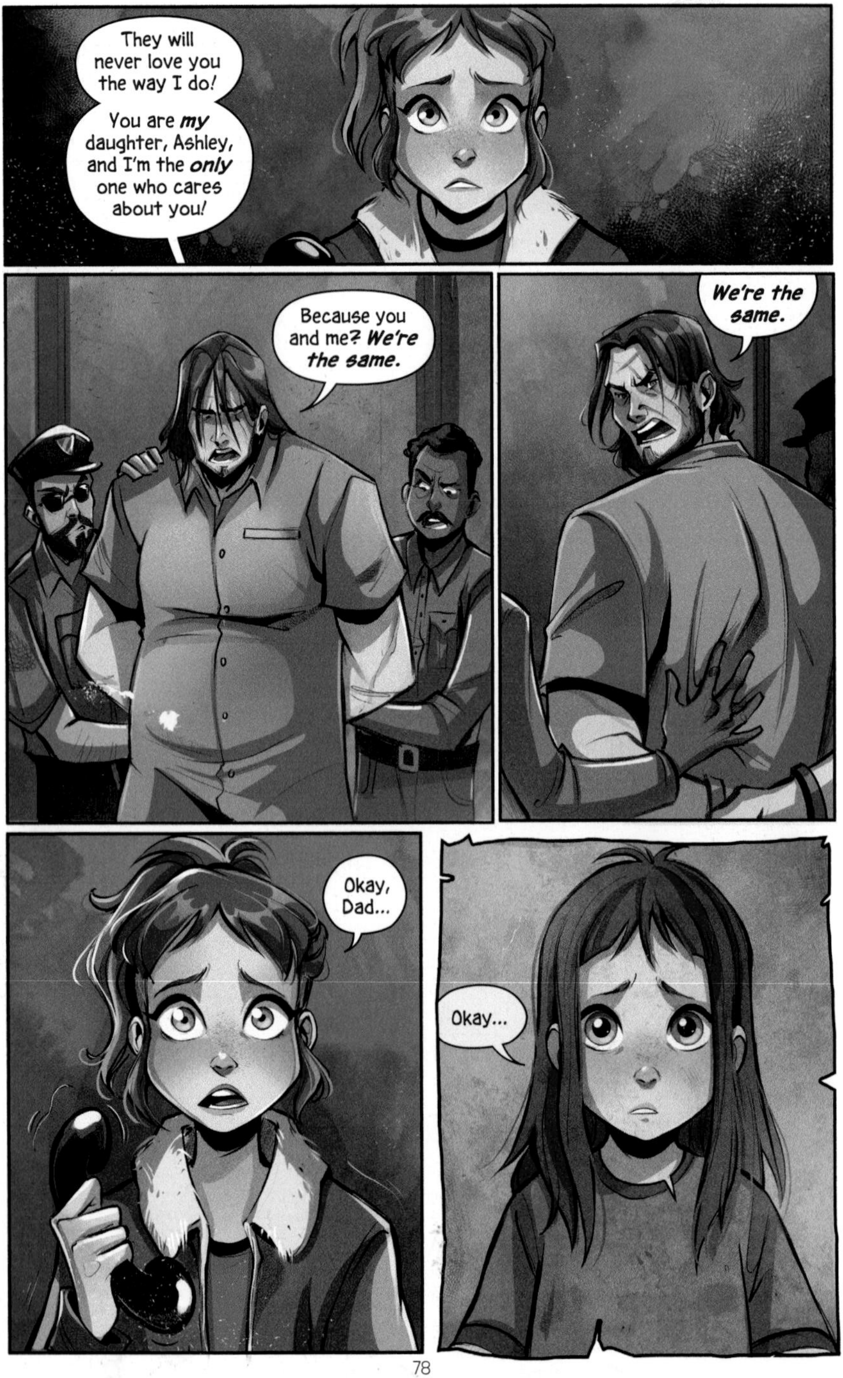

They will never love you the way I do!
You are *my* daughter, Ashley, and I'm the *only* one who cares about you!
Because you and me? *We're the same.*
We're the same.
Okay, Dad...
Okay...

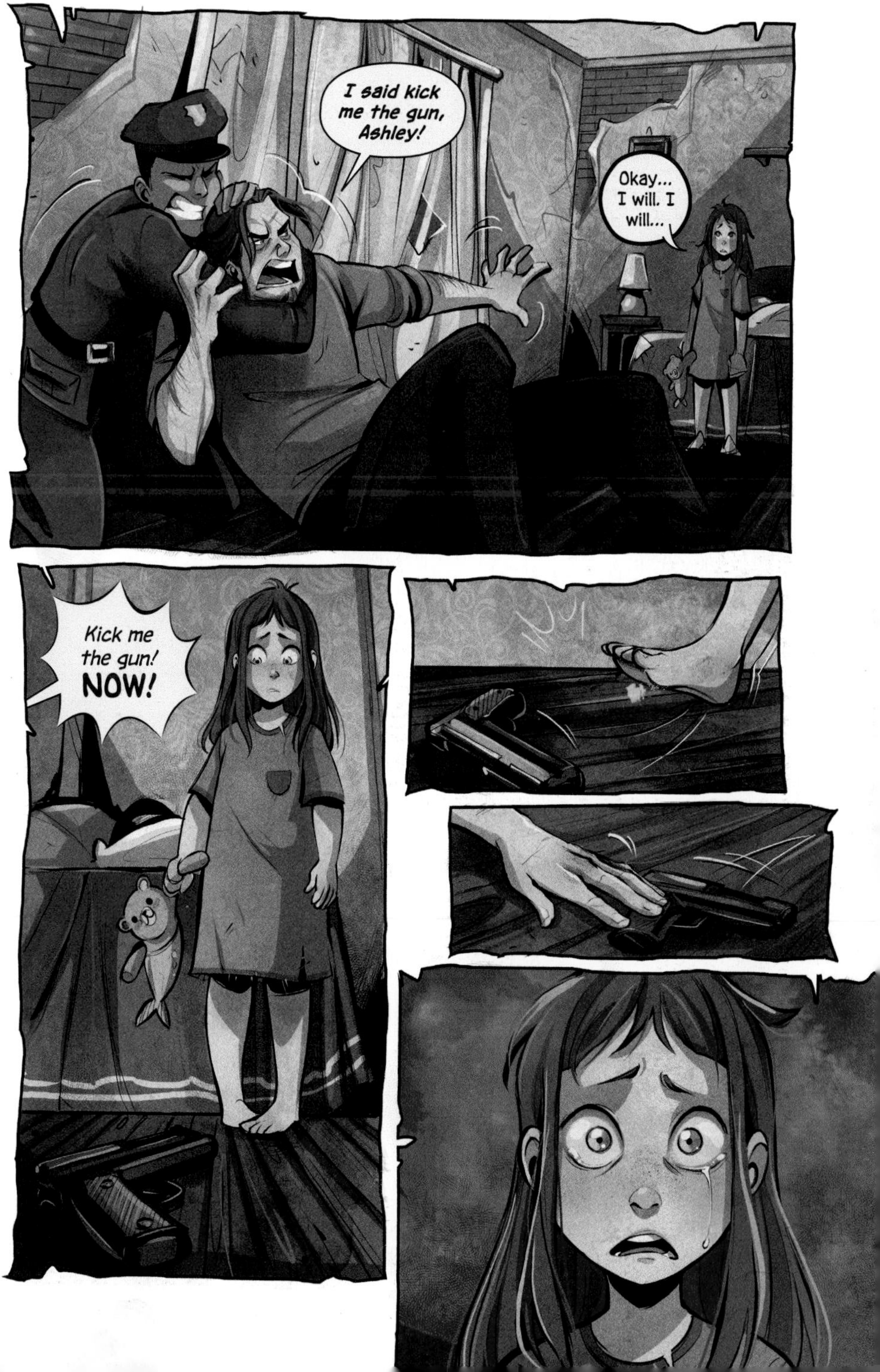
I said kick me the gun, Ashley!
Okay... I will. I will...
Kick me the gun! NOW!

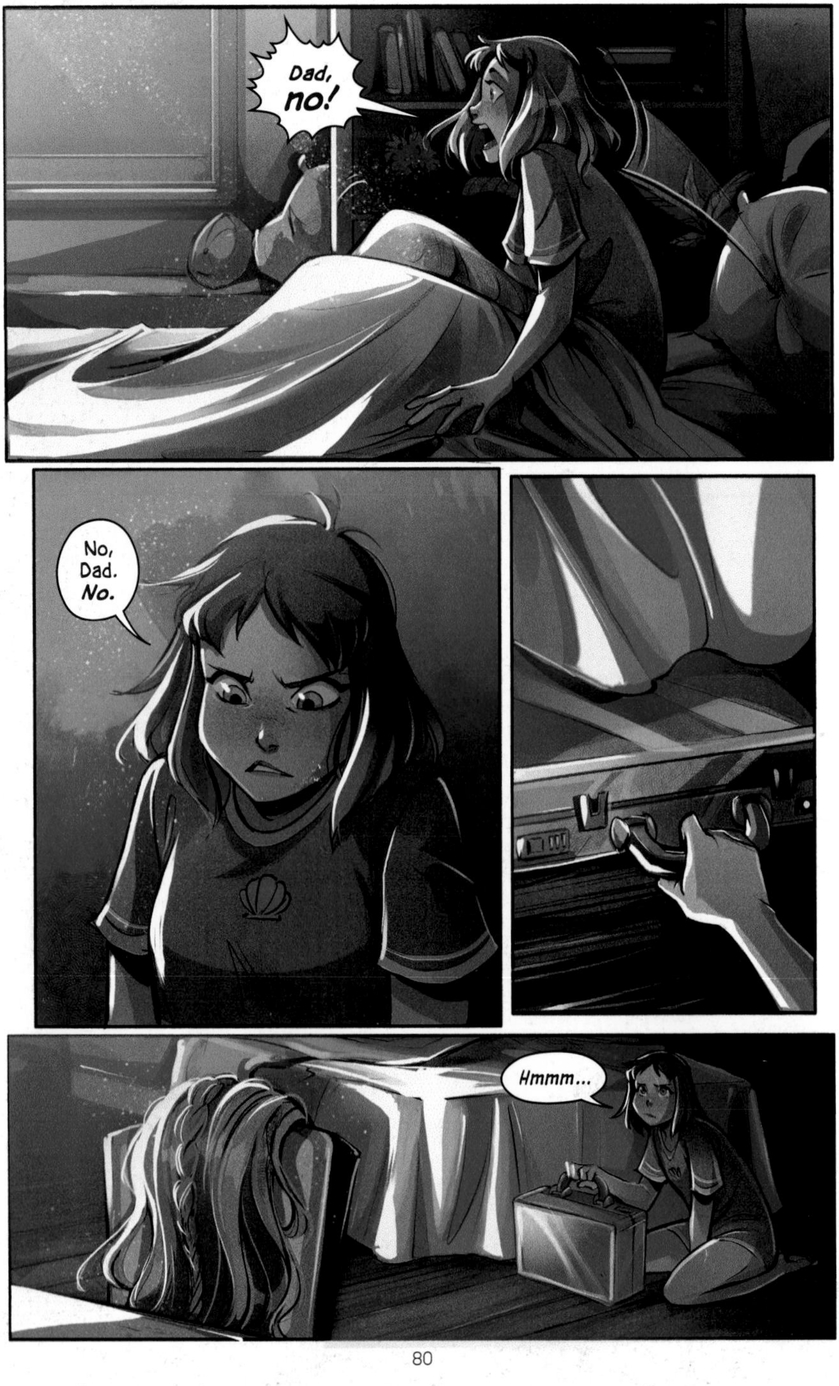
Dad, no!
No, Dad. No.
Hmmm...

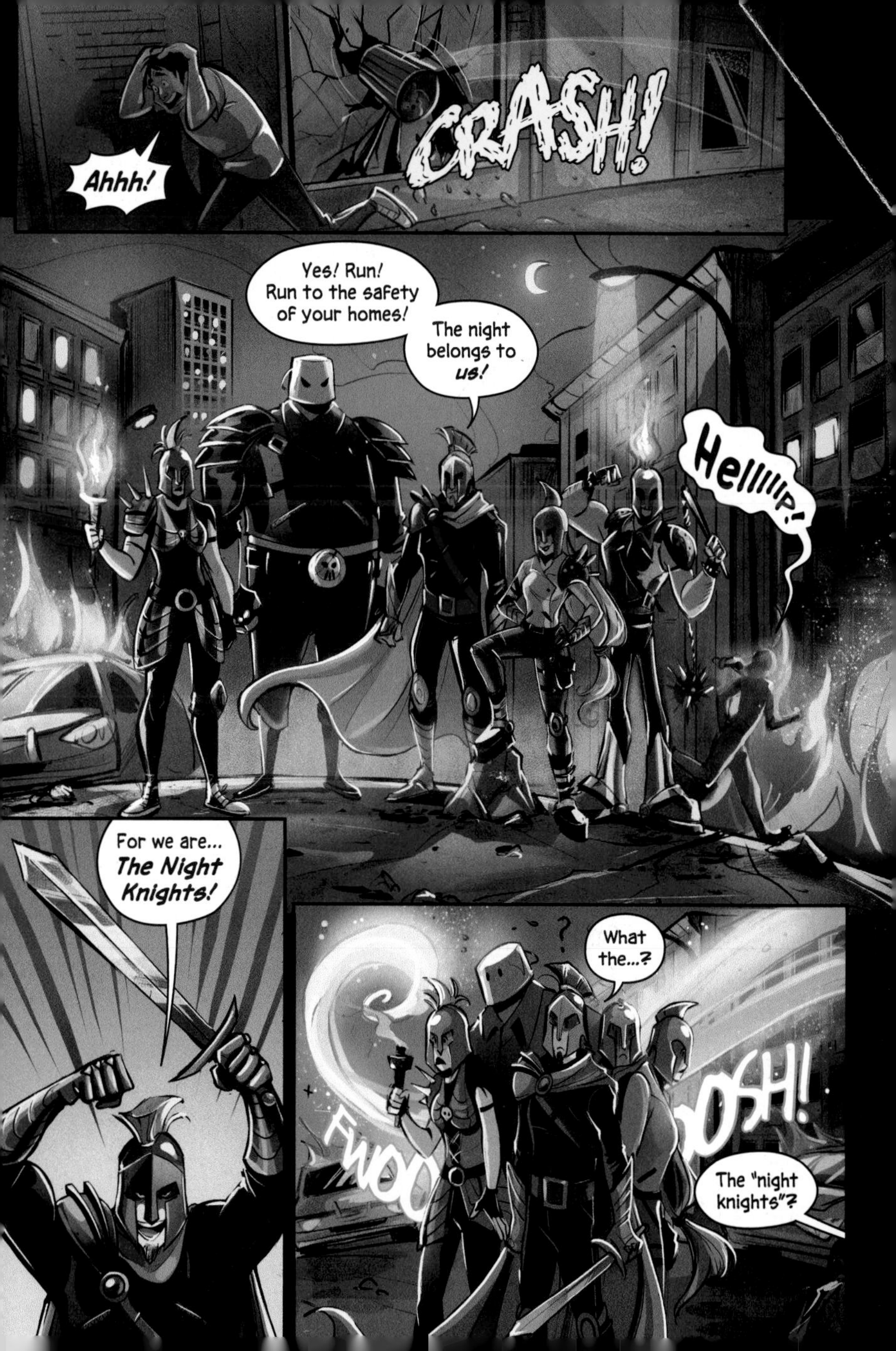
Ahhh!
CRASH!
Yes! Run! Run to the safety of your homes!
The night belongs to *us!*
Helllllp!
For we are... *The Night Knights!*
What the...?
FWOOOSH!
The "night knights"?

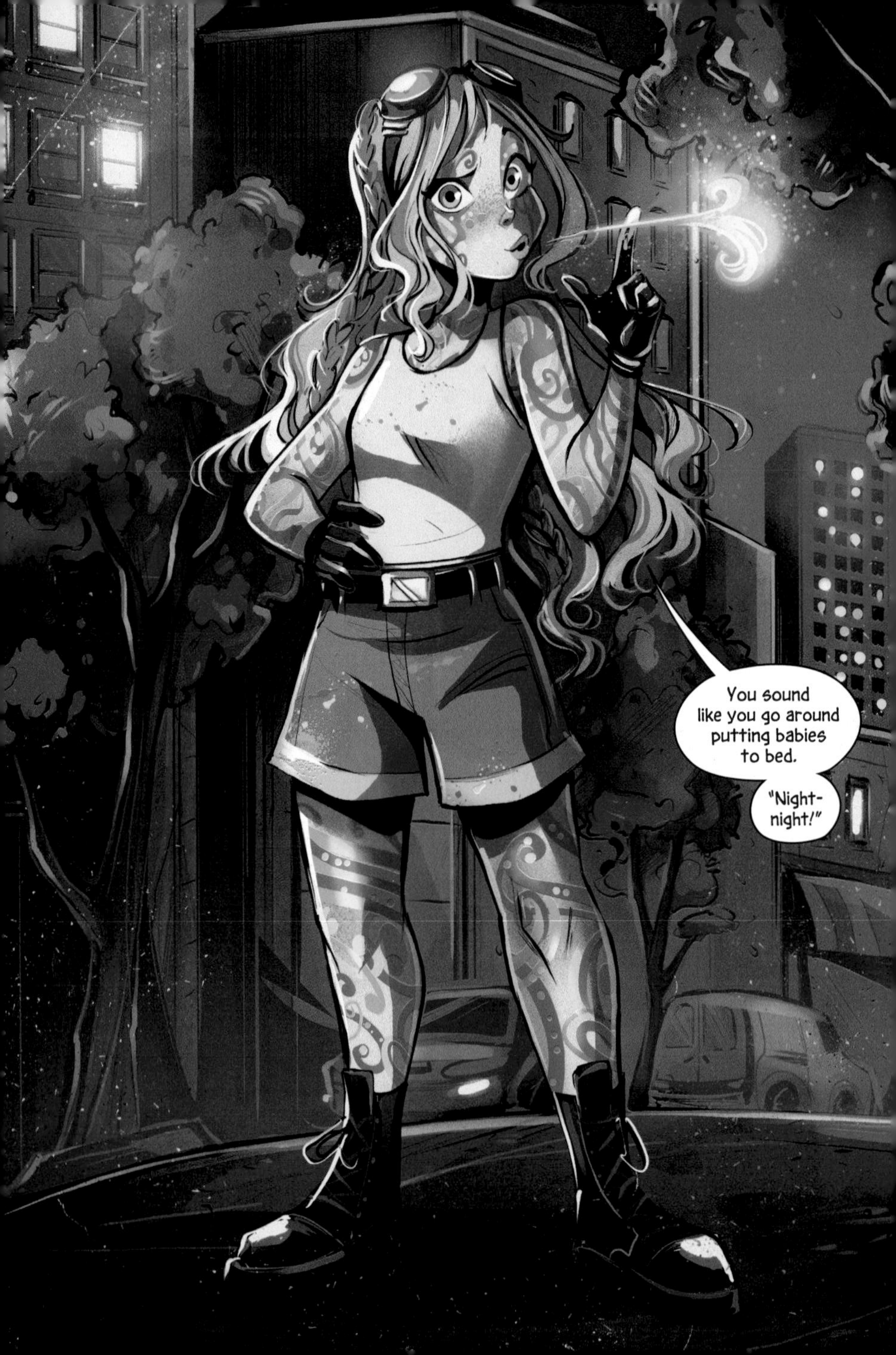
You sound like you go around putting babies to bed.
"Night-night!"

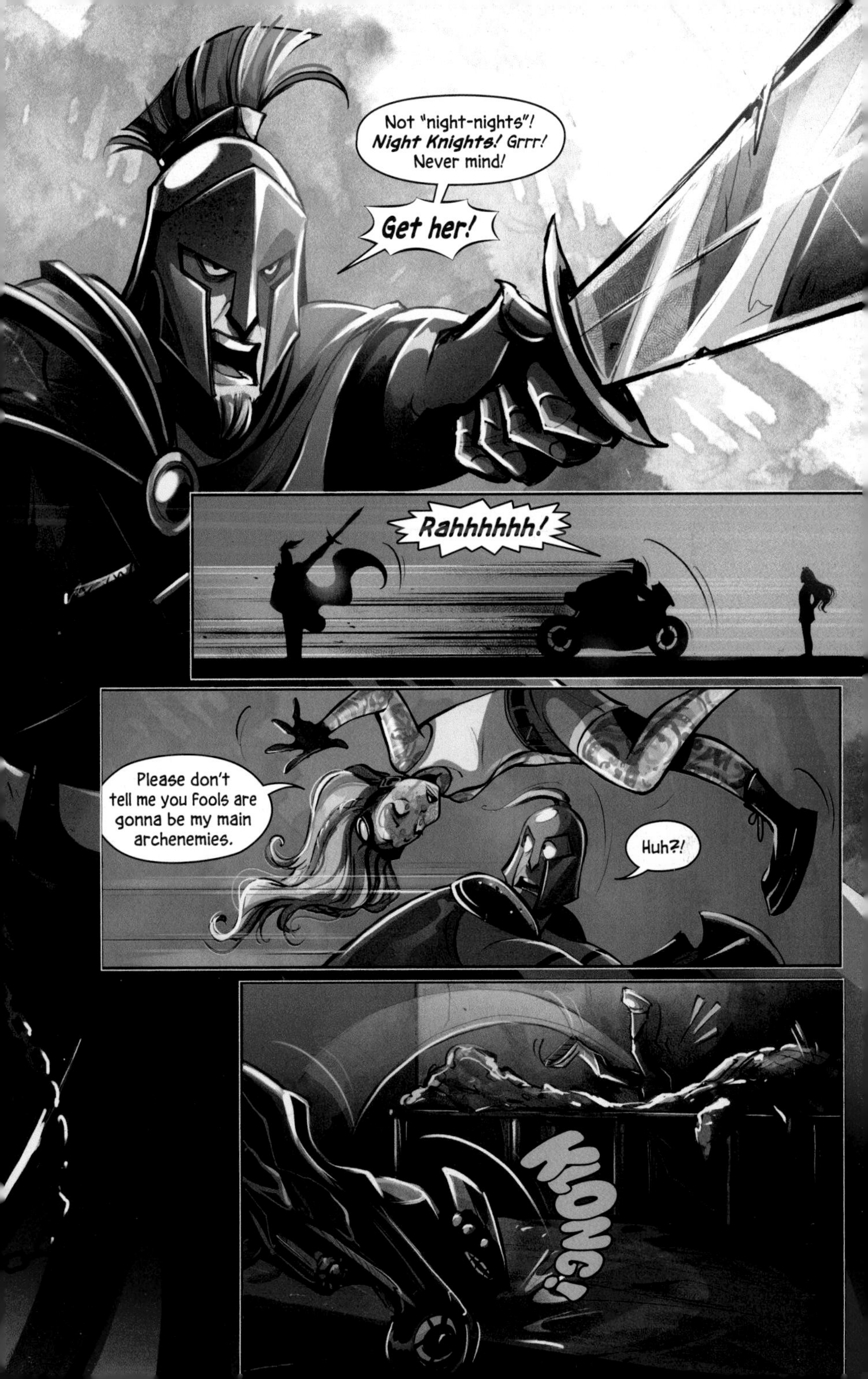
Not "night-nights"! *Night Knights!* Grrr! Never mind!
Get her!
Rahhhhhh!
Please don't tell me you fools are gonna be my main archenemies.
Huh?!
KLONG!!

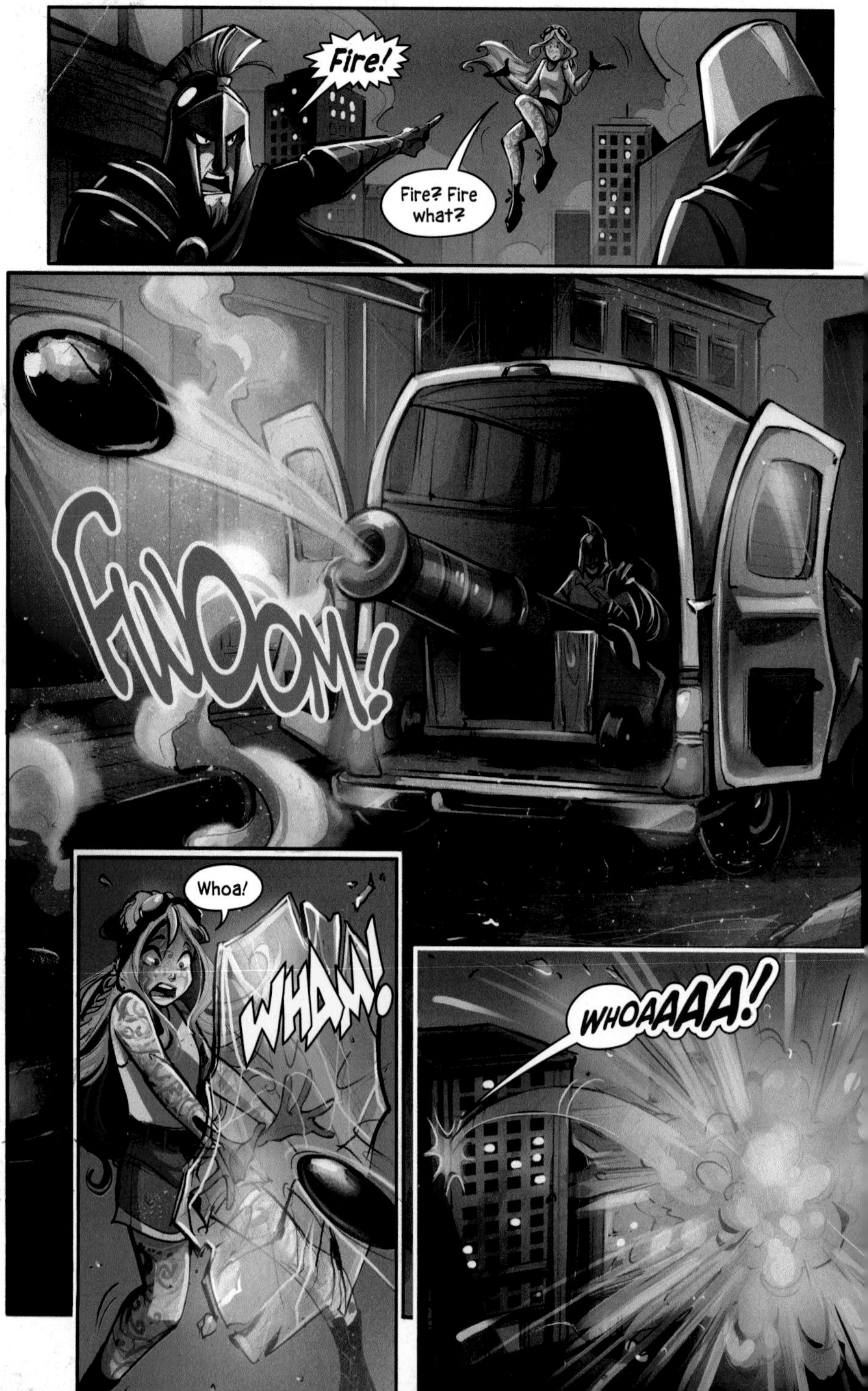
Fire!
Fire? Fire what?
FWOOM!
Whoa!
WHAM!
WHOAAAA!

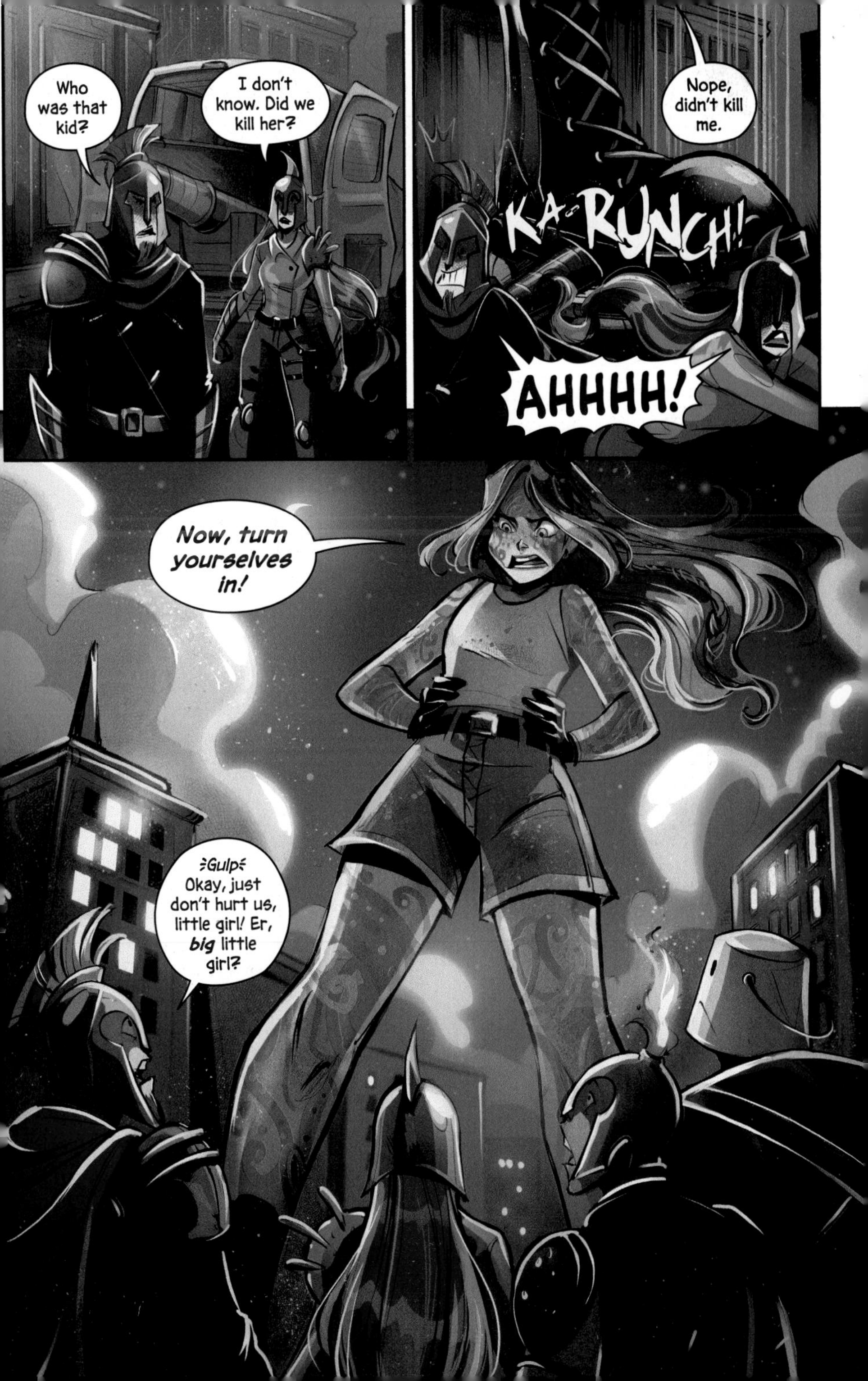
Who was that kid?
I don't know. Did we kill her?
Nope, didn't kill me.
KA-RUNCH!
AHHHH!
Now, turn yourselves in!
Gulp
Okay, just don't hurt us, little girl! Er, big little girl?

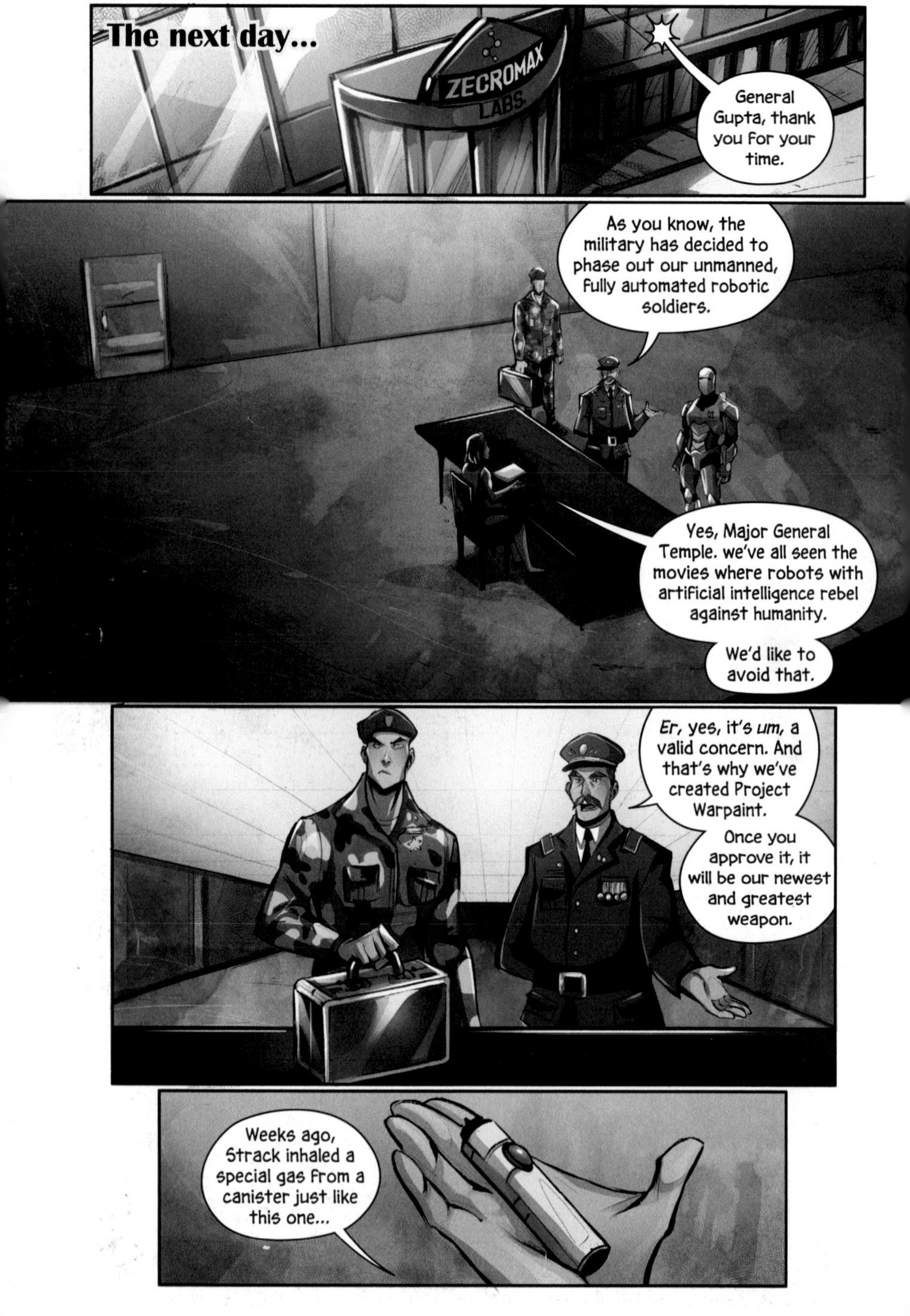

The next day...
ZECROMAX LABS.
General Gupta, thank you for your time.
As you know, the military has decided to phase out our unmanned, fully automated robotic soldiers.
Yes, Major General Temple. we've all seen the movies where robots with artificial intelligence rebel against humanity.
We'd like to avoid that.
Er, yes, it's *um*, a valid concern. And that's why we've created Project Warpaint.
Once you approve it, it will be our newest and greatest weapon.
Weeks ago, Strack inhaled a special gas from a canister just like this one...

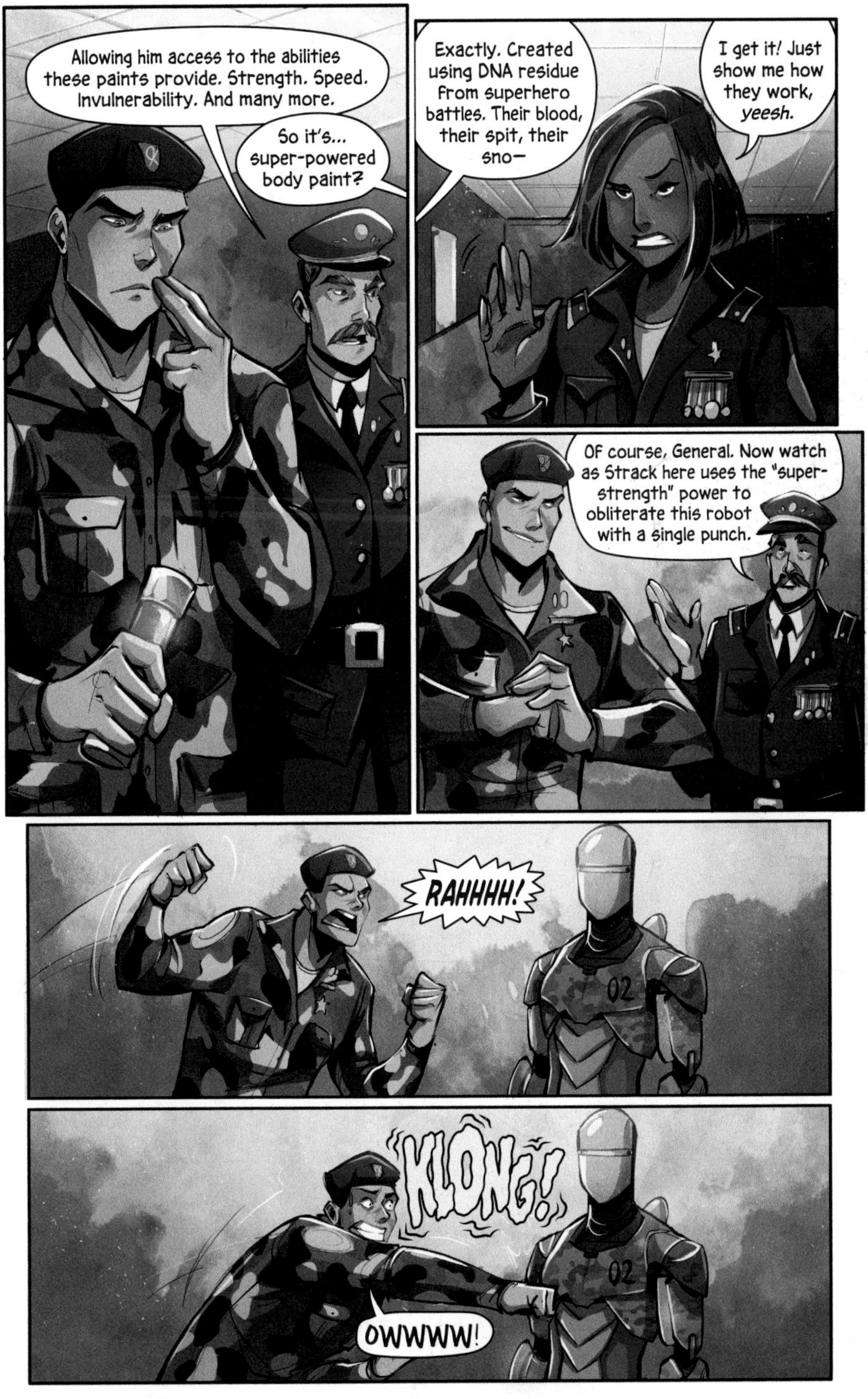
Allowing him access to the abilities these paints provide. Strength. Speed. Invulnerability. And many more.
So it's... super-powered body paint?
Exactly. Created using DNA residue from superhero battles. Their blood, their spit, their sno—
I get it! Just show me how they work, *yeesh.*
Of course, General. Now watch as Strack here uses the "super-strength" power to obliterate this robot with a single punch.
RAHHHH!
02
KLONG!
02
OWWWW!

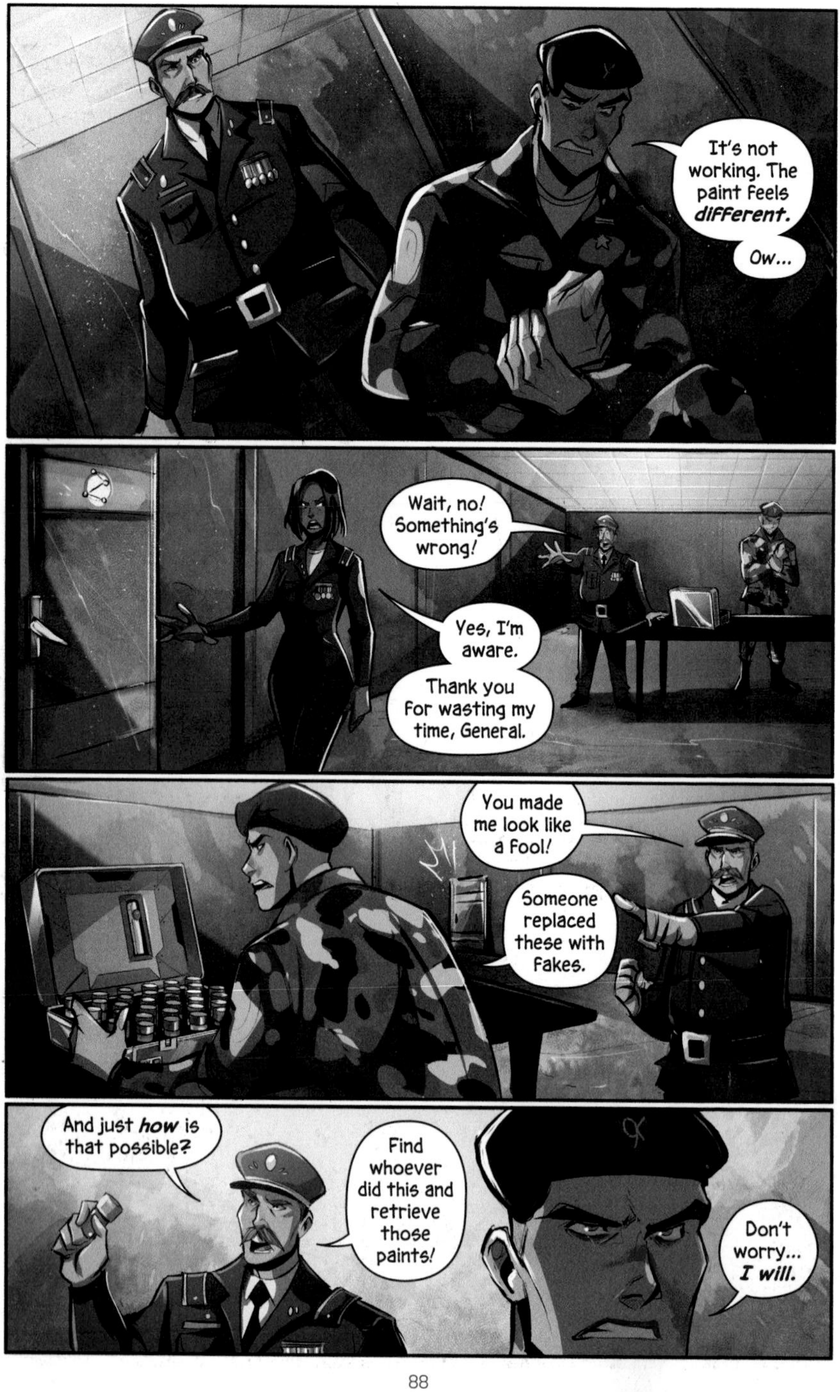
It's not working. The paint feels *different.*
Ow...
Wait, no! Something's wrong!
Yes, I'm aware.
Thank you for wasting my time, General.
You made me look like a fool!
Someone replaced these with fakes.
And just *how* is that possible?
Find whoever did this and retrieve those paints!
Don't worry... *I will.*

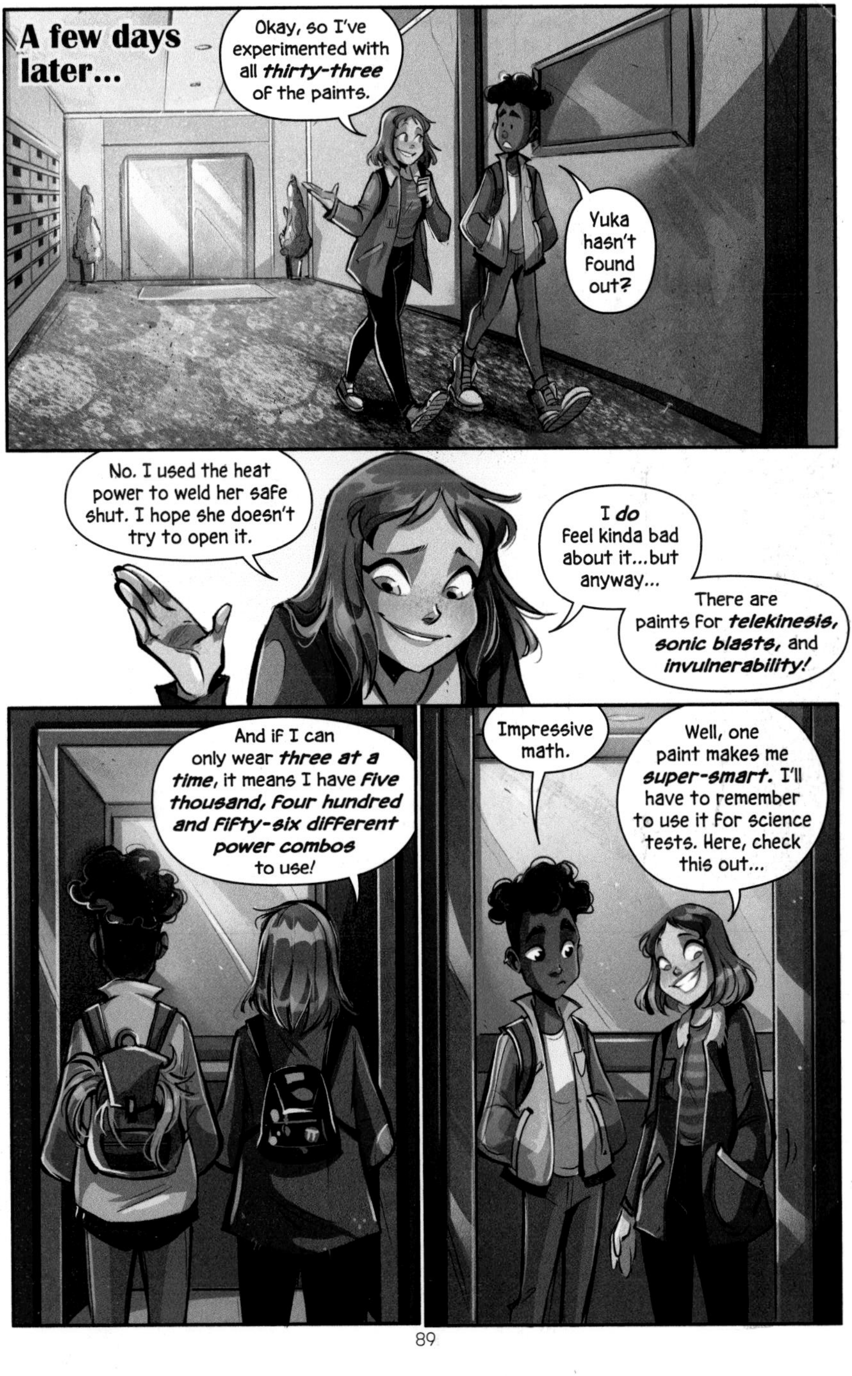
A few days later...
Okay, so I've experimented with all *thirty-three* of the paints.
Yuka hasn't found out?
No. I used the heat power to weld her safe shut. I hope she doesn't try to open it.
I *do* feel kinda bad about it...but anyway...
There are paints for *telekinesis, sonic blasts,* and *invulnerability!*
And if I can only wear *three at a time*, it means I have *five thousand, four hundred and fifty-six different power combos* to use!
Impressive math.
Well, one paint makes me *super-smart.* I'll have to remember to use it for science tests. Here, check this out...

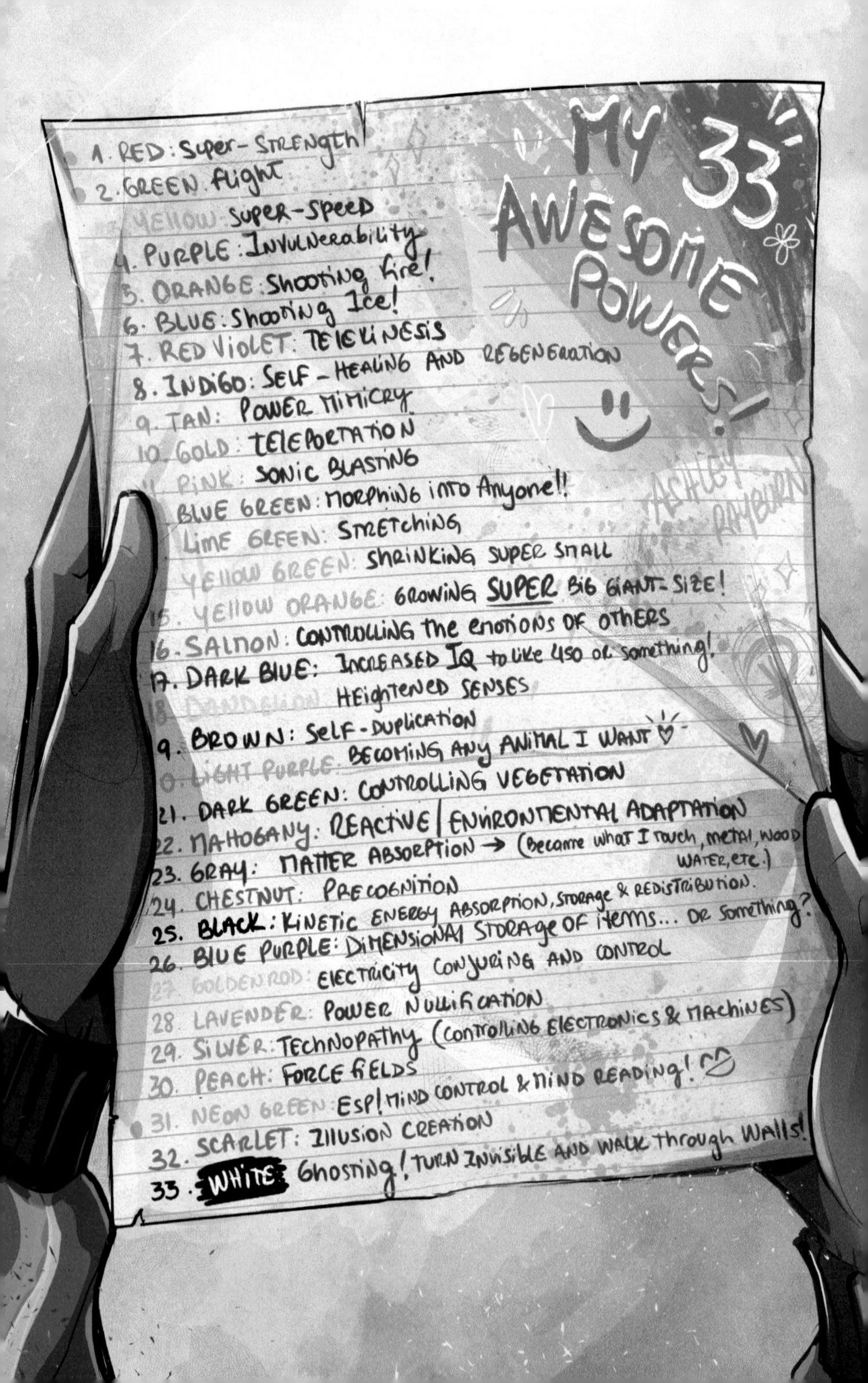

MY 33 AWESOME POWERS!
1. RED: Super-Strength
2. GREEN: Flight
YELLOW: Super-Speed
4. PURPLE: Invulnerability
5. ORANGE: Shooting fire!
6. BLUE: Shooting Ice!
7. RED VIOLET: TELEKINESIS
8. INDIGO: SELF-HEALING AND REGENERATION
9. TAN: POWER MIMICRY
10. GOLD: TELEPORTATION
PINK: SONIC BLASTING
BLUE GREEN: MORPHING INTO ANYONE!!
LIME GREEN: STRETCHING
YELLOW GREEN: SHRINKING SUPER SMALL
15. YELLOW ORANGE: GROWING SUPER BIG GIANT-SIZE!
16. SALMON: CONTROLLING THE EMOTIONS OF OTHERS
17. DARK BLUE: INCREASED IQ to like 450 or something!
18. DANDELION: HEIGHTENED SENSES
19. BROWN: SELF-DUPLICATION
LIGHT PURPLE: BECOMING ANY ANIMAL I WANT
21. DARK GREEN: CONTROLLING VEGETATION
22. MAHOGANY: REACTIVE | ENVIRONMENTAL ADAPTATION
23. GRAY: MATTER ABSORPTION → (Became what I touch, metal, wood water, etc.)
24. CHESTNUT: PRECOGNITION
25. BLACK: KINETIC ENERGY ABSORPTION, STORAGE & REDISTRIBUTION.
26. BLUE PURPLE: DIMENSIONAL STORAGE OF ITEMS... OR SOMETHING?
27. GOLDENROD: ELECTRICITY CONJURING AND CONTROL
28. LAVENDER: POWER NULLIFICATION
29. SILVER: TECHNOPATHY (CONTROLLING ELECTRONICS & MACHINES)
30. PEACH: FORCE FIELDS
31. NEON GREEN: ESP! MIND CONTROL & MIND READING!
32. SCARLET: ILLUSION CREATION
33. WHITE: GHOSTING! TURN INVISIBLE AND WALK THROUGH WALLS!
ASHLEY RAYBURN

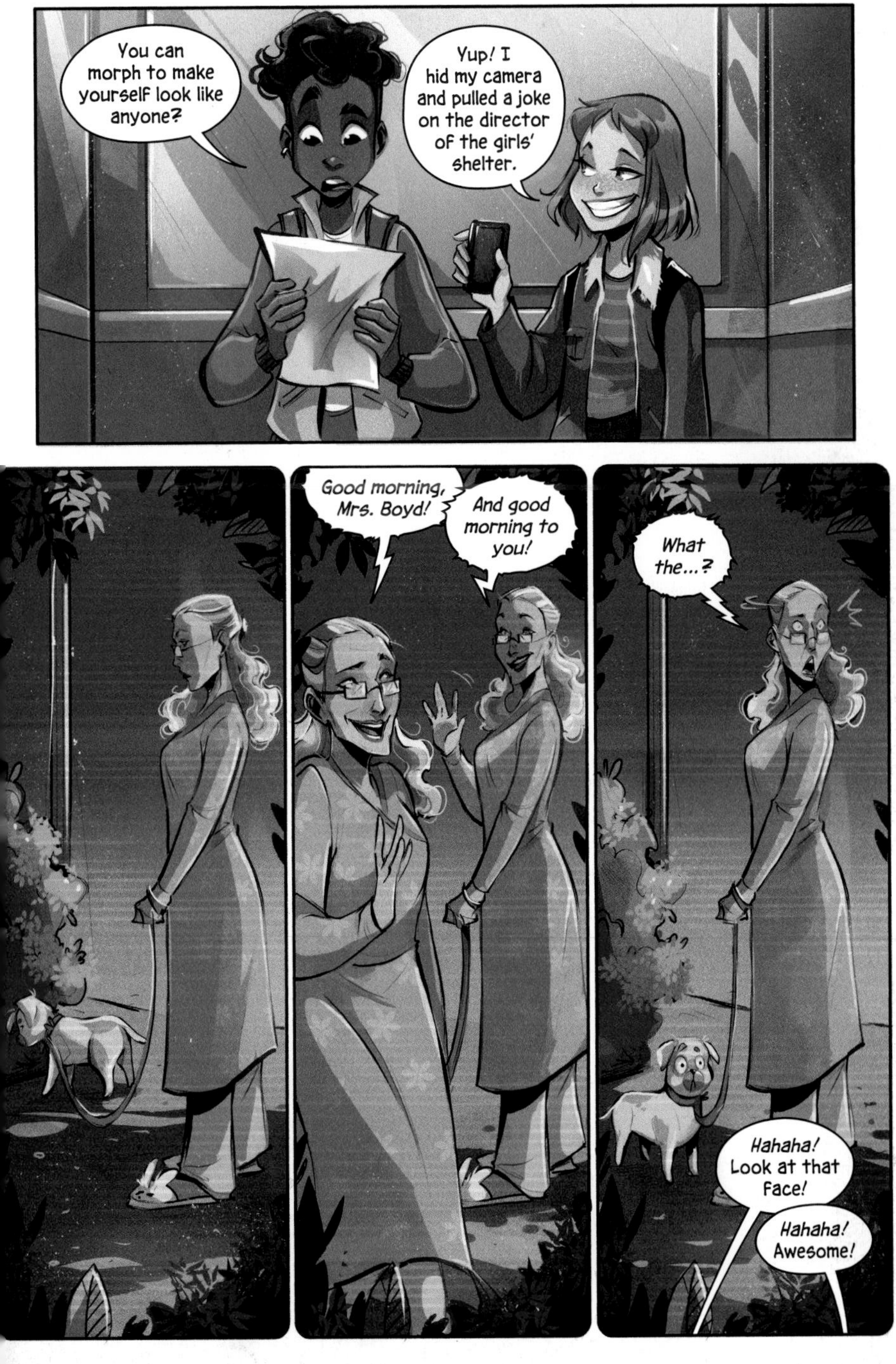
You can morph to make yourself look like anyone?
Yup! I hid my camera and pulled a joke on the director of the girls' shelter.
Good morning, Mrs. Boyd!
And good morning to you!
What the...?
Hahaha! Look at that face!
Hahaha! Awesome!

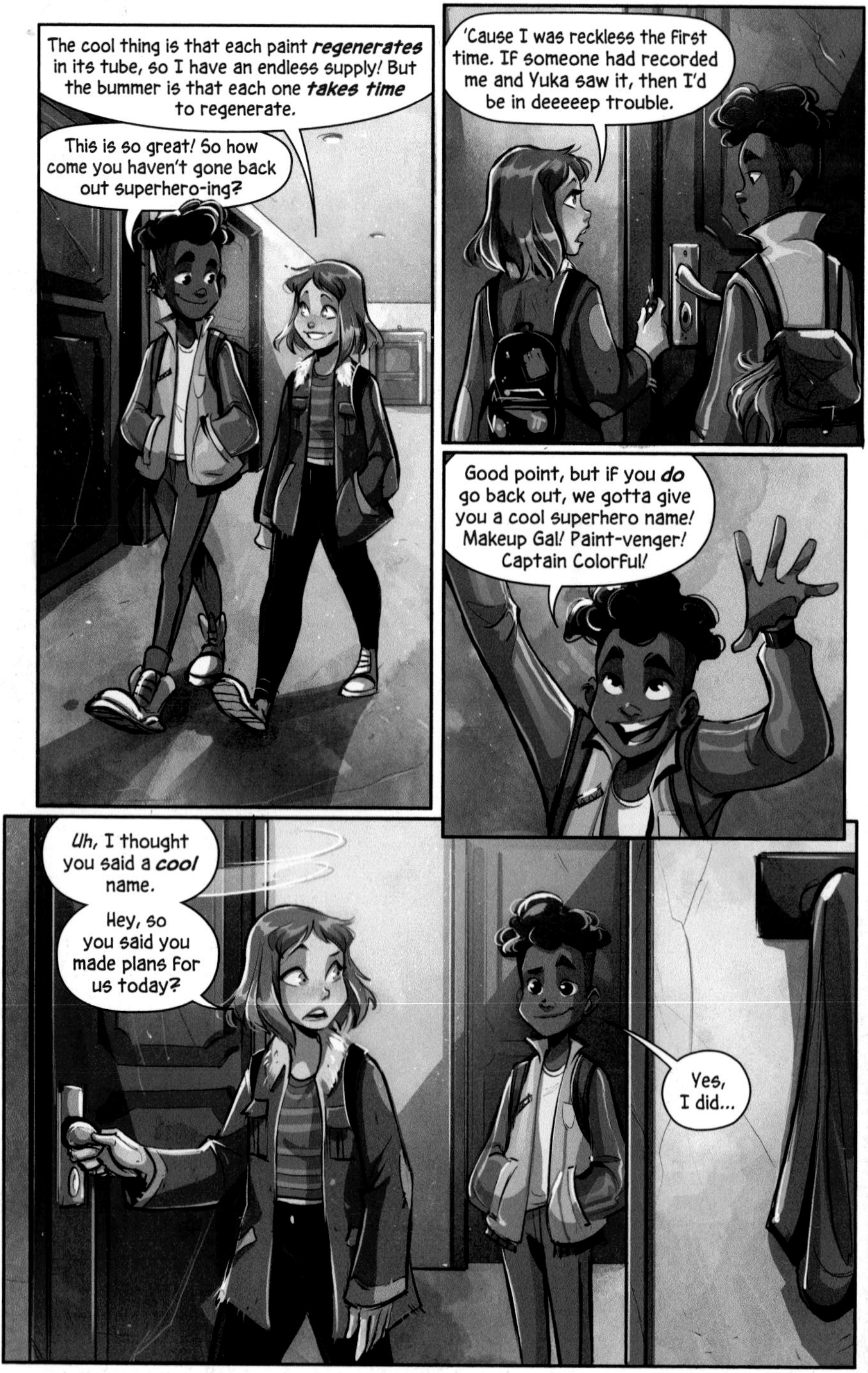
The cool thing is that each paint *regenerates* in its tube, so I have an endless supply! But the bummer is that each one *takes time* to regenerate.
This is so great! So how come you haven't gone back out superhero-ing?
'Cause I was reckless the first time. If someone had recorded me and Yuka saw it, then I'd be in deeeeep trouble.
Good point, but if you *do* go back out, we gotta give you a cool superhero name! Makeup Gal! Paint-venger! Captain Colorful!
Uh, I thought you said a *cool* name.
Hey, so you said you made plans for us today?
Yes, I did...

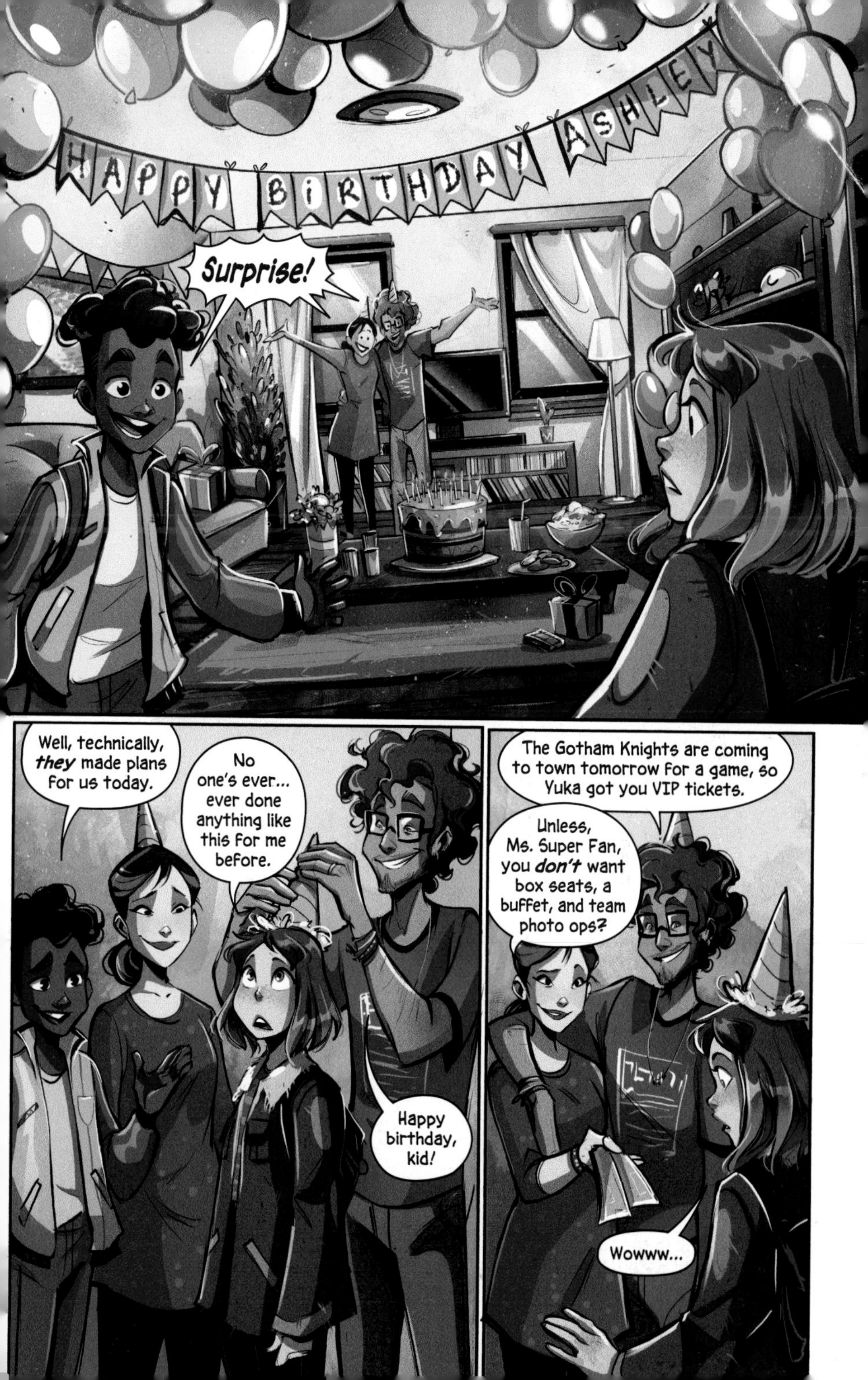
HAPPY BIRTHDAY ASHLEY
Surprise!
Well, technically, *they* made plans for us today.
No one's ever... ever done anything like this for me before.
Happy birthday, kid!
The Gotham Knights are coming to town tomorrow for a game, so Yuka got you VIP tickets.
Unless, Ms. Super Fan, you *don't* want box seats, a buffet, and team photo ops?
Wowww...

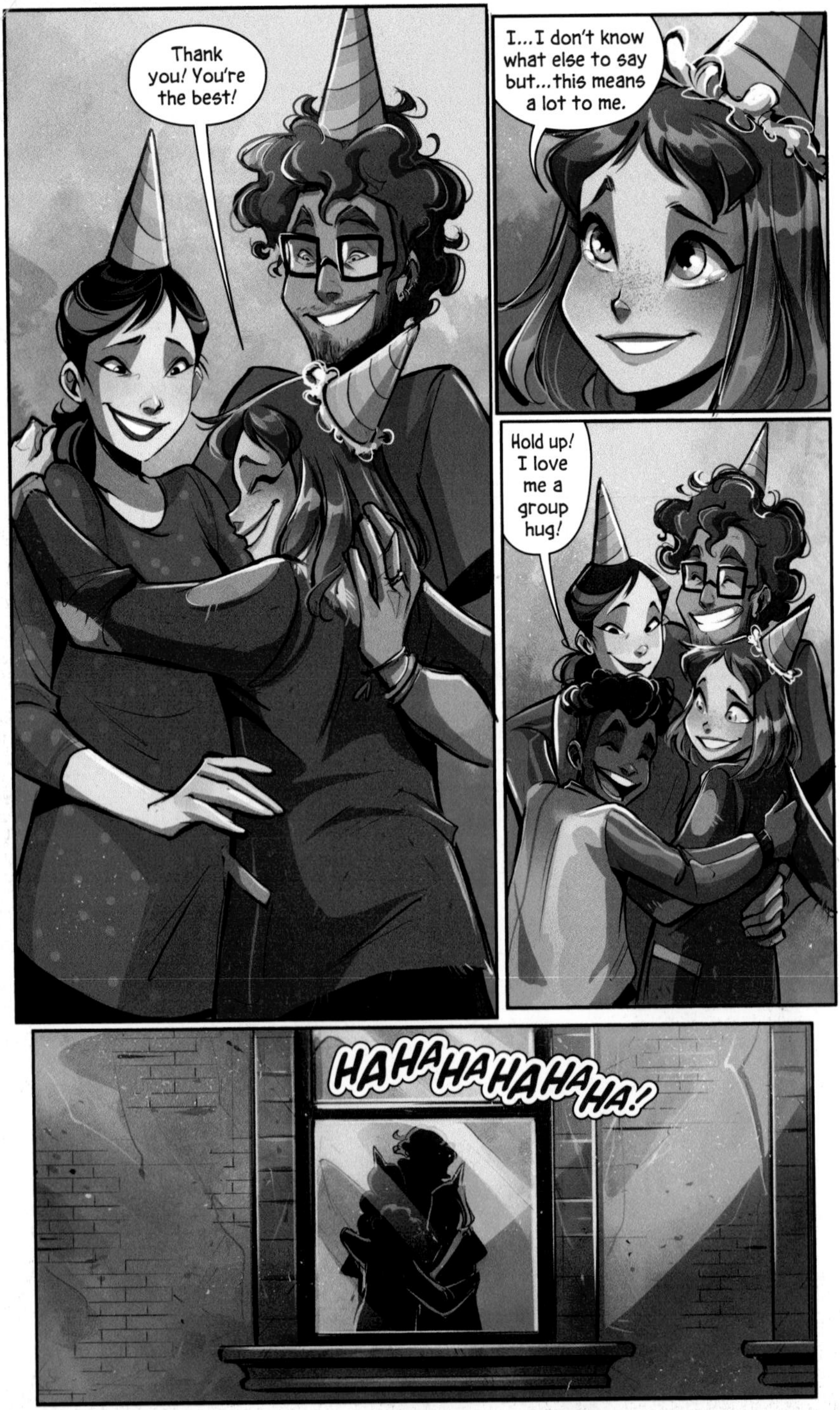
Thank you! You're the best!
I...I don't know what else to say but...this means a lot to me.
Hold up! I love me a group hug!
HAHAHAHAHAHAHA!

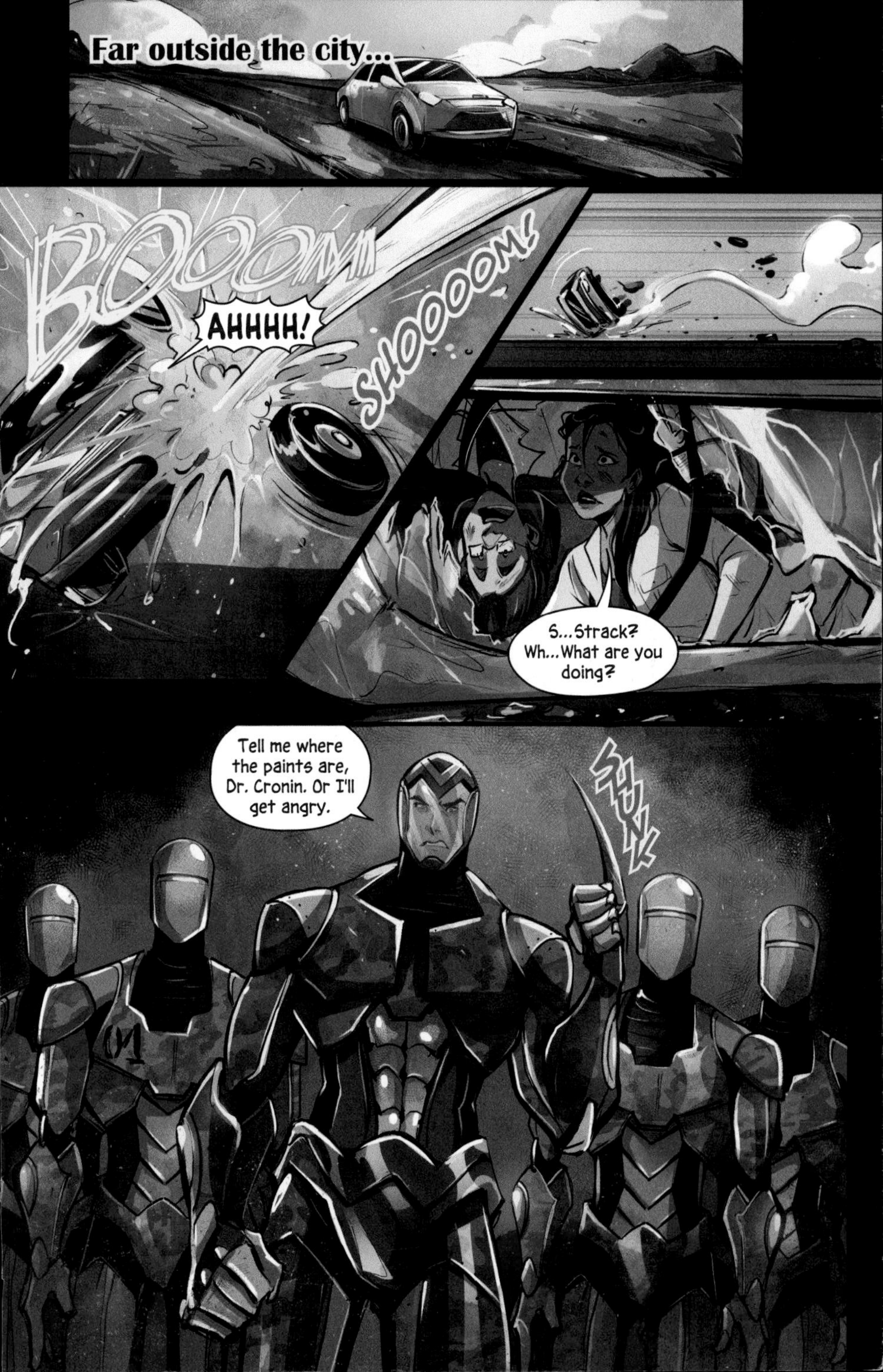
Far outside the city...
BOOOOM!
AHHHH!
SHOOOOM!
S...Strack? Wh...What are you doing?
Tell me where the paints are, Dr. Cronin. Or I'll get angry.
SHUNK

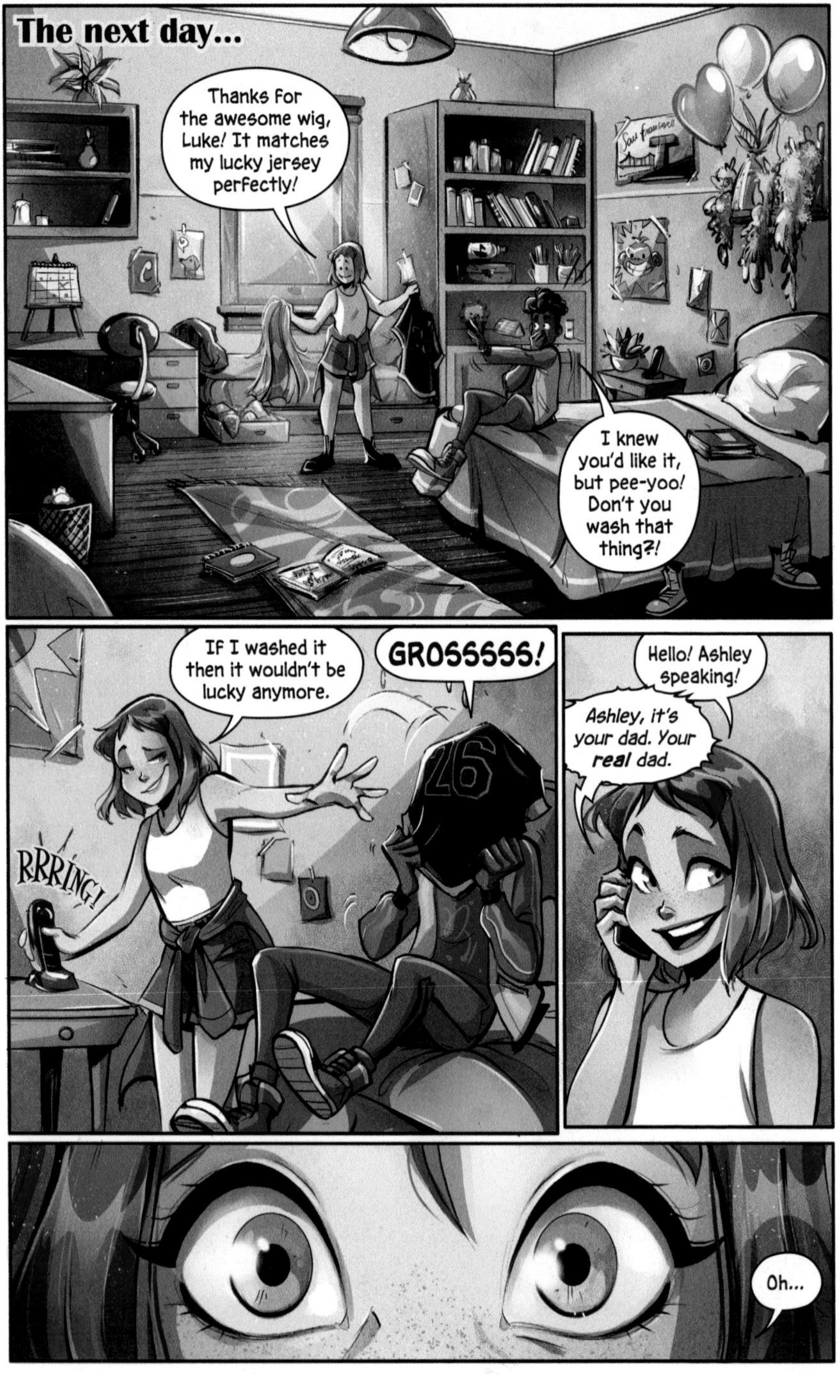
The next day...
Thanks for the awesome wig, Luke! It matches my lucky jersey perfectly!
I knew you'd like it, but pee-yoo! Don't you wash that thing?!
If I washed it then it wouldn't be lucky anymore.
GROSSSSS!
RRRING!
Hello! Ashley speaking!
Ashley, it's your dad. Your *real* dad.
Oh...

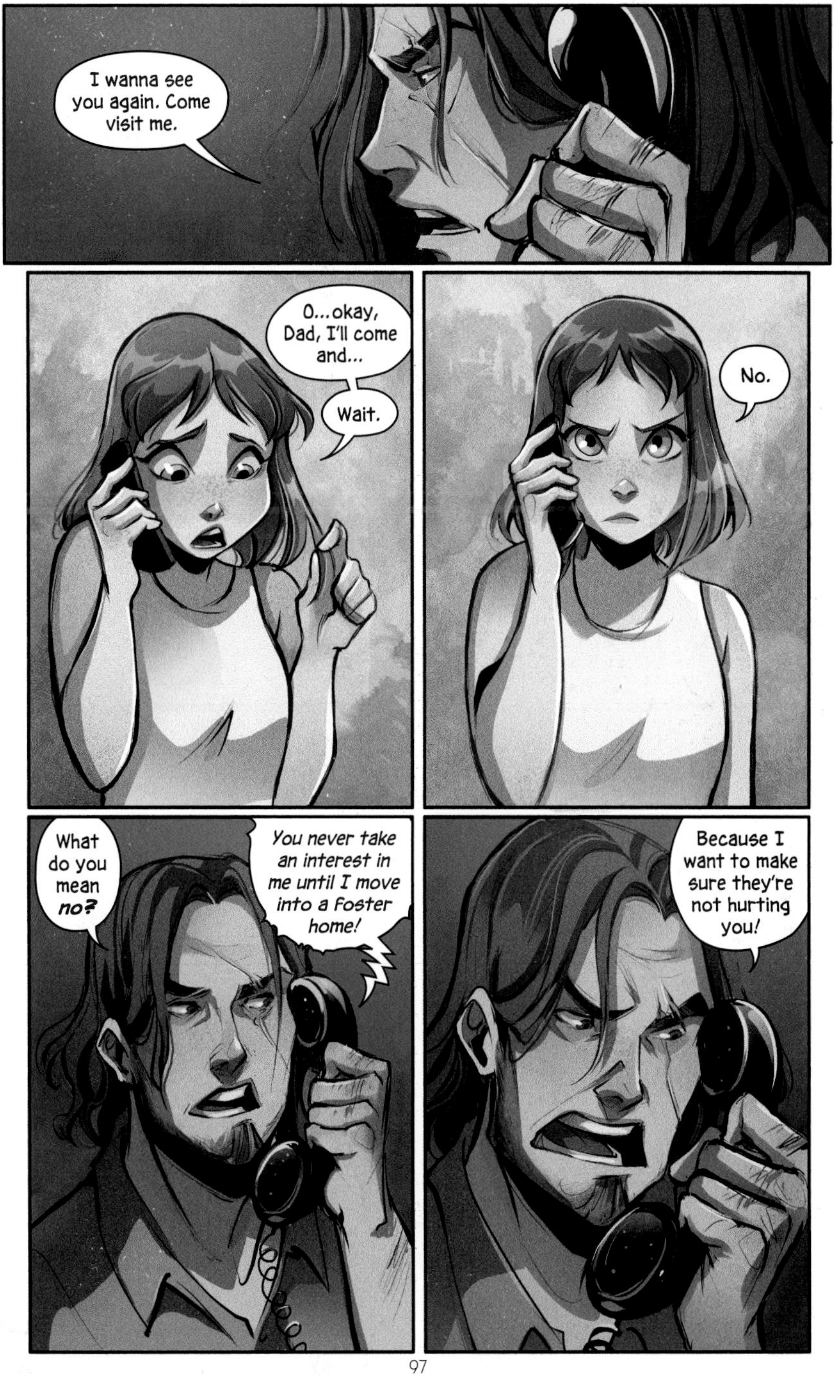
I wanna see you again. Come visit me.
O...okay, Dad, I'll come and...
Wait.
No.
What do you mean *no?*
You never take an interest in me until I move into a foster home!
Because I want to make sure they're not hurting *you!*

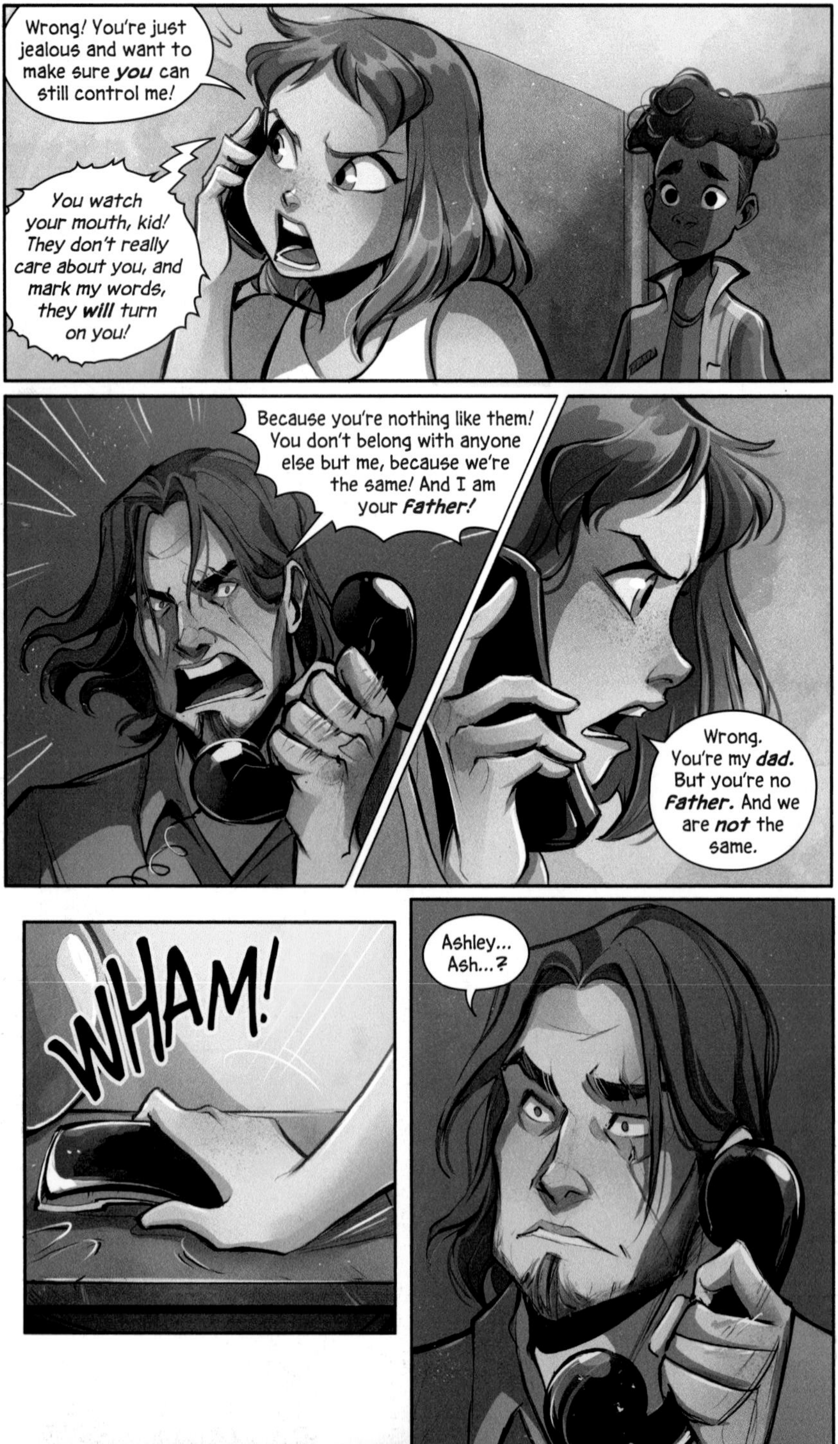
Wrong! You're just jealous and want to make sure ***you*** can still control me!
You watch your mouth, kid! They don't really care about you, and mark my words, they ***will*** *turn on you!*
Because you're nothing like them! You don't belong with anyone else but me, because we're the same! And I am your ***Father!***
Wrong. You're my ***dad.*** But you're no ***Father.*** And we are ***not*** the same.
WHAM!
Ashley... Ash...?

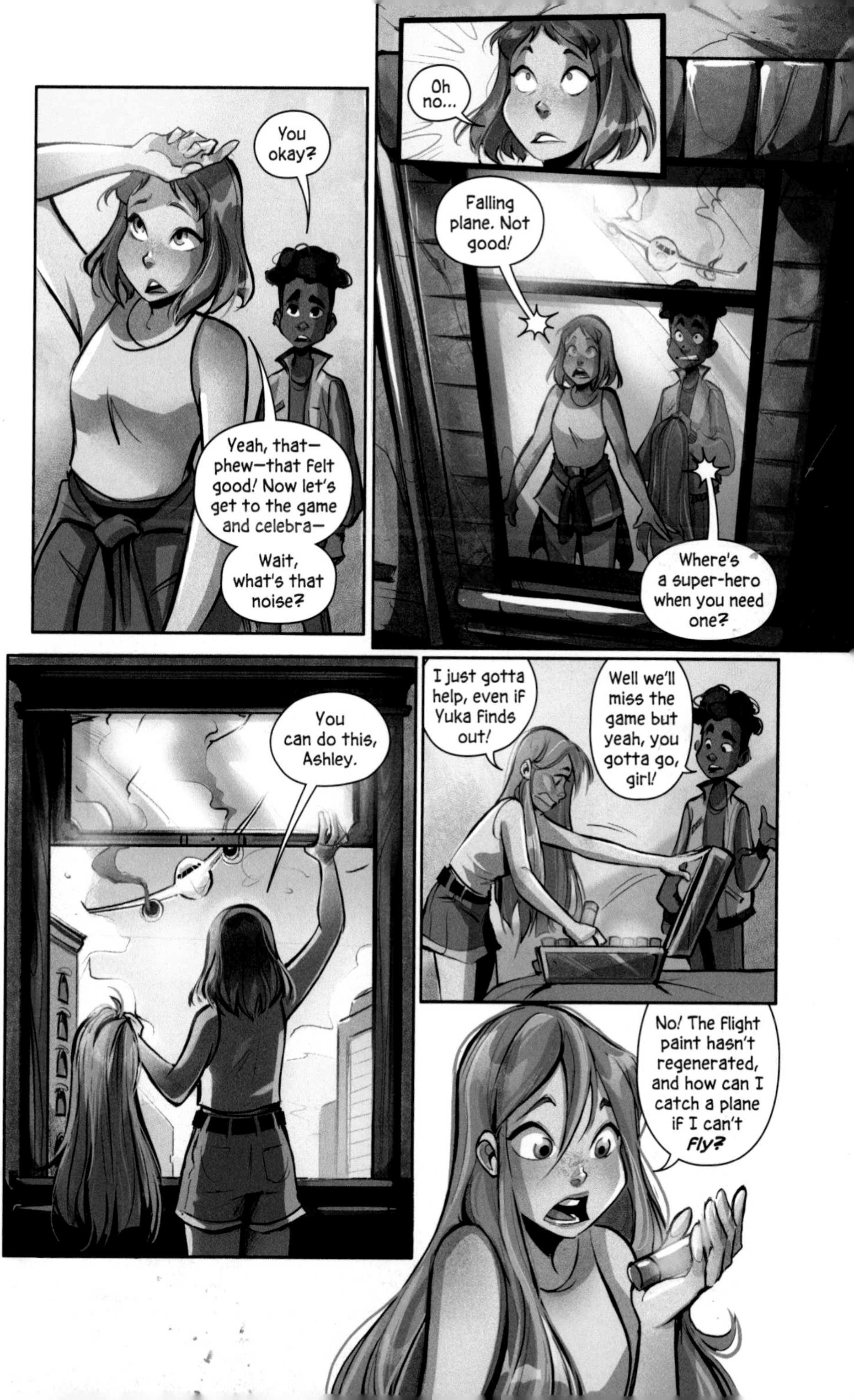
You okay?
Yeah, that—phew—that felt good! Now let's get to the game and celebra—
Wait, what's that noise?
Oh no...
Falling plane. Not good!
Where's a super-hero when you need one?
You can do this, Ashley.
I just gotta help, even if Yuka finds out!
Well we'll miss the game but yeah, you gotta go, girl!
No! The flight paint hasn't regenerated, and how can I catch a plane if I can't *fly?*

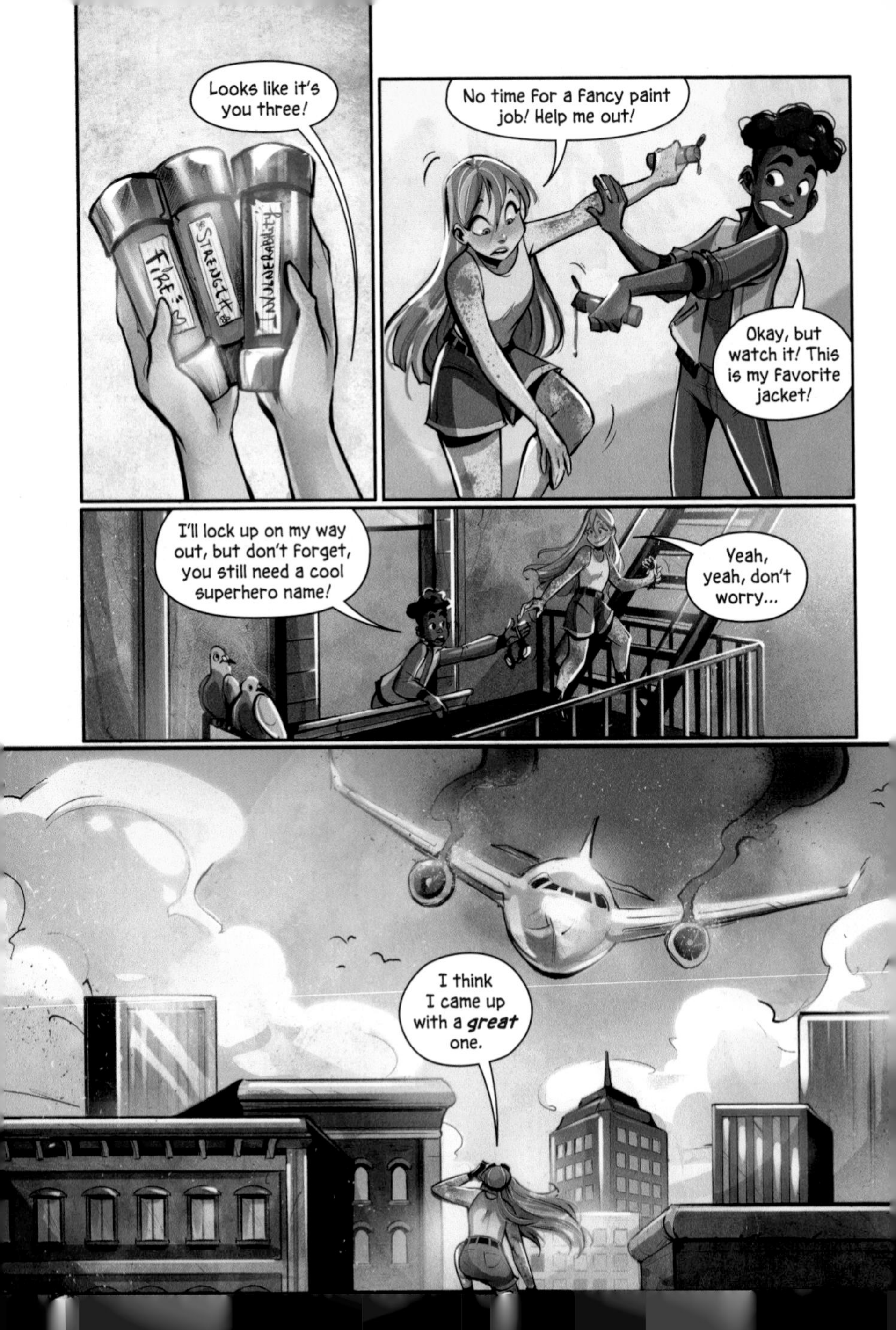
Looks like it's you three!
FIRE
STRENGTH
INVULNERABILITY
No time for a fancy paint job! Help me out!
Okay, but watch it! This is my favorite jacket!
I'll lock up on my way out, but don't forget, you still need a cool superhero name!
Yeah, yeah, don't worry...
I think I came up with a *great* one.

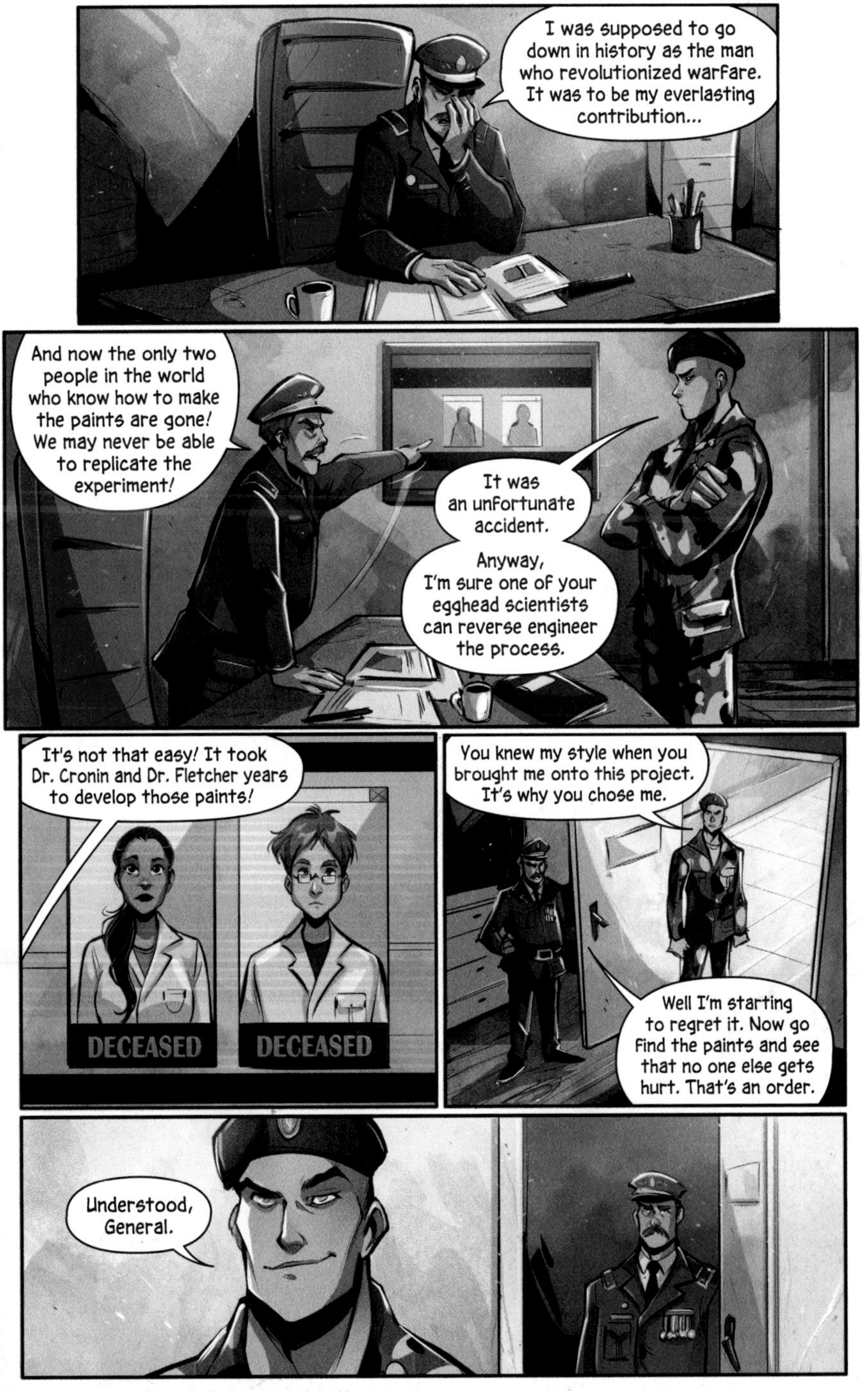
I was supposed to go down in history as the man who revolutionized warfare. It was to be my everlasting contribution...
And now the only two people in the world who know how to make the paints are gone! We may never be able to replicate the experiment!
It was an unfortunate accident.
Anyway, I'm sure one of your egghead scientists can reverse engineer the process.
It's not that easy! It took Dr. Cronin and Dr. Fletcher years to develop those paints!
DECEASED
DECEASED
You knew my style when you brought me onto this project. It's why you chose me.
Well I'm starting to regret it. Now go find the paints and see that no one else gets hurt. That's an order.
Understood, General.

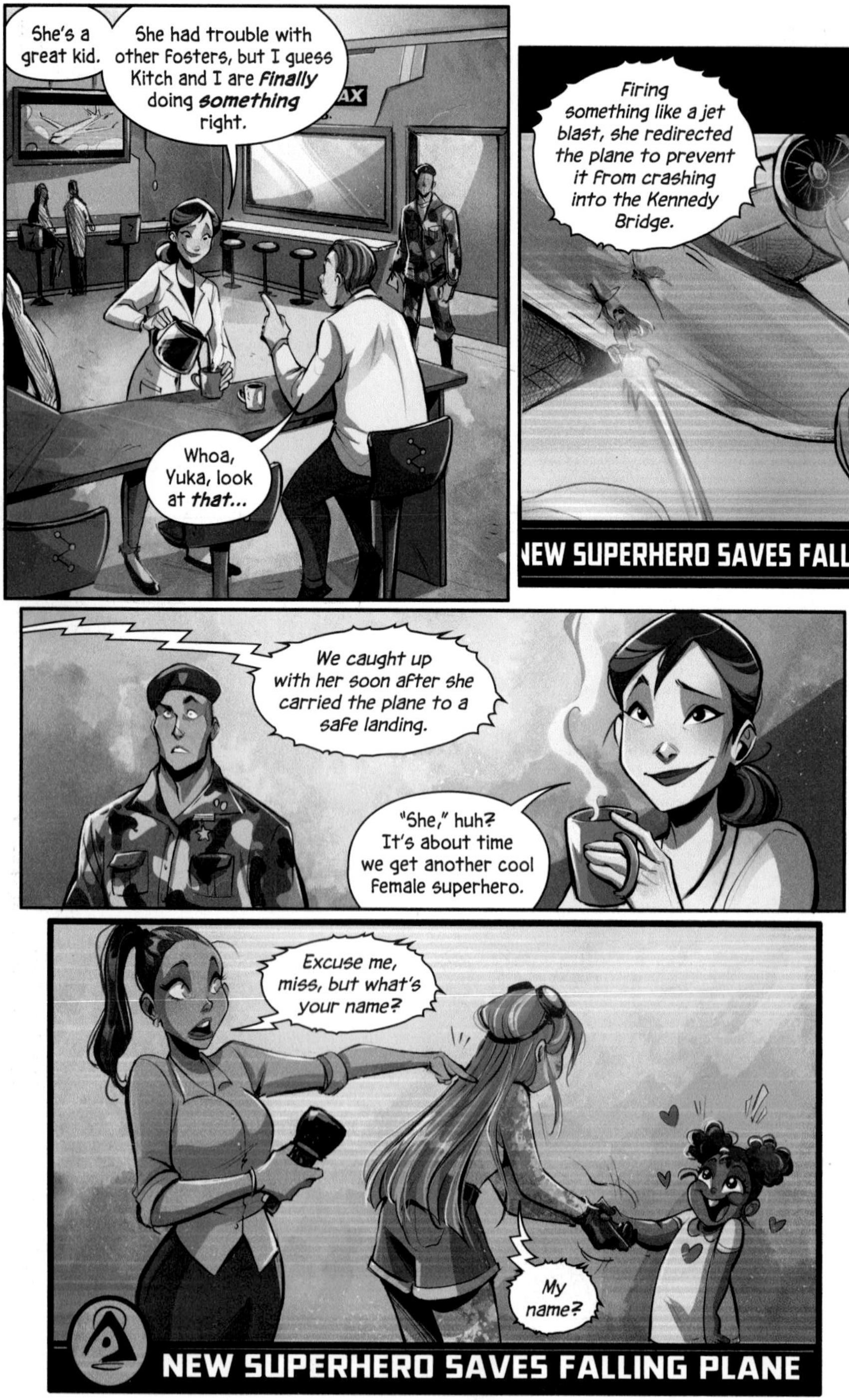

She's a great kid.
She had trouble with other fosters, but I guess Kitch and I are *finally* doing *something* right.
Whoa, Yuka, look at *that*...
Firing something like a jet blast, she redirected the plane to prevent it from crashing into the Kennedy Bridge.
NEW SUPERHERO SAVES FALLI
We caught up with her soon after she carried the plane to a safe landing.
"She," huh? It's about time we get another cool female superhero.
Excuse me, miss, but what's your name?
My name?
NEW SUPERHERO SAVES FALLING PLANE

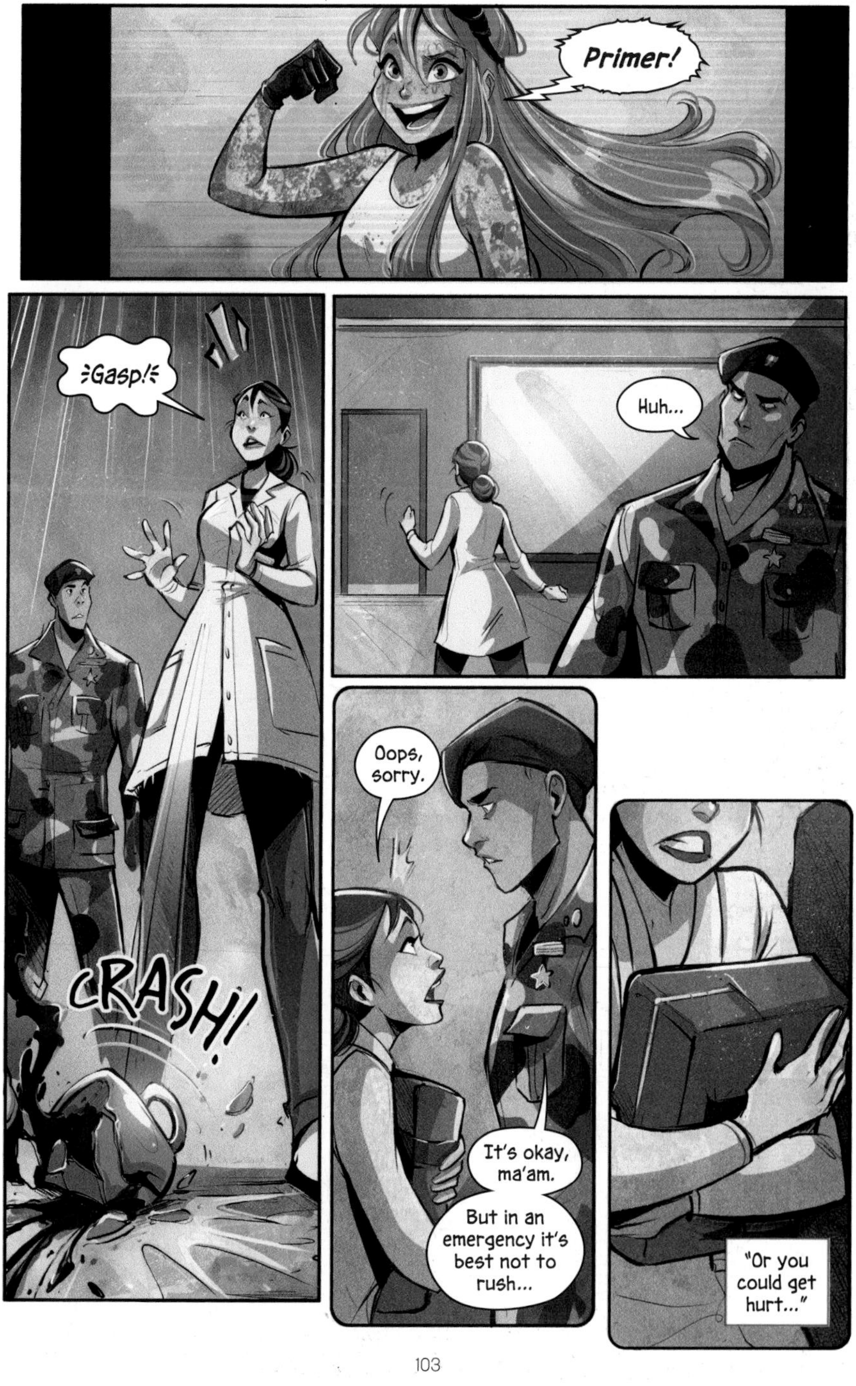
Primer!
Gasp!
CRASH!
Huh...
Oops, sorry.
It's okay, ma'am.
But in an emergency it's best not to rush...
"Or you could get hurt..."

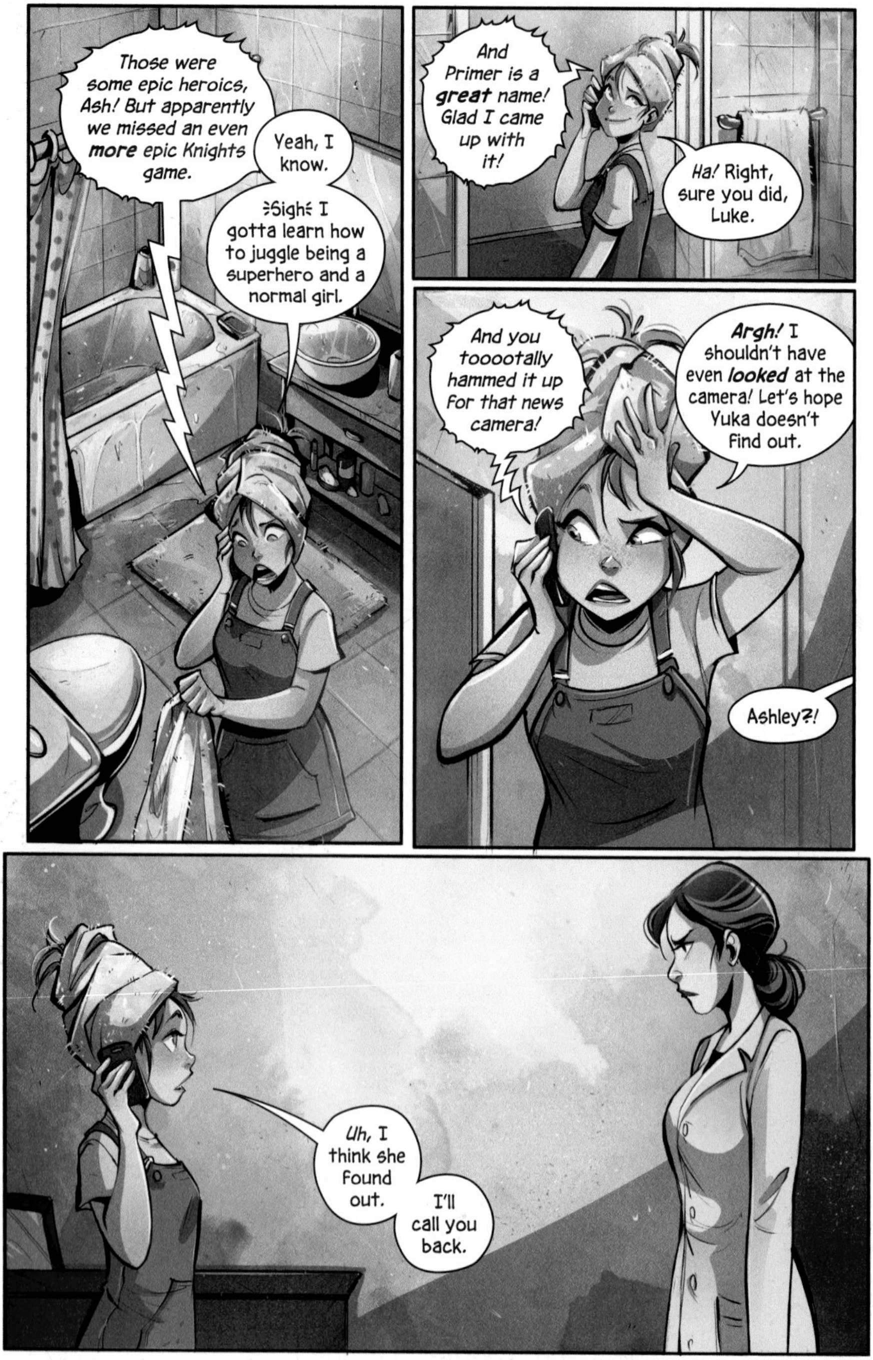
Those were some epic heroics, Ash! But apparently we missed an even **more** epic Knights game.
Yeah, I know.
⋛Sigh⋚ I gotta learn how to juggle being a superhero and a normal girl.
And Primer is a **great** name! Glad I came up with it!
Ha! Right, sure you did, Luke.
And you tooootally hammed it up for that news camera!
Argh! I shouldn't have even **looked** at the camera! Let's hope Yuka doesn't find out.
Ashley?!
Uh, I think she found out.
I'll call you back.

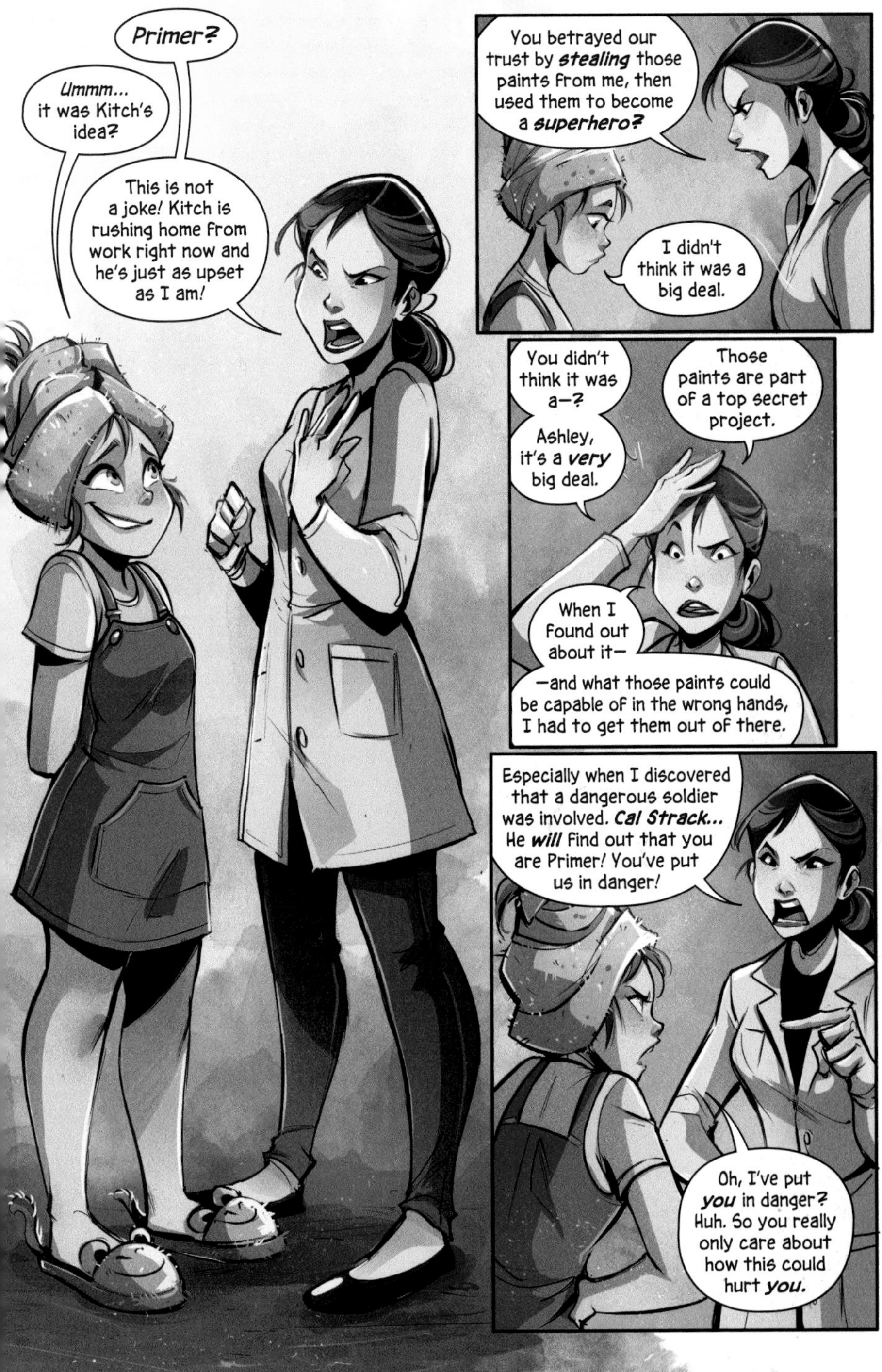

Primer?
Ummm... it was Kitch's idea?
This is not a joke! Kitch is rushing home from work right now and he's just as upset as I am!
You betrayed our trust by *stealing* those paints from me, then used them to become a *superhero?*
I didn't think it was a big deal.
You didn't think it was a—?
Ashley, it's a *very* big deal.
Those paints are part of a top secret project.
When I found out about it—
—and what those paints could be capable of in the wrong hands, I had to get them out of there.
Especially when I discovered that a dangerous soldier was involved. *Cal Strack...* He *will* find out that you are Primer! You've put us in danger!
Oh, I've put *you* in danger? Huh. So you really only care about how this could hurt *you.*

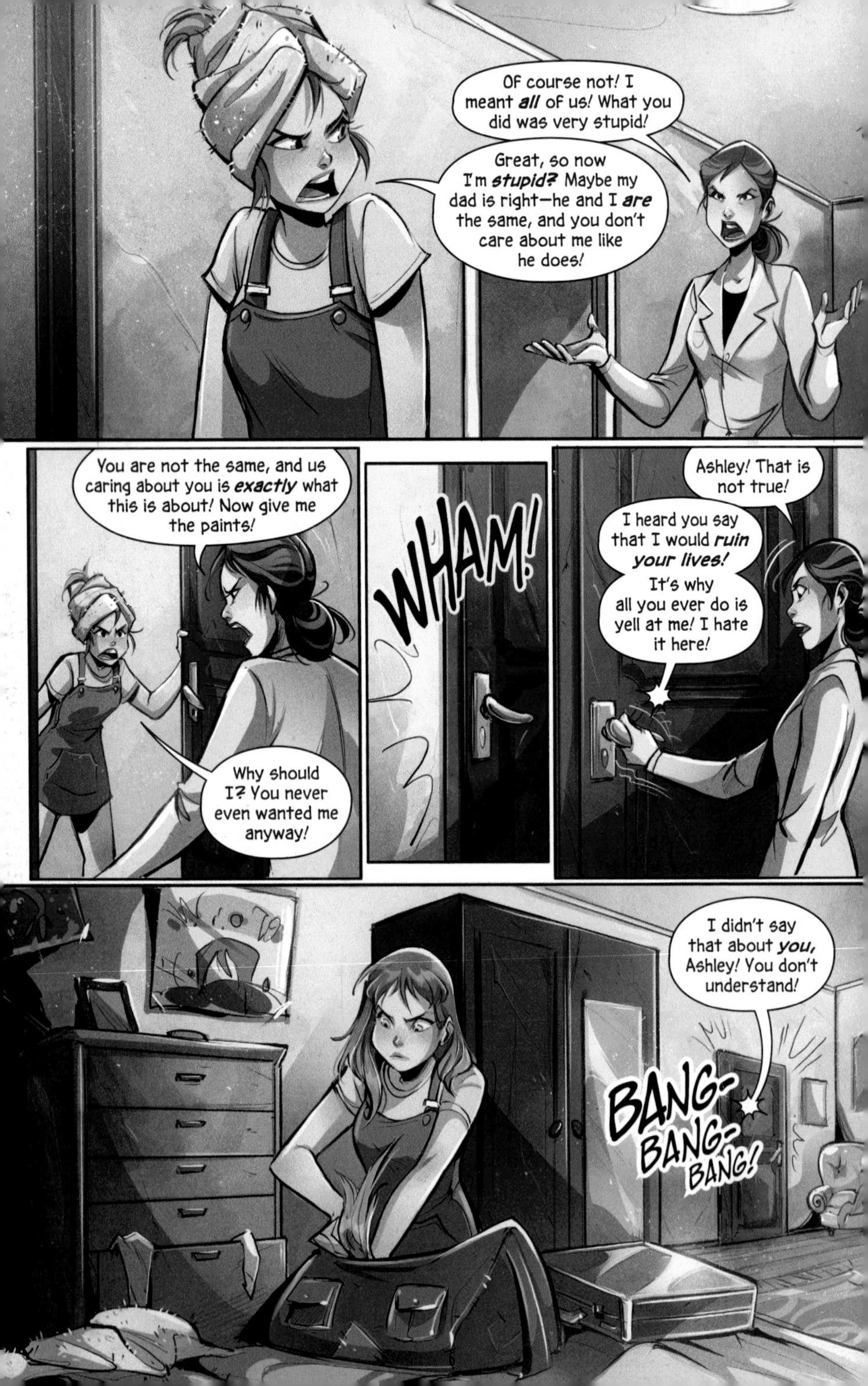
Of course not! I meant *all* of us! What you did was very stupid!
Great, so now I'm *stupid?* Maybe my dad is right—he and I *are* the same, and you don't care about me like he does!
You are not the same, and us caring about you is *exactly* what this is about! Now give me the paints!
Why should I? You never even wanted me anyway!
WHAM!
Ashley! That is not true!
I heard you say that I would *ruin your lives!*
It's why all you ever do is yell at me! I hate it here!
I didn't say that about *you,* Ashley! You don't understand!
BANG-BANG-BANG!

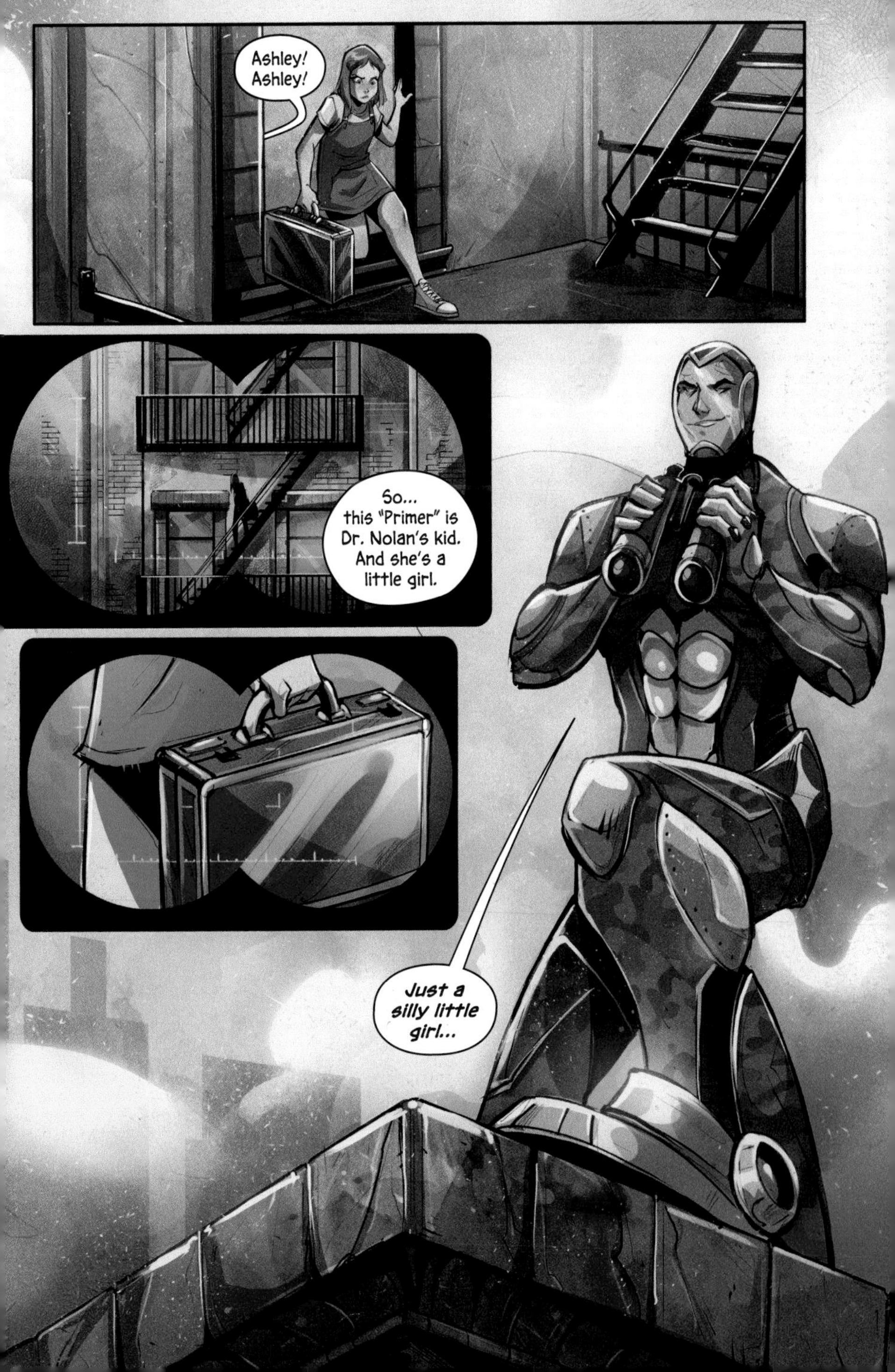
Ashley! Ashley!
So... this "Primer" is Dr. Nolan's kid. And she's a little girl.
Just a silly little girl...

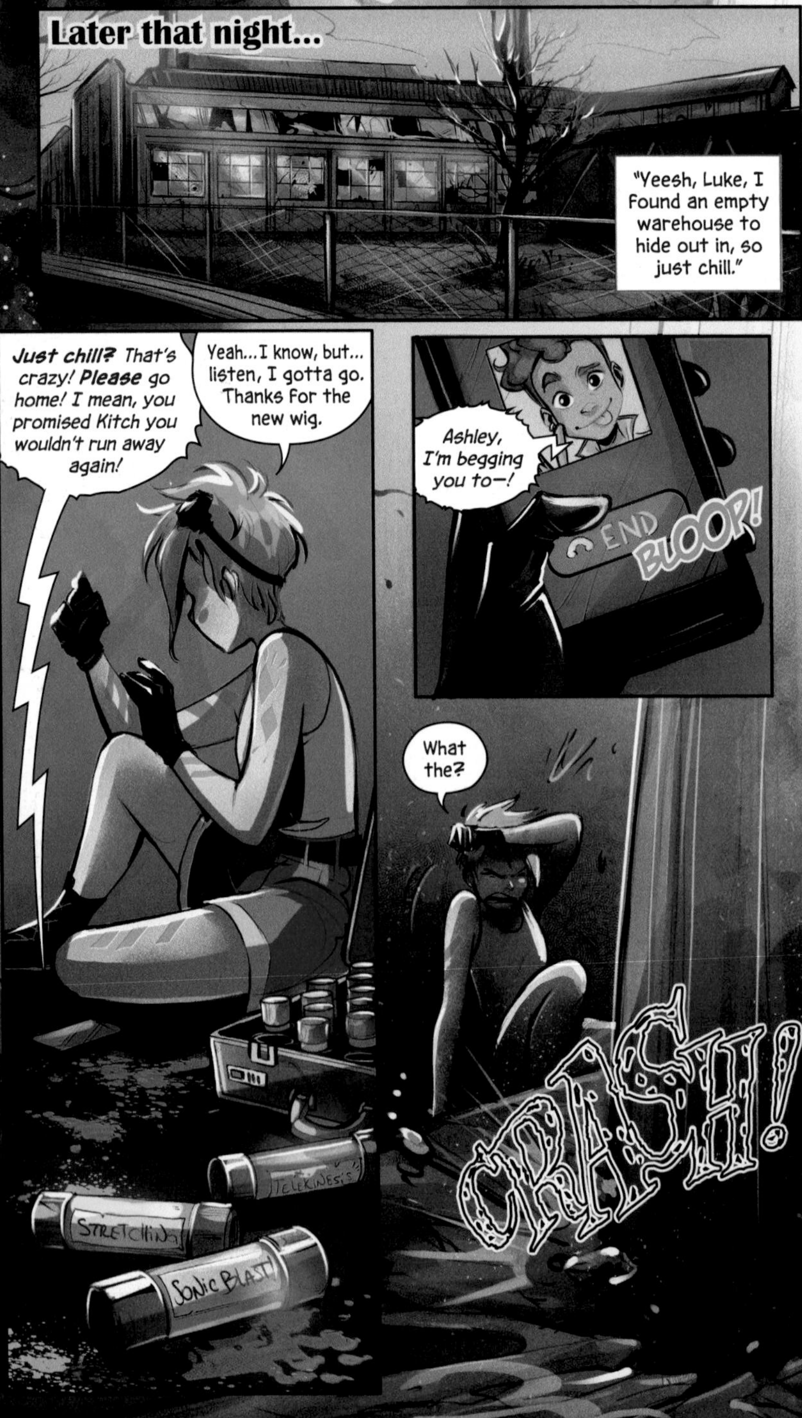
Later that night...
"Yeesh, Luke, I found an empty warehouse to hide out in, so just chill."
Just chill? That's crazy! Please go home! I mean, you promised Kitch you wouldn't run away again!
Yeah...I know, but... listen, I gotta go. Thanks for the new wig.
Ashley, I'm begging you to—!
END
BLOOP!
What the?
TELEKINESIS
STRETCHING
SONIC BLAST
CRASH!

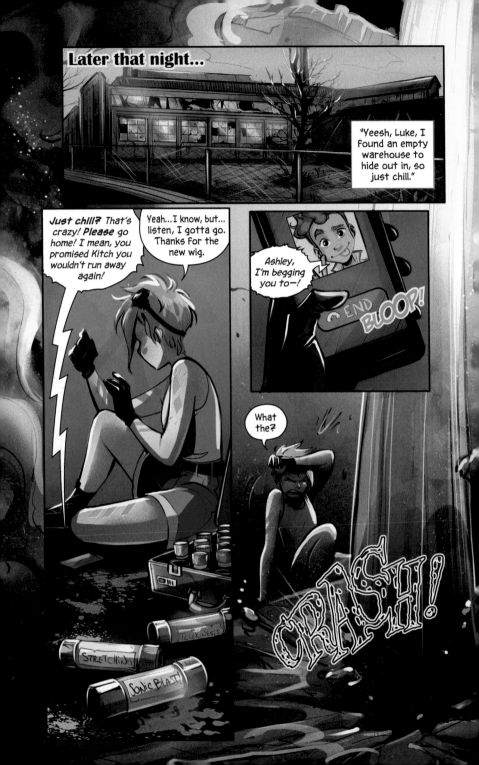

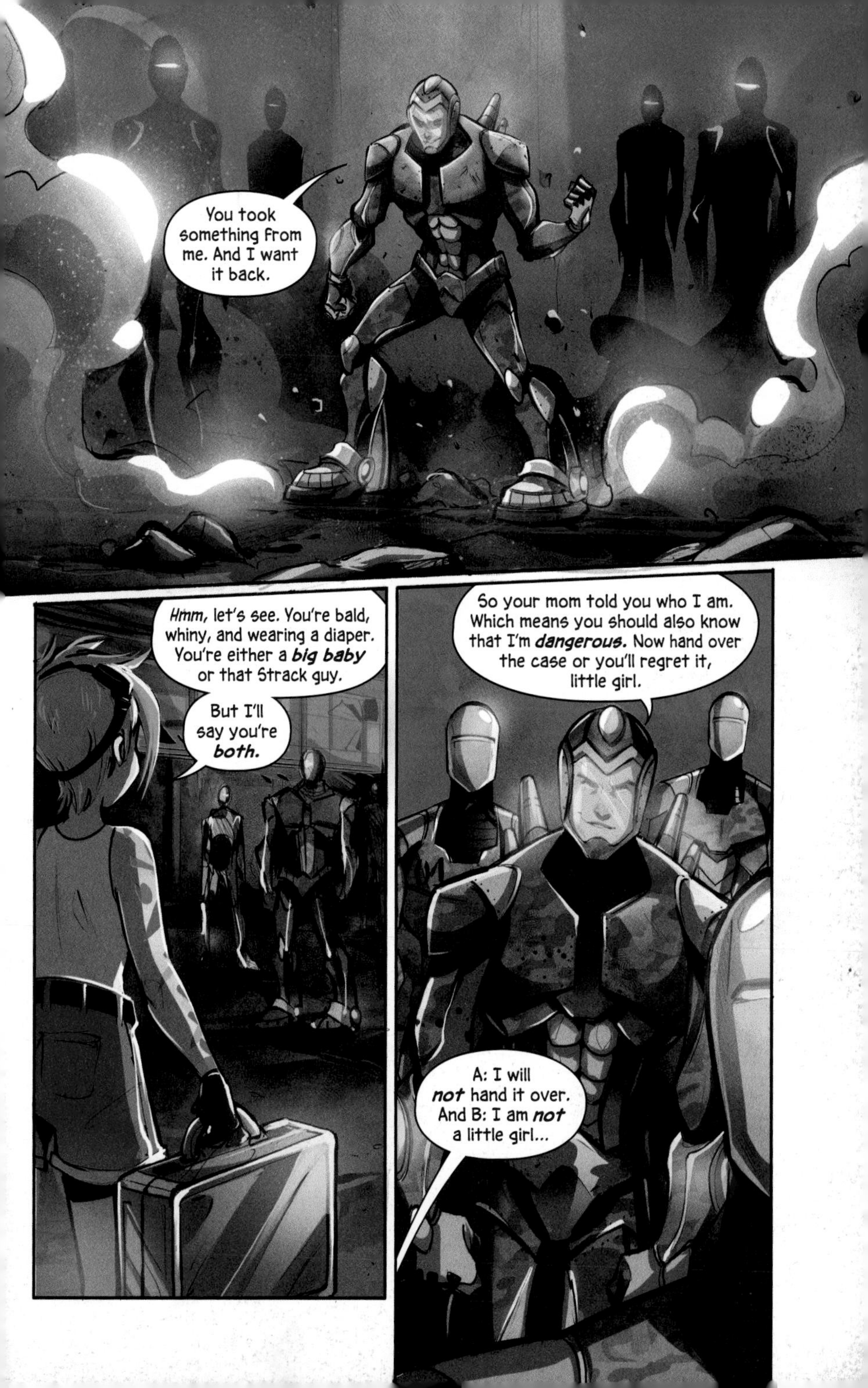
You took something from me. And I want it back.
Hmm, let's see. You're bald, whiny, and wearing a diaper. You're either a ***big baby*** or that Strack guy.
But I'll say you're ***both.***
So your mom told you who I am. Which means you should also know that I'm ***dangerous.*** Now hand over the case or you'll regret it, little girl.
A: I will ***not*** hand it over. And B: I am ***not*** a little girl...

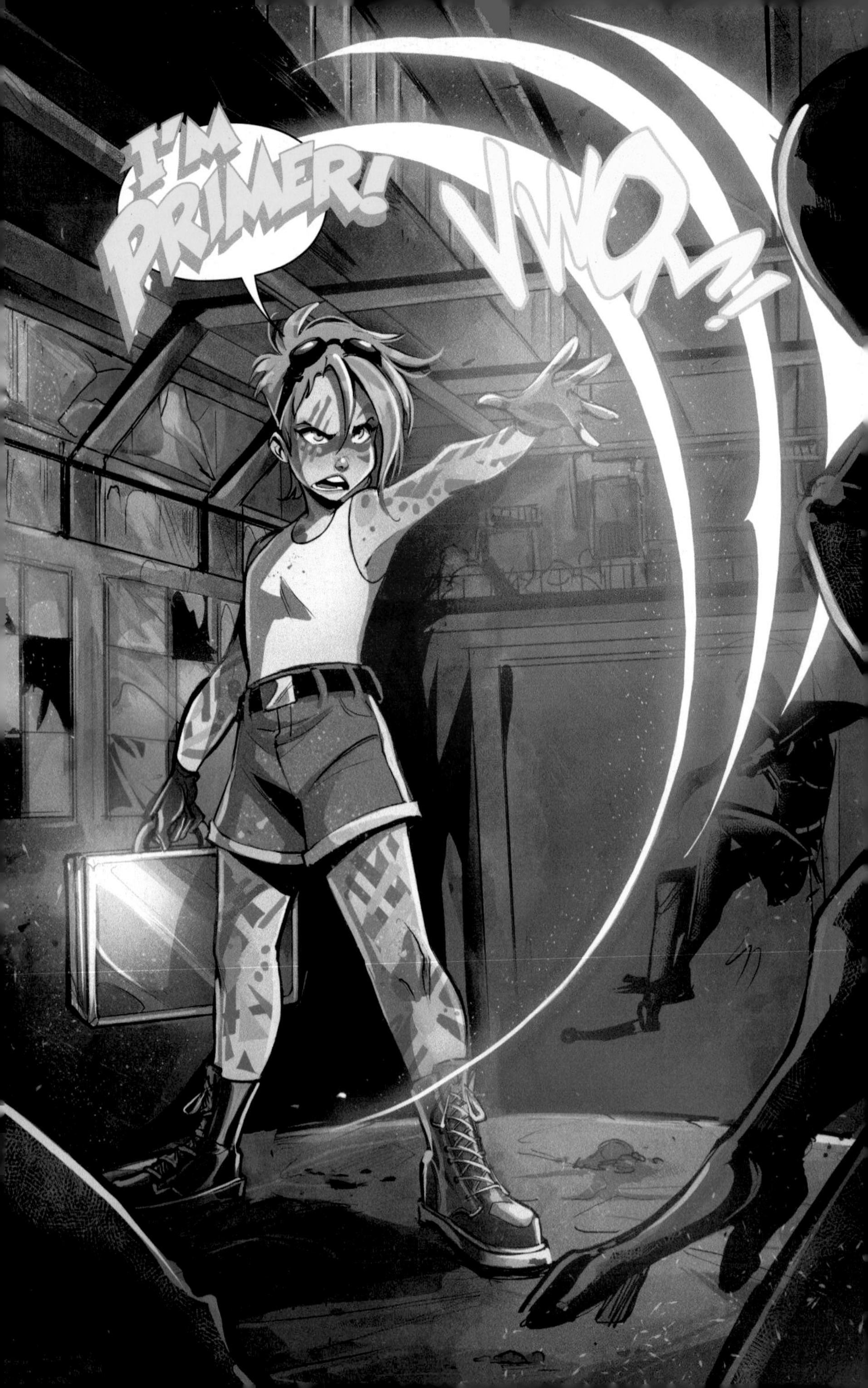
I'M PRIMER!
VWOM!!

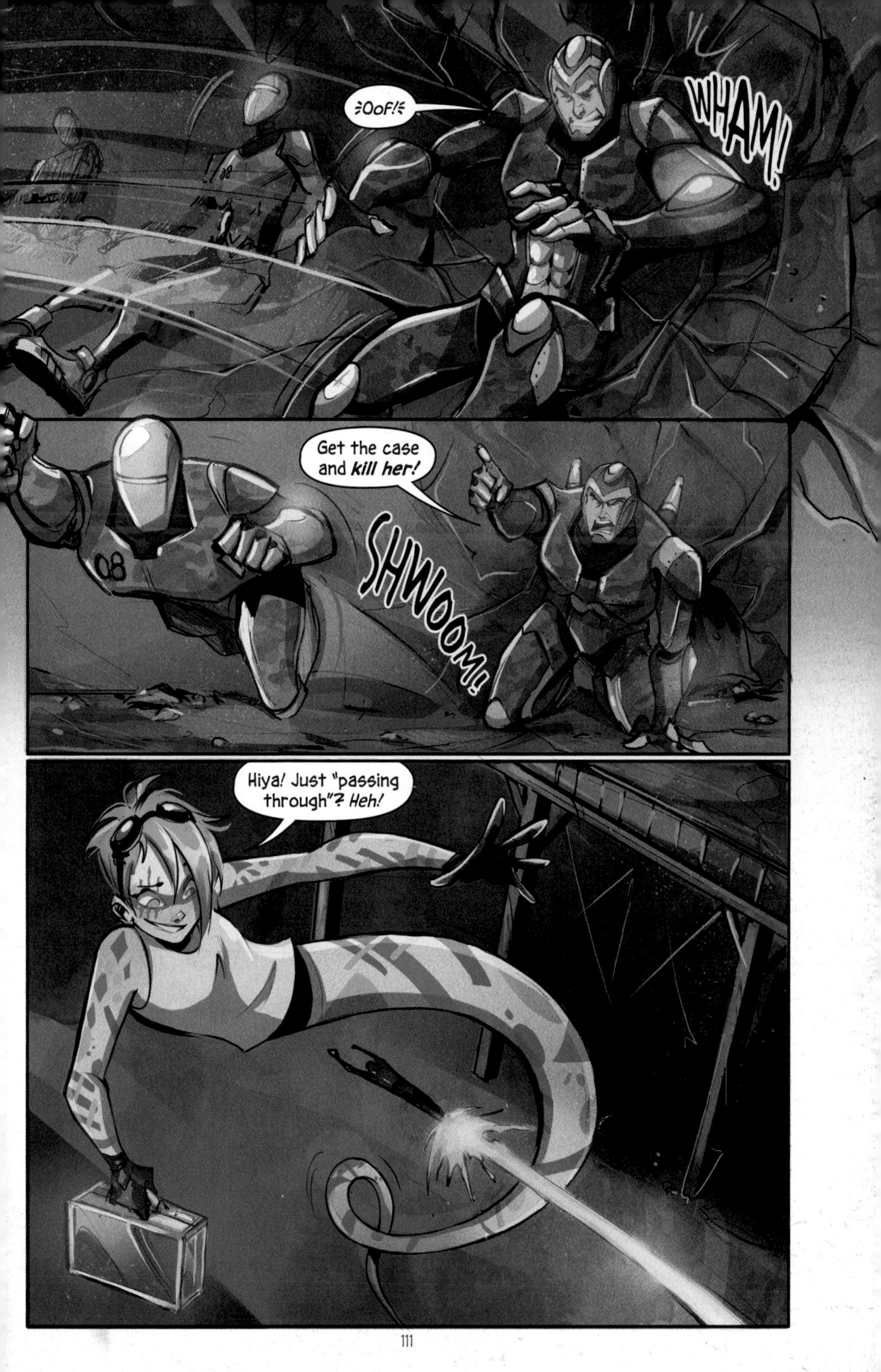
Oof!
WHAM!
Get the case and *kill her!*
SHWOOM!!
Hiya! Just "passing through"? *Heh!*

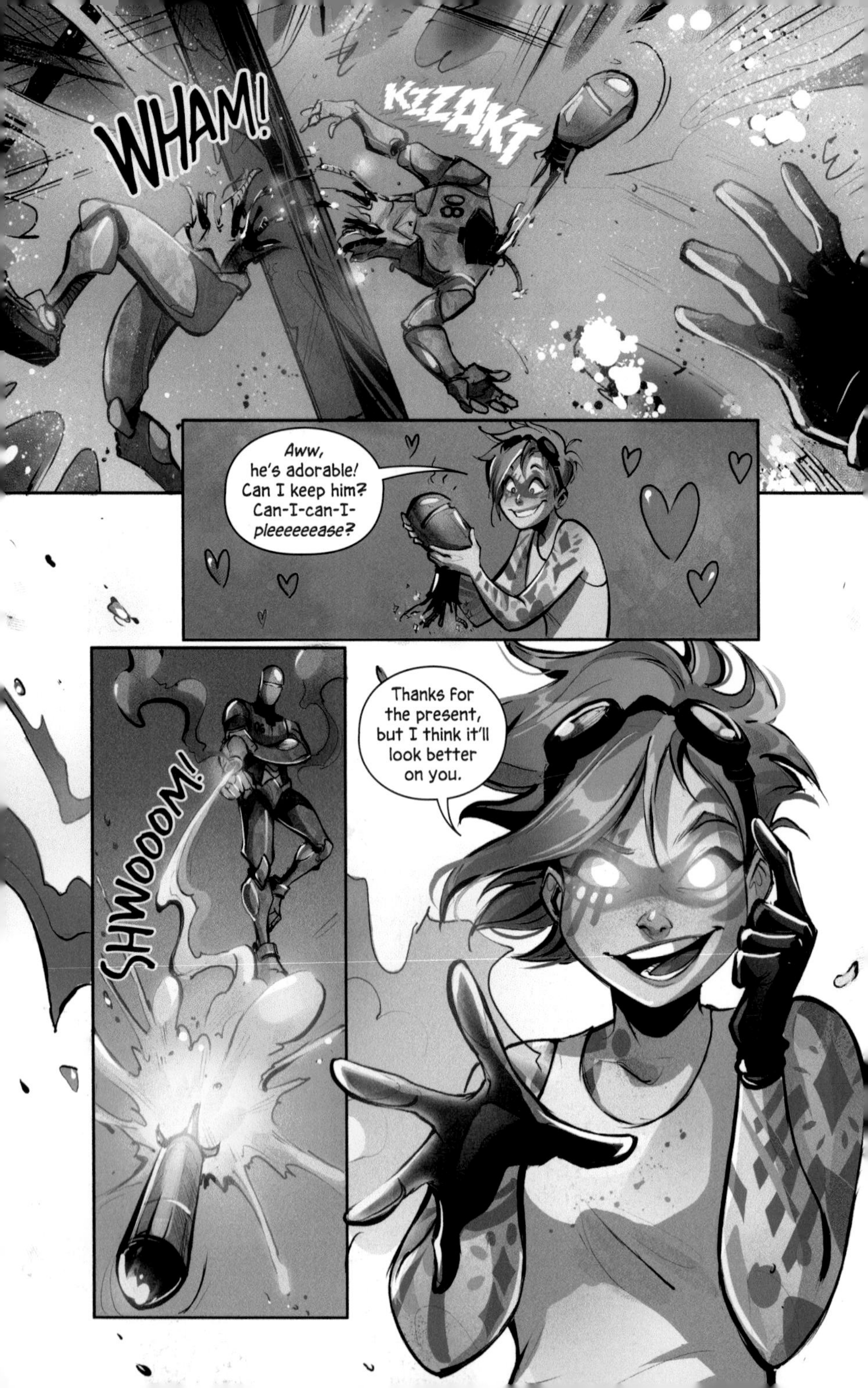
WHAM!
KIZAKT
Aww, he's adorable! Can I keep him? Can-I-can-I-pleeeeeease?
SHWOOOM!
Thanks for the present, but I think it'll look better on you.

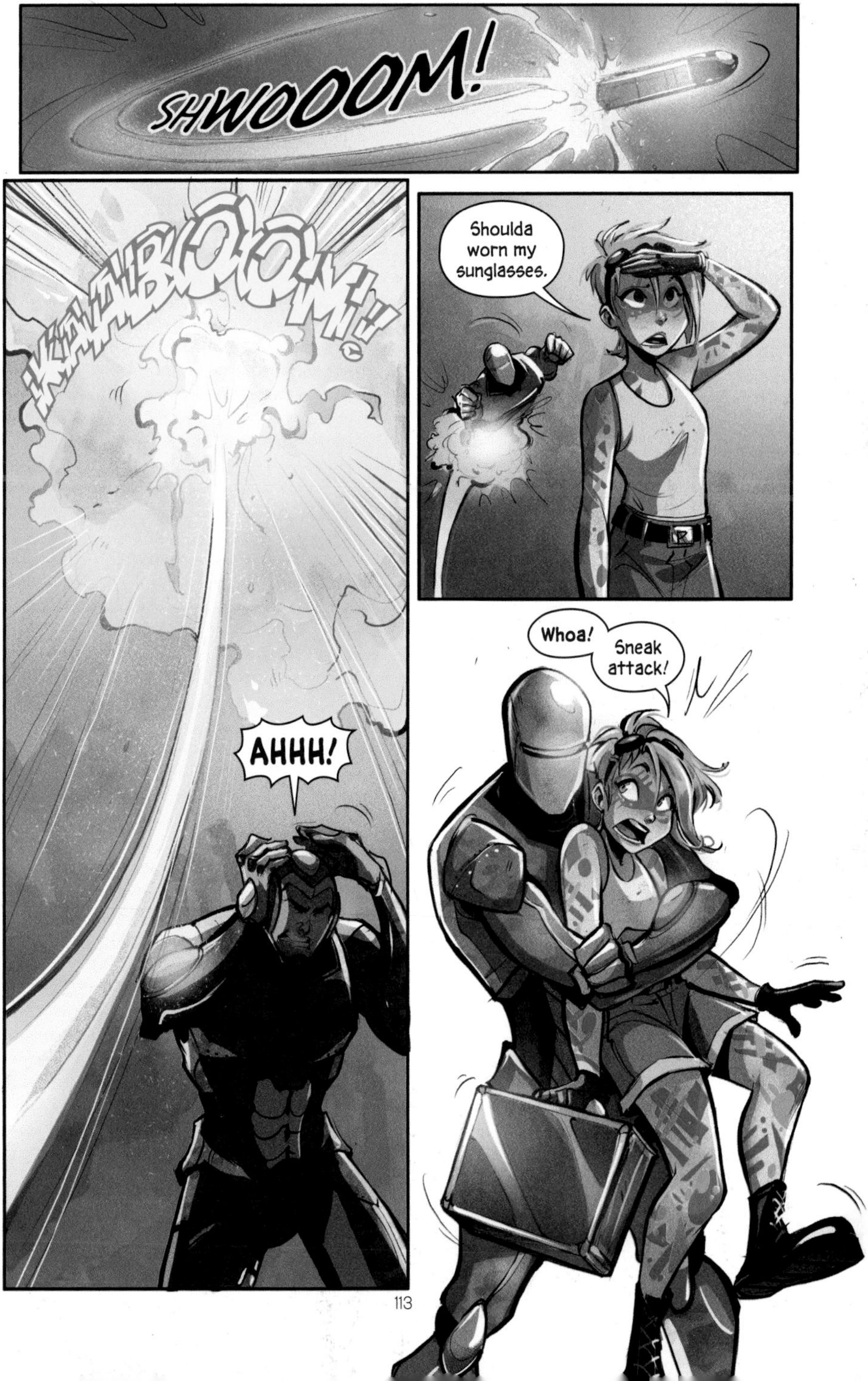
SHWOOOM!
KAHBOOM!!
AHHH!
Shoulda worn my sunglasses.
Whoa!
Sneak attack!

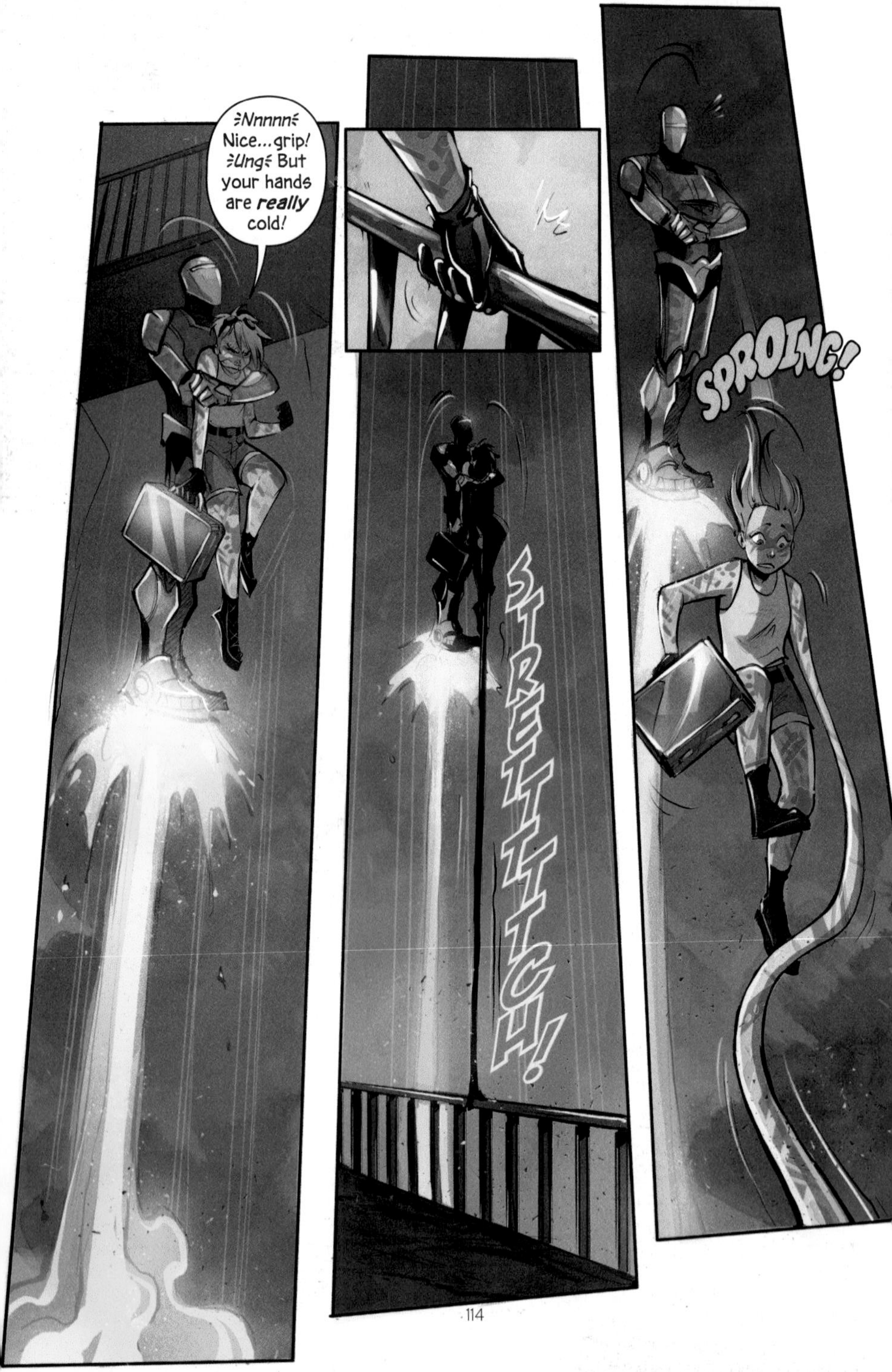

≡Nnnnn≡ Nice...grip! ≡Ung≡ But your hands are *really* cold!
STRETTTTCH!
SPROING!

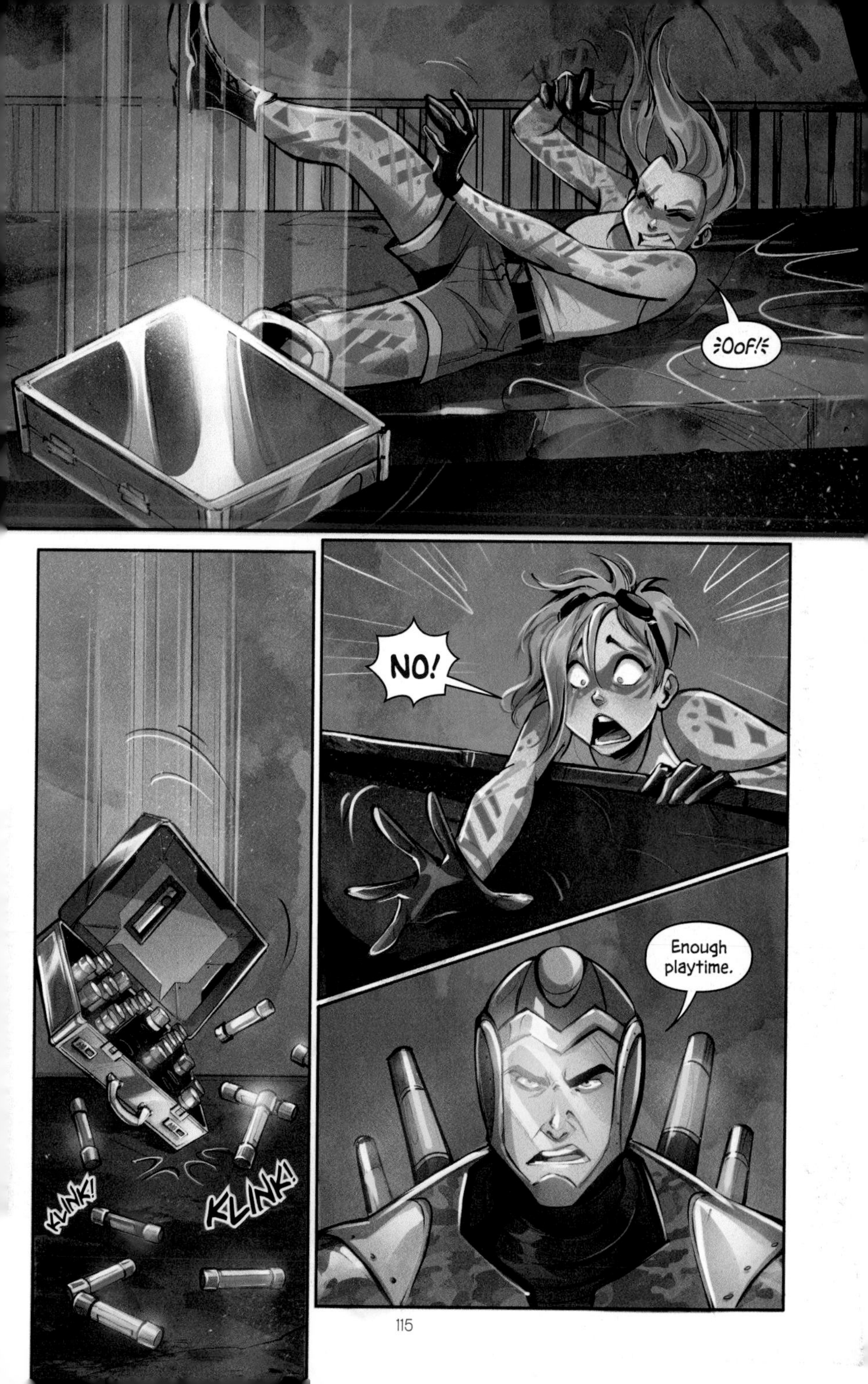
Oof!
KLINK!
KLINK!
NO!
Enough playtime.

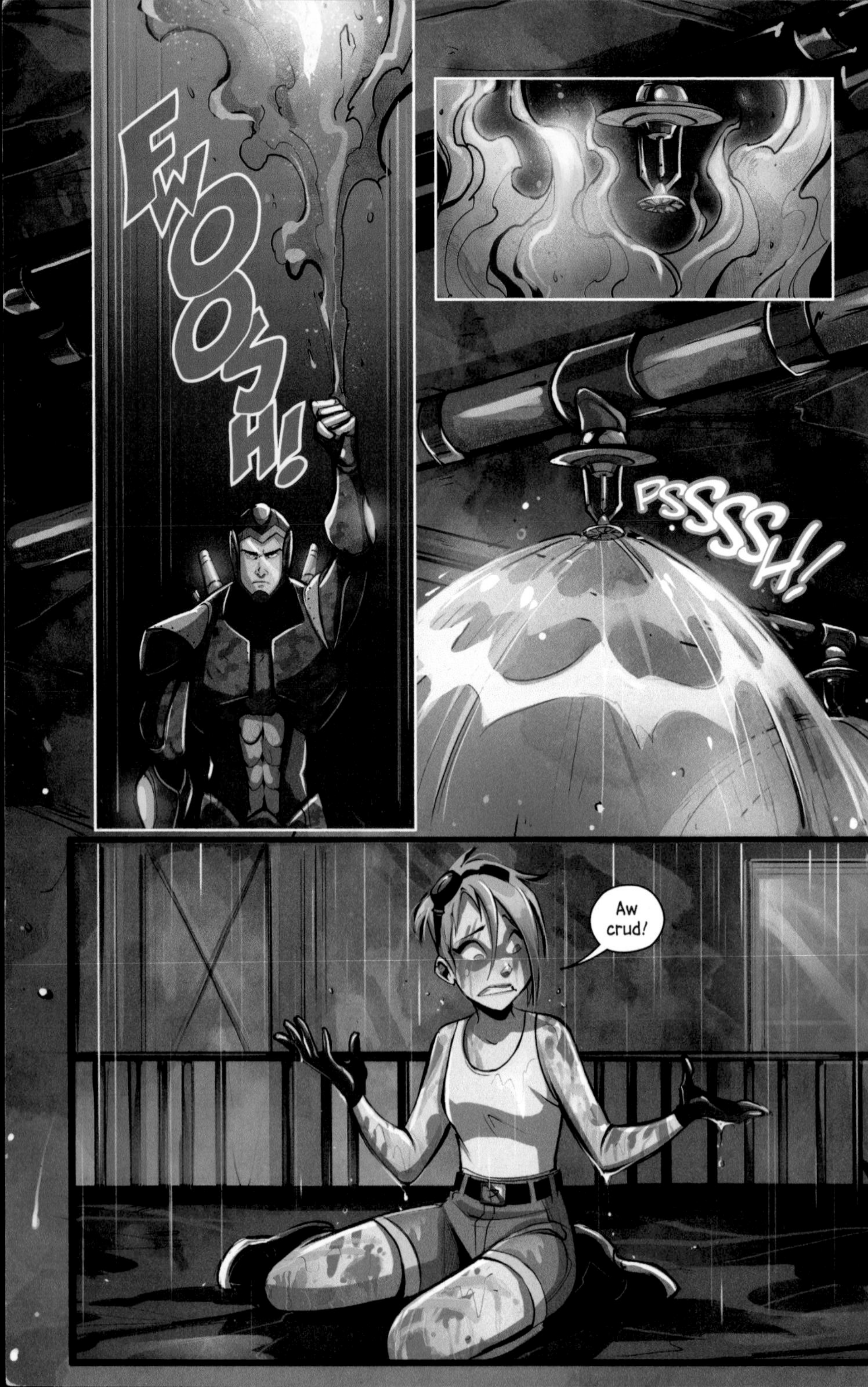
FWOOSH!
PSSSSH!
Aw crud!

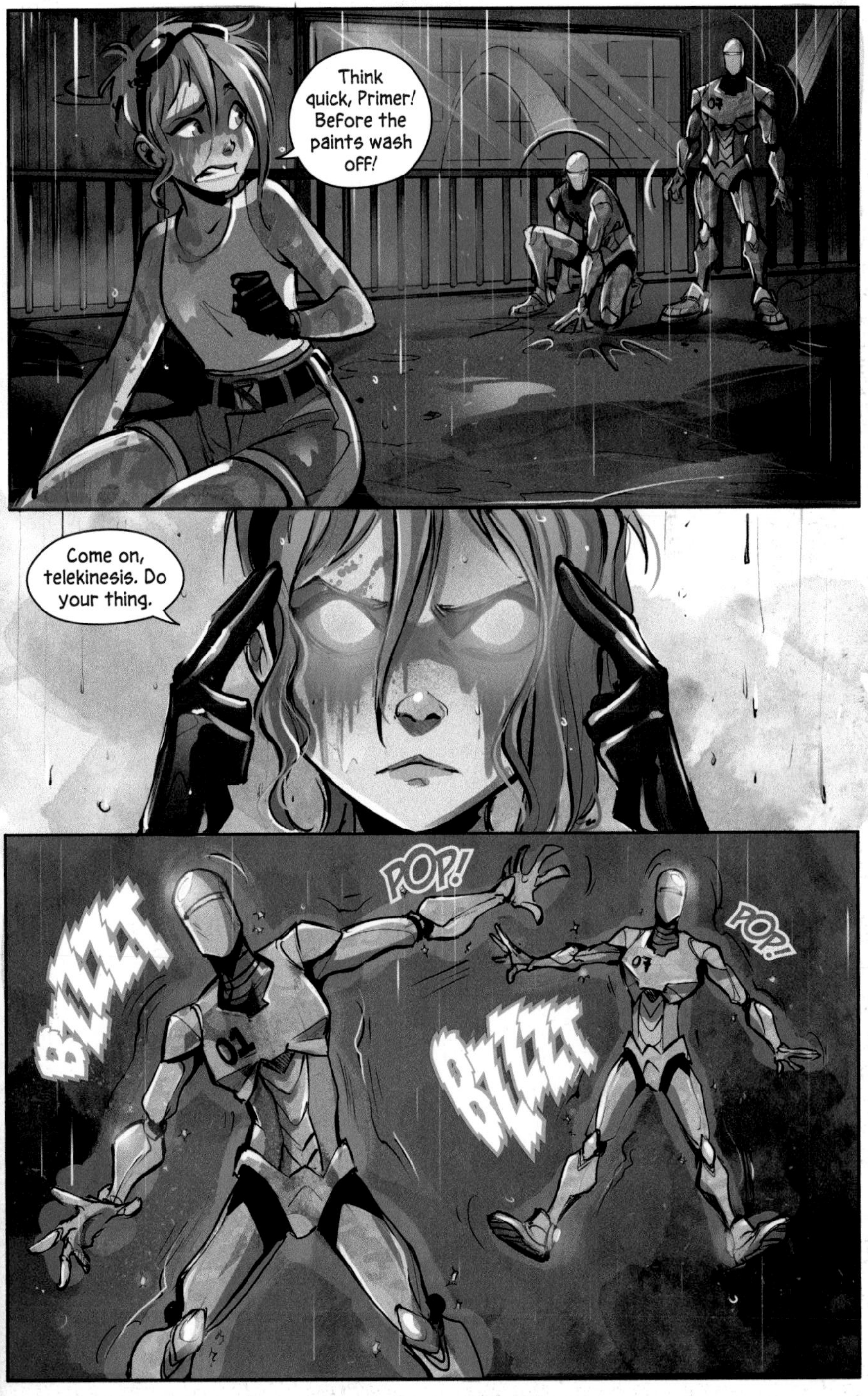
Think quick, Primer! Before the paints wash off!
Come on, telekinesis. Do your thing.
POP!
POP!
BZZZT
BZZZT

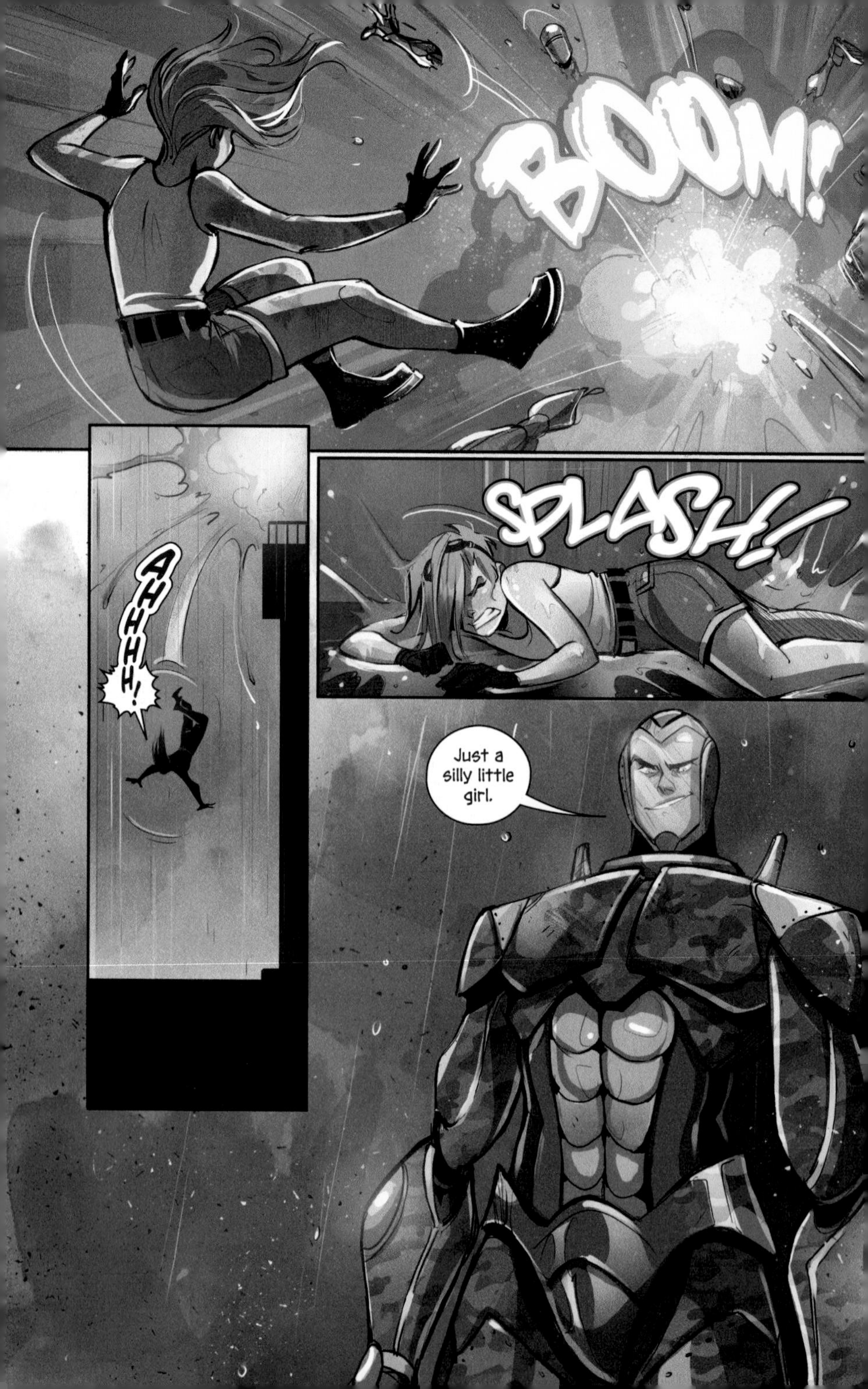
BOOM!
AHHHHH!
SPLASH!!
Just a silly little girl.

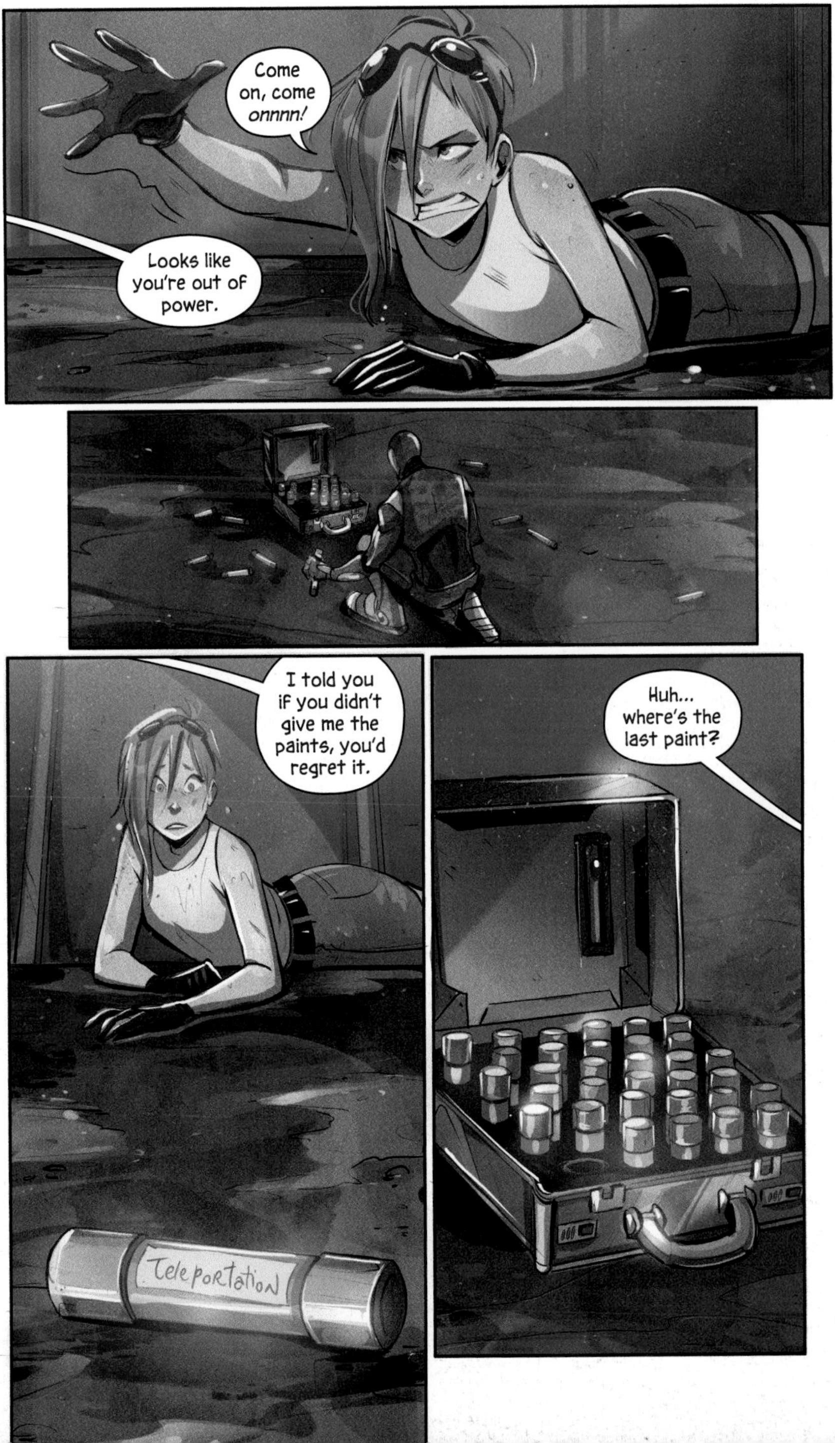
Come on, come onnnn!
Looks like you're out of power.
I told you if you didn't give me the paints, you'd regret it.
Teleportation
Huh... where's the last paint?

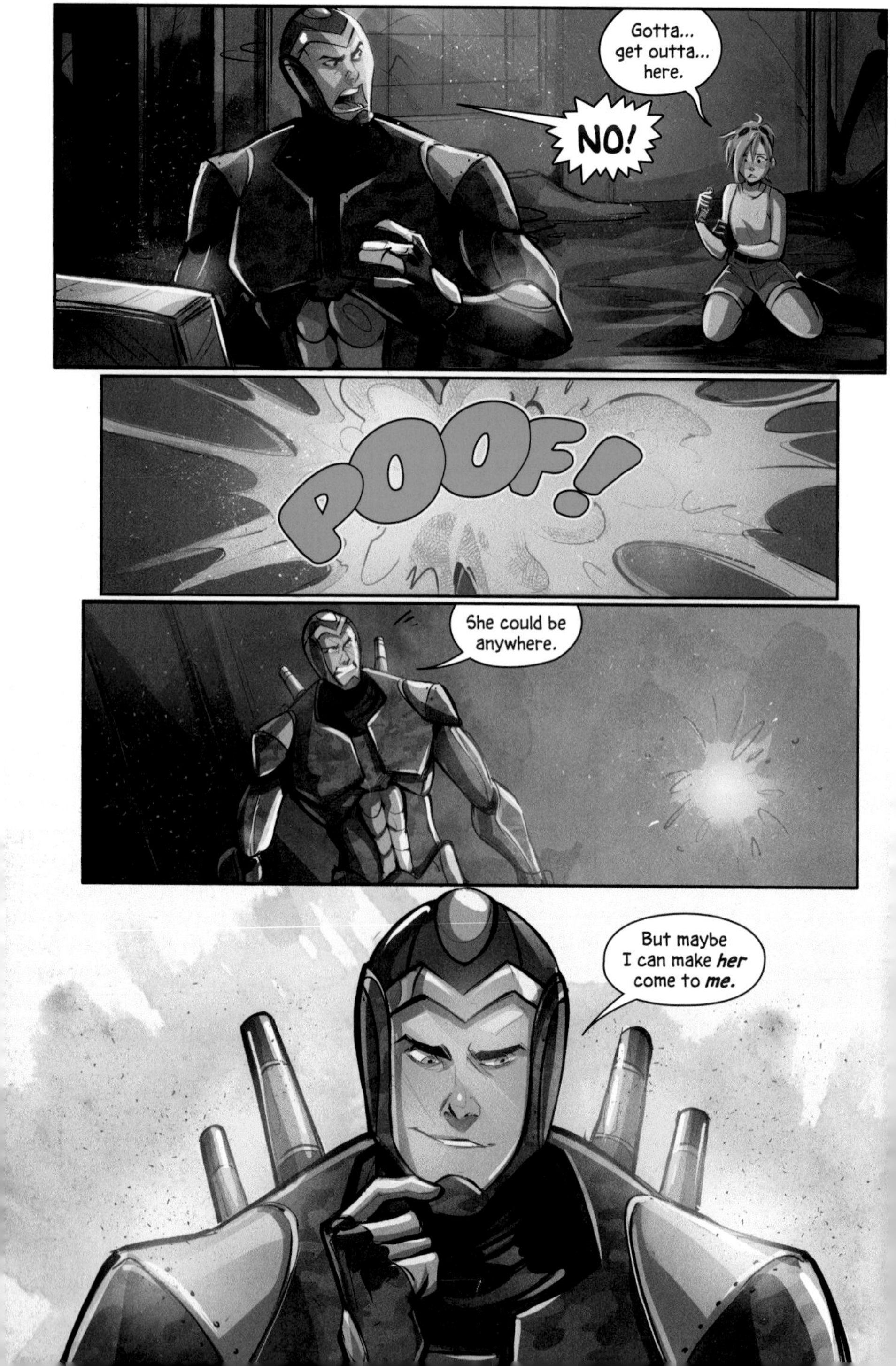
Gotta... get outta... here.
NO!
POOF!
She could be anywhere.
But maybe I can make *her* come to *me.*

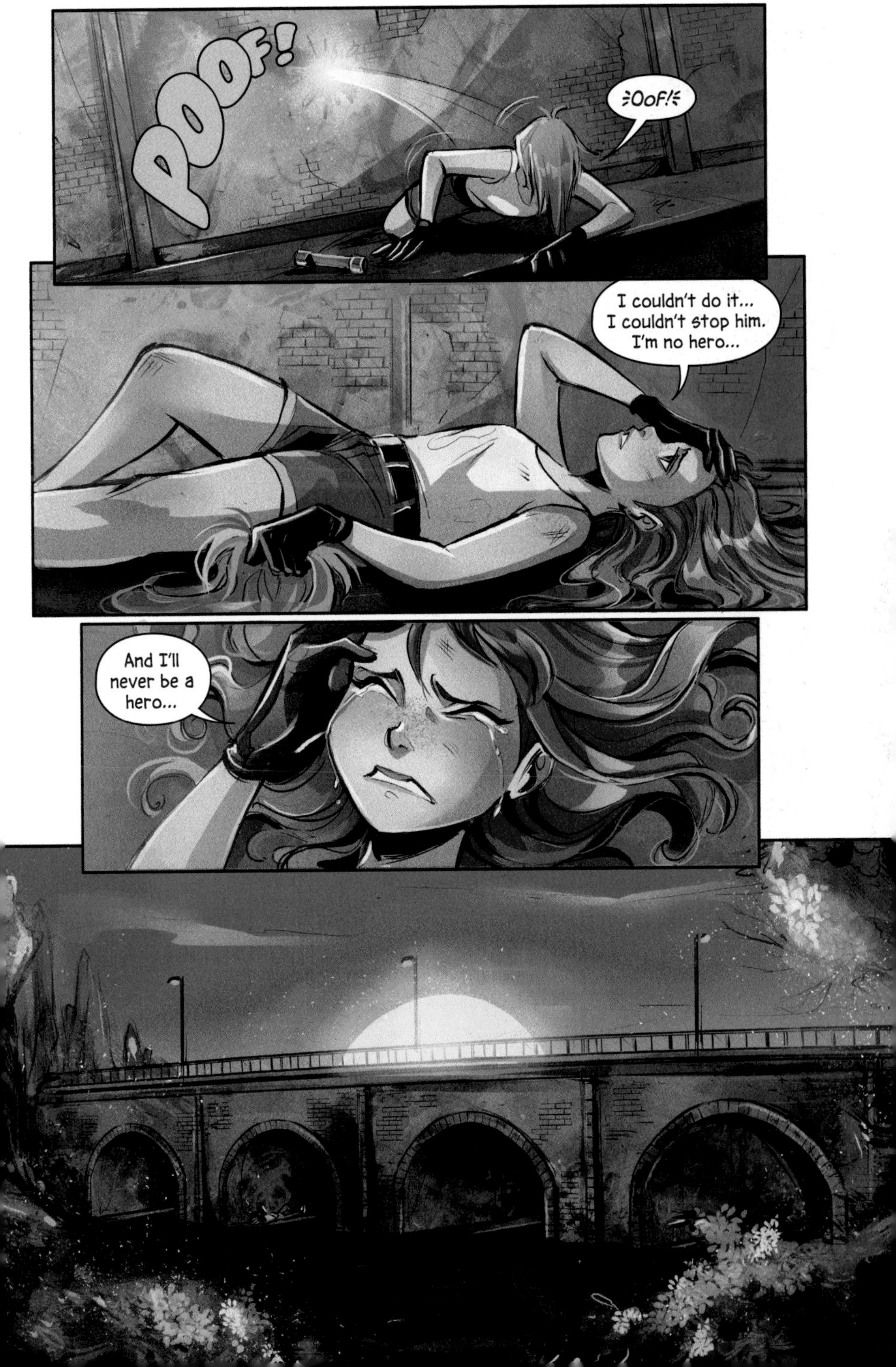
POOF!
OOF!
I couldn't do it... I couldn't stop him. I'm no hero...
And I'll never be a hero...

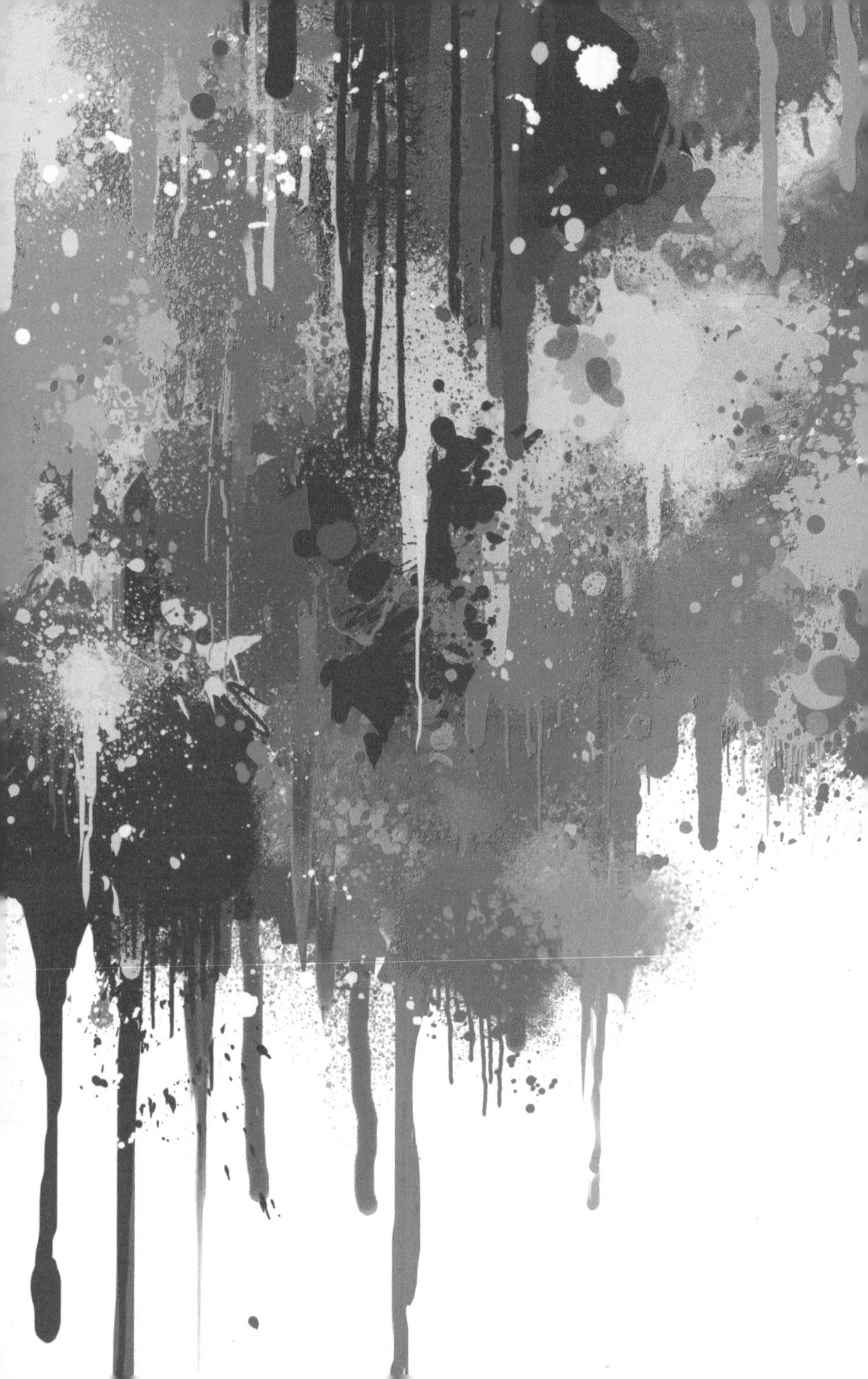

chapter 4
True Colors

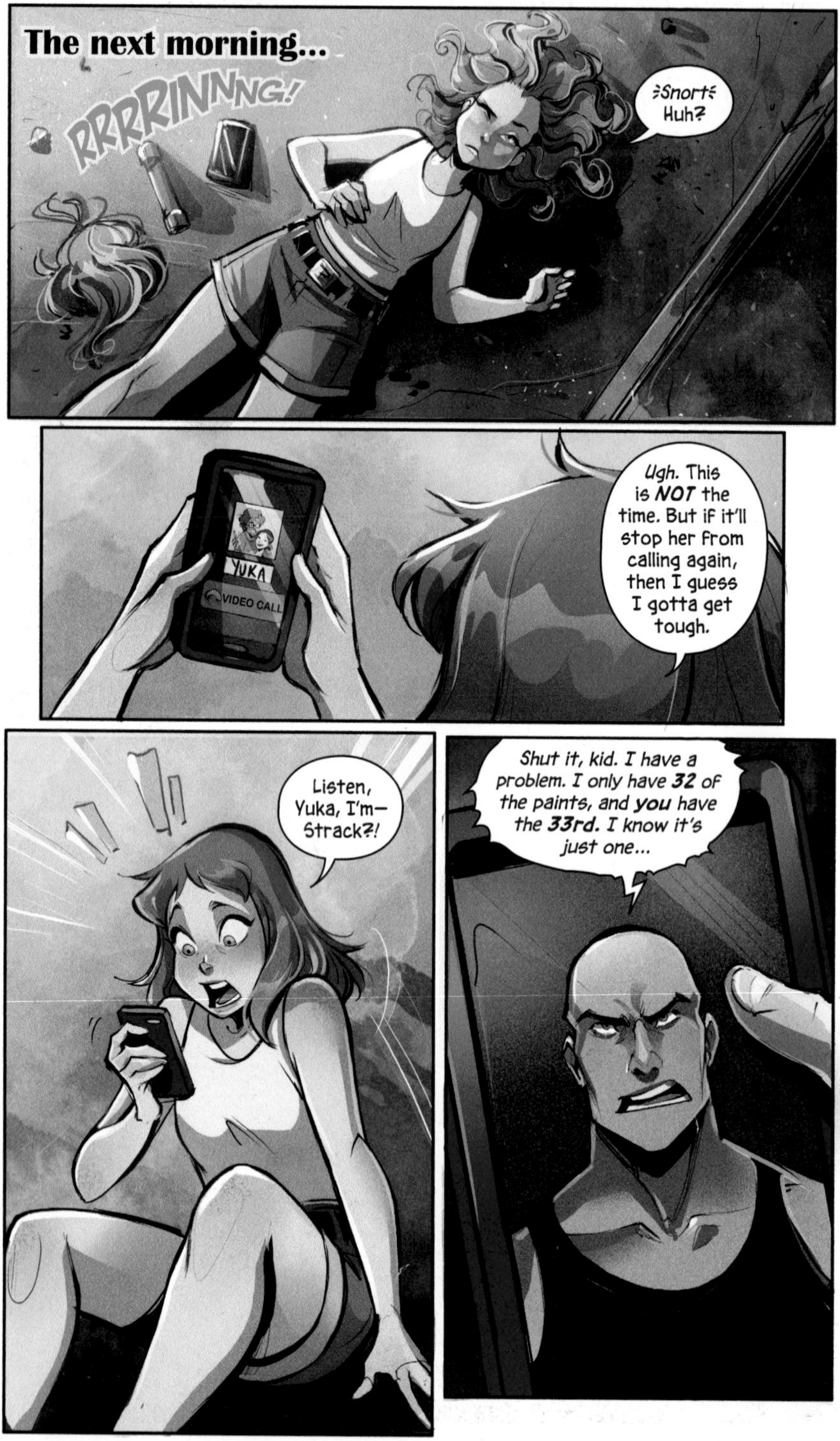
The next morning...
RRRRINNNNG!
Snort
Huh?
YUKA
VIDEO CALL
Ugh. This is NOT the time. But if it'll stop her from calling again, then I guess I gotta get tough.
Listen, Yuka, I'm— Strack?!
Shut it, kid. I have a problem. I only have 32 of the paints, and you have the 33rd. I know it's just one...

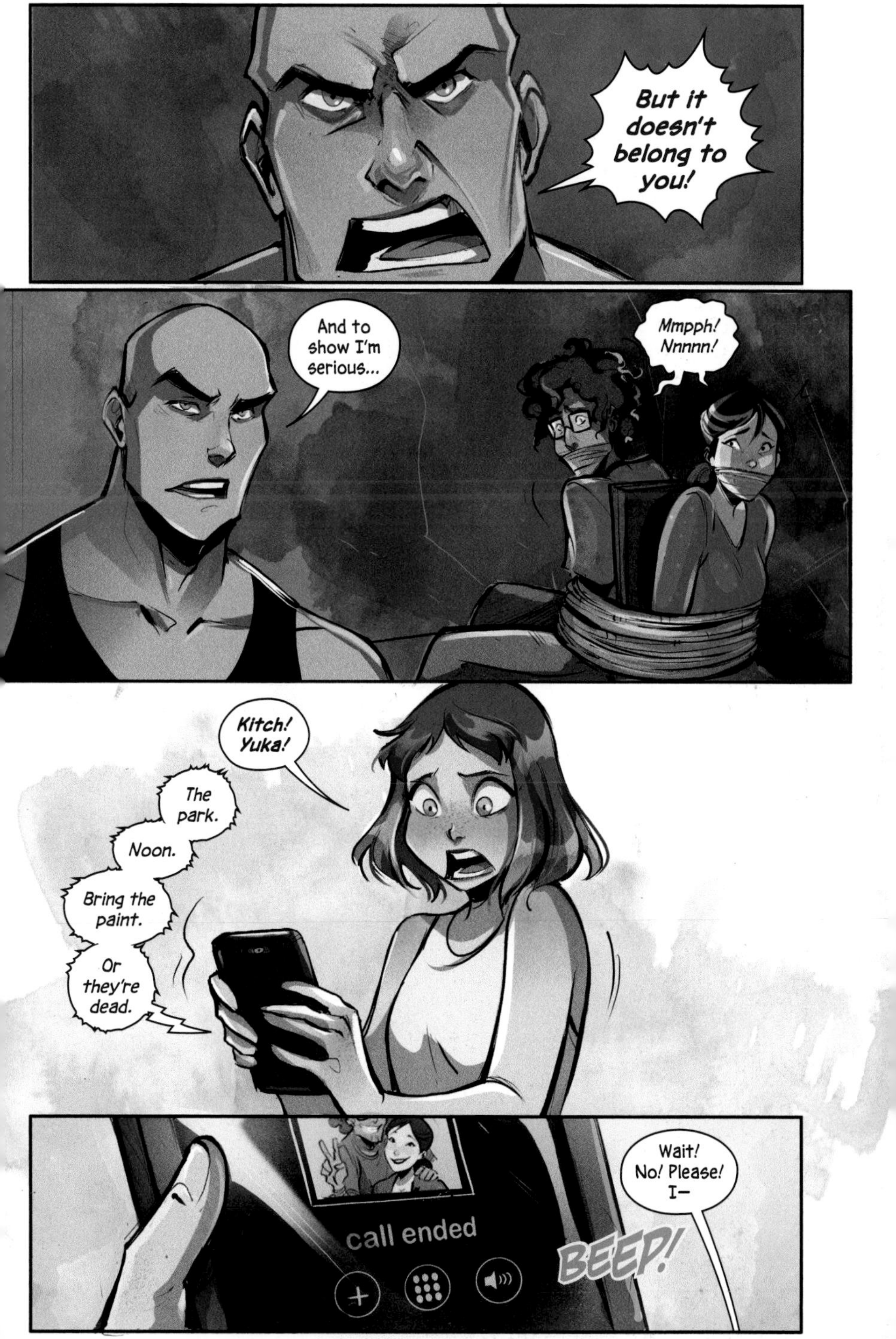
But it doesn't belong to you!
And to show I'm serious...
Mmpph! Nnnnn!
Kitch! Yuka!
The park.
Noon.
Bring the paint.
Or they're dead.
call ended
Wait! No! Please! I—
BEEP!

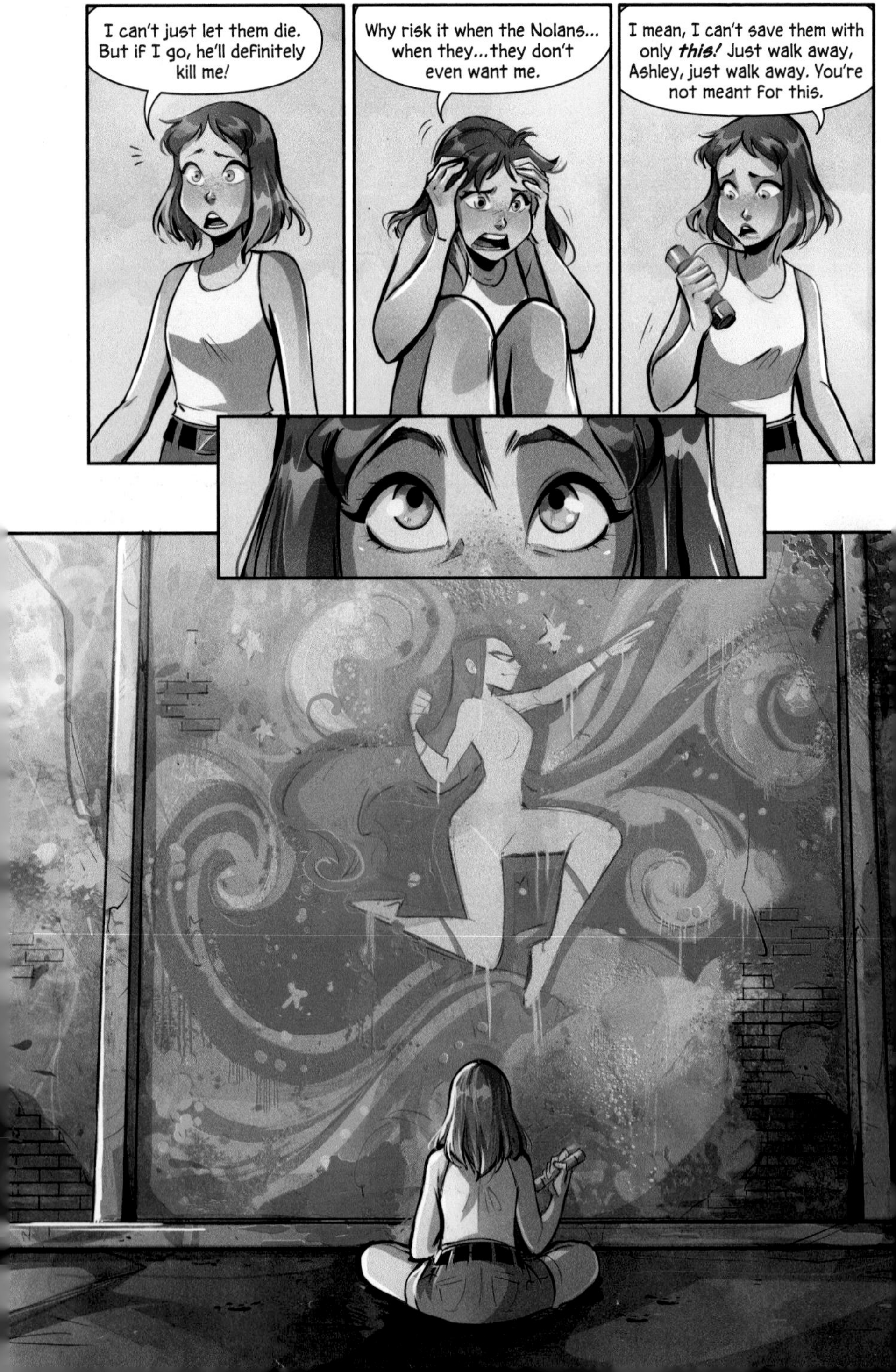
I can't just let them die. But if I go, he'll definitely kill me!
Why risk it when the Nolans... when they...they don't even want me.
I mean, I can't save them with only *this!* Just walk away, Ashley, just walk away. You're not meant for this.

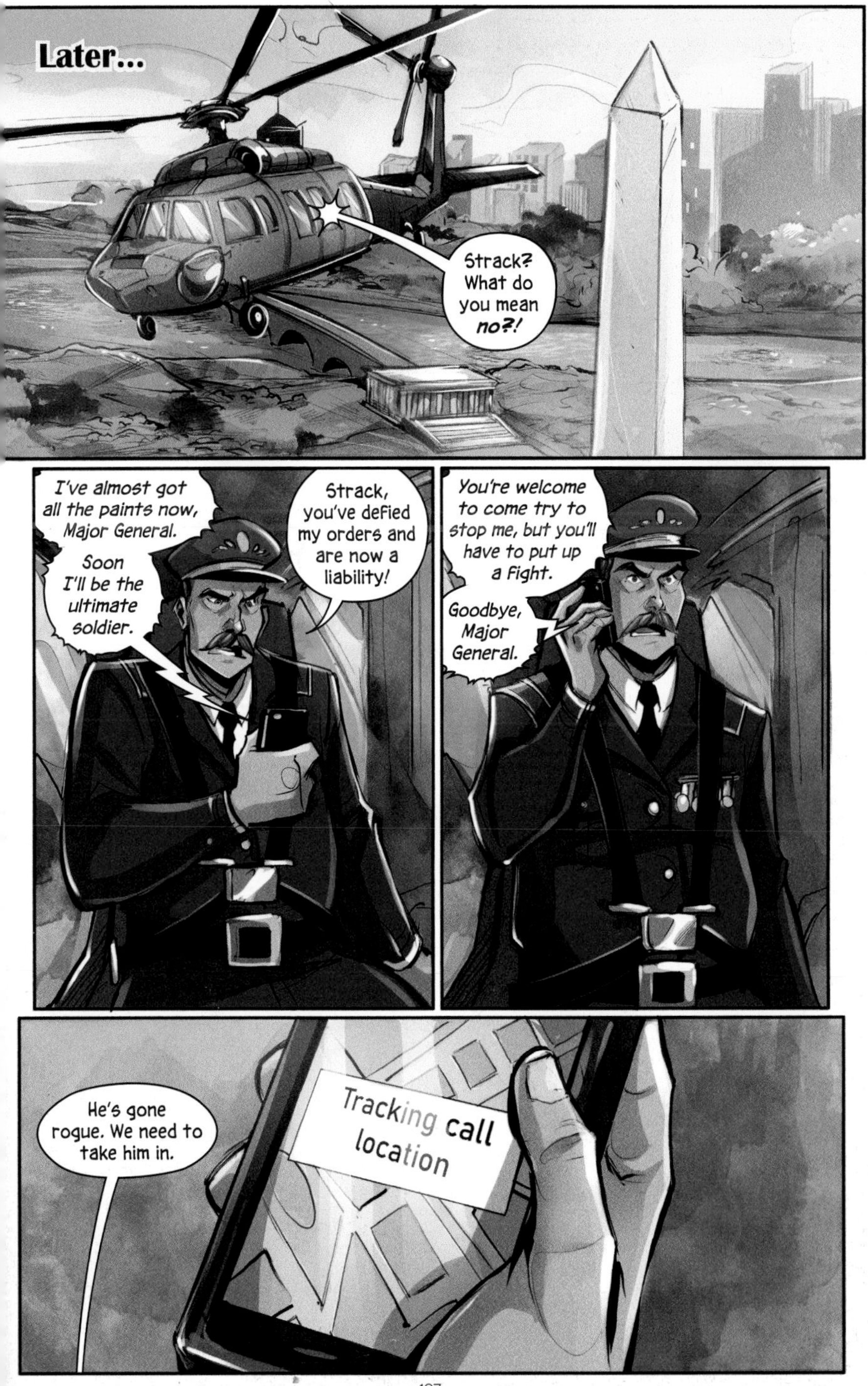
Later...
Strack? What do you mean no?!
I've almost got all the paints now, Major General.
Soon I'll be the ultimate soldier.
Strack, you've defied my orders and are now a liability!
You're welcome to come try to stop me, but you'll have to put up a fight.
Goodbye, Major General.
He's gone rogue. We need to take him in.
Tracking call location

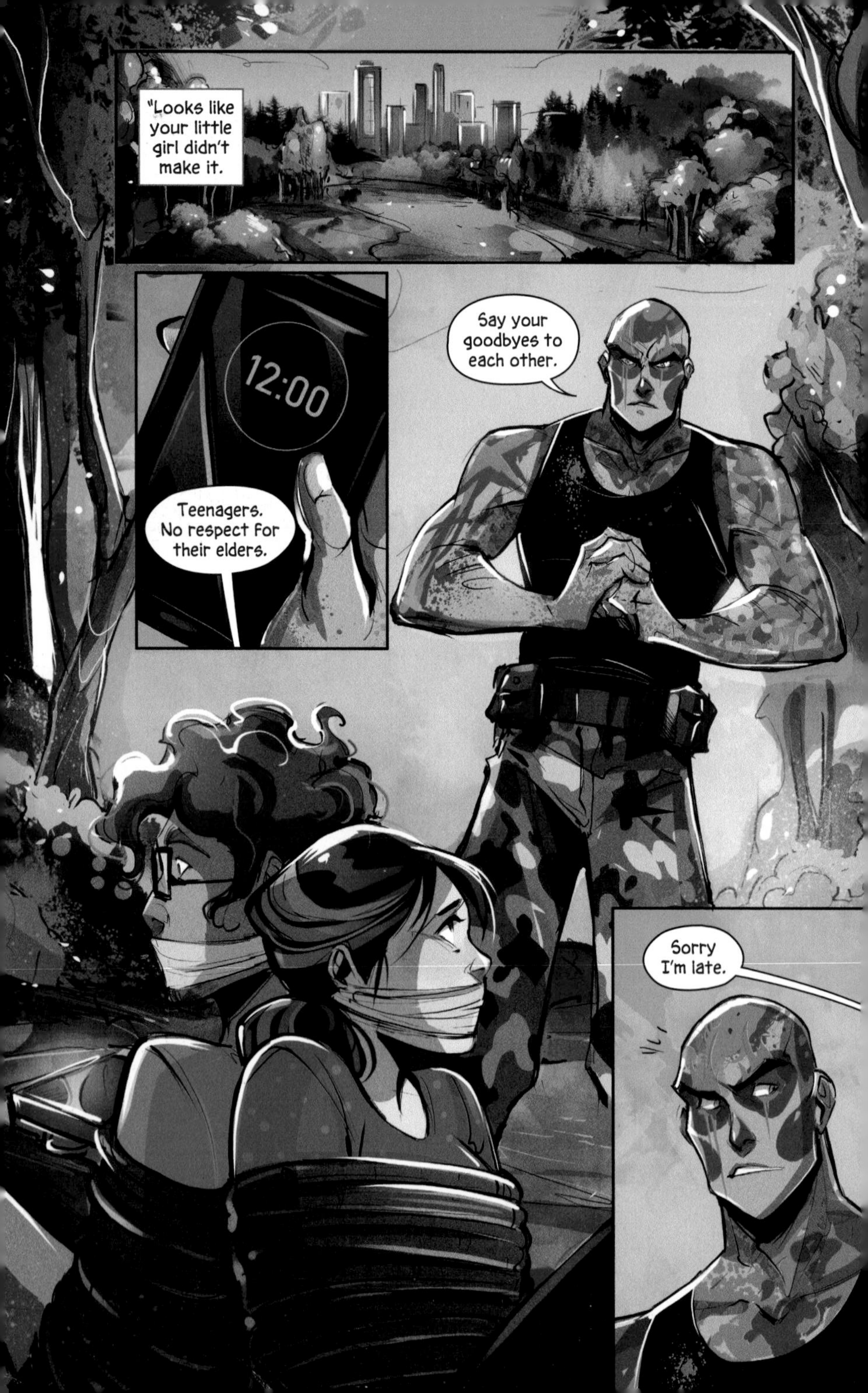
"Looks like your little girl didn't make it.
12:00
Teenagers. No respect for their elders.
Say your goodbyes to each other.
Sorry I'm late.

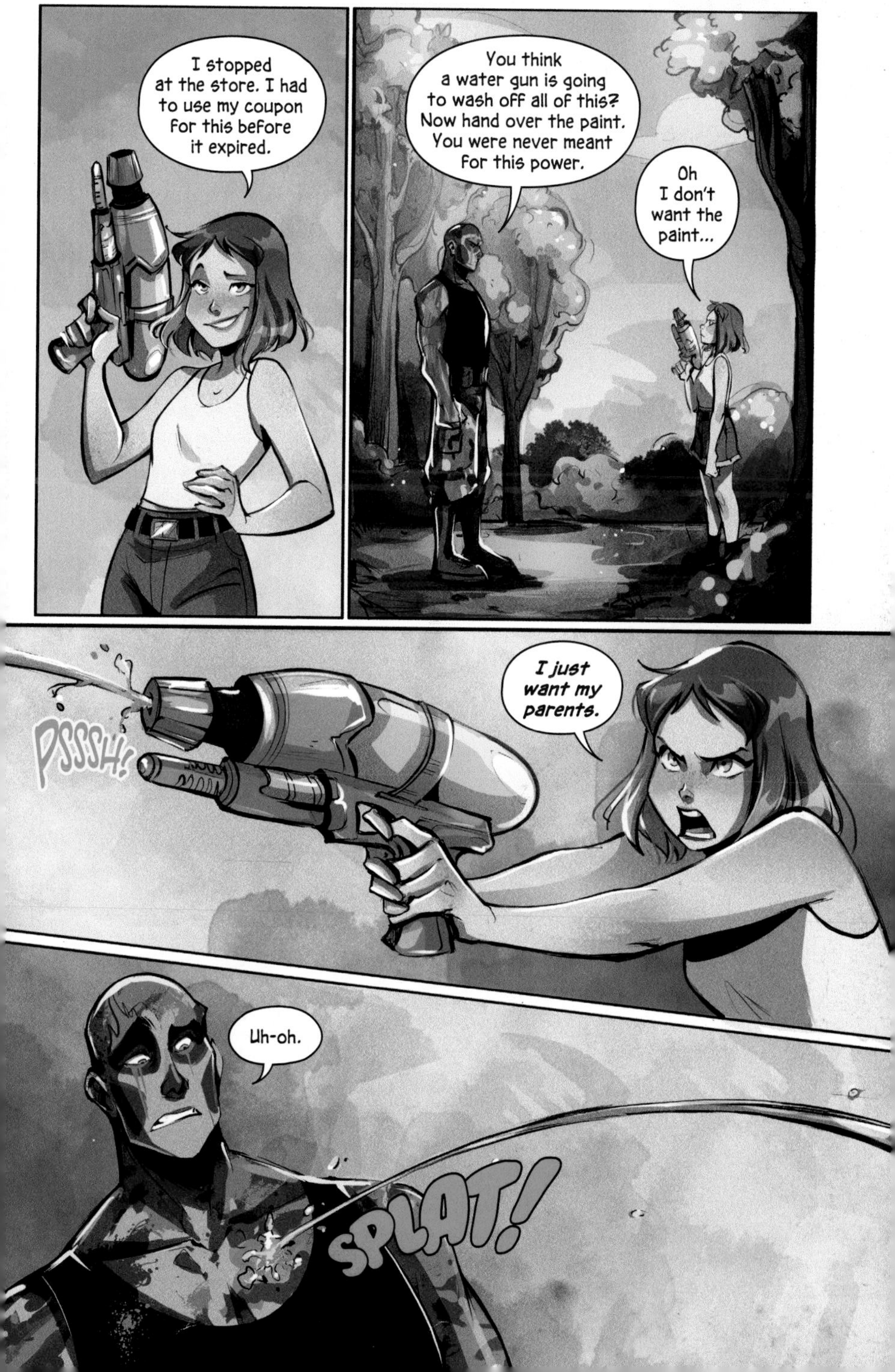
I stopped at the store. I had to use my coupon for this before it expired.
You think a water gun is going to wash off all of this? Now hand over the paint. You were never meant for this power.
Oh I don't want the paint...
PSSSH!
I just want my parents.
Uh-oh.
SPLAT!

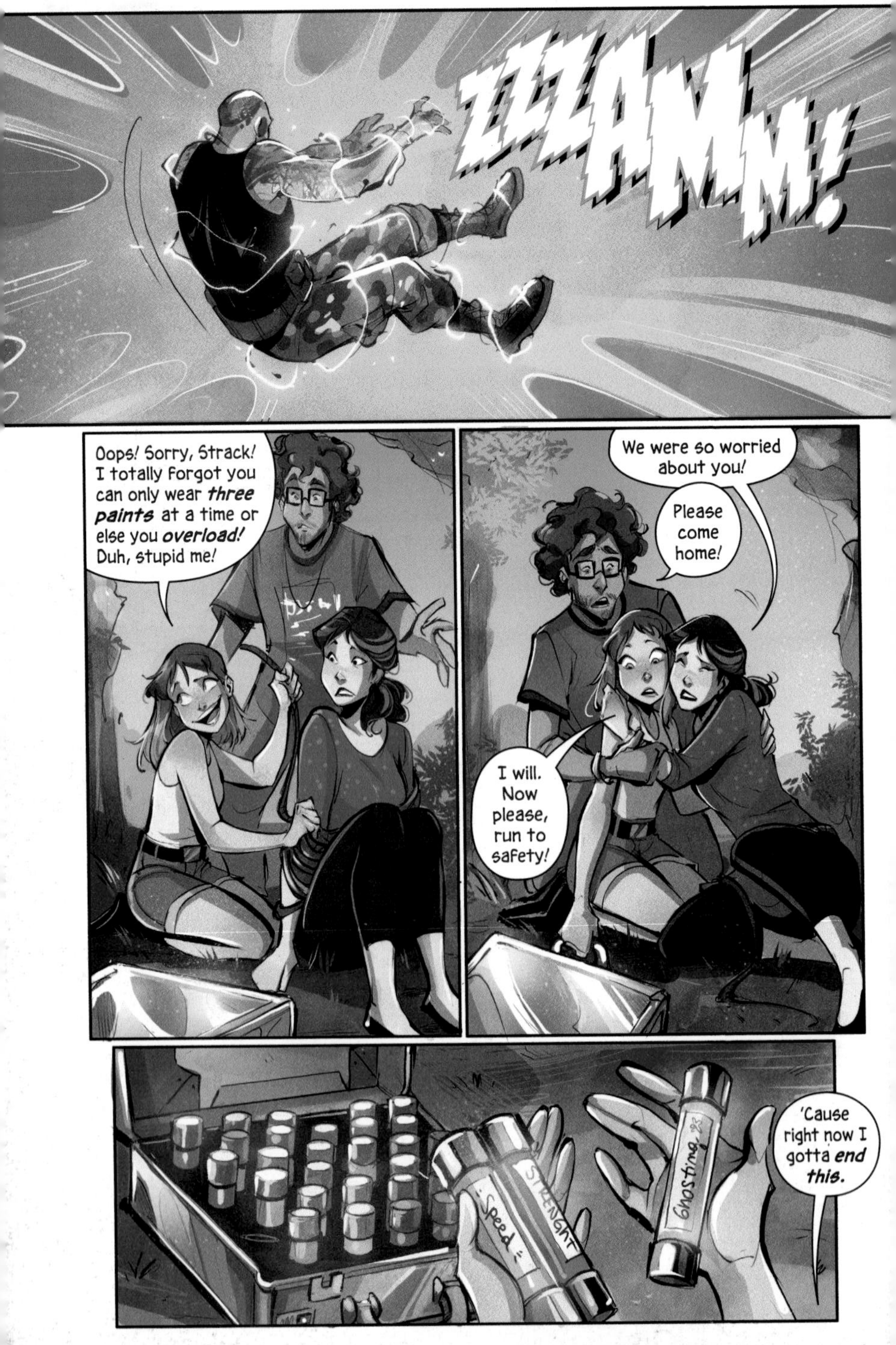
ZZZAMM!
Oops! Sorry, Strack! I totally forgot you can only wear *three paints* at a time or else you *overload!* Duh, stupid me!
We were so worried about you!
Please come home!
I will. Now please, run to safety!
'Cause right now I gotta *end this.*
Speed
STRENGHT
Ghosting

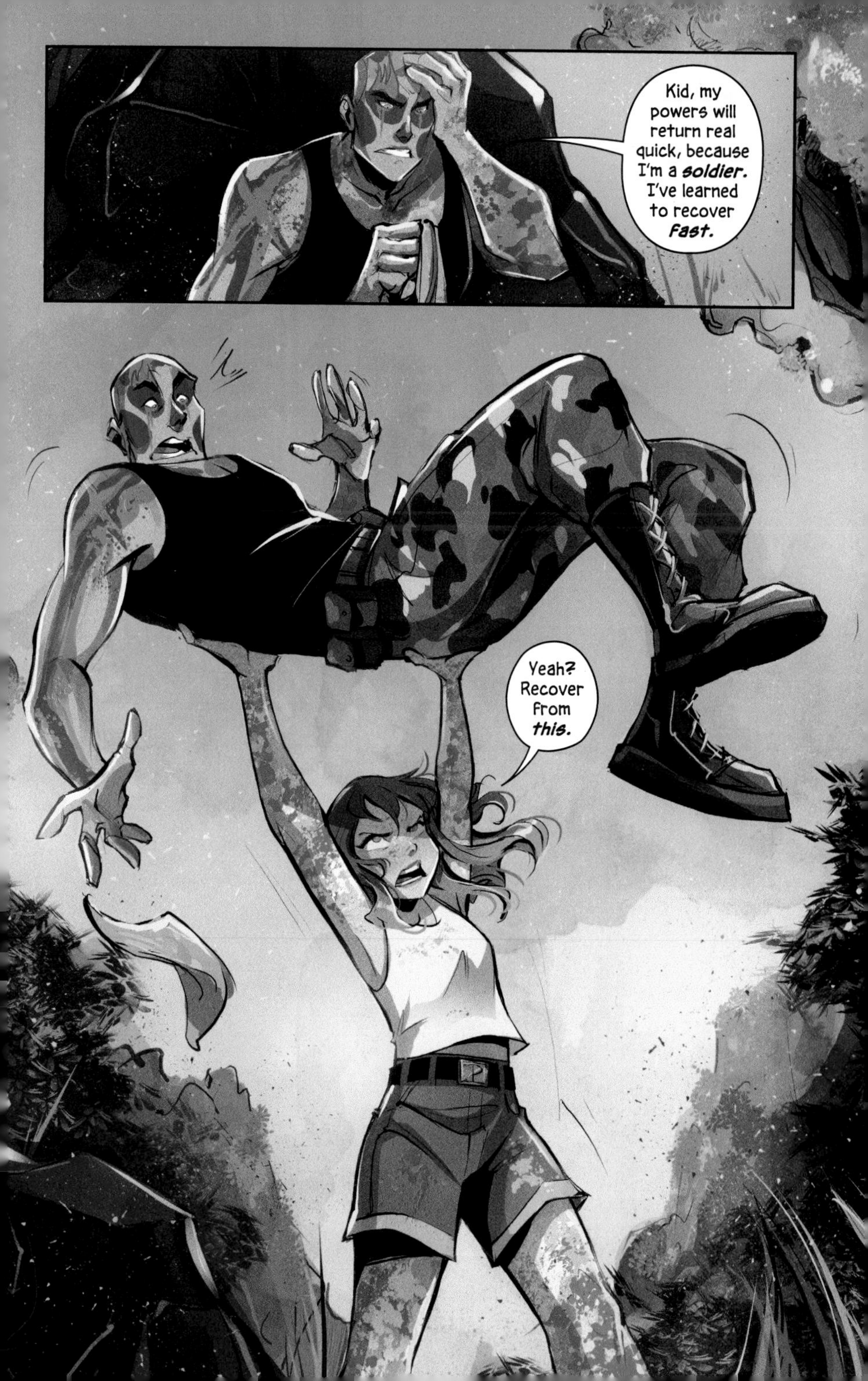
Kid, my powers will return real quick, because I'm a **soldier.** I've learned to recover **fast.**
Yeah? Recover from **this.**

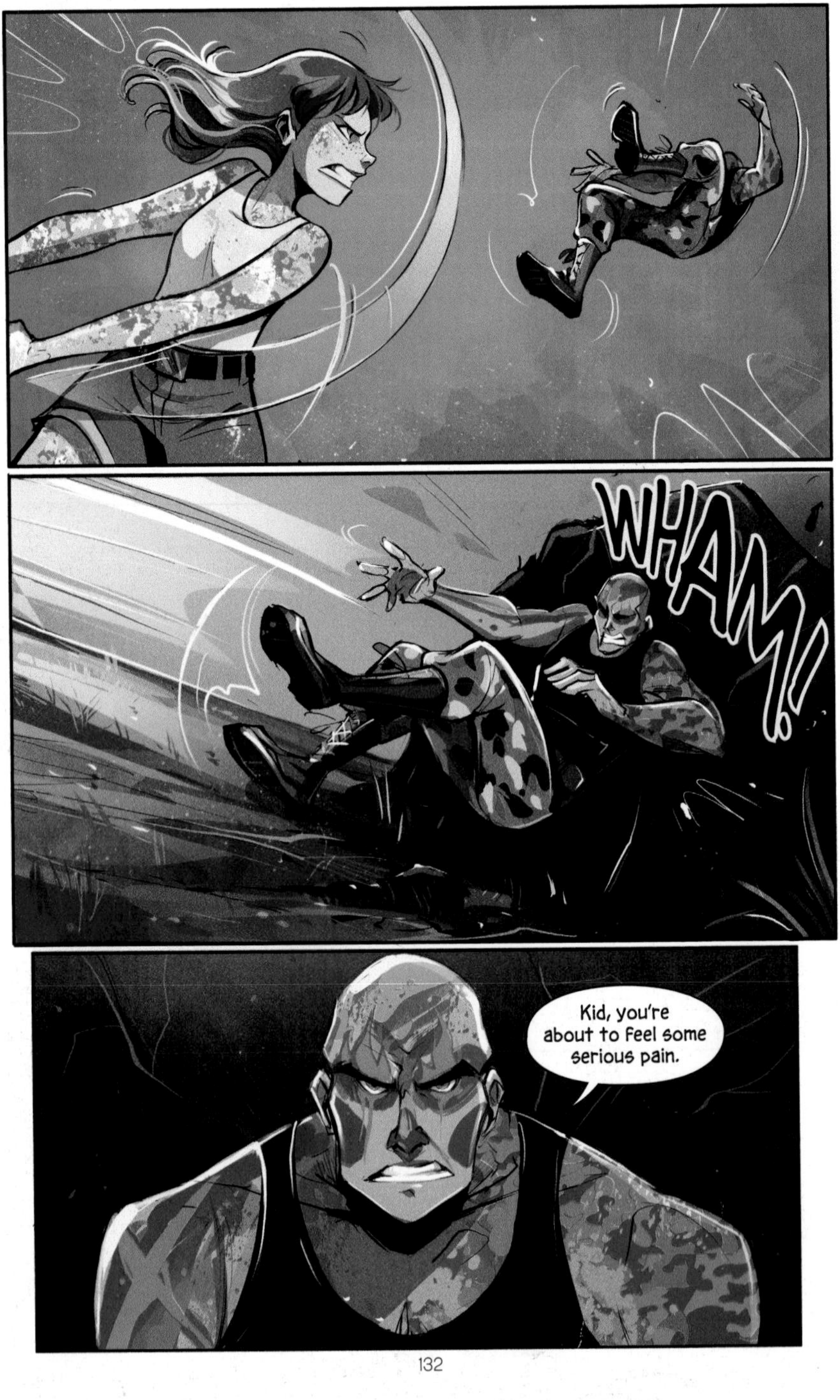
WHAM!
Kid, you're about to feel some serious pain.

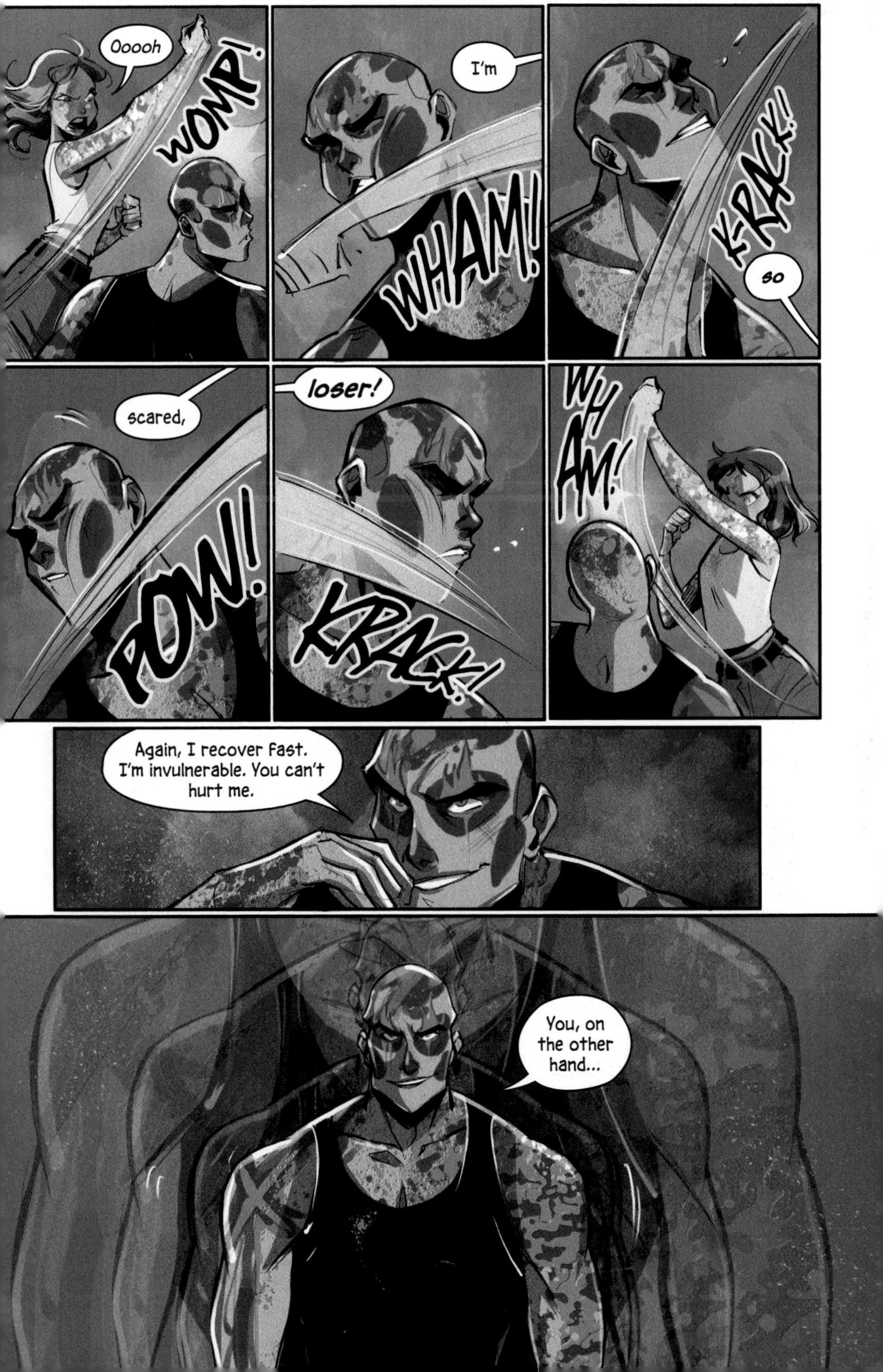

Ooooh
WOMP!
I'm
WHAM!
KRACK!
so
scared,
POW!
loser!
KRACK!
WHAM!
Again, I recover fast. I'm invulnerable. You can't hurt me.
You, on the other hand...

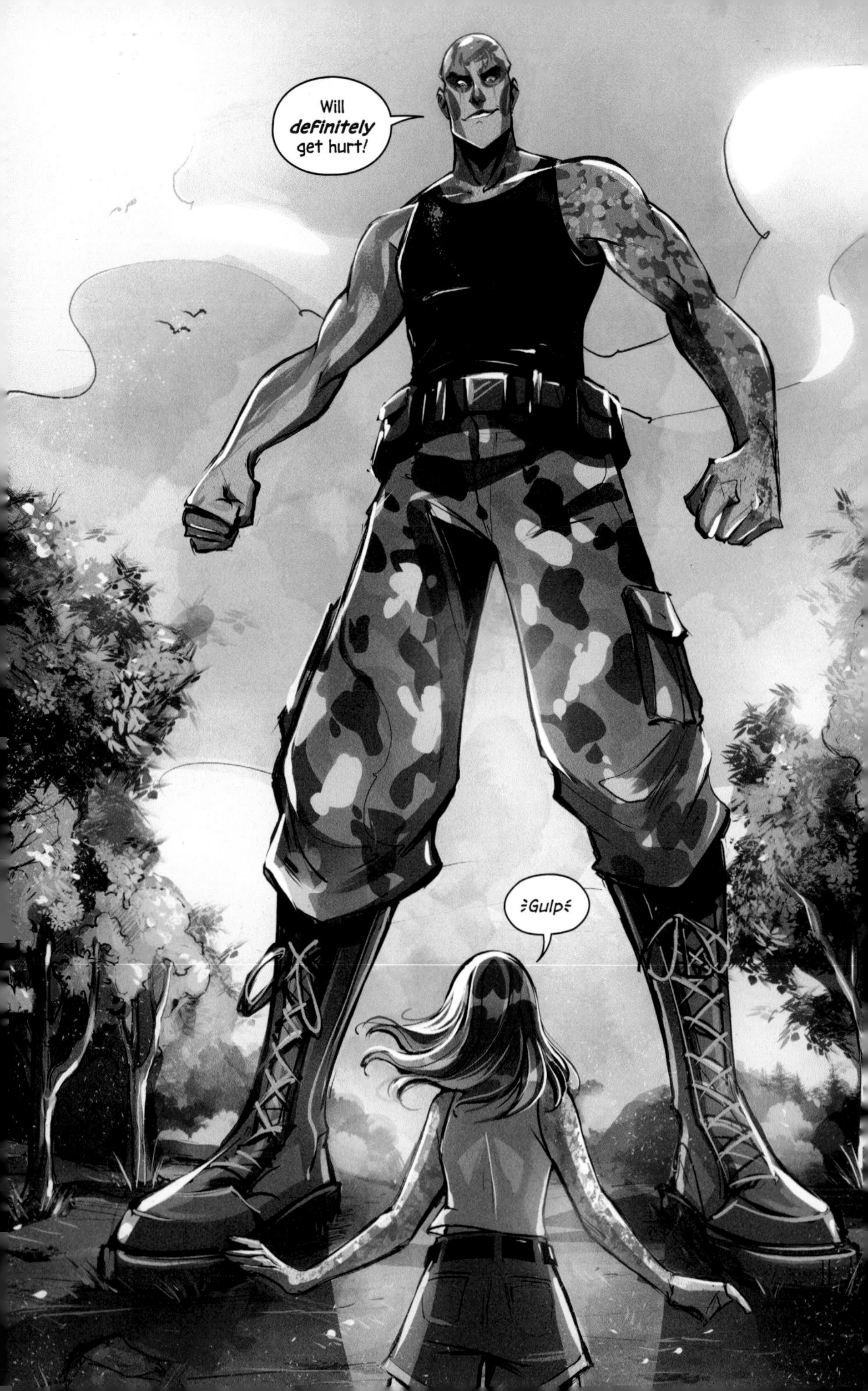
Will *definitely* get hurt!
Gulp

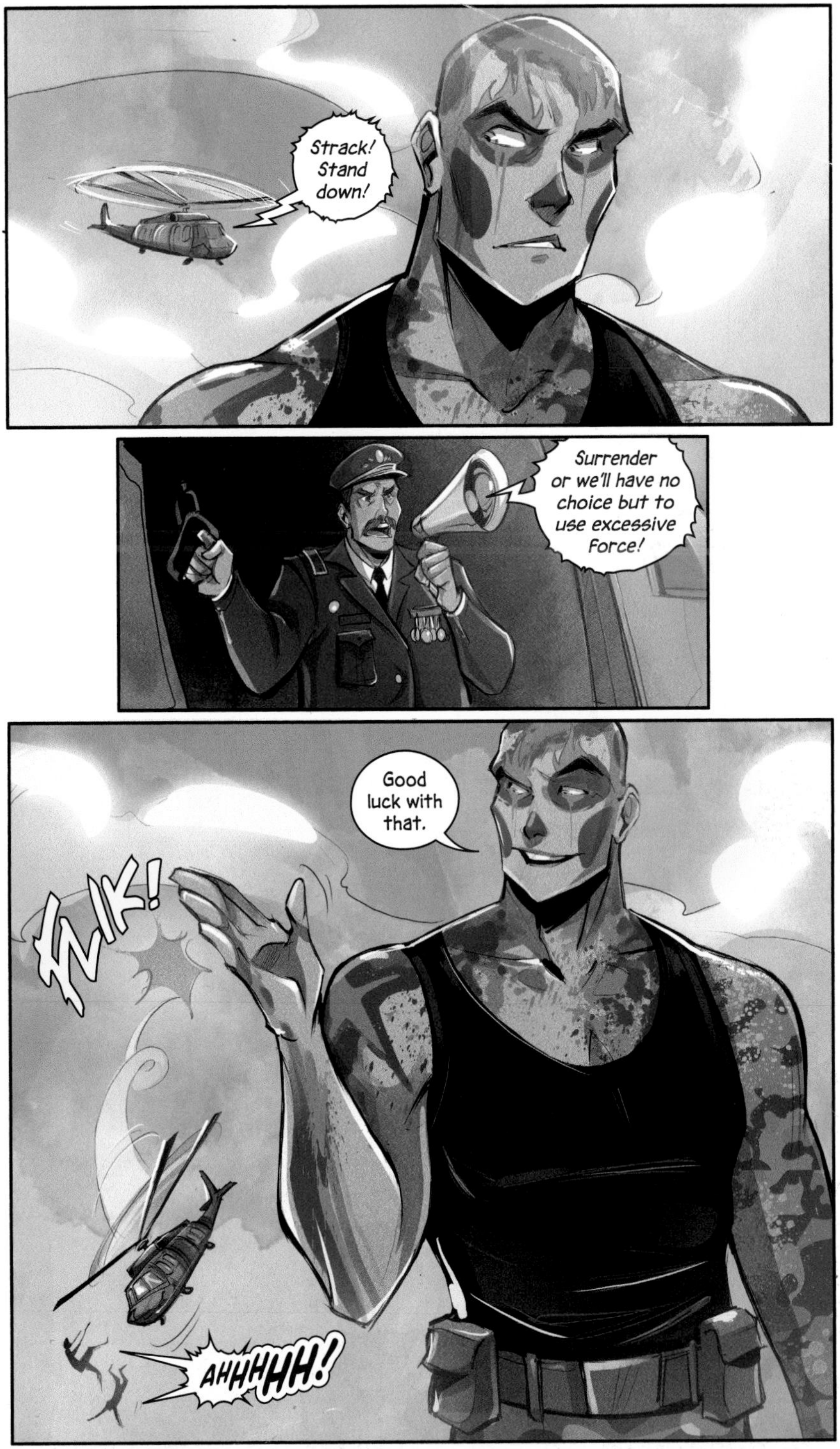
Strack! Stand down!
Surrender or we'll have no choice but to use excessive force!
Good luck with that.
FZLIK!
AHHHHH!

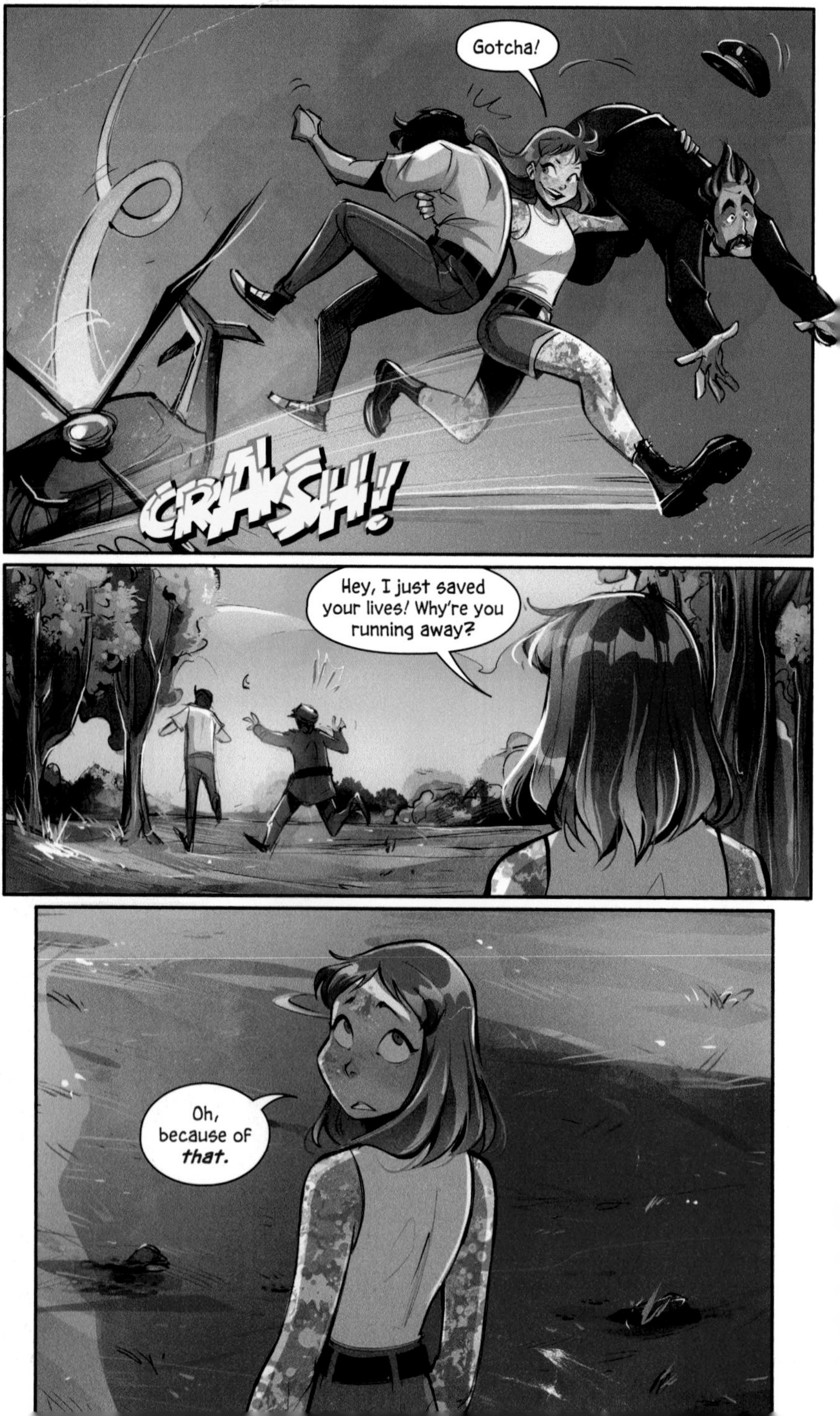
Gotcha!
CRASH!!
Hey, I just saved your lives! Why're you running away?
Oh, because of *that.*

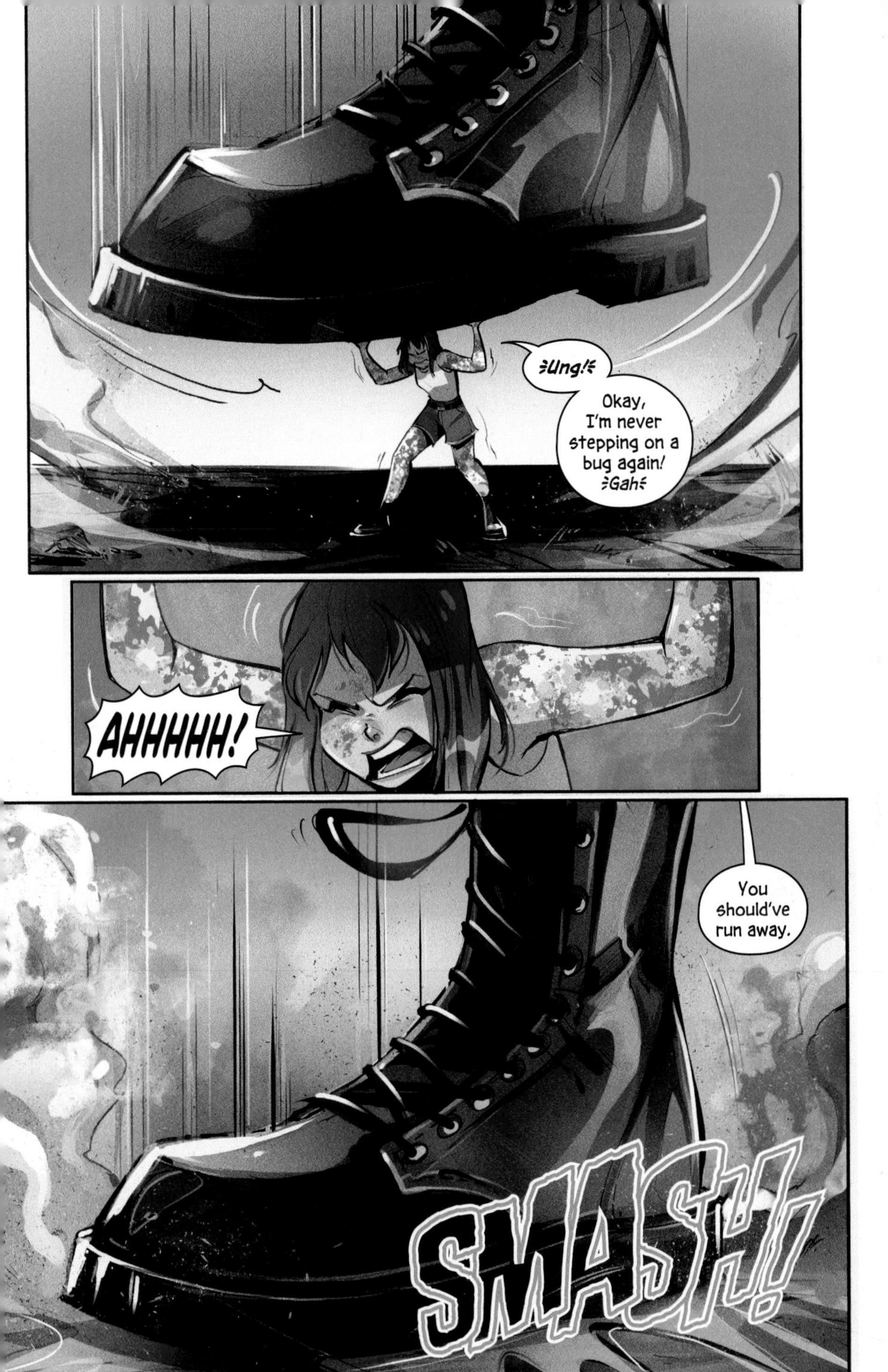
Ung!
Okay, I'm never stepping on a bug again! Gah
AHHHHH!
You should've run away.
SMASH!

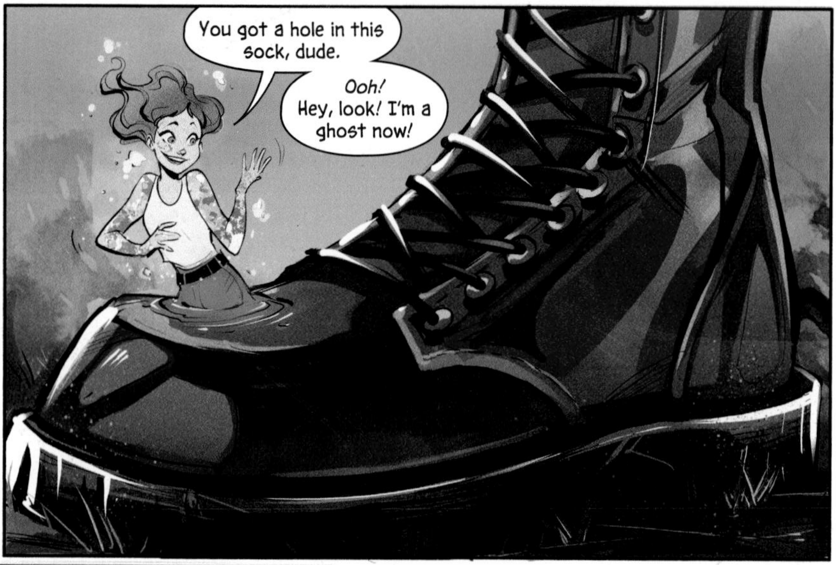
You got a hole in this sock, dude.
Ooh! Hey, look! I'm a ghost now!
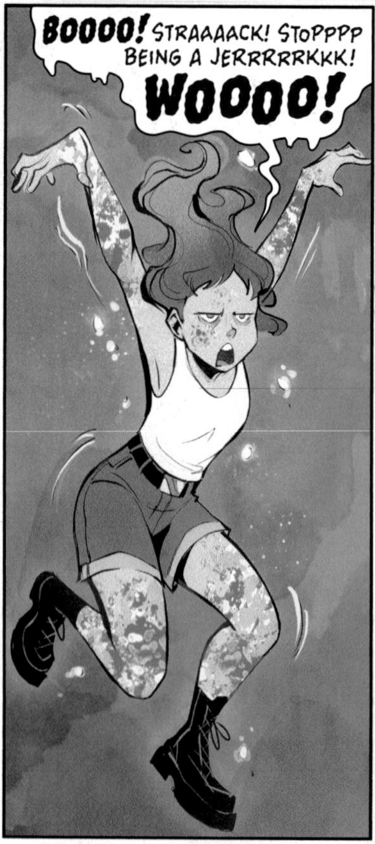
BOOOO! STRAAAACK! STOPPPP BEING A JERRRRRKKK! WOOOO!
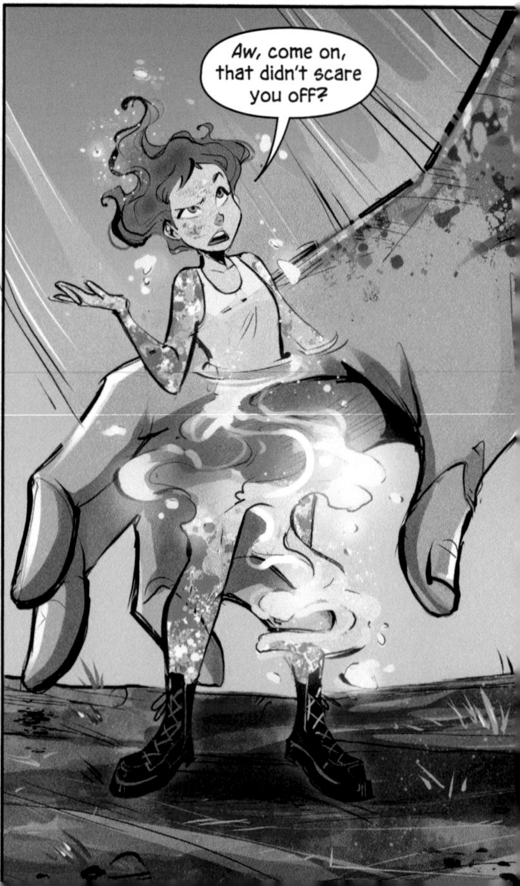
Aw, come on, that didn't scare you off?

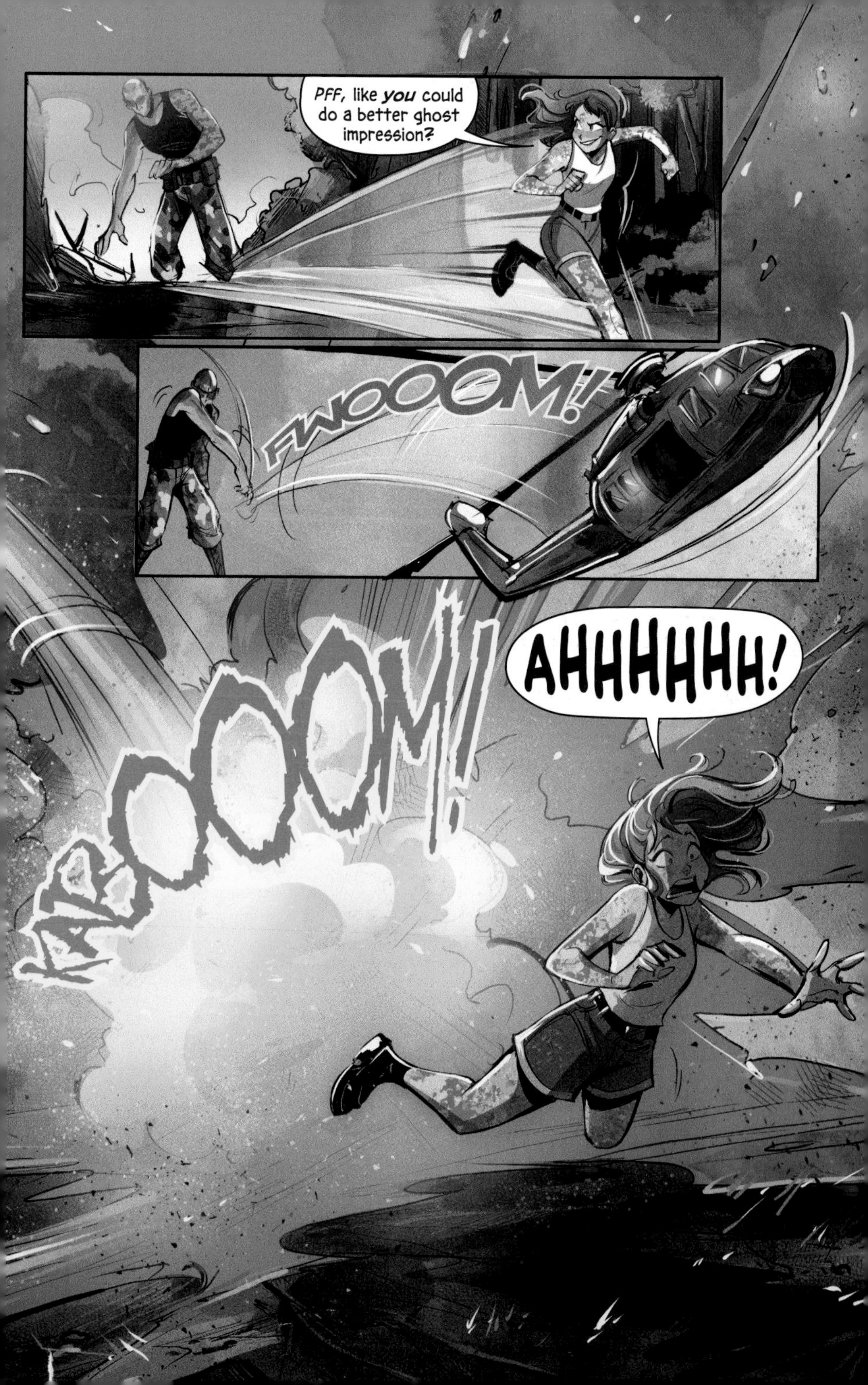
PFF, like *you* could do a better ghost impression?
FWOOOOM!
KABOOOM!
AHHHHHH!

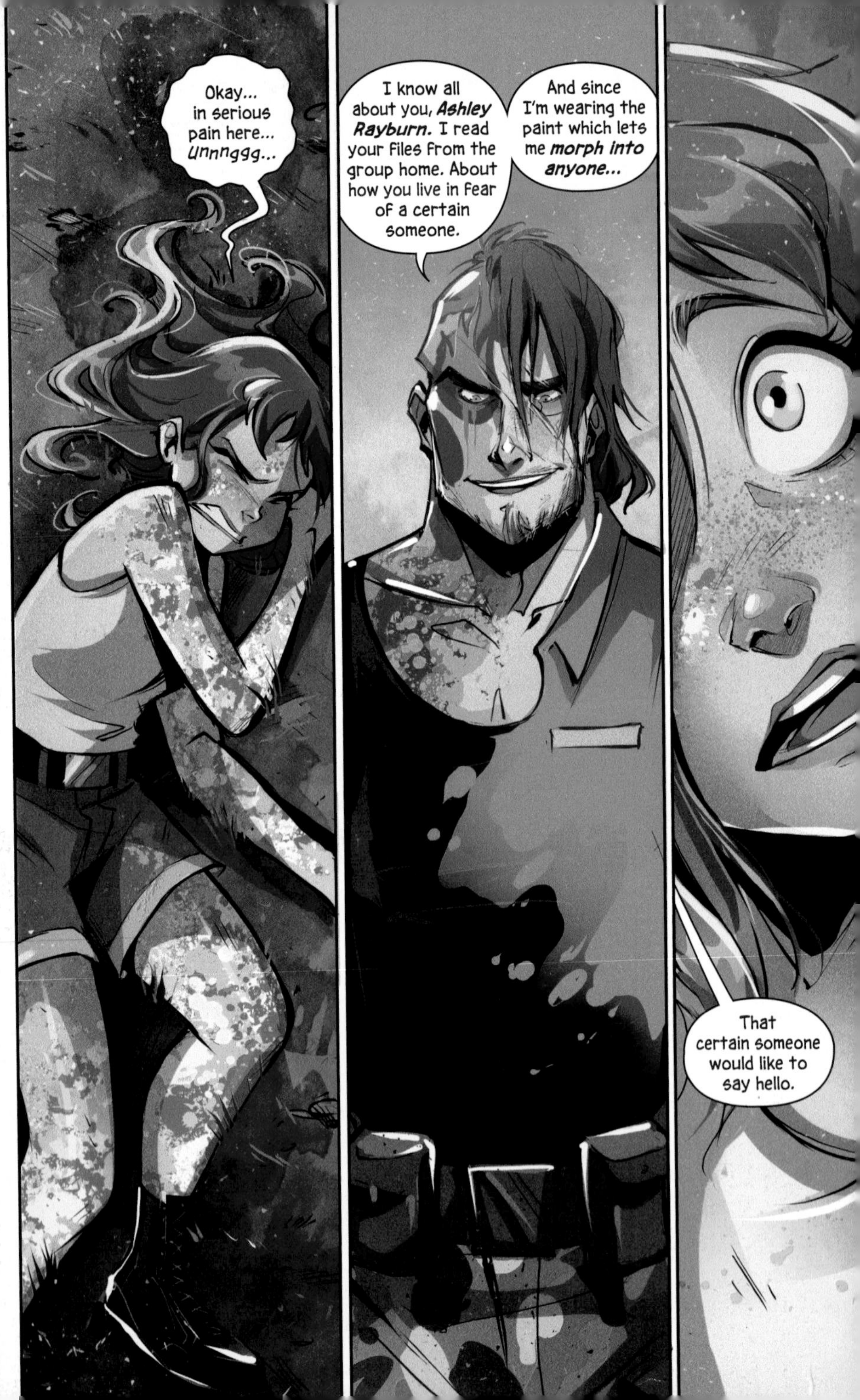

Okay... in serious pain here... Unnnggg...
I know all about you, *Ashley Rayburn.* I read your files from the group home. About how you live in fear of a certain someone.
And since I'm wearing the paint which lets me *morph into anyone...*
That certain someone would like to say hello.

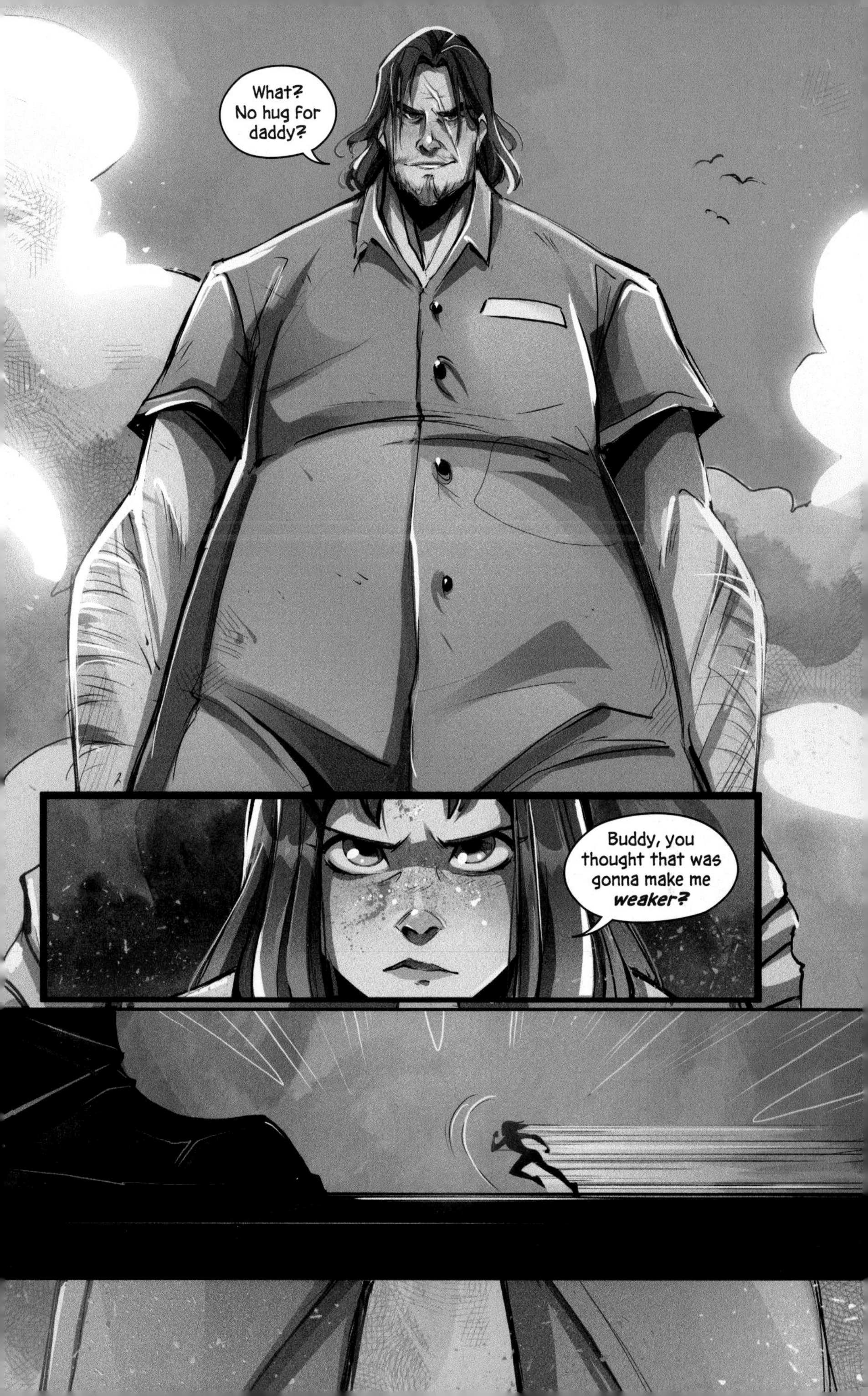
What? No hug for daddy?
Buddy, you thought that was gonna make me *weaker?*

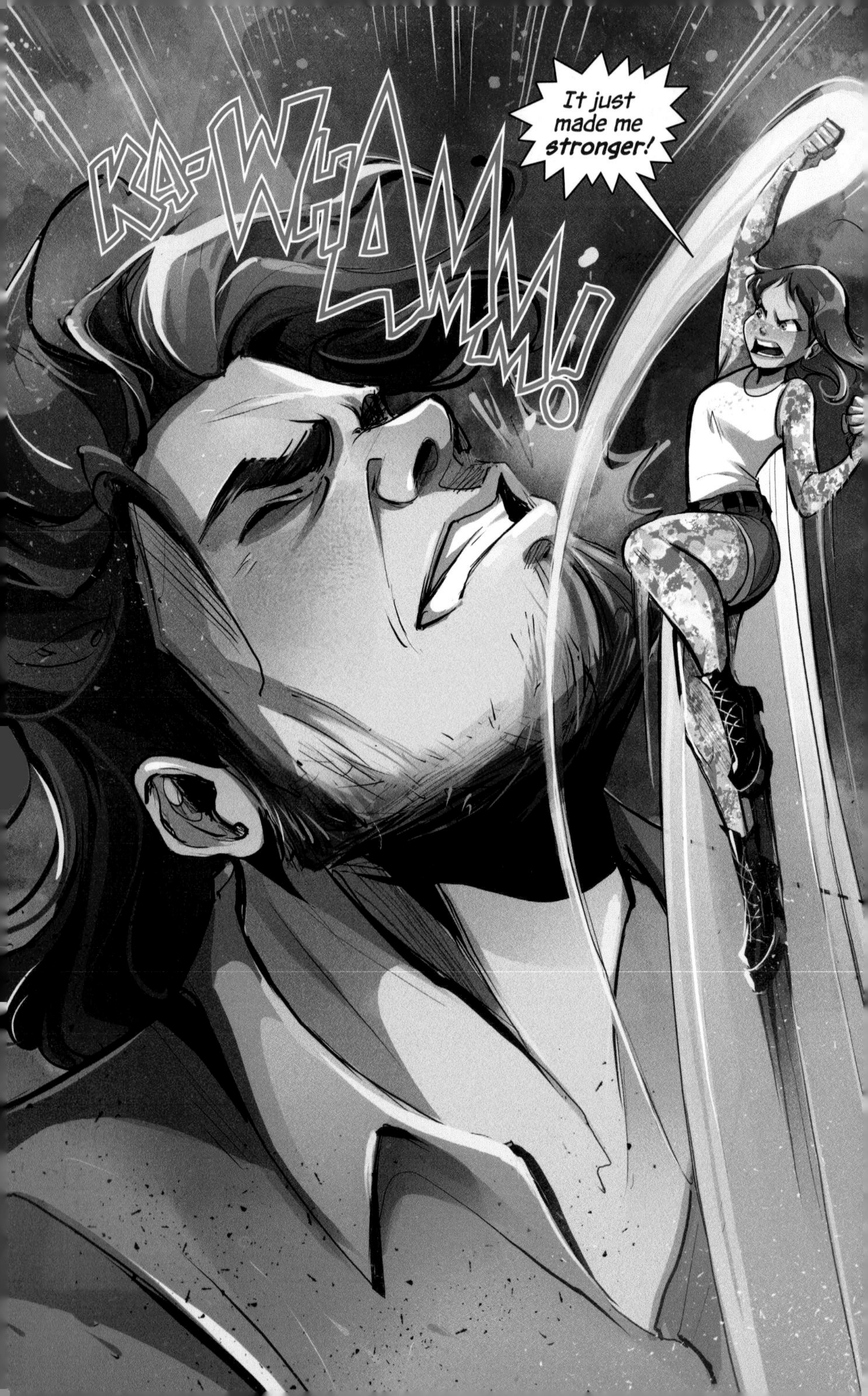
KA-WHAMMM!
It just made me stronger!

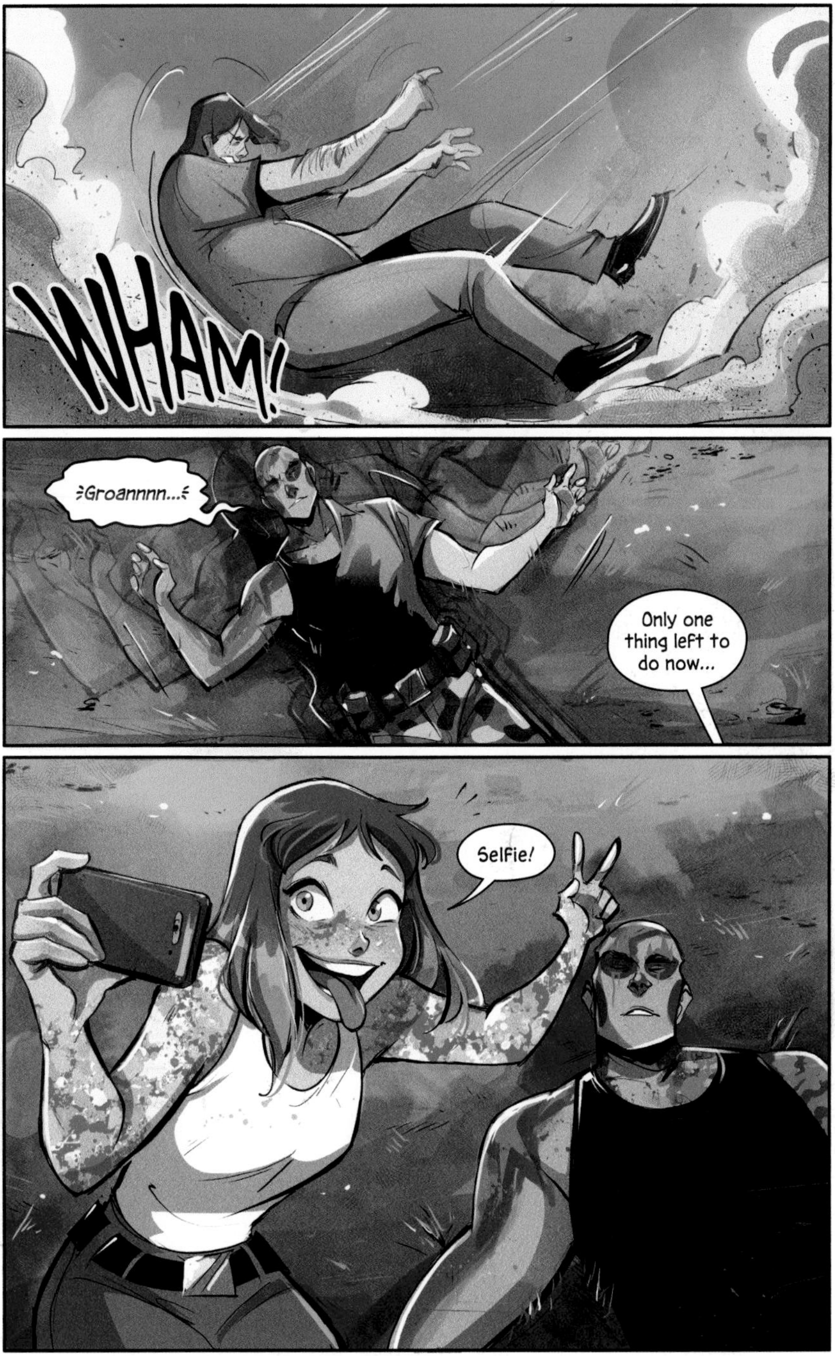
WHAM!
Groannnn...
Only one thing left to do now...
Selfie!

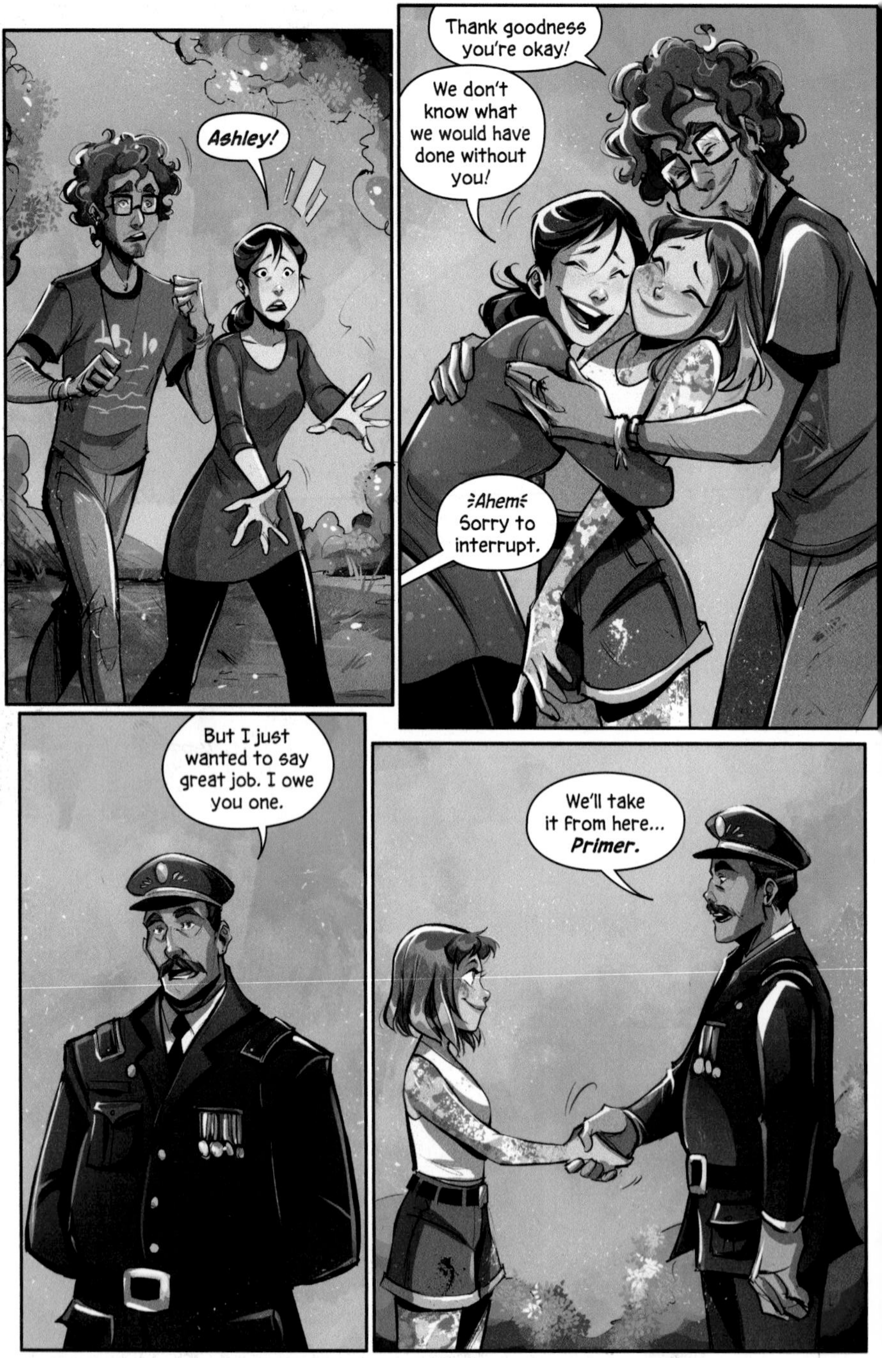
Ashley!
Thank goodness you're okay!
We don't know what we would have done without you!
=Ahem= Sorry to interrupt.
But I just wanted to say great job. I owe you one.
We'll take it from here... Primer.

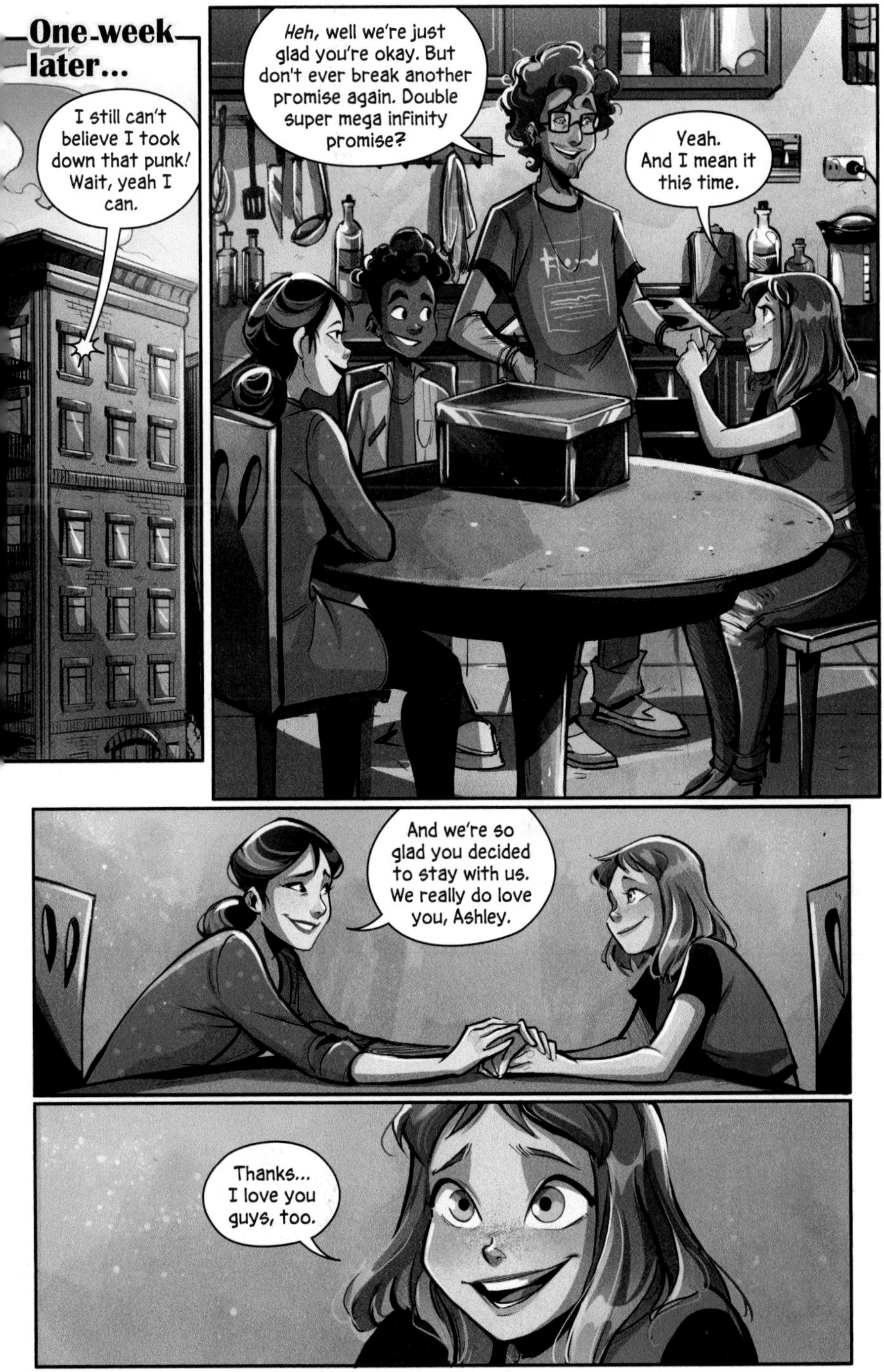
One-week later...
I still can't believe I took down that punk! Wait, yeah I can.
Heh, well we're just glad you're okay. But don't ever break another promise again. Double super mega infinity promise?
Yeah. And I mean it this time.
And we're so glad you decided to stay with us. We really do love you, Ashley.
Thanks... I love you guys, too.

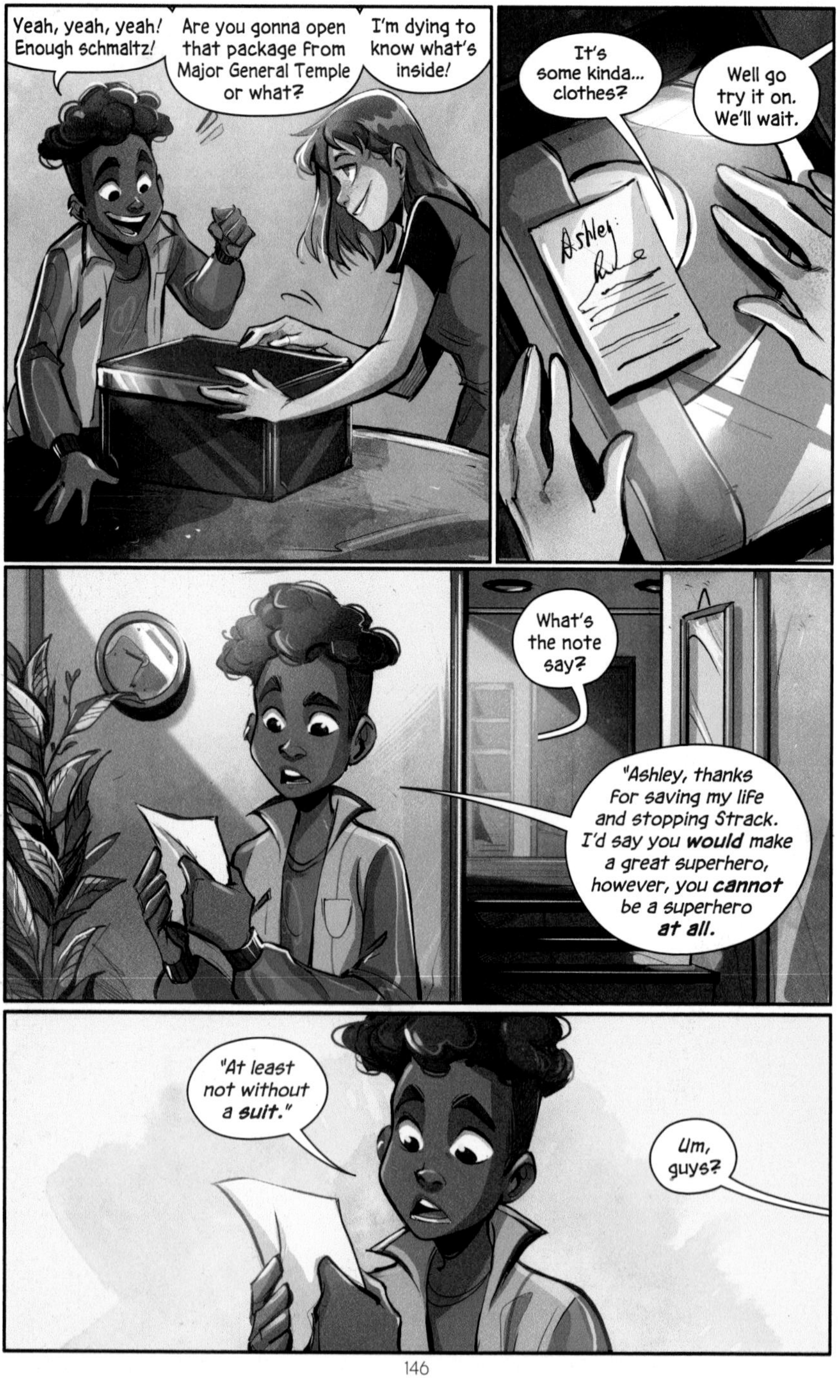
Yeah, yeah, yeah! Enough schmaltz!
Are you gonna open that package from Major General Temple or what?
I'm dying to know what's inside!
It's some kinda... clothes?
Well go try it on. We'll wait.
Ashley:
What's the note say?
"Ashley, thanks for saving my life and stopping Strack. I'd say you **would** make a great superhero, however, you **cannot** be a superhero **at all.**
"At least not without a **suit.**"
Um, guys?

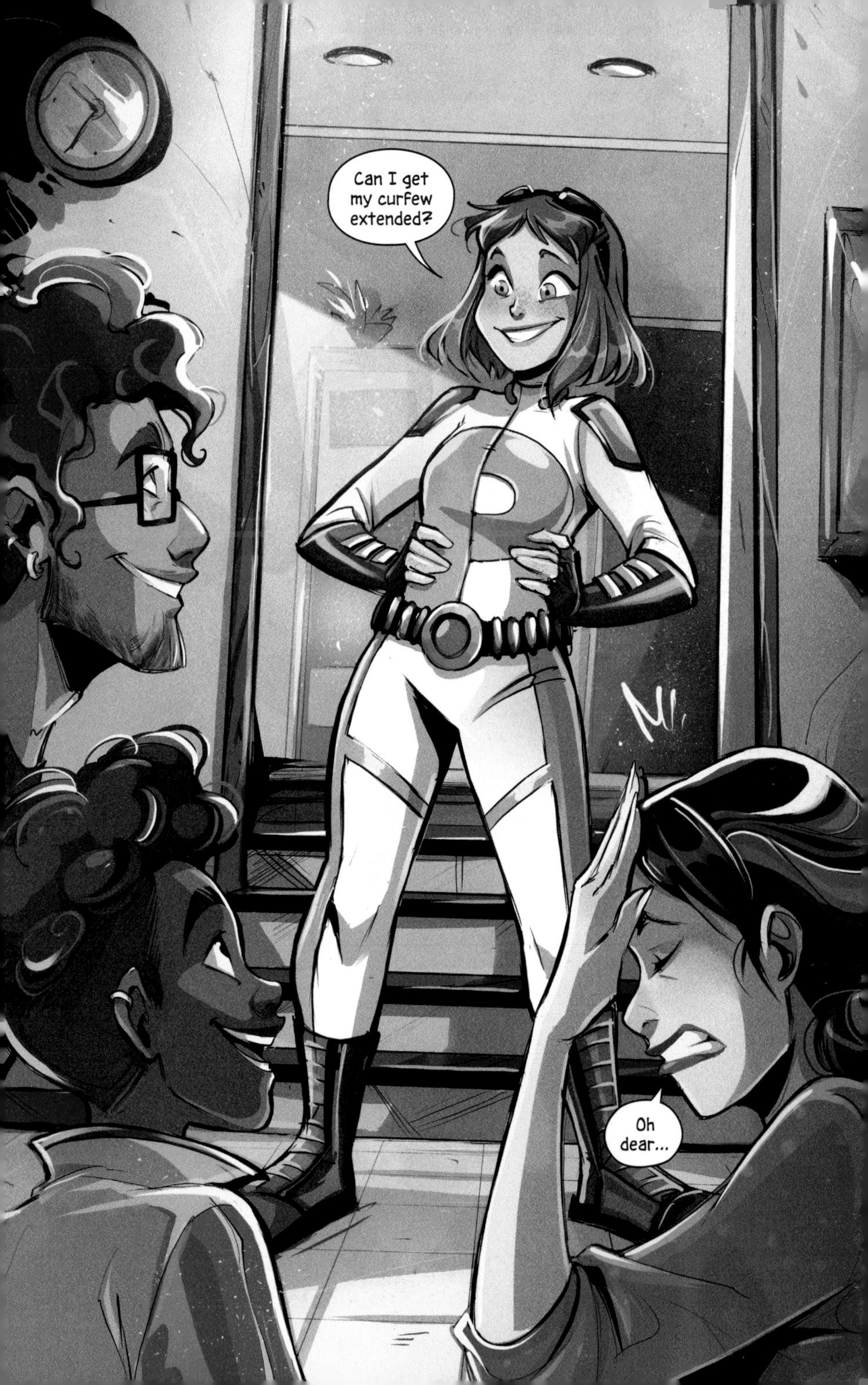
Can I get my curfew extended?
Oh dear...

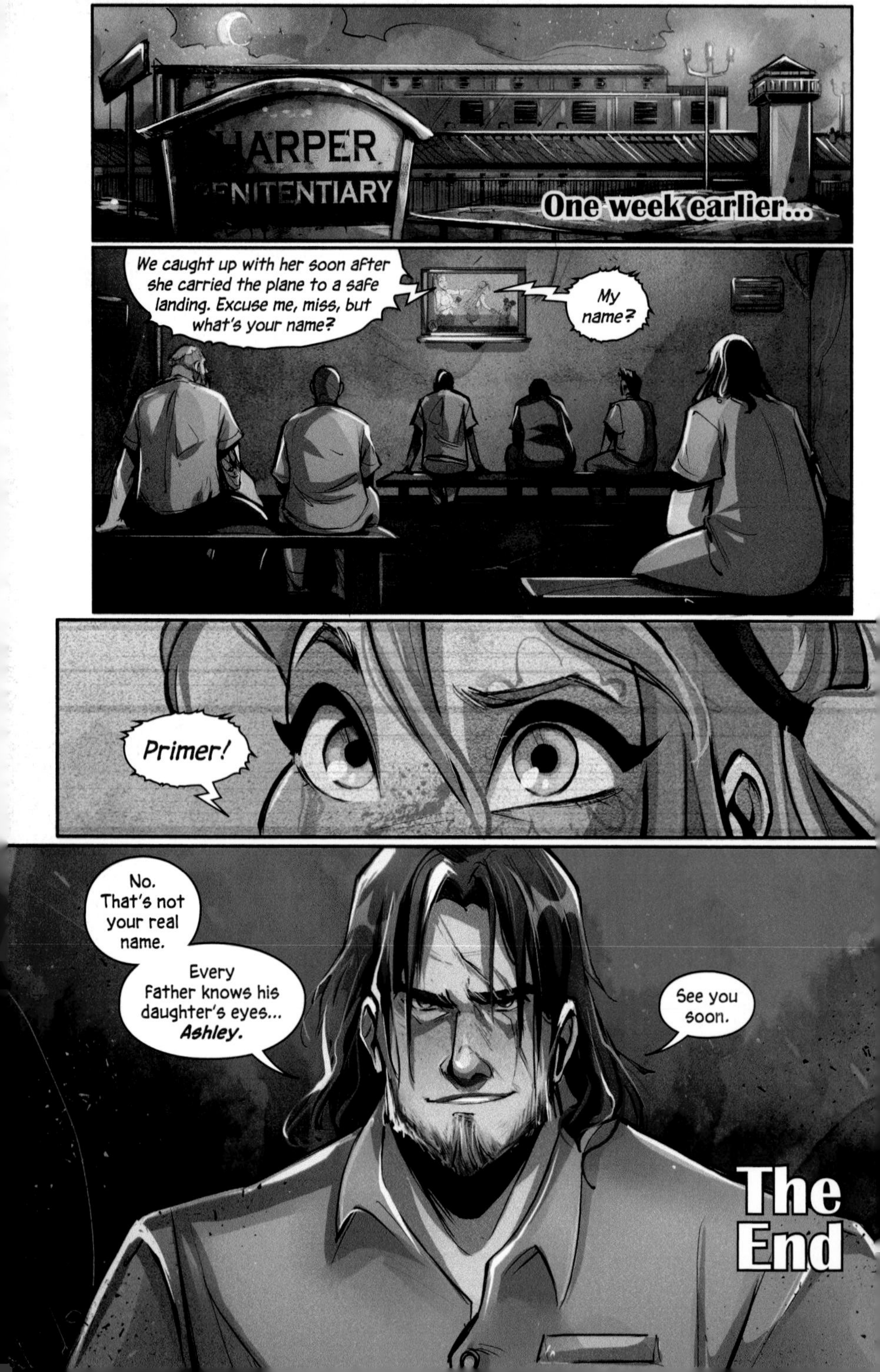
HARPER
PENITENTIARY
One week earlier...
We caught up with her soon after she carried the plane to a safe landing. Excuse me, miss, but what's your name?
My name?
Primer!
No. That's not your real name.
Every father knows his daughter's eyes... Ashley.
See you soon.
The End

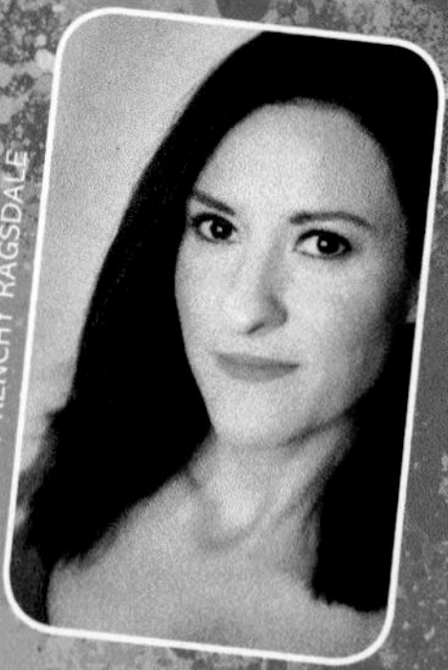

PHOTO BY KENCHY RAGSDALE

Jennifer Muro is the writer of the Lucasfilm series *Star Wars: Forces of Destiny*. She's also written for *Justice League Action*, *Lego DC Super Hero Girls*, and Marvel's *Spider-Man*, and she is currently working on the *Critical Role: The Legend of Vox Machina* series.

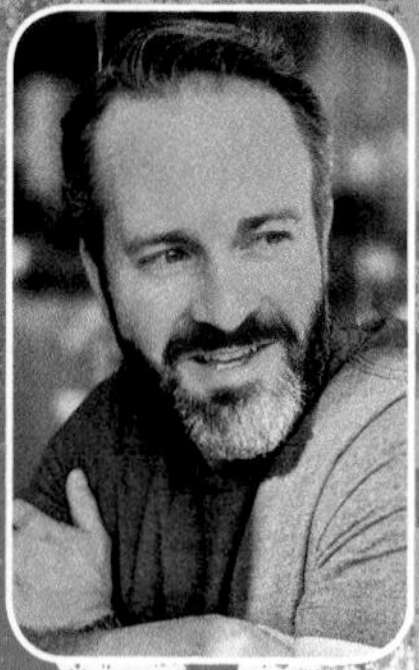

PHOTO BY ALISON HAISLIP

Since 2004, **Thomas Krajewski** has been writing animation for Nickelodeon, Disney, Warner Bros., the BBC, and Cartoon Network. Series he has worked on include *Teenage Mutant Ninja Turtles*, *Iron Man*, *Looney Tunes*, *Scooby-Doo and Guess Who?*, and *The Fairly OddParents*. He is also the head writer on the Netflix series *Buddy Thunderstruck*.

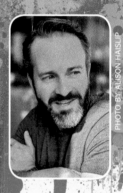

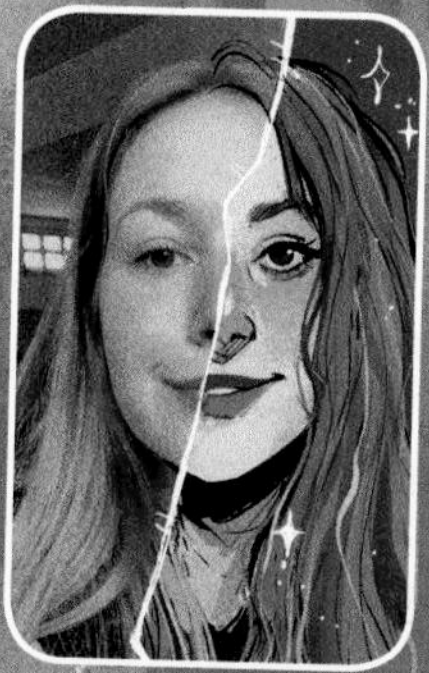

PHOTO AND ART BY GRETEL LUSKY

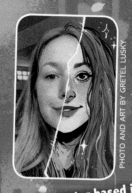

Gretel Lusky is an illustrator based in Buenos Aires, Argentina, where she studied visual arts at the National University of the Arts. She started her career in the animation industry as a visual development artist and character designer for 2-D and 3-D animated shorts, TV series, and feature films. She continued working on a variety of projects including editorial work, book covers, and concept art for video games. Nowadays she is pursuing her long-term dream of doing comics.

From *New York Times* bestselling author Grace Ellis (*Lumberjanes*) and artist Brittney Williams (*Goldie Vance*) comes a new story about 13-year-old Lois Lane as she navigates the confusing worlds of social media and friendship.

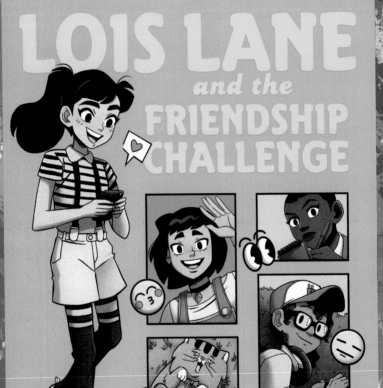

NEW YORK TIMES BESTSELLING AUTHOR OF LUMBERJANES **GRACE ELLIS**

LOIS LANE
and the
FRIENDSHIP CHALLENGE

illustrated by
BRITTNEY WILLIAMS

Keep on reading for a sneak peek of
Lois Lane and the Friendship Challenge!

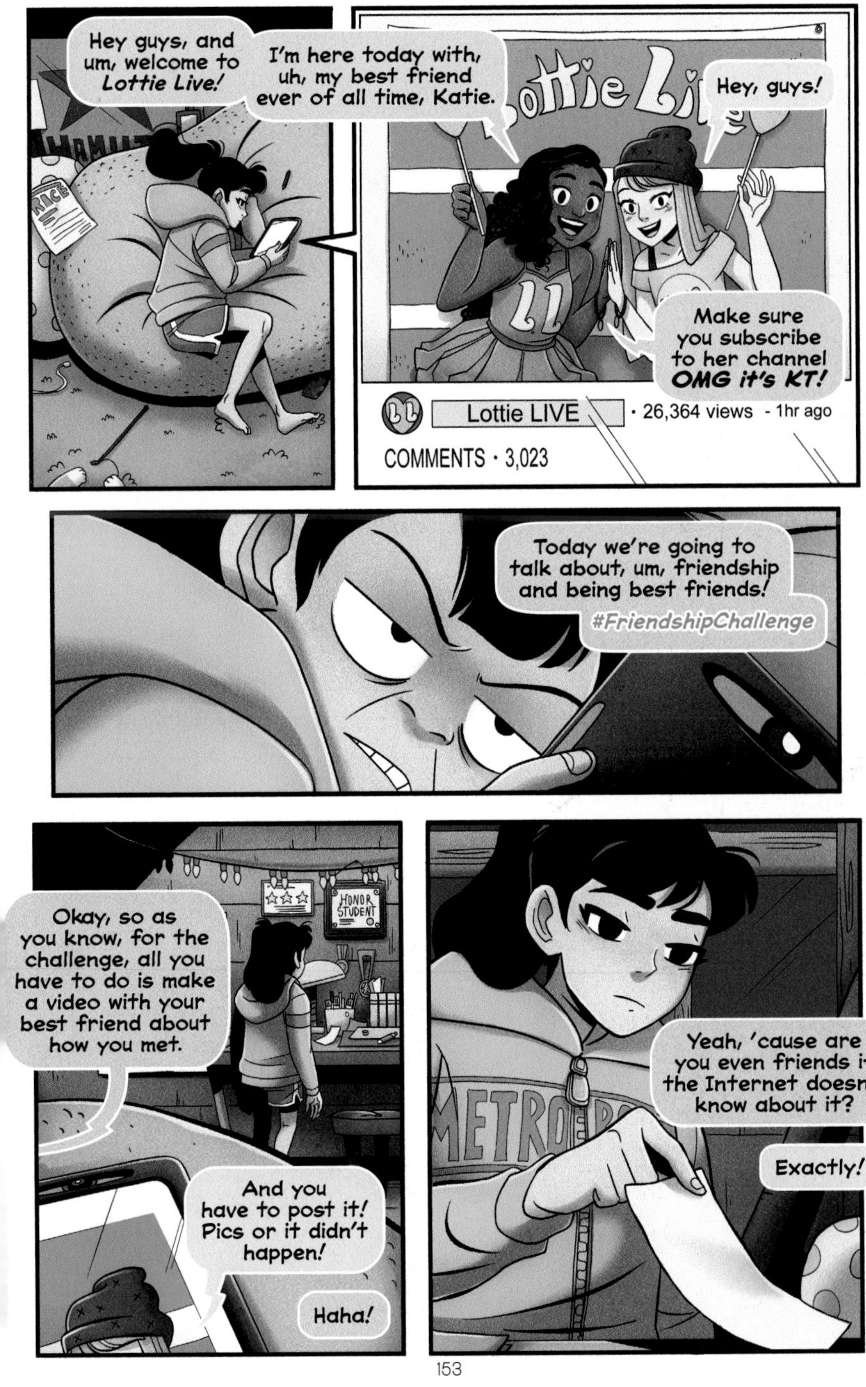
Hey guys, and um, welcome to Lottie Live!
I'm here today with, uh, my best friend ever of all time, Katie.
Hey, guys!
Lottie Live
11
Make sure you subscribe to her channel OMG it's KT!
Lottie LIVE
• 26,364 views - 1hr ago
COMMENTS • 3,023
Today we're going to talk about, um, friendship and being best friends!
#FriendshipChallenge
HONOR STUDENT
Okay, so as you know, for the challenge, all you have to do is make a video with your best friend about how you met.
And you have to post it! Pics or it didn't happen!
Haha!
Yeah, 'cause are you even friends if the Internet doesn't know about it?
Exactly!

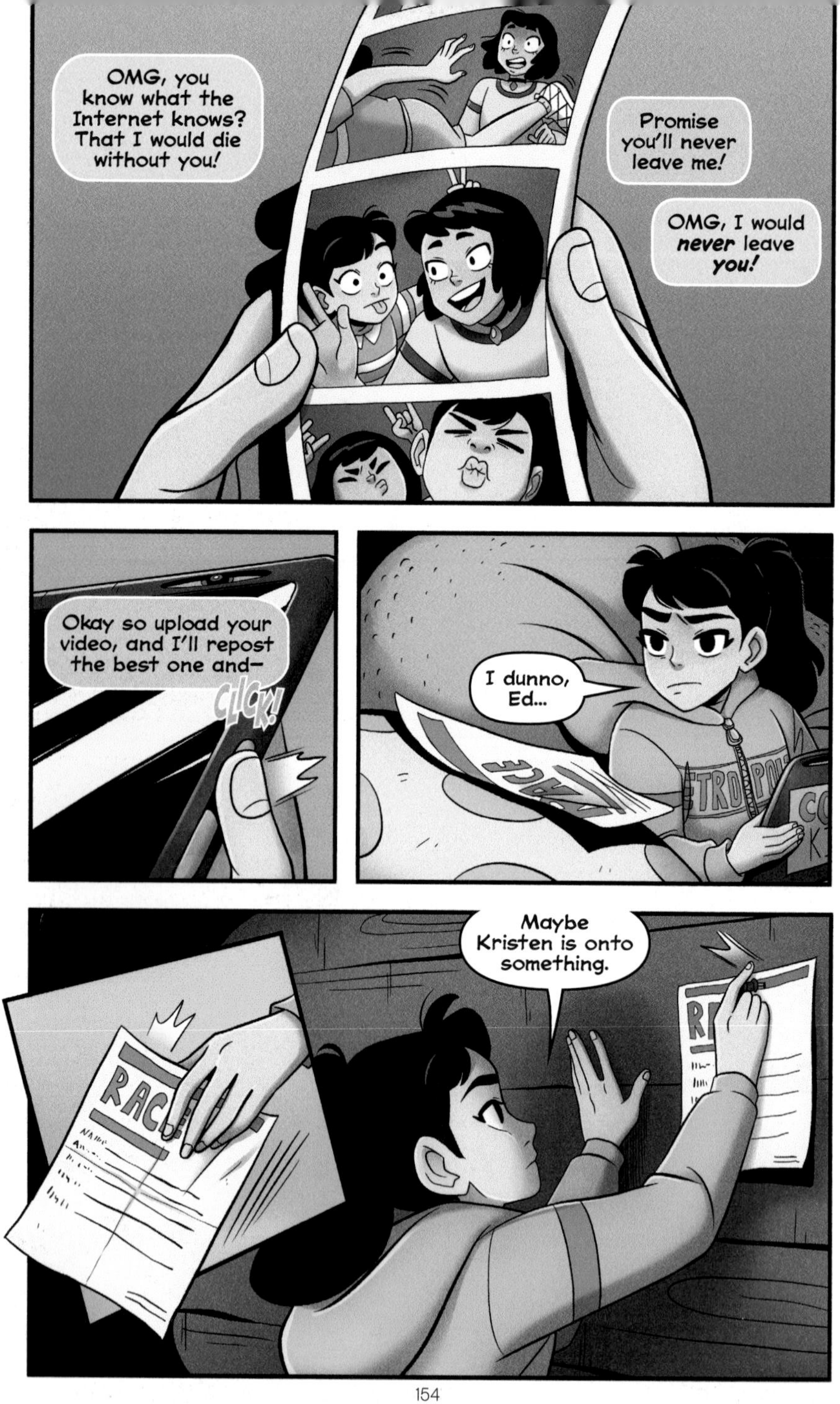
OMG, you know what the Internet knows? That I would die without you!
Promise you'll never leave me!
OMG, I would never leave you!
Okay so upload your video, and I'll repost the best one and—
CLICK!
I dunno, Ed...
Maybe Kristen is onto something.
RACE

Hmm.

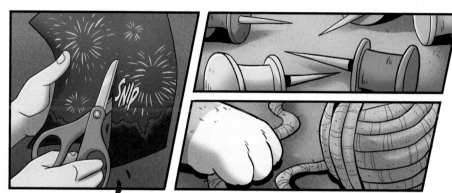

SNIP

OUCH!

IZZY is the RINGER!

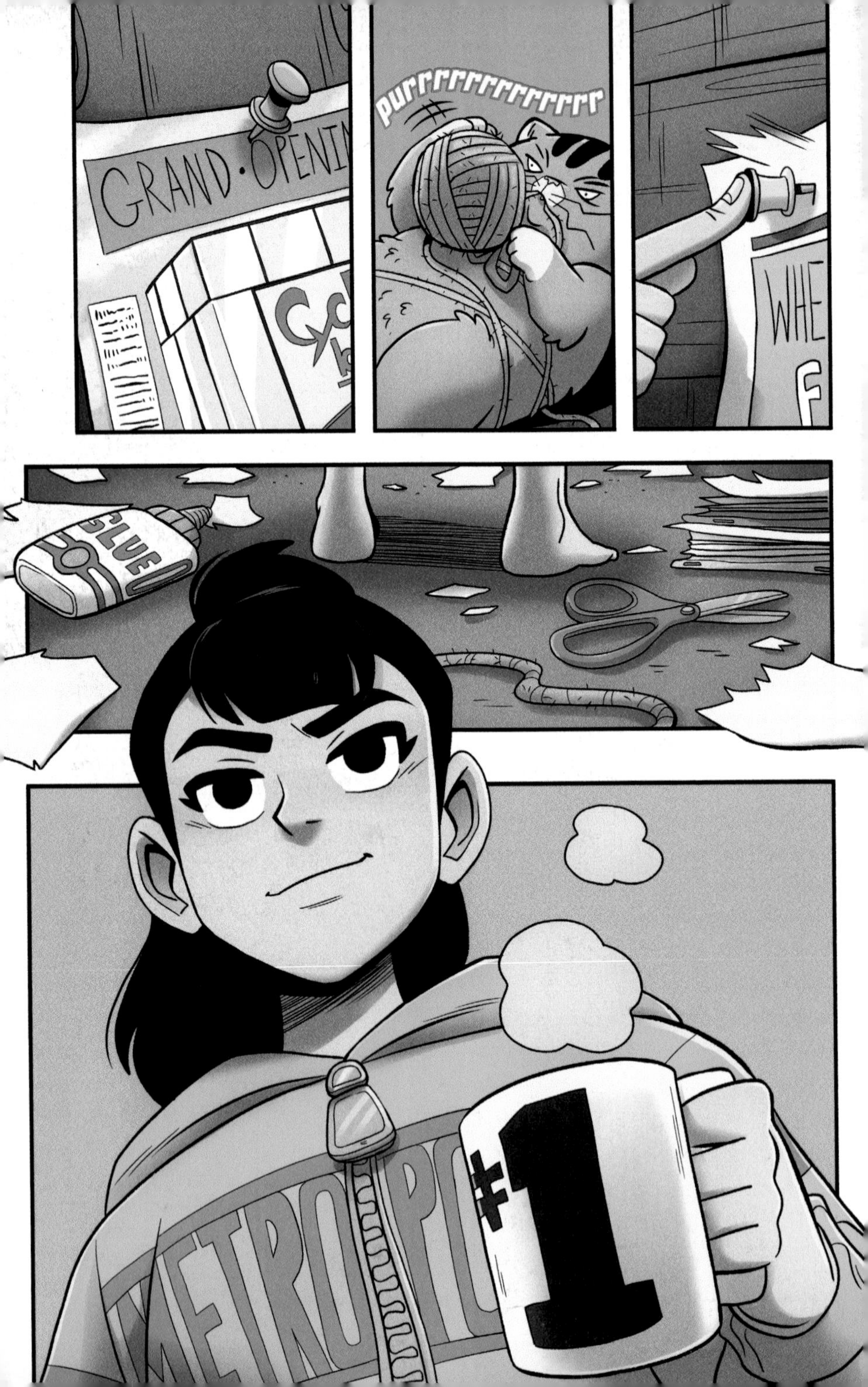

GRAND · OPENI
purrrrrrrrrrrrr
WHE
F
GLUE
METROPO
#1

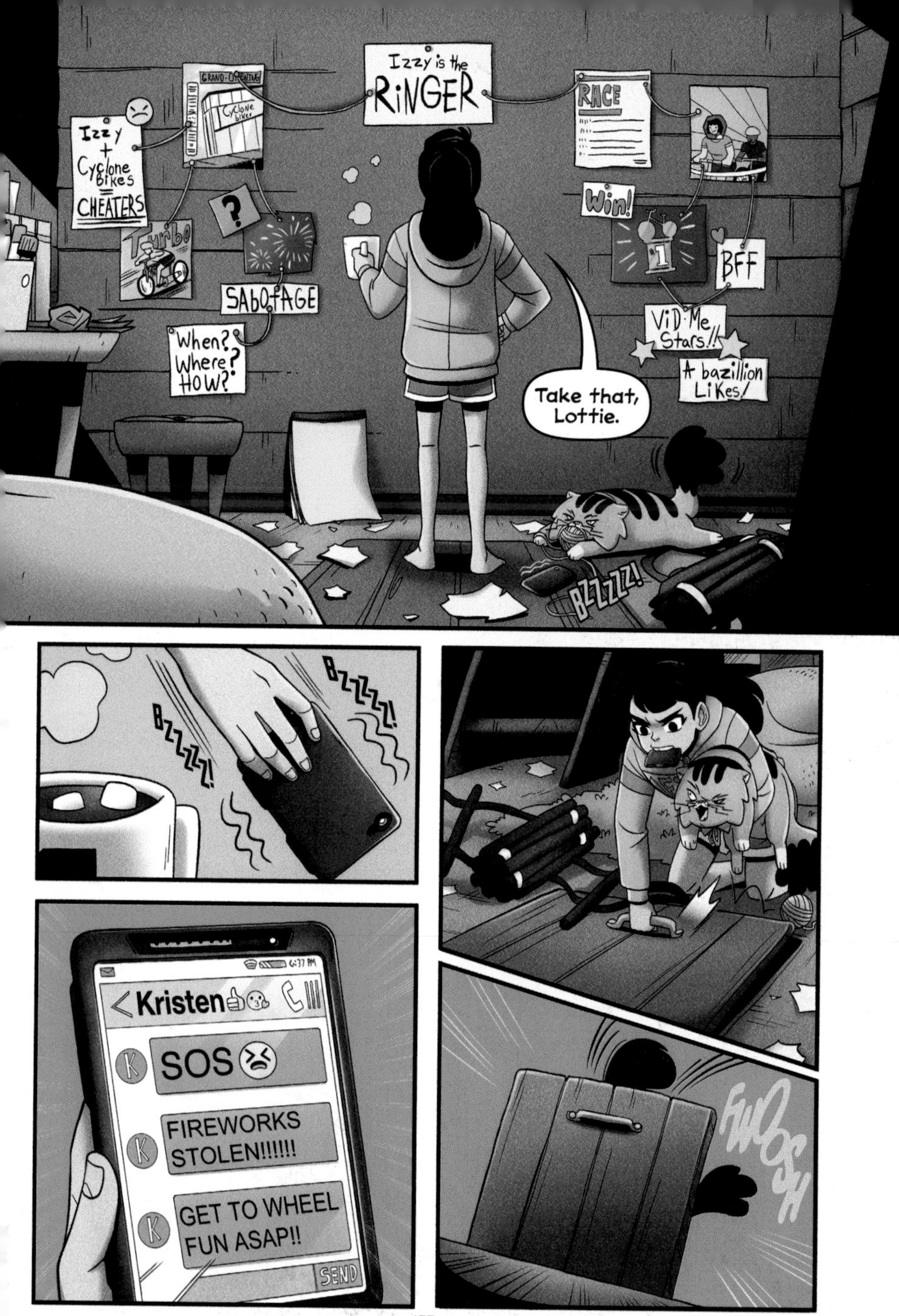
Izzy is the RiNGER
GRAND OPENING
Cyclone bikes
Izzy + Cyclone Bikes = CHEATERS
Turbo
?
SABOTAGE
When? Where? HOW?
RACE
Win!
#1
BFF
ViD Me Stars!!
A bazillion Likes!
Take that, Lottie.
BZZZZZ!
BZZZZZ!
BZZZZZ!
Kristen
SOS
FIREWORKS STOLEN!!!!!!
GET TO WHEEL FUN ASAP!!
SEND
FWOOSH

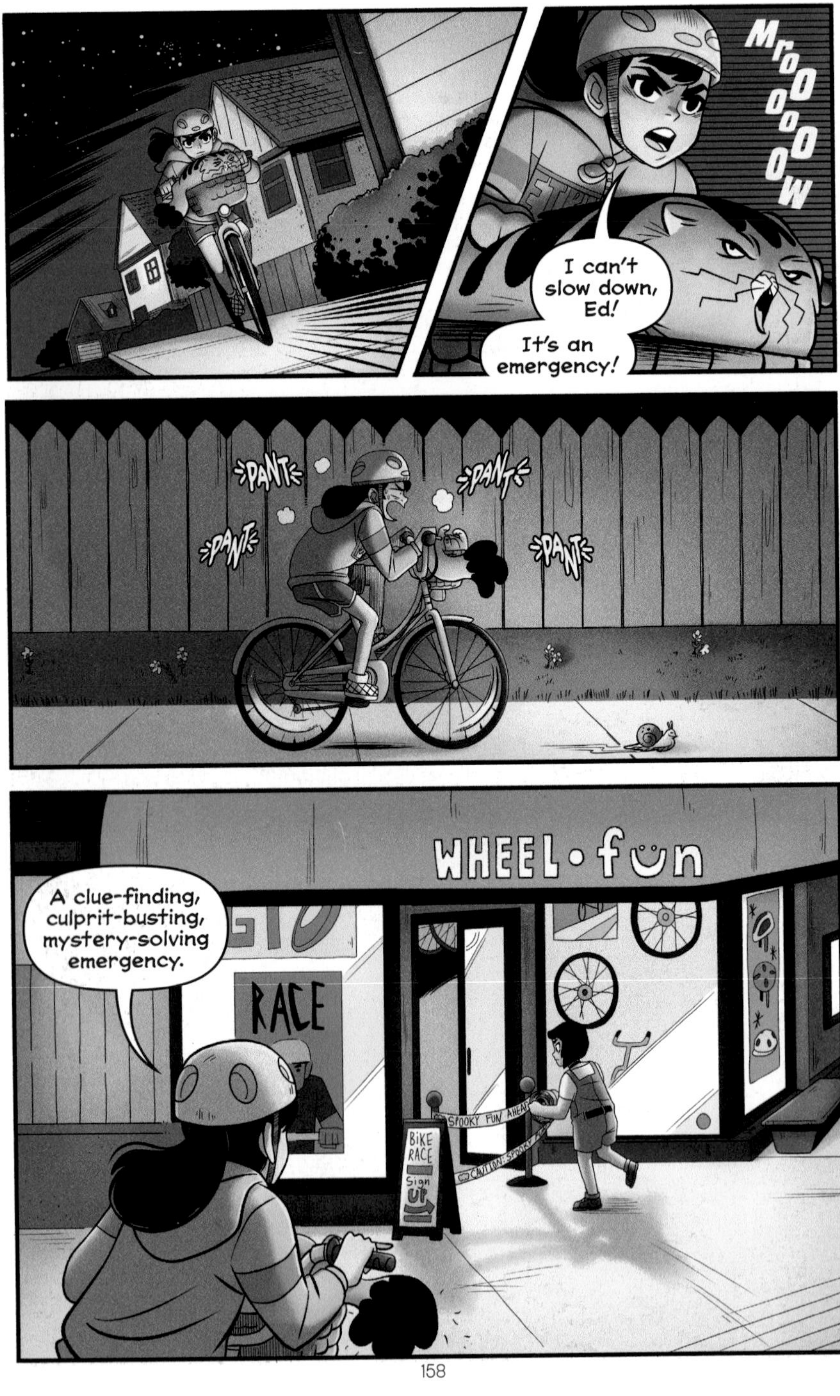
Mroooooow
I can't slow down, Ed!
It's an emergency!
PANT
PANT
PANT
PANT
WHEEL • fun
A clue-finding, culprit-busting, mystery-solving emergency.
RACE
SPOOKY FUN AHEAD
CAUTION: SPOOKY
BIKE RACE Sign UP

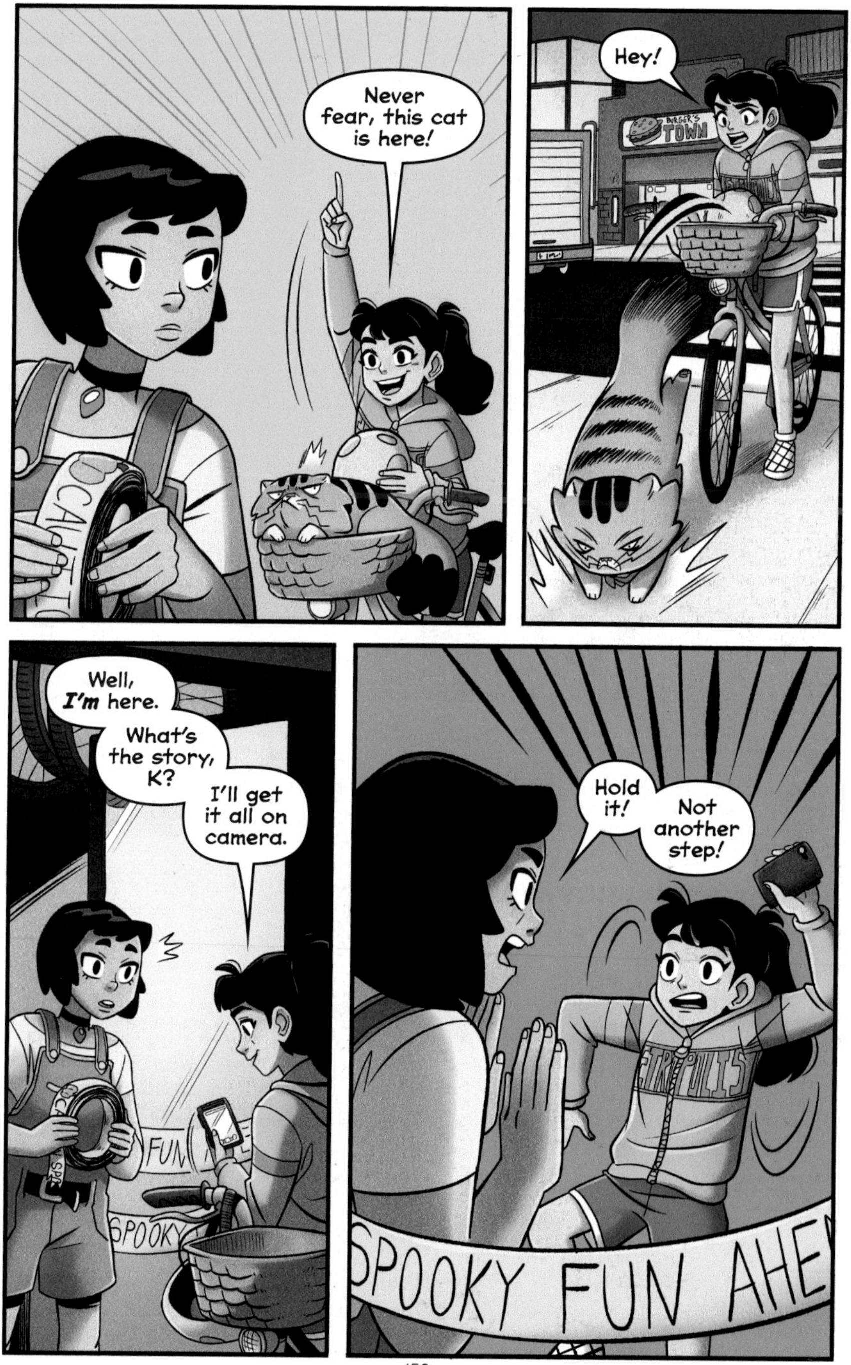
Never fear, this cat is here!
Hey!
BURGER'S TOWN
Well, *I'm* here.
What's the story, K?
I'll get it all on camera.
Hold it!
Not another step!
SPOOKY FUN AHE

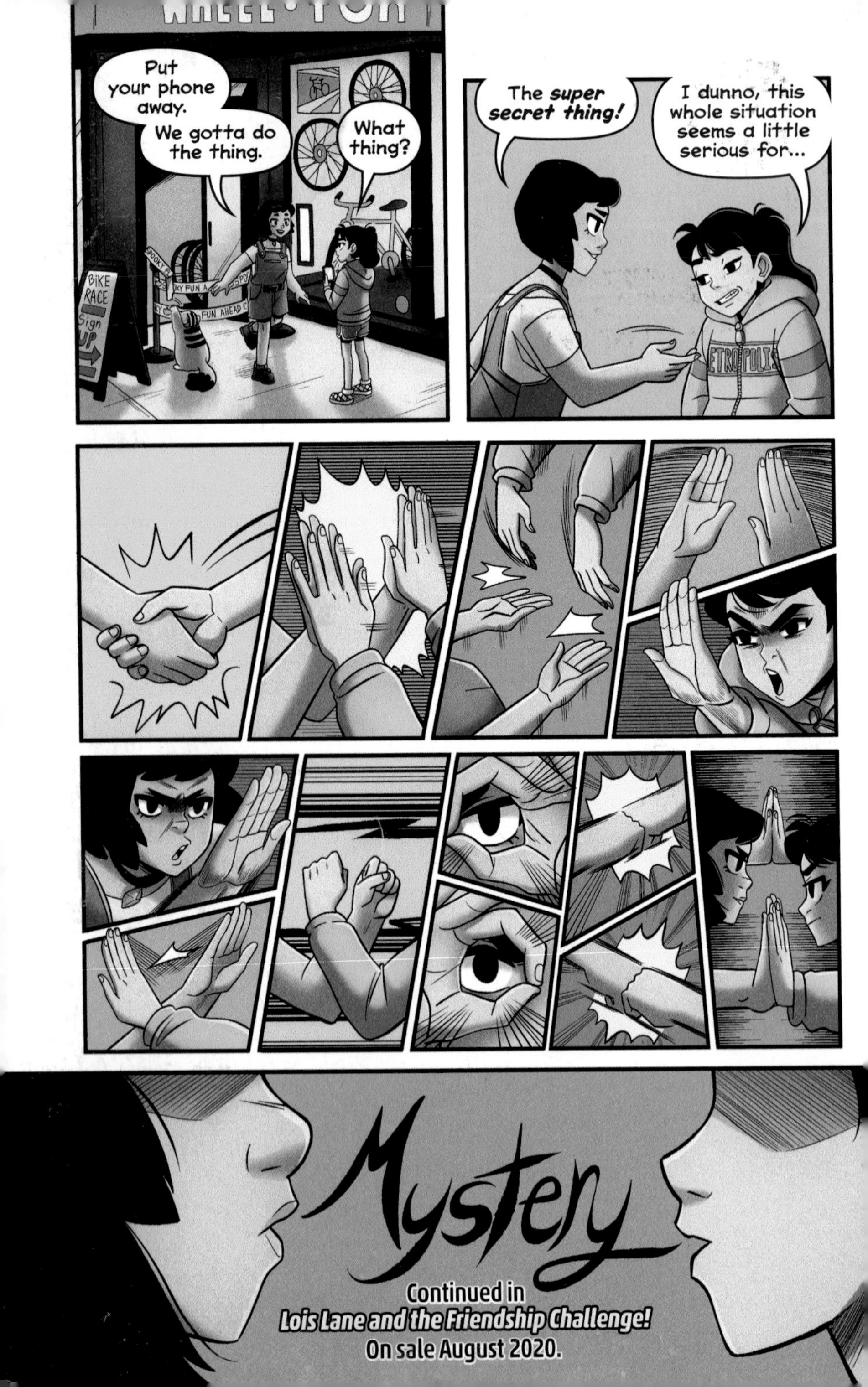
Put your phone away.
We gotta do the thing.
What thing?
BIKE RACE Sign UP
The *super secret thing!*
I dunno, this whole situation seems a little serious for...
Mystery
Continued in
Lois Lane and the Friendship Challenge!
On sale August 2020.